PRAISE FOR AUSTIN CLARKE'S
The Polished Hoe

"Lyrical . . . seductive . . . hypnotic. . . . In this politically engaged novel, we are reminded that when it comes to colonialism, one never comes to any sort of final understanding."
—*Houston Chronicle*

"Magnificent. . . . *The Polished Hoe* oozes unrequited love and seduction under duress. Clarke conjures lush, lyrical images that pull the reader deeper into his space."
—*San Antonio Express-News*

"Dazzling. . . . The novel's eerie magic derives from Clarke's exploitation of voices . . . stipled, like Morrison's *Song of Solomon*, with music and singing games. . . . Language in *The Polished Hoe* does more than express experience, it embodies it."
—*Publishers Weekly*

"A well-crafted novel. . . . If the literary gods are feeling fair . . . Clarke will now receive attention from U.S. readers."
—*Austin American-Statesman*

"The story will captivate readers."
—*Daily Oklahoman*

"Endlessly fascinating . . . creatively executed. . . . *The Polished Hoe* is certain to be met with critical acclaim in the United States."
—*Booklist*

"A complex story . . . that deftly reveals an abominable state of sexual oppression and racist tyranny and the revenge both can invoke."
—*Library Journal*

AUSTIN CLARKE is a professor of literature and has taught at
Yale, Brandeis, Williams, Duke, and the Universities of Texas
and Indiana. He assisted in setting up a Black studies program
at Yale in 1968, after which he became the cultural attaché of
the Embassy of Barbados in Washington, D.C. He lives in
Toronto, Canada.

THE
POLISHED
HOE

A NOVEL

Austin Clarke

Amistad

An Imprint of HarperCollins*Publishers*

A hardcover edition of this book was published in 2003 by Amistad,
an imprint of HarperCollins Publishers.

HarperCollins books may be purchased for educational, business, or sales
promotional use. For information, please write: Special Markets Department,
HarperCollins Publishers Inc., 10 East 53rd Street, New York, NY 10022.

Originally published in Canada in 2002 by Thomas Allen Publishers,
a division of Thomas Allen & Son Limited. Reprinted by arrangement with
Thomas Allen Publishers.

Grateful acknowledgment is made to Derek Walcott for permission
to print from *Omeros*.

FIRST AMISTAD PAPERBACK EDITION 2004

Printed on acid-free paper

The Library of Congress has catalogued the hardcover edition as follows:
Clarke, Austin.
The polished hoe / Austin Clarke.—1st ed.
p. cm.
ISBN 0-06-055565-3
1. Women—West Indies—Fiction. 2. Plantation owners—Fiction.
3. Women murderers—Fiction. 4. Plantation life—Fiction.
5. West Indies—Fiction. 6. Mistresses—Fiction. I. Title.
PR9199.3.C526P65   2002b
813'.54—dc21   2003052189

ISBN 0-06-055762-1 (pbk.)

05 06 07 08 PDF/RRD 10 9 8 7 6 5

For Gladys Irene Clarke-Luke
My Mother.

That victory was hers,
and so was his passion; but the passionless books
did not contain smell, eyes, the long black arm, or his

knowledge that the island's beauty was in her looks

—Derek Walcott, from *Omeros*

PART ONE

"MY NAME IS MARY. People in this Village call me Mary-Mathilda. Or, Tilda, for short. To my mother I was Mary-girl. My names I am christen with are Mary Gertrude Mathilda, but I don't use Gertrude, because my maid has the same name. My surname that people 'bout-here uses, is either Paul, or Bellfeels, depending who you speak to . . ."

"Everybody in Flagstaff Village knows you as Miss Bellfeels, ma'am," the Constable says. "And they respects you."

"Nevertheless, Bellfeels is not the name I want attach to this Statement that I giving you . . ."

"I will write-down that, ma'am, as you tell it to me. But . . ."

"This Sunday evening," she says, interrupting him, "a little earlier, round seven o'clock, I walked outta here, taking the track through the valley; past the two stables converted into a cottage; past the sheep pens and the goat pens, and fowl coops; and through the grove of fruit trees until I came to the Front-Road, walking between two fields of canes. In total darkness. But I knew the way, like the back of my two hands. Now, where we are in this Great House is the extremity of the Plantation Houses, meaning the furtherest away from the Main House, with six other houses, intervening. These consist of the house the Bookkeeper occupies; one for the Overseer, Mr. Lawrence Burkhart, who we call the Driver—that's the smallest house; one for the Assistant Manager, a

Englishman, which is the third biggest after the Main House; and there is a lil hut for the watchman, Watchie; and then there is this Great House where we are. The Main House have three floors, to look over the entire estate of the Plantation, like a tower in a castle. To spy on everybody. Every-other house has two floors. Like this one. That would give you, in case you never been so close to this Plantation before, the lay of the land and of things; the division of work and of household."

"I sees this Plantation only from a distance, ma'am. I know it from a distance only," the Constable says.

"It was dark, and I couldn't see even my two hands outstretch in front of me. I took the way from here, right through the valley where the track cuts through it. I could make out the canes on both sides of me; and I could hear them shaking, as there was a steady wind the whole evening; the kind of wind that comes just before a heavy downpour of rain, like before a hurricane. They were 'arrows' shooting-out from the tops of canes. Crop-Season, as you well-know, is in full swing; and the Factory grinding canes, day and night. You could smell the crack-liquor, the fresh cane juice, strong-strong! What a sweet, but sickening smell cane juice is, when you smell it from near!

"Wilberforce, my son, who was home earlier, is my witness to the hour I left . . .

"Have I told you about Wilberforce, yet? No? Pardon me. The memory is fading, Constable, the memory. The mind not sharp no more, and . . . very often . . . What was I telling you about?"

"You was talking about your son, Mr. Wilberforce, the doctor, ma'am."

"Yes! Wilberforce! My first-born. He isn't really the first of my thrildren I give birth to. He's the one outta the three who lived-past childbirth.

"Wilberforce, always with his head always inside a book, I keep telling him that with all that book-learning retain in his head, if he's not careful, he going burst his blasted brains!

"He, I gave birth to, in the year nineteen . . . I told you that, didn't I?"

"You didn't tell me when Mr. Wilberforce born, ma'am."

"Nevertheless. Two more thrildren I had. A boy and a girl. I gave them the names I intended to christen them with, if they had-live. William Henry. Two names I took from a English magazine. And Rachelle Sarah Prudence, the girl. Lovely English names I named my two dead thrildren with. One died eighteen months after the first one. The boy.

"My third-born, Wilberforce, became therefore my first-born. A mother's pride and joy.

"Wilberforce went to the best schools in this Island of Bimshire. Then overseas. He travel to countries like Italy, France, Austria and Europe; and when he return-back here to this Island, he start behaving more like a European than somebody born here. But, at least, he came back with his ambition fulfill. A Doctor. Of Tropical Medicines.

"Whereas, had the other two thrildren survive, I wanted them to follow in the path of the Law. They would have made such lovely barsters-at-Law! You don't think so?"

"Yes, ma'am," the Constable says.

"My sweet boy-child, William Henry; and lovely Rachelle Sarah Prudence, the girl.

"Yes, Constable. Me. I, Mary-Mathilda . . . I, Mary Gertrude Mathilda, although I don't use Gertrude, as I told you . . ."

"Yes, ma'am."

". . . left inside-here at seven o' clock this evening, and walked the four hundred and something yards from here to the Plantation Main House, and it take me fifteen minutes time to arrive there; and . . ."

"Which night you mean, ma'am, when you left your residence of abode?"

"Which night I took the walk? Was it Saturday night, last night, or tonight Sunday night, is what you getting at?"

"I mean that, too, ma'am. But what I really getting at, is if the moon was shining when you leff your home and place of abode, on the night in question, walking to your destination? Or if you was walking in the rain. 'Cause with rain, I have to refer to footsteps. They bound to be footprints . . ."

"If there are footsteps, those would be my prints in the ground, Constable. Bold and strong and deep-deep; deep-enough for water to collect in them. Deep-enough to match the temperriment I was in. I can tell you that my determination was strong.

"It was dark-dark, earlier tonight. But in that darkness, I was not hiding from anybody. Not from the Law; not from God; not from my conscience, as I walked in the valley of the shadow of darkness and of death. No. There was no moon. But I was not a thief, craving the darkness, and dodging from detection. Oh, no!

"A long time ago, before tonight, I decided to stop walking in darkness.

"With that temperriment and determination of mind, I first-started, on a regular basis, to polish my hoe. And to pass a grinding-stone dip in car-grease, along the blade, since September the fifteenth last-gone; September, October, November just-pass, is three months; and every day for those months, night after night as God send, more than I can call-to-mind. And I have to laugh, why, all-of-a-sudden, I went back to a hoe, I had-first-used when I was a girl, working in the cane fields, not quite eight years of age. The same hoe, weeding young canes, sweet potato slips, 'eight-weeks' yams, eddoes, all those ground provisions.

"This hoe that I used all those years, in the North Field, is the same hoe I used this Sunday night.

"If it wasn't so black outside, you could look through that window you sitting beside, and see the North Field I refer to, vast and green and thick with sugar cane, stretching for acres and acres, beyond the reach of your eyes, unmeasuring as the sea . . .

"So, no, Constable. I was not seeking the shadows of night, even though the moon wasn't shining!

"I already stated to you that at seven o'clock, the hour in question, it was like a full moon was shining, by which I mean, as the saying in this Village goes, a full-moon alters the way men behave—and women, too!—turns them into lunatics, and—"

"Pardon me, ma'am. But on the telephone to the sub-station, in your perlimary Statement to Sargeant, Sargeant say that you say the night was dark, and no moon wasn't shining. Is so, Sargeant tell me to write down your Statement, in my notebook, using your exact words. So, I hope that I not stating now, in-front-'o-you, what you didn't state, nor intend to state, in your telephone Statement, ma'am?

"Sargeant send me to get your Statement offa you before he come himself. All we know is what you say when you call, that something happen, and you want Sargeant to come, and take your Statement, first-hand, from you. We don't know what happen and we don't yet know what is the circumstances. Sargeant would look after that. He say to say he have another important assignment. I am consequently here until Sargeant comes. But Sargeant coming . . ."

"Soon, I hope."

"Sargeant soon will be here."

". . . and so, what I mean by a bright night and the moon shining, is merely a comparison of my disposition towards darkness and light; something, as Wilberforce calls it, like the ironies of life. *Ironies*. He uses it all the time, and would say, 'Sitting down to eat food is full of ironies.' 'Life is full of ironies.' 'A full moon is full of ironies.' That is Wilberforce favourite word for it. *Ironies*.

"When there is a full moon, people behave strange. But tonight, with no moon at all, my behaviour was still strange, granted.

"Tonight, a Sunday, in spite of no moon, the act that I committed, however the people in this Island wish to label it, is not a act, or behaviour of a woman ruled by a full moon; nor of a woman who chooses darkness over light, to move in, or to hide her act in.

"My footprints that you say might be evidence, was, in the darkness, strong footprints, if not stronger even than my temper-riment itself. And my act went along with that. I was determined. And deliberate. Because I knew what my cause was. And I had a cause."

The lights dip from their brilliance; and for just one second, it is dark in the front-house, where they are; dark, as when, long ago, the wind would run through these same windows, and brush aside the flames from the mantles of the large acetylene lamps that have *Home Sweet Home* printed in white letters on their polished lamp-shades. Just for one moment, that moment that it takes for a mouse the same colour as the carpet to steal into a corner.

But wind cannot play those tricks with the electric lighting. The two bulbs hang low, just above their heads, from two long, ugly brown electrical wires, on which, during the day, and especially late at night, flies and other bugs make their homes, and their graves; and are stuck to death.

The wind continues pushing itself through the windows, and brings on its breath the smell of flowers, poinsettia and lady-of-the-night and the strong smell of sugar-cane juice from the Factory. And the lingering intoxicating smell of burnt sugar canes; and the pungency of burnt cane trash, comes into the front-house with them . . .

"From the time, way-way back, when Ma, my mother, out of need, sent me while I was still a lil girl, seven or eight, to the Plan-tation to work in the fields, from that time, I had a cause. And in particular from that day, when the midwife delivered Wilberforce, I have had a cause.

"And I am very sorry to have to talk this way to you, a Constable, sitting in my front-house, on a Sunday night, filling in for Sargeant, who promise me faithfully, to come later, and take my Statement.

"Incidentally, Sargeant and me, went-school together. Did you know that? He was always inquisitive. Always hunting-down answers.

And lizards which he put in cigarette boxes, as coffins, to bury them. Now, we are from two different sides of the paling. But . . ."

"How I should write-down your name, in its official status, ma'am?"

"My name is Mary-Mathilda. My full name is Mary Gertrude Mathilda. But I drop Gertrude because of my maid."

"The whole Village know your names and your surnames, ma'am. And they worships you."

"It began, this whole thing, many-many years ago, on a Sunday. A Sunday morning, close to midday, about ten-to-twelve o'clock. We were in the Church Yard of Sin-Davids Anglican Church. Near the graves and tombs and tombstones; where they buried English-men and sailors from Lord Horatio Nelson's fleet that went down in these waters.

"I remember that my shoes were burning my feet. And I had slip them off. To ease the pain. All through the sermon that the Vicar, Revern Dowd, was delivering from the pulpit, so high and powerful; above my head; high as the water tank in the Plantation Yard . . . I couldn't follow one word that Vicar Dowd was talking, from so on high. His words were too big for me.

"Some words passed my ear, though. I remember that Revern Dowd had-take his sermon from One, Sin-Peter, three, seven-teen. Whether I remember it on my own, or Ma had-remind me afterwards, Revern Dowd was saying how it is more better for a man to suffer for his well-doing, than for his evil-doing. I remem-ber only those words, from that Sunday.

"It is better, if the will of God be so, that a man suffer for well-doing, than for evil-doing.

"Those were the words. I have walked with that text in my heart, since that Sunday. And if, right-now, you open my Bible there on that mahogany centre-table with the white crochet-cloth on it, you will see the text, mark by a palm-leaf cross from last Palm Sunday, One, Sin-Peter, three, seventeen . . .

"It is better to suffer for well-doing, than . . .

"I was a lil girl, then; no more than seven or eight; in such pain from my new shoes. My new shoes weren't purchase new, from Cave Shepherd & Sons, the Haberdasheries store down in Town. They was a pair that the youngest daughter of Mr. Bellfeels had grown outta. Hand-me-downs. Not through inheritance; but castaways. They were new to me, though. Mr. Bellfeels daughter, Miss Emonie, was the same size as me, in clothes and in height. But her shoes pinched like hell, because her feet were white feet; and very narrow.

"That Sunday morning was in the Easter season! It was Easter Even."

"If you don't mind me saying so, ma'am," the Constable says, "Easter is the time I like best outta the whole year o' going-church. Easter! Easter morning, with the singing of carols and psalms! '*O, all ye beasts of the sea!*'

'*Praise Him, and glorify Him, forever!*'

"And the sermon does be so sweet. But long. And then, after Easter, is Easter bank holiday! And flying kites! And holding goat-races!"

"The Collect that Sunday, the morning of Easter Even . . . though I can't naturally call-to-mind the entire Collect, I remember this passage: '. . . *and that through the grave, and the gate of hell, we may pass to our joyful resurrection . . .*'"

"What that mean, ma,am," the Constable says.

"*Resurrection,*" she says.

"*Amen!*" the Constable says.

"*We may pass to our joyful resurrection. Amen.*'"

"For the carol-singing and the sermons, gimme Easter to Christmas, any Sunday morning, ma'am!"

"So, it was that on that same Sunday morning, Ma introduce me to this powerful man. Mr. Bellfeels. He wasn't Plantation manager then; just a field overseer. A driver, as we labourers called such men. Mr. Bellfeels the Driver.

"Ma was in the gang of women weeding in the North Field. In

time, that same North Field was assign to me. And in time, because I was young and vigorous, I became the leader of the same gang of women.

"The sun was bright that Sunday morning of Easter Even. And it was in my face. So, I couldn't see his eyes. Mr. Bellfeels looked so tall, like the pulpit or the water tower, that I had to hold my head back, back, back, to look in his face. And still, I couldn't see his face, clear. This man who looked so tall, and me, a little girl, in pain from wearing his own daughter's shoes that was killing me.

"The sun was playing tricks in his face, too. So, neither of the two of we could see the other person too clear. But he could see my face, because he was looking down.

"Then, Mr. Bellfeels put his riding-crop under my chin, and raise my face to meet his face, using the riding-crop; and when his eyes and my eyes made four, he passed the riding-crop down my neck, right down the front of my dress, until it reach my waist. And then he move the riding-crop right back up again, as if he was drawing something on my body.

"And Ma, stanning-up beside me, with her two eyes looking down at the loose marl in the Church Yard, looking at the graves covered by slabs of marble, looking at the ground. Ma had her attention focused on something on the ground. My mother. Not on me, her own daughter.

"I could smell the rich, strong smell of the leather, just like the leather in the seats and upholstery of the Austin-Healey motor-car that Mr. Bellfeels own. Like the smell of new leather rising in my nose, when I stand in the shoemaker's galvanized shack, and watch him stitch-round the sole, with his awl, making a pair of boots. That smell. That smell of leather. And the feel of leather of the riding crop, passing over my dress, all over my body, as if it was his hand crawling over my body; and I was naked.

"That Sunday morning, in the bright shining sun, with Ma stanning-up there, voiceless, as if the riding-crop was Mr. Bellfeels finger clasped to her lips, clamped to her mouth to strike her dumb to keep her silence, to keep her peace. From that Sunday morning, the meaning of poverty was driven into my head. The sickening power of poverty. Like the smell of leather, disintegrating from animal skin into raw leather, curing in water; soaking in clean water that becomes mildew, before it is tanned and turn into leather, when it is nothing more than pure, dead, rotten, stinking skin. From a animal.

"'*So, this is lil Mary!*' Mr. Bellfeels say.

"'*Yes,*' Ma told Mr. Bellfeels, '*This is my little Mary.*'

"'*Good,*' Mr. Bellfeels say.

"And not a word more. And then, all of a sudden, the sun that had-went suddenly behind a cloud came out again, and was shining more brighter, and the light had-changed the same way, as in the story that we listened to in Sunday school from *Bible Stories for Children*. Like a miracle of light, this brightness . . . and in this brightness cut short, there was this darkness; and in this blackness, Mr. Bellfeels disappeared.

"And me and Ma walked home. Not a word pass from Ma to me, in our entire journey from the Church Yard, passing the houses on the Plantation property, the Great House, the cottage made from two stables, passing the Pasture some distance from the Harlem Bar & Grill rum shop, cross-over Highgates Commons and Reservoir Lane, the crossroads that divide the Village from the Plantation, through the cane-brake, through the gully, through the other gullies growing Guinea grass and Khus-Khus grass; circumventing the North Field, and fields and lands of the Plantation . . . it was the season for dunks. And we picked a few, and ate them while walking, as our journey consisted of a distance of some length, a mile, a mile and a half from Sin-Davids Anglican Church, to our house beside the road, but in the tenantry, on Plantation land.

"That Sunday, we had the usual food after Church. Me and Ma. Dry-peas and rice. The peas was prepared as doved-peas. The rice cooked with a lil salt beef boil-down-in-it, to add flavour.

"Yes, that Sunday afternoon, after we left the Church Yard and Mr. Bellfeels, we ate roast chicken, doved-peas, and some sweet potatoes that Ma had-stole from the very North Field, the Friday afternoon; one-or-two potatoes, hide-way in her crocus bag apron. We had to steal from the Plantation, to make-do.

"'*I borrow these offa the Plantation*,' she told me the Friday, smiling and happy. '*In other words, I steal them, Mary-girl!*'

"Constable, you don't know those days! Lucky you! Days of hardships. But days of great joy and spirit, nevertheless. The joy of a tough life. Cutting and contriving. If you didn't have it, you found a way to get it. Or a neighbour would come to your rescue.

"Or you steal it. All of us, regardless to position, place, complexion, the Ten Commandments, we-all exacted something from the Plantation. A head of eddoes pull-up outta the ground; you brek-off a piece of cane and suck it, to bring up the gas outta your stomach; pull-off a few red-tomatoes offa the vine in the Plantation kitchen garden; and hide them in a crocus bag.

"Every last man-jack, all of us, devout Christian-minded men and women attending Sin-Davids Anglican Church, three times a Sunday, going to Mothers Union every Wednesday night as God send, we all extracted our due from the Plantation.

"But we paid. We paid dear. With our lives. Every-last-one-of-us!

"Well, you shouldn't be a stranger to this history. You were bred and born right here, in this Village, in this Island of Bimshire. You see? Here I go, wandering-off again . . ."

"I learning a lot o' history from you, ma'am. My mother and my gran-mother tell me some o' the history of here."

"You remember Clotelle, then? Clotelle who leff-back three nice lil girl-thrildren, when death grab her sudden, and unaware?

"Clotelle, who was always dress in black. From head to foot, mourning like a N'Eyetalian-'snora, as if mourning for a dead husband? Only thing, Clotelle never had one.

"But the Sunday morning, just before Matins, they found Clotelle henging from the tamarind tree in the Plantation Yard? And nobody didn't know how she got there? And it was Ma who Mr. Bellfeels ordered to cut down Clotelle, cause the Plantation-people was too ashamed and embarrass, and too scornful to touch a dead-body? And how, following after all the fuss that Clotelle mother made over the sudden death of her only child, they held the attopsy. And lo and behold, the attopsy disclose that Clotelle was five months' heavy, in the family-way! But it didn't take tummuch for the whole Village to know who the father was? And . . ."

"I hear this from my gran-mother. They made a calypso on Clotelle."

"It climb to number one on the hit parade. It was a sweet calypso, too. It lasted one week . . .

"Ma tell me when that sad tragedy happened to Clotelle. Ma tell me that she saw Clotelle laying down in the cane-brake, with her face washed in tears; and bleeding; and that it was later the same night, in all the rain, that Clotelle climbed up the tamarind tree; and how Clotelle had-use pieces of cloth that she rip-off from her own dress, with all the blood and all the man's semen staining it; and how Clotelle make a rope outta her own dress, and wrap-it-round the highest branch she could reach in the tamarind tree, and the rest you know. Yes. The rest you know. The *ironies* of history and of life, as Wilberforce like to say. Henging from the tamarind tree, in broad daylight the next day Sunday morning, they found Clotelle, just as Mr. Darnley Alexander Randall Bellfeels, and Mistress Bellfeels, and the two girl-thrildren, Miss Euralie and Miss Emonie, was stepping down the verandah of the Plantation Main House, to cross the gravel path, to get in the Austin-Healey motor-car, the chauffeur holding the door open for them to get in, to be driven to attend Matins at Sin-Davids Anglican Church, 'leven-o'clock-in-the-morning; butting and bounding the school-house building where you went to Elementary School."

There is total deep silence. It seems as if the room descends also into darkness. Silence and darkness. And when the darkness rises, and the silence is broken, it is her voice humming the chorus of the calypso that remembers Clotelle's tragedy, that made the hit parade.

"'*Who full she up,*
And tie she up,
Could cut she down.'

"Golbourne, now . . ."

"I remember the whole song," the Constable says. "My gran-mother tell me that the tamarind tree in the Plantation Yard that Clotelle henged herself from is a famous tree. One day, during slavery, my gran-mother say, they henged a slave, after they give him forty lashes, with a balata, for stealing a fowl; and they henged him from the same tamarind tree as Clotelle was henging from; and following ever-since from that day, all the tamarinds that this tamarind tree bear, have seeds the shape of a man's head. The head of the slave that they flogged and afterwards henged. Right here in Bimshire."

"You have a good memory. You are going to make a proper de-tective, following in the footsteps of Sargeant. Yes. Your gran knew the history of this Island backwards."

"Concerning the calypso, the part you just sang, that is the chorus . . ."

"You have the memory of a barster-at-Law."

"I used to sing it!"

"Golbourne, now . . . as I was saying, is a different story. Today, anybody who was to rest his two eyes on Golbourne, walking-'bout Flagstaff Village, with his goadies bulging through his pants, meaning his two enlarge testicles, the size of two breadfruits, wob-bling-'bout inside his oversize pants, built specially by the tailor to commodate Golbourne's two things, anybody who see Golbourne in his present state would conclude that Golbourne born so. Not at all, Constable! Golbourne wasn't born with this disfiguration, looking like the Frenchman-fellow Wilberforce talks about, the man

who used to ring the bells of Notre Dame Cathedral Church, some-
where in Paris-France. The Hunchback! Oh, no! Golbourne was a
model of manhood. One of the most masculine men to ever walk
this earth! Golbourne was such a man, in his prime, that I-myself . . .

"But that night, twenty, twenty-something years ago, walking-
cross the gap leading from the Plantation to the Village, holding
hands with the nursemaid to the Plantation thrildren, walking her
home, his bicycle in his next hand, Lord! Mr. Bellfeels two motor-
car headlights picked them out, as he was returning from seeing a
movie at the Empire Theatre. Those two high-beam lights picked
Golbourne out before Golbourne could jump in the gutter to
safety, and hide. That was the night-before. The Saturday. And Mr.
Bellfeels lay-wait for Golbourne the following night, the Sunday,
to see if he was going walk-home the nursemaid.

"That tragic night was a dark night. Mr. Bellfeels was in the
canes of that section of the North Field, hiding. The canes were tall
and green. And when Mr. Bellfeels stop beating Golbourne with
his riding-crop, followed-up with kicks from his brown leather
Wellingtons, in Golbourne's two groins, what you see today, in
respect of the sameness in posture with the Hunchback of Notre
Dame, is the direct result of the venom in the beating administered
by Mr. Bellfeels on Golbourne.

"Mr. Bellfeels, that avaricious man, had his hand buried inside
Golbourne's pot. All this came out in the wash. Mr. Bellfeels had-
wanted everything for himself. A man with such needs and wishes,
my God!"

"My gran-mother tell me that Golbourne was the fastest body-
line fast-bowler the Island o' Bimshire ever produce," says the Con-
stable. "Appearing for the Flagstaff First Eleven Cricket Team,
Golbourne, my gran-mother tell me, was more faster than Voss,
the great Australian fast-bowler. Golbourne was like a freight
train, with the new ball. Men uses to tremble when they had to
face Golbourne, opening the bowling from the Plantation End,
whiching is the north end, near the North Field. Men uses to wet

their pants . . . I beg your pardon, ma'am . . . when the captain
send them out to face Golbourne."

"Yes, opening from the North Field, with the new ball!"

"Golbourne tek eight wickets one Saturday. In the first innings.
For fifteen runs. Is still the record in the whole Wessindies. And
before the first water-break, not to mention before lunch. In three
overs, when a over was still eight balls per over!"

"But the worst was Pounce," Mary-Mathilda says. "Pounce
never trouble a living-soul. Well-mannered? Would doff his cloth
hat to the littlest, most humble person; and likewise, to the most
lofty. Saying, 'Good morning, my-lady,' to every woman. 'Good
evening, sir!' to child and adult-man alike. But won't enter a church
if yuh gave him a jimmy-john full of the strongest Mount Gay dark
rum. But never a Sunday pass that you didn't see Pounce stanning-
up at the same church window, *outside*; but in full view of the pul-
pit, for Passover, for Easter and for Christmas. And there Pounce
would be; listening to every word that drop from the lips of Revern
James, Pastor of the Church of the Nazarene, just down Reservoir
Lane, by the West Field.

"Pounce came from a poor family, but decent. And it was only
for a few sweet potatoes, and pulp-eddoes, you hear me, Constable?
Not even a whole hole of potatoes, then. I counted them myself.
Cause Mr. Bellfeels had the lack of decency to bring the *same* pulp-
eddoes and sweet potatoes that he shoot Pounce for, injuring him
with a gun loaded with course-salt, to Ma; and ask Ma to cook
them in the pigeon-pea soup she was making for his dinner. That
son-of-a-bitch! Pardon my French, Constable . . ."

"I didn't hear you use no bad-words, ma'am. My two ears close!"

"Ma was working inside the Plantation Main House, by this time,
as nursemaid, following the consequences to Golbourne's former
girlfriend, who died all of a sudden, one Monday night. From the
pining and a broken heart, appears. There were three sweet pota-
toes and four pulp-eddoes Pounce tried to steal. I counted them
myself. One, two, three. Three. And one, two, three, four. Four.

They didn't even weigh much more than one pound! From the North Field. I was now leading a gang of slightly older women, weeding the sweet potato slips, of that North Field . . .

"Constable, I am rambling again! I don't know what got-me-off on this topic, talking about the history of this place. But this Plantation touch all of we. All our lives was branded by this Plantation. You see it there, with its tall chimney belching smoke from the Factory grinding canes at this time of year, Crop-Season; and with the smell of cane-juice boiling; and the noise of the Factory itself, the machineries that is always brekking-down. And this sweet, sickening smell, a smell that sticks to your clothes, and to your mind, like the rawness and the scales from fish, from a piece of shark that many a evening I watched Ma scale in the kitchen of that same Plantation Main House, when she was promoted from being a field hand, to combination nursemaid; later, to Chief Maid. The position was nothing more than chief-cook-and-bottle-washer! I am talking now about the War-days, the First World War, Ma's days. Nevertheless, the times I am now talking about is World War Two, when it look as if a real World War was taking place right-here-in-Bimshire. We didn't have no concentration camps. The people living in this Village wasn't put behind no barbed wire, such as what Wilberforce tell me was the treatment of many, Jews and non-Jews, and people called Gypsies . . . Constable, I always thought that a Gypsy was the name for a woman with a lovely voice! Those bad things happened in the outside-world; in Europe. But in this part of the universe, the Wessindies, nobody didn't torture nobody, nor squeeze nobody balls, by applying pliers, or lectricity to anybody testicles to pull the truth from outta him. Nobody down here suffer-so. Nor behave brutal-so. But, according to the *ironies* of life, as Wilberforce would say, it was the same suffering, historically speaking, between living on this Plantation and living-through the War in Europe. Much of a muchness. When you think of it. The same War. The same taking of prisoners. The same bloodshed. And the same not taking of no prisoners. So, in the eyes of Europe, we couldda been the same as Jews. It was war, and the *ironies* of war. It was *war*, Constable.

"Lord, I remember these things as if it was yesterday. The Friday evening before the Sunday in the Church Yard, when Mr. Bellfeels passed his riding-crop, as if it was his hand, all over my body . . . round four or five the Friday evening . . .

"A lorry had just crawl-over the hill, in low gear, right in front our house; and that lorry was packed to overflowing, with canes; so much so that the lorry driver had to slow down, and change from low gear into the jewel gear, to get over the hill, poor fellow. The weight of the canes, the age of the lorry, the smoke and the exhaust from the engine was almost burying Mr. Broomes the lorry driver; poor soul; and when he back-down, back into the jewel gear, in order to get over the crest of the hill, Mr. Broomes, poor fellow, was almost buried alive in all this smoke and exhaust; and then, this pullet. A Bardrock hen. The stupid fowl decide at this very same minute, whether she got blind by the smoke and the exhaust, or else was thinking that day had turn-into night, through the smoke from the old lorry engine, decided to cross the road; and *blam!* Mr. Broomes tried his best to slam-on the brakes— *Scrrrrrrreeeenk!*—but too late. The pullet lay fluttering. Mr. Broomes, poor fellow, couldn't extricate himself from outta the cab of the lorry fast-enough; or in time to rescue the Bardrock; or, put it in the cab and carry it home to his wife; nor could he stop the lorry. It was still on the incline of the hill. And a minute later, the whole lorry of canes start backing-back, by itself, back down the hill; and as Mr. Broomes was occupied with the safety of the lorry, and the load of canes, he couldn't think about laying claim to the pullet; plus, all the feathers was now joining-in with the clouds of exhaust smoke. I was looking out the window seeing all this, when Ma in the kitchen, hearing the screeling of the brakes, and the racket from the fowl, start screaming.

"*Take it! Take it!*' Ma say. '*Take it, before somebody-else! Quick, before anybody see you taking it!*'

"Ma had just come home, carrying her crocus bag apron full with sweet potatoes, in one hand, and her weekly wages, in the other.

" *'Quick, Mary-girl, before anybody see!'*

"Well, I tell you, Constable, that that Friday evening was the day I committed my first act of sin.

"But, I tell you also, that that Bardrock pullet was put in warm water with lil salt and lime juice, to draw it, Friday evening and all Saturday; and on the Sunday morning, into the iron buck-pot with some eschalots, fresh thyme, lard-oil and hot nigger-peppers. And it grace our table the next day, Sunday, the same Sunday that after Church, I came face-to-face the first time, with Mr. Bellfeels.

"We had that chicken with doved-peas, as I told you. I am relating these foolish things to you, at a time like this, when I should be giving you a Statement of my deeds and misdeeds, in this stage of my life. But . . ."

"Better late than never, ma'am," the Constable says.

"This is my history in confession, better late than never, which in your police work is a Statement. And I wonder, as I sit here this Sunday evening, why I am giving you this history of my personal life, and the history of this Island of Bimshire, altogether, wrap-up in one?"

"Ma served me the part of that Bardrock hen that has the wishbone, and . . ."

"Did you break-it-off, for luck?"

" *'Wish,'* Ma tell me, whilst she was sucking-out the two eyes from the chicken head. *'Wish, Mary-girl! Wish for the whirl. For the stars! You may be a poor, only-child of a poor, confuse mother . . . but the wish you wish, can still be rich! And big! Wish big! God will bring your wish to fruitions, and make you a powerful woman, on this very Plantation. So, wish big, Mary-girl! Wish!'*

"Ma's hand, slippery from holding the chicken head, slip-off the wishbone, so the whole wishbone remain inside my fingers, whole. Was it my fate?

"Well, Constable, I carried that wishbone for years; hoeing in

the North Field with it; tending elementary school with it, pin-to-
my dress; everywhere. I would sit in Sunday School and run my
hand over it, and dream as I followed the words in the Bible story
of Daniel in the lions den; and the flight of the Israelites walking
miles and miles over the hard, scorch earth, crossing the Arabian
Desert . . . is it the Arabian Desert, or the Sahara . . . crossing the
Sahara; and all those rock-stones and cracks in the ground and in
their feet, just like how the ground here in Bimshire gets hard and
dry when the sun come out following a downpour of rain. And I
would catch myself in these daydreams and fantasies, far-far from
that little Sunday School classroom, at the back of the church,
travelling miles and miles away from this Island of Bimshire. Pic-
turing myself in foreign countries, in Europe and in Germany—
even during the War—in Rome-Italy, living like a N'Eyetalian
countessa, dress in a white gown, a robe edged in silver and gold
piping; and with goblets of wine, and bowls of grapes and olives,
laid out before me; and I am reclining, as I see Eyetalian countessas
nowadays, in some of the magazines my son subscribes to, recline.

"I had some fantastic daydreams and fantasies, in those days,
Constable!

"And sometimes at night, sitting down here in this front-house
studying my head; and listening to Wilberforce talk about his trav-
els, the Danube, the river, so blue; crossing the Alps in a aeroplane
coming from Rome-Italy, the place which made him think of 'The
Ride of the Valkyries'; Austria and Vienna, where they can dance
the waltz, and the polka in Poland, so nice; and throughout the
whole night! Englund and even Scotland, after which I got my
name, Mary, from one of their mad Queens. All those places I vis-
ited in my dreams and fantasies, while studying, while listening to
my son, Wilberforce.

"However, I had visited those places in daydreams, even before
I gave birth to Wilberforce!

"But I never visited Latin-Amurca. Nor any place in the Wess-
indies. And I wonder why?

"I won't tell you, since you are nothing but a boy, where exactly on my dress, on my person, I carried that wishbone! But I held on to it, as if I expected a full-grown Bardrock pullet to spring-up from that lil wishbone, and grace our dinner table, every Sunday after that first Sunday, for Ma and me, until I became a woman and could provide more better.

"And every day, in all that time, ten or maybe eleven years, I made a wish on that wishbone; a wish *never-ever* to forget Mr. Bellfeels; and how he moved the riding-crop over my entire body, as if he was taking off my clothes, and then taking off my skin. And every time my hand touch that wishbone I take a oath to myself to never to forget to give him back.

"Can I ask you a question, Constable, before I stray more farther? It's a personal question."

"You could axe me any question; or anything, ma'am. I hold it as a privilege if you cross-examine me."

"Before I ask. That bell. On the table, touch it for me. Let's see what Gertrude is up to. She's too quiet . . . Thank you, Constable."

"I touch the bell."

"Thanks. The personal question. Do you attend Church?"

"You mean if I goes to Church? Or if I belongst to a particular 'nomination, or congregation? Well, the answer is part o' both. What I mean by that is this. I goes to Church, but on Easters mainly. And then, Christmas, for the five o'clock service in the morning. Or if somebody that I know dead. Or pass away. Or, or if a friend o' mine is getting henged, meaning getting married, and . . ."

"You know God, then, don't you, Constable?"

"I really and truly don't know, ma'am, if I know God. Or if God know me. I don't know God in the way I getting to know you, though, ma'am. I don't know if I should know God more better, or less better than I knowing you. We was never that close, meaning God and me.

"The only other thing I could say in regards to knowing God, is that I learned about God in elementary school. Every afternoon at Sin-Davids Elementary School for Boys, we had oral Scripture. That is where I went-school.

"You may not remember this, ma'am, but I uses to help you round the yard when I was a lil boy. 'Specially in the long vacation, June, July and August. I uses to sweep-up the yard with a coconut broom; feed the sheeps and the other stocks; wash-down the pigpens; and burn the trash and dry-leaves, in a' empty oil drum."

"And what is your name?"

"I name Bennett. Granville Chesterfield Bennett Browne. But they calls me Benn, ma'am. My proper name is Bennett."

"And you're a Constable in the Force!"

"Yes, ma'am."

"You have a nice name."

"My gran-mother give me these big-names."

"Years and years ago, Constable . . . after Wilberforce finished at the same Sin-Davids, and start attending Harrison College . . ."

"I went as far as Six Standard. And straight outta Six Standard, I join the Force."

"You did well, too! And your gran-mother gave you three nice names. Anglican?"

"Yes, ma'am."

"Confirmed?"

"Well, not exactly."

"It must be the police work. Oh, here Gertrude comes!"

"Evening, Mistress. Good evening, Constable."

"Good evening, ma'am," the Constable says.

"Constable, is there anything at all I can offer you? Cocoa-tea, or anything?"

"A cup o' cocoa-tea, please," the Constable says. "I don't normally drink cocoa-tea, but as I on duty, ma'am . . ."

"Good! Cocoa, then. Bring the Constable a nice glass of milk, Gertrude. He could mix-in the cocoa on his own. I'll have my usual . . ."

The Constable, who is about twenty-two years old, has a head shaven almost to its shining pate, as if it is purposely done this way to fit the policeman's peak cap, issued too small. He is handsome in his night uniform of black serge tunic and trousers; "for the occasion, boy; for the grave occasion," Sargeant had told him; and beside him, on the floor, he has rested his cap, that has a red band round the side. He is sitting up, in a straight-backed mahogany tub-chair; and is watching Gertrude with one eye; and with his other, Miss Mary-Mathilda Bellfeels—he calls her Miss Bellfeels, as she is known in the Village—to see if she is watching him watch Gertrude.

Gertrude is well-built, not fat, but with large breasts, round face, large brown eyes and a well-padded behind—a "big botsy," he calls it. Gertrude's skin is like velvet, black and smooth. She is five feet seven inches. The Constable sees her as a very appealing woman, for the first time, in this new light; but before tonight, and previously, on his own rounds, he would see her coming from Wednesday night prayer meetings, and revival meetings, particularly during Crop-Season; and in all these years, he never had eyes for her; never looked at her with lust. Because of the competition from other men, among them Manny who owns the Harlem Bar & Grill. So he went his way, and she hers. And then, on that Friday night, when the annual Harvest Festival of the Church of the Nazarene, where she was a Sister, ended, with the clapping and the shouting and the singing and the testifying and the sound of the joyful tambourines late in the humid, sweating air and in her spirit, Constable saw Gertrude holding Sargeant's hand, entering a field of canes.

He looks at her now, as she comes into this front-house, twice the size of the house in which he was born and still lives; facing him; the two of them thrown together in this Great House, with its shining floors, whose wood give off the smell of freshly polished mahogany, and the smell of Hawes Furniture Polish; surrounding him with a smell of sweet sexual sweetness he imagines coming from her; and he lowers his eyes to watch her small, dainty feet, bare; uncovered; not dressed in washercongs, or even Indian slippers. They are greased with coconut oil. Yes. It is the coconut oil that he smells. Not the polished mahogany furniture, nor the Hawes Furniture Polish.

Gertrude moves silent as a cat, over the thick Persian carpets. He can see the sinews on the insteps of her feet; he can see how they change form when she walks; he sees the lighter colour of skin of her heels, from the rest of the rich black colour of her instep. Dots of red nail polish, the colour of blood, decorate eight toes. The nails of her little toes are too small to accommodate even one drop of this red blood.

The Constable can see also the outline of her panties, as she moves in front of the light from the bright bare, naked bulbs that reach two feet above the table on which the bell that he rang, *pling!*, stands. And he imagines her panties are pink, and plain and without an embroidered edge round the legs and waist; and he can see clear through to them, with the help of his imagination and the naked bulbs, to the thick hair between her legs, and better still, just as she holds her body over, without bending her knees, to open the doors of an ornate cupboard; and from it, take a large decanter of crystal cut glass.

The Constable thinks of panties, made of soft sea-island cotton, bought on time from the Indian merchants whom he sees coming through the Village on Sundays, just as food is being served in Village kitchens. The Constable closes his eyes and sees Gertrude naked in his new lust, as she pours a drink into a glass. The glass has a large belly. A round belly. Large and round, like the belly of the Vicar of the Anglican Church, the Reverend Mr. M. R. P. P. Dowd, M.Th. (Dunelmn)——Master of Theology; and the Constable makes a wish, and his wish is Gertrude's voice talking to him; and he smiles, for his wish has at last been granted; and she is telling him, "*Yes, come and take it*"; but it is not Gertrude's voice: it is Mary-Mathilda, the

woman sitting beside him, whose voice he is hearing, who is say-
ing, "Come and take it, your milk. Would you like something else,
Constable?"

"The milk would do, ma'am."

"Constable's milk, and the brandy then, please," she says to
Gertrude, who is still in the room; and to the Constable, "Are you
sure you won't like something more strong than milk? In all my
born days, I never met a police who drinks milk!"

"I loves milk, ma'am."

"Now, I am curious to know, Constable, if you ever had some-
thing you couldn't part with? A *taw-ee*. A nail. Piece of lead-pencil.
A button. Anything. Like it was a, a kind of . . . obsession you had.
Like something religious. Wilberforce been telling me that the
Catholics in Rome-Italy have obsessions like these. The Catholics
we have in this Island, small in numbers, since we are basically
English and Anglicans, and high-Anglicans to-boot, are like those
Catholics in Rome-Italy. People with obsessions. I don't think that
Anglicans have obsessions of such colour and nature, though. Do
you? Wilberforce tells me that Catholics walk with a string of
beads in their hand, or round their neck; and when they die, they
insist, either in their Will, or in their last wishes, that that string
of worrying beads, that is what they call them, worrying beads,
be buried with them, in their coffin. Isn't that something? Mr.
Bellfeels told me that the man who fathered him had his gold
pocket watch and gold chain buried with him in his coffin, accord-
ing to his last Will and Testament; and that just before the grave
diggers pile-on the mould to bury the coffin, the undertaker jump-
in the grave, saying that he forget to take off all the silver orna-
ments from offa the coffin; and he unscrewed the oval hole for
viewing the corpse; and quick-so, before the mourners could blink,
bram!, the expensive gold pocket watch with matching gold chain
was rip-outta the corpse hands, and almost was inside the under-
taker paws before Mr. Bellfeels intervene.

"But when Mr. Bellfeels tell me that story, all I could do was laugh. *'I snap-on my right hand 'pon the fucker's wrist, and squeeze,* Mr. Bellfeels say he say, *and the fucker drop the watch in my left hand. With my right hand, I was choking the fucker. This is the same gold pocket watch you see me wearing all the time. My father watch.'*

"Mr. Bellfeels say that most Plantation-people want to carry their riches with them, to the grave. And they live just like that. Isn't that something?

"Poor people, on the other hand, leave-back their poorness for their offsprings to inherit. And their miseries. That is something!

"Well, that is the story about my wishbone. I lived with it, like I was a Catholic. And it lived with me, too. Carrying it all that time, from the age of eight, and for fifteen to twenty years, made it turn it into an ornament.

"But I need to get back to my Statement. I am sorry. I am sure that Sargeant did not send you here to listen to me wandering-off about wishbones and obsessions. You are here about the matter in question, and my preliminary Statement."

"But I enjoying listening to you talk about the history of the Island," the Constable says. "To-besides, we need to know the whole background to a person, for a Statement to be a statement worth its salt. Sargeant is coming. Sargeant pick me to proceed him, because he didn't want to come himself and upset you, by being the first to open the 'vestigation, and have to axe you questions that he have to axe you, because of his position. Sargeant say he can't cross the threshold of this Great House, just so, and precede to axe you questions. Sargeant tell me to tell you to-don't get worried. He not digging too deep into your business, as he and the majority o' Flagstaff people know the history of the Plantation. As aforemention, ma'am, Sargeant tell me to tell you so. Your son the doctor looks after Sargeant. We all know that. Been looking after Sargeant for years now, ma'am; and never-once charge Sargeant a copper-penny, for consultations, medicine, tablets nor proscriptions. Sargeant, as you know, have the pressure. High blood pressure. And your son is who save his life, by looking after Sargeant. Sargeant have the nerves, too. Tension and stresses from the job. We know how important you and your son is to the people of this Village. Sargeant say to tell you that he send his respects, under the circumstances."

"Under the circumstances."

"What is the real circumstances, though, ma'am? I have to put this in my report."

"Do you always drink milk when you are vestigating and taking Statements?"

"No, ma'am. I doesn't drink milk at all, but in your presence I would drink it."

"But you still like it."

"Suppose so. But I didn't get enough when I was small."

"Just milk?"

"Ulcers, too, ma'am. Occasionally, I takes something strong. Like at a wedding, or when Sargeant invite me at him, to hear the new piano that his daughter send-down from Amurca, two Christmases ago. From Brooklyn, I think, is where she lives."

"You play yourself?"

"Just a few chords. Tinklelling the ivories."

"Look at this Steinway. This Steinway is a gift, twenty-five years ago, when Wilberforce was five. Mr. Bellfeels wanted his son to have the same things in this Great House as his two daughters, Miss Euralie and Miss Emonie, had when they were growing up in the Plantation Main House.

"Wilberforce got the same as them.

"Gifts! Gifts is funny things, Constable. They could tie you to a person. And then you can't untie yourself, nor extricate your independence from that person. The knot round your neck is too tight. Gifts are unhealthy; but there are gifts. So, sometimes, you have to accept them with a smile, and a skin-teet, meaning you are far from sincere.

"There were always gifts, expensive gifts that really could not buy-me-off, even with the generousness buried inside the gifts themselves. Gifts were not enough.

"That old Steinway there, been standing like a dumb person, with no power of words. Mr. Steinway's tongue cut out. Ten-fifteen years, now.

"Wilberforce learned to play on it. And Miss Grimes smacked Wilberforce knuckles three evenings a week, learning his scales. Every four o'clock, Monday, Wednesdays and Friday, straight from Harrison College.

"One night, during this time, Mr. Bellfeels came over, and I offered him something to drink; and he took a Tennents Stout. That was his drink, when he was a more younger man. In later life, he switch to white rum. And that, plus a few more things, was what I couldn't stomach in him. Belching as he swallowing the Tennents. No class. A few coppers rackling-'bout inside his pockets, yes. But no class. The right complexion and colour of skin for living high-on-the-hog, in this Island, yes. But class? Not one bloody ounce. The man would break wind, pass gas in front of me, and his son—fart, then!—even carrying on this behaviour home, in front o' Miss Euralie and Miss Emonie. Mistress Bellfeels, his wife, in one of the few exchanges we ever had, told me such.

"I have seen Ma, whilst she was his maid, iron dozens of hand-kerchiefs, every Friday evening, rinsing-and-starching them on the Thursday; white cotton ones, with a light-blue border in all of them. And never-once Mr. Bellfeels used a handkerchief. Index finger gainst one nostril, and *phew!* Splat in the road, and watch the thick green stuff slide over a rock and disappear in the ground.

"I don't know how I managed to stomach his weight laying-down on top of me all those years; breeding me and having his wish; and me smelling him; and him giving-off a smell like fresh dirt, mould that I turned over with my hoe, at first planting, following a downpour of rain, when all the centipees and rats, cockroaches and insects on God's earth start crawling-out in full vision and sight, outta the North Field.

"And a man of his means! To live like that! And never think of dashing a dash of cologne, or some Florida Water over his face and under his two armpits . . ."

She stops talking, as she dabs a handkerchief at her mouth; and then at her right eye; and then at her left eye. The Constable sits and wonders why women always wipe their lips first, when it is their eyes that express the emotion they no longer want to disclose.

Her body shakes a little. In his eyes, she is a woman past desire; a woman who wears her dress below the knee; a powerful, rich, "brown-skin" woman; a woman to fear. He remembers her screaming at him when he was her yard-boy, because he had not swept the garbage clean from the yard; that was years ago; and he can still hear her high-pitched voice that sent chills down his back. But each evening, when he was leaving, she placed a brown paper bag into his hand, told him, "Tell your mother I say how-d." The paper bag contained large and small tomatoes, cucumbers, red peppers, three eggs and leftover chicken legs for his mother; a brown sugar cake and a penny for himself.

He pulls himself together now; puts all thought of Gertrude, and thoughts of this rich, brown-skin woman's plight, out of his mind; and recaptures the dignity of being a Constable in the Constabulary of the Island of Bimshire Police Force.

He must not let this woman's personal appeal and her physical attractiveness affect his concentration.

He must not, under the circumstances, let her soften his duty to conclude his preliminary Statement; nor, considering the act in question, have her ruffle his thoughts on Gertrude.

He is once more a Constable in the Constabulary.

So, he straightens his shoulders and sits erect in the straight-backed tub-chair.

She does the same thing with her posture, in her chair, and smiles with him.

She looks very beautiful to him, at this moment. Tempting as his grandmother told him she was, as a little girl. *"Many a man' heart skip a beat after that Tilda, before she even reach her teens. Any man would want to ravish Tilda's beauty and virginity. But she save everything for Bellfeels."*

". . . And the nights Mr. Bellfeels came over, I remember how Wilberforce, then in Third Form, beginning to take Latin and Greek, the boy was so happy to hear his father play those lovely old tunes. In foxtrot time, mainly. And 'Ole Liza Jane.' 'Carry Me Back to Ole Virginny.' And the one that Wilberforce liked best, 'Banjo on My Knee.'

"You shouldda seen the three of us! Father. Mother. And child. And then, Wilberforce and me! Jumping-round on the carpets in this front-house! Skinning our teet, and imitating the rhythms of dancing like if we were Amurcan Negroes. Doing a jig.

"Years later, Wilberforce who had-spend time in France and Germany and Rome-Italy, was now at Oxford and the Imperial College, in Tropical Medicines, studying to be a doctor, learning about malarias and sleeping sickness, from-where he would write letters to me, usually once a week, though they didn't reach these shores till months later, sometimes, specially during the War; nevertheless, in two letters, in two consecutive weeks, flashing-back to those nights when Mr. Bellfeels play 'Ole Black Joe' on the Steinway, Wilberforce tell me in the two letters . . . and these are his own words . . . *'We carried on like slaves'*—Wilberforce exact words— *'like slaves on a plantation, we put on that pantomine to entertain that man, and were ignorant, and did not know the ironies in our behaviour.'*

"Wilberforce loves the dirt his father walk on. That much you must know. But, for me to see and to hear the chastisement in the tone of his words . . .

"Since those letters arrive, this Steinway never had its lid lifted again after those words of reproach.

"It hurt my heart to know what betrayal of life we lived without knowing it! And had to live!

"Those evenings, Mr. Bellfeels would throw in a waltz; and a piece of the Classics, now and then. But he played 'Banjo on My Knee' every Saturday night. And 'Ole Black Joe.'

"Yes. Those Saturday nights were nights of Amurcan Negro songs, mainly. And even if I was in my vexatious moods, I still learn a lot from listening. Both in this Great House where he put me in, as the mother of his three thrildren, to live, even although only one of the thrildren survived past childbirth, and when I worked in the Main House. Yes, William Henry, named after two kings. Decease soon after birth. Rachelle Sarah Prudence, named after English ladies-in-waiting. Decease likewise, following birth. And Wilberforce. The living boy. Wilberforce Darnley Alexander Randall Bellfeels. W. D. A. R. Bellfeels, M.D., Doctor of Tropical Medicines, as Revern Dowd like to address him. Yes.

"I mothered Mr. Bellfeels outside-thrildren, and for that he put me in this Great House, and he gave them the name of Bellfeels, even to William Henry and Rachelle Sarah Prudence, before they dead.

"That is something in his favour, I suppose.

"Mr. Bellfeels never-even suggest I use his surname, to mean whatever the use of that name mean, in these circumstances. But I know what it could mean. I also know that behind my back, the Villagers call me Miss Bellfeels the Outside-woman. Gertrude told me. I forced it out of her. But praise God, he make my three thrildren, two dead and one still in the quick, legitimate and respectable citizens of Bimshire, bearing the name of Bellfeels. The name Bellfeels, for all the badness it conjure up, and mean to me personally; and the reputation it have in Flagstaff Village, is . . . well . . .

"On Sundays, when the sun cool-off a bit, you could find me in the Church Yard, looking down at the two slabs of white marble covering the graves of my two thrildren who passed-way."

William Henry Bellfeels, R.I.P. Rachelle Sarah Prudence, R.I.P.

"One Sunday evening, near seven o' clock, just before Evening-song-and-Service is to begin, I see the back of this man, in the

Church Yard, bending down looking at the same two white marble slabs. Him. Mr. Bellfeels! Years ago that happened.

"Write-this-down in your black notebook, what I was saying, before I got sidetracked by talking about my three thrildren . . . Yes. Write-this-down . . ."

She looks up from her lap, and sees that the Constable's eyes are closed; and she stops talking for a moment, waiting to see if he will stir from his slumber; but his eyes remain closed; and his breathing is a bit loud; and she concludes with some resignation that he is asleep. The night is long. It moves at a slow pace. The night takes on the desultory pace of her words and of her recollections. Realizing he is fast asleep, she continues talking, nevertheless.

"Serving at Mr. Bellfeels table, my first elevation from out the fields, when I was a more younger woman, and was only bearing his weight on my belly, every Saturday night, regardless to whether I was having my menses, or not . . . Yes!

"That low-class bastard! Pardon my French, Constable, although you fast-asleep.

"Yes. I remember 'The Blue Danube.' And all those foxtrots he would play. People in those days used to dance so formal and lovely, wearing long dresses, with the men in long swizzle-tail coats, looking like undertakers and penguins. But the elegance! In those days! The *ironies* of elegance! And at the Crane Beach Hotel where the really rich, the really white people, went; or at the Marine Hotel down in Hastings District, where the lower-class Plantation-people who were really not white, went. The Marine Hotel was the class to which Mr. Bellfeels belong, by birthright. To the red-nigger Marine Hotel crowd, down in Hastings.

"But you should have seen the tribes of them dancing! Those were the days! I wish those days would come back, for the sake of my son Wilberforce, who is approaching the age for marrieding. Is time he find a woman to spend his life with. Yes. For Wilberforce sake, and for the sake of the art of dancing, I wish those days would return-back.

"In those days, the men of this Island *knew* how to dance! The Aquatic Club on Bay Street, down in Town, was another popular place. In those days, a person even with a complexion such as mine, 'a brown-skin bitch,' as I happen to know is what Gertrude calls me, not even a brown-skin bitch like me, could get-past that iron gate. Unless I was working there, as a servant. And at that, they had a entrance for servants, with a hand-painted sign, saying SERVANTS ONLY. Yes."

The Constable opens his eyes, looks around, convinces himself that he did not actually fall-off to sleep; and becomes alert, fiddling with his black notebook. She watches him; and smiles.

"Now, Wilberforce, being of a even more lighter complexion than me, don't have that trouble. You see what I mean? Yes. The Aquatic Club. The place where the best dancing was danced to the best music. The Percy Greene Orchestra, plus the Coa Alleyne Orchestra. Big bands, boy! Led by two black musicianers from right here in Bimshire. Two of the *best*! In the whole Wessindies! Nor only in Bimshire.

"Did you know that the Percy Greene Orchestra played once for Majesty? Yes.

"Yes! The King, George-the-Fiff, was in the Island once . . . he wasn't really King then, not yet, he would later become King . . . and they held a dance, a Ball, what am I saying? A Ball. At the Aquatic Club. Proper; and decent, for His Majesty, George-the-Fiff. I know all this because Ma who—God rest her soul—was now promoted from weeding in the North Field, to a position within the kitchen staffs of the Plantation Main House, having a more higher status and position, as a consequence, but getting the same field-hand wage; and the Bookkeeper at the time, none other than Mr. Bellfeels, was appointed Chairman of the Royal Ball, by the Social Events Committee of the Marine Hotel, to be stage manager of the Ball held at the Aquatic Club, plus being in charge of making arrangements for transportation in private cars and hiring hired cars from Johnson's Stables; for making the banners and screamers, streamers; and buntings; for blowing up the red-white-and-blue balloons; for making-sure that the ball-room floor was waxed, and shining like dogs stones—as the saying goes—and slippery as ice; and just as treacherous; so that if a man step-off, and didn't hold his balance, like Harry-on-the-ice, mov-ing his body in time to the rhythm of some of the slowest pieces of waltz-music that the Percy Greene Orchestra would play; if that man wasn't *good!* and didn't have perfect balance, nor a knowledge of waltzes, how to move his body in time to the rhythm, how to make his footwork move in and out to the intricate movements, he was in *bare* trouble! A man wasn't a man unless he could dance on that Aquatic Club floor, wax to a vexatious perfection! If he moved the *wrong* way, or turned too fast on that floor, wax like a sheet of ice, *brugguh-down!* Flat on his arse. In full view of the invited cou-ples, and the eyes of the staffs looking-on through the glass hole in the swing-door leading to the kitchen.

"So, Mr. Bellfeels axe Ma to help-out that night, with the serving of the sangwiches and the eats and the drinks. Ma, and the other staffs of the Plantation, plus the servants of the rich white people; people like the two leading barsters-at-Law in the Island; the Solicitor-General; the doctors and business people; the Vicar, Revern Dowd; the manager-owner of Cave Shepherd & Sons, Haberdasheries down in Town, all of them-so contributed their personal staffs to the loyal service of the Royal Ball in honour and by Appointment to the King, George-the-Fiff. Ma and all of them were dressed in ser-vant uniforms, black; with white aprons, white caps, starch-and-ironed; and hard-hard-hard like deal board. Black stockings and black leather shoes. Yes!

"You shouldda seen Ma! Ma looked so beautiful. Like a queen! Pretty-pretty. Like a, like a movie-screen star. Like a young Mary Pickford!

"Yes. And, you should have seen the Bimshire ladies and gentle-men that night. It was like a fairyland, like Alice in Wonderland, like starlights burning on a Fiff of November, Guy Fawkes Day, as the King, George-the-Fiff, was in all his regalias and majesty and metals . . . medals, weighing-down his shoulder blade, poor fellow, since, as he was in the flesh, such a diminnative small man to have to bear all those regalias and insignias pin to his chest, Ma say.

"And the King made a big-big point, that night. His Majesty dance with *all* the Bimshire ladies. Every last one. And not only the ones that were white, when they were presented to him, and wasn't . . . and the King, poor fellow, who couldn't tell who-from-who, since they all looked white to him, traipsed the light-fantastic with every blasted one o' those whores! . . . Ma tell me so.

"Ma tell me, also, something that hit me in the pit of my stomach. The strangest utterance. Ma tell me she wished she was *somebody-else* that night. To be able to take part in that Ball, dress in a long dress sweeping the floor, and dance with *her* King, George-the-Fiff; and take her rightful place in the Receiving Line of that gala; and she wished she was not who she was, a field hand, a harlot, a tool for a man who came into her house, small as it was, humble as it was, after the gala was over, and the Ball had come to its end with the playing of 'God Save the King,' and after the kitchen staffs had clean-up . . . And *robbed* her of her maiden. Yes!

"Took her virginity away from her.

"She had the right colour, as you can see from my own complexion, for him to want her. But not light-enough to warrant admission on her own oars, and cross the iron gates of the Aquatic Club, to attend the Ball for her king, His Majesty, George-the-Fiff! She had the looks, as you can see she handed down in me. She had everything. Except the accident of borning in the right bedroom. Ma. My mother. God rest her soul.

"There is a story-and-a-half I could tell you about the doings and the happenings in this small Island of Bimshire! Stories to make your head curl! Stories and skeletons bigger than the square-mile-area of this Island.

"It took Ma until she was on her deathbed before she could empty her heart and tell me. And seek her redemption before God called her to her judgment.

"Psalm 51, Constable, in the *Book of Psalms*.

"Have mercy upon me, O God, according to thy lovingkindness.

"Ma was reading this Psalm in the Bible, for days and days, just before she died. As a warning to me, she eventually confess. But he, Mr. Bellfeels, was already inside my system.

"She was sixteen the night it happened. When he *took* her.

"She went to her grave, at the ripe age of seventy-eight.

"Sixty-one, sixty-two years. Three-score-and-two, she carried that burden like I carried my wishbone, in secrecy, like a skeleton; speechless, and with no utterance. A stain on a white dress, in the wrong place, and that won't come out, regardless of the bleaching you put it through. A obsession, just like I walked with my wishbone. Not one iota passed her lips. Three-score-and-two years. A whole lifetime. Vouchsafe in the books of the Old Testament.

"Women of her generation knew how to carry burdens. And how to bury them. Inside their hearts. Concealed in their blood. They were strong women, then. Tough women. Women who gave birth in the fields today, and returned to raise their hoe and lift their load two afternoons later; within forty-eight hours. In the same fields. Yes."

She takes the fat-bellied crystal glass from the mahogany side table, and raises it to her lips. She makes no sound as she takes a sip. She places the snifter back onto the white doily in the middle of the rich, brown, shining table made by the Village joiner and cabinetmaker, from mahogany wood, in the shape of a heart. Three others, scattered through the large front-house, are in the shape of a spade, a diamond and a club. Each has the same white crocheted doily on it. One has her Bible.

"Ma lost the baby conceived in rape, the night His Majesty, *her* King, George-the-Fiff, danced in Bimshire. 'My God, the blood.' That is all Ma said. That is all she remember. It was my great-gran,

Ma's gran-mother, with her knowledge of bushes and vines and leaves used for medicines; and cures; plus a lil touch of obeah and witchcraft, that saved Ma. Ma say that Gran brought this knowledge with her from Almina, in Africa. My great-gran. Yes.

"She had a name that sounded African. But I could never pronounce it, the right way. It sounded something like *Agne Beraku*; but in time, it went completely outta my mind, altogether. I do not know my great-gran's African name. Yes.

"I would see her, my great-gran-mother, just before she pass-away, bent almost in half; her face scenting the bushes; picking and picking; putting a leaf or a twig or a stem inside her mouth and chew on it, to test it; and then spitting it out; with her braided-up grey hair slipping out from underneat her white head-tie, and hanging low to the ground, searching-through worthless rocks and stones as if they were precious pearls and corals, picking a twig from this bush, a twig from the next; and putting all of them in her apron. Gran wore a apron, even when she was long-past-working in people kitchens. She spent most of her life in the kitchen at the Aquatic Club. It's a wonder to me, knowing what she must-have-went-through in them days, that she didn't put a lil twig from the wrong bush, or a stem of Poison Ivy, a lil-lil piece of the root, in the tureens of turtle soup those bastards liked her to cook for them! Yes.

"My great-gran. Her apron was like a badge of honour. In her apron, always white and starch-and-ironed, and pleated in straight lines from her waist down to below her two ankles, she would put those bushes—sersey bush, Christmas bush, miraculous bush, lignum-vitae bush, soursop leaves and leaves from the puh-paw trees, tamarind tree leaves and sugar-apple leaves . . . I don't remember the other bushes! But I know that the sersey bush is what did the trick. Sersey bush that Gran boiled thick-thick until it came like tar; bitter and black; and that poor little girl, my ma, no more than seventeen, or sixteen, was made to drink that tar-tea every morning at five o' clock, until Mr. Bellfeels vim was worked out of her system. And at every six o' clock every evening, Gran put Ma in a bush bath, and soaked her until the sin, and the stain, and the mistake, came out in the form of blood. Yes!

"It take three days and three nights, with Ma's gran-mother sitting sleepless in a upright chair, for Ma to regain her salvation, and have release from the thing that Mr. Bellfeels sowed inside her, inside Ma.

"But blood was always in our lives. Blood, and more blood . . . and that is why I did what I did."

Sargeant moves through the blackness of the night, like a brown worm, sluggish and silently; burrowing in the wet, soft mud and soil of the acres and acres of Plantation lands surrounding him. There are no street lights in Flagstaff Village. Sin-Davids Anglican Church, on the northeast edge of the Village, stands like a fortress covered in green crawling ivy, and buried in blackness. Sargeant cannot even make out the church tower; and only because he was born in the Village and has seen the Church in its stationary stoutness, day after day, a witness to the sins of the entire Village, can he tell you, by pointing in this black night, that the Church is still there.

Sin-Davids Elementary School for Boys, and Sin-Davids Elementary School for Girls, have no light over their entrances. They never had.

The only lights in this part of the Village are the two naked, powerful bulbs which hang like testicles over the verandah of the Plantation Main House. Everything else is in darkness.

So, on this night, Sargeant, on duty as the Village's only detective, disconnects the gears in his three-speed Raleigh bicycle, and smiles in the thick dark night as he realizes that the black polished frame of the bicycle contributes to the invisibility which he relishes, as he pedals like a thief throughout the back roads and fields: inspecting and spying, "'vestigating," looking for suspects, and for women, wherever they may happen to be, before heading for the rum shop, where he will pause, even though he is late in getting to the Great House, and take a snap of overproofed dark Mount Gay Rum, offered free by the owner of the rum shop, Mr. Mandeville White, Manny to Sargeant, as an indication of Sargeant's office and status in the Village, and as a down payment in exchange against future protection, and the protection of secrets, some mutual, some personal, all serious; and the occasional offer of an item, evidence no longer essential to a case being "'vestigated": a wristwatch, a bicycle pump, perhaps; and once, a leather wallet dropped by a man fleeing the clutches of the husband of the woman he was fooping. Sargeant kept the money. Four pounds sterling, and seven shillings. He then tore up the identification card, and the photos of the wife and child of the "fornicater," before he offered the empty wallet to Manny. Manny paid him five shillings, or one hundred and twenty cents, and a snap of Mount Gay, for the brown buckled-back gentleman's wallet, that had *Genuine Leather, English Made*, stamped into its rich Moroccan-red leather, in gold lettering.

Sargeant dislikes what his duty says he has to do tonight. Visit Miss Mary-Mathilda at the Great House. He has to face her before it gets much later. He does not want to take her Statement. If he could avoid it, postpone, forget it, have Vicar Dowd go in his place, ask her to leave the Great House where she lives with her son, the doctor, his doctor; have her leave Bimshire, "emigrade" and just go away . . . Englund, Amurca; live in Brooklyn with the other thousands of illegal people from Bimshire; "escape" to Venezuela, Brazil, even Cuba, Panama, in the Canal Zone, then . . . *anywhere* but here in Bimshire; and he would do anything, but have to face her . . .

He is trained as a detective, to look and to behave brave, even when he is scared. Still, Sargeant does not like this darkness. It frightens him.

Many nights, moving along the narrow track that separates the North Field from the South Field, he would pause often, imagining that he hears the sound of a man moving in the canes, trampling the dried trash; and this would make him grip his truncheon round its thick brown girth, its leather strap wrapped tight round his fingers, as he grips it now; and his body would become tense as steel; and so, stunted by fear, he would listen to the swishing sounds of footsteps deep within the vast, dark bowels of the thick cane fields, swaying in the South Field and the North Field; wondering all the time how he will apprehend this man who intrudes upon his peace, and who delays the pause for refreshment at the rum shop, for the shot glass of Mount Gay Rum whose taste is so enticing.

Sargeant knows about Amurca and Canada from magazines of those countries that carry stories of murders and "'vestigations" by the Federal Bureau of Investigation, the FBI; and the Royal Canadian Mounted Police, the RCMPees; in the swallowing swamps of Southern Florida filled with alligators; and in the deep snows of the Canadian North, where, as he read, a man could freeze to death in two minutes flat, if he stands outside on a street in a town named Winnapeg-Manitoba, in November and December and January and February, when the temperature in fifty-three degrees below zero; and he knows that the FBI and the RCMPees enforce the Law carrying guns; and he wonders why the authorities, the Commissioner of Police and the Solicitor-General and the Governor of this Island, in charge of his personal safety, balk against arming a man like him; arming him against the violence of all "these blasted criminals" hiding in cane fields, in his Village, in his jurisdiction, trampling the blasted trash a man have to do his business on.

So, Sargeant carries only a truncheon. It is the weapon to protect him from criminals. It is officially issued by the Police Force. It is made out of local wood. Mahogany, perhaps; or lignum vitae. But, in addition, privately, and secretly, Sargeant carries a bull-pistle, a whip made from the cured penis of a Zeebu bull, soaked in water and linseed oil; hidden in a long narrow side pocket custom-made into his trousers.

Tonight, he hears the dried trash swishing in the canes that surround him like the sea; and the crushing sound of the criminal's footsteps, magnified on the cane trash, at the bottom of the field, like a carpet six inches thick; and on this carpet of cane trash,

Sargeant himself, on a slow night, would take a woman, Gertrude, Miss Mary-Mathilda's maid, more often than others, and would lie; and then lie-down on her belly; and turn over on his back, and dream; and then when he has had his orgasm, which he does not stifle but announces with a "Jesus Christ!" because the field is vast, and he can be loud and still no one would hear his ecstasy; he would then roll over, putting the woman, Gertrude, more often than others, on his belly, and look past her head, right at the skies, and start to count the stars, identify for her the constellations, Orion, the Big Dipper, Neptune, constellations he read in a book his daughter, Ruby, sent to him from Brooklyn, the only ones he memorized; and actually identify the stars he counted, because the sky was dark blue and the stars were like emeralds. But now, tonight, the sky is black and there are no stars. The noise of the criminal's footsteps on the trash, in the middle of the field, comes closer to him; and makes him grip his truncheon, tighten its leather strap, until he can feel the pain in his fingers. The strap is twisted tight round his right fist, perfect for the delivery of a quick, deadly blow.

He grips his searchlight. It is almost two feet long, issued specially to sargeants and detectives tracking criminals. And he waits. He holds his bicycle against his waist, and waits and waits in this thick, voiceless darkness.

It was so peaceful and satisfying when he was last in this field of canes, near the same spot he is now, about ten o'clock in the night, two Fridays ago, when the trash was thick and soft almost as the mattress of his own bed; and the woman beside him, Gertrude, was silent; and as he lay on her, he smelled the thick richness of the sugar-cane trash, and hoped, in a loose moment that did not last too long for what he was doing, that a centipede from the thick black soil would not crawl from beneath the trash, and ramble up his trousers leg, and put a sting in his testicles.

Sargeant counted stars again that night. And saw Orion and the Big Dipper.

He goes over that last night now, as he stands, hardly breathing, ready to pounce upon the criminal in the canes.

The sounds of feet are moving. Coming towards him. No wind is blowing. He looks up, and he is covered in the same blackness of the skies as the night surrounding him. His mouth is dry. His palate is like sandpaper. He fears that he may not be able to cry out for help. But even if his mouth was not dry, and he could scream for assistance, in the blackness of the night, thick as if it has body to it, like a substance, a thickness you can measure, no one will hear his wail for assistance. No man—or woman—in the Village, will come to Sargeant's rescue, even if he heard him calling out. Sargeant is a policeman. A Crown-Sargeant. No Villager will come to rescue a policeman.

The sounds of the feet he hears are louder now. They are like the voice of the Vicar that pounds magnified through the loud-speaker placed on a tripod in the Pasture of Flagstaff Commons, where athletic games are held, when the Vicar announces entrants for the fifty-yard and one-hundred-yard foot races, on the day of the Sin-Davids Anglican Church Annual Picnic; a voice that hits the eardrums.

The footsteps are waves pounding in Sargeant's ears, and this sound of water weakens him further, for he cannot swim. He cannot move. He stands with his body against the steel frame of the bicycle.

Only once before, in his fifteen years in the Police Force, before he was promoted to Crown-Sargeant, has he come this close to the nausea born of deep fear—and from the snapping of rum—that caused him to vomit.

The quickest sedative now, for his nerves and to appease his high blood pressure, would be a double shot of strong dark Mount Gay Rum, straight-without-ice; and he wishes he was sitting in the dimly lit "Selected Clienteles Room" of the rum shop, on a wooden bench that has no back, cozy amongst his friends. But he must watch this strong dark rum. His doctor, Wilberforce, the son of the woman he has to take the Statement from, has warned him about rum.

This is the second time in his career that Sargeant must accept that a murder, part and parcel of being a detective, has turned him into pulp.

There was that first time . . .

Sargeant had arrived at the scene of that crime, on the wet thick Khus-Khus grass near the entrance to the Plantation Main House; and had pulled back the brown crocus bag that Watchie, the night watchman, had covered the body with; and he saw the young woman, naked; with her throat marked by a red line, tight and as clear as if it was a necklace of red pearls, a choker, eaten into her flesh from ear to ear; and her body striped in blood, with the dark brown soil from the crocus bag that had held sweet potatoes, collected in the folds of the sack, powdering her skin, reddened, in thick clotting marks that followed the direction of the string of red pearls, the direction and the hatred of the butcher knife that the atopsy said she had used, after she had tied herself up to the highest, most convenient limb of the tamarind tree, with a rope ripped from her own clothes; when the rope faltered, she could not hang herself, could not take her own life, could not die clean as she had wanted to do. The butcher knife told the story.

Sargeant had vomited then. O, Clotelle! Clotelle, Clotelle . . .

The sight of her body ravaged by this violence took him back to the cane trash in the North Field, months ago . . . He had sat beside her just three Fridays before, in a revival meeting at the Church of the Nazarene. Clotelle. Yes.

Now, with the same beating fear that is mixed with the courage of fate and destiny, like a man exhaling his last gasp of energy, Sargeant is actually being propped up only by the sturdy steel of his Raleigh bicycle.

Footsteps in the cane field coming towards him, magnified by the dryness of the trash, become louder and more foreboding. He turns his searchlight on. The truncheon in his hand is like an extended right arm. The footsteps become noisier; and his heart is pounding; and just as he is wondering how deadly to make his blow, two dogs locked in sex, and joined like Siamese twins at the genitals, struggle clumsily out of the canes.

"Jesus Christ!" Sergeant says. And laughs. The dogs retreat into the thickness of the North Field. Sergeant unbuttons the fly of his heavy black serge trousers. His urine splatters on the cane trash. He shivers as he pees. His pee splatters on his policeman's black boots.

Sargeant is thirsty now. He wants his snap of rum. Tonight, he will have three. Rum is the blood of the Island.

The rum shop is a small building, of one gabled roof, made of deal board, and unpainted; and it is built like an afterthought, on to the rest of the main house. Architecturally, it is nothing more than a "shed-roof." Manny built the rum shop years ago, in one Saturday afternoon and a Sunday morning, with the help of men and boys— and some women—in the Village; their help induced by four tins of Fray Bentos corn beef, Wibix soda biscuits, pork chops fried in lard, and two jimmy-johns of Mount Gay Rum.

There is one door, reached by climbing two raw blocks of coral stone, cut from the Village Quarry. When the rains come, the two blocks shake, and move from their moorings a little, and cause some customers to lose their balance, and bang their bodies against the door posts.

The rum shop is lit by acetylene lamps that require pumping, and whose mantles resemble crocheted booties for dolls. They are all white. These acetylene lamps burn with more fierce brilliance than low-watted electric bulbs. They burn throughout the night, like peeping eyes, even when there is no customer in the Selected Clienteles Room.

Sargeant has to wonder why Manny, Village rum shop proprietor and Village butcher, never got electricity installed in the rum shop, as in the main part of his house, named Labour Bless.

"I can't afford 'lectricity offa the blasted lil money these hand-to-mout' people does-pay me to kill a pig for them!" Manny explains.

In the verandah of Labour Bless, which runs along three sides of the house, made of coral stone and deal board, Manny has an acetylene lamp, which guides his "selected clienteles" on dark nights when there is no moon.

Labour Bless is the name Manny christened his house with, after he returned from Cuba where he worked cutting sugar cane.

"And from the loins of my labour," Manny told Sargeant, "and blasted hard labour it was, at that! In that Cuban heat? In August? Jesus Christ! Offa that labour, I build this wall-house. It take me five years to complete, but it is mine!" Pride was reflected in the name of the house, even though spelled in English; and in the house itself.

"If I had-remember enough Spanish, Labour Bless woulda been spell-out in 'Paniol!'"

The acetylene pump-lamp on the verandah is not burning tonight. This to Sargeant is some kind of omen.

But he rides on, from the vicinity of the North Field, in low gear, in the unending darkness. He continues his patrolling of the Village, taking a dirt track bordered by canes. The canes have sharp leaves like razor blades, and with the overhanging branches of the pigeon-pea trees, these two obstacles bite into his face, missing his eyes, and sear his hands. He knows the lay of this land like the keyboard of the piano he plays on Fridays for his friends and for Constable. As he moves in this black night, he feels better, now that the first incident of his patrol was nothing more threatening than two screwing dogs.

"Blasted dogs. No breeding!"

And he, a big man, this powerful Crown-Sargeant, felt his life was in danger. He had felt so cowardly, so exposed.

"Imagine! *Me*, scared? What could scare me, a big Crown-Sargeant in His Majesty's Royal Constabulary Force of Bimshire?"

Sargeant talks to himself all the time, especially on dark nights, patrolling the back lanes, in the black, quiet Village. He talks to himself when he is off duty; when he is at home alone; when he is bathing in the sea at five o'clock every morning; when he is walking up the aisle in the Choir. He talks to himself in the Court of Common Pleas, while he waits to give evidence.

Instinctively, he passes two fingers of his right hand over the silver embroidery of the three stripes edged in red on his shoulder; and the two fingers linger for a further moment, on the large Imperial Crown that sits above the stripes. He adjusts the bicycle clips on his trousers legs, around the ankles; pushes the heavy brown truncheon back into its leather sheath; and flashes the searchlight in a wide arc, making figures in the black night air, like a child holding a starlight on Guy Fawkes Day.

He rides on, with the gear of his three-speed bicycle ticking softly and slowly, in low. The sound is like the music of the Police Marching Band, playing a tune of sad death and remembrance, a march composed by Sousa, as he wades through a narrow track, in a dark valley of tall sugar canes cut out between the North Field and the South Field. And he whistles, in a clear, sharp tone, this road-march tune, without knowing whether the tune is by Sousa, or by some other composer of martial music:

"*It's a long way to Tipperary,*
It's a long way to go,
It's a long way to Tipperary . . ."

Sargeant cannot put the sight of Clotelle's body out of his mind. For years after he had taken the Statement that showed the cause of her death; and whenever he rode his three-speed bicycle through the ticking black nights, each sudden noise, each movement, the shaking of a pigeon-pea tree branch, perhaps a footstep from within the vast cane fields, made him see, all over again, the thick clotting blood that covered the gaping wound left by the weapon the murderer had used.

The crime was not suicide. It was murder. He thought about this crime, its flesh and blood and the savagery a sharp knife could take on, whenever on a Saturday afternoon he went to the rum shop to visit Manny, to shoot the breeze, as he stood within the paling of Manny's backyard, and saw how Manny butchered-up the huge pig from which he would make black pudding-and-souse, a Village delicacy of boiled pig features: feet, ears, snout, jowls of the head, the tongue, gristle and bones, feet and ears pickled in lime juice with diced cucumber, chopped thyme and hot nigger-peppers, following all this activity, and Manny's dexterity with a long knife, Sargeant could understand how easy it was for him to see Clotelle all over again.

And one Saturday morning, he arrived in the backyard and found Manny with his hands deep within the entrails of a slaughtered pig, pulling out the intestines, the heart and the liver and the blood; then cutting the head from the body; and cleaning the head; scrubbing off the black silk hairs with a stone and then with a razor blade and with boiling water. Part of the head, from the neck down, looked like the head of a young woman, bathed in blood. Like Clotelle's head.

And now, after a quick drink that he will snap back in the rum shop, without water to kill its sting, without respecting the caution given by his doctor, Wilberforce; after three quick snaps of rum, he will have the courage and the strength to face another tragedy; but worse than that, because of duty, he will be forced to take a Statement from a woman he has lusted over for years, from Miss Mary-Mathilda at the Great House. She is a woman he has known since childhood. It is a knowledge that was shaped by the distance that controlled status and complexion, and that tested love itself. A woman he still loves, but dare not tell her; a woman who, years before, had caused his small heart to palpitate, and his tom-pigeon to throb in little spasms . . .

He will need more than three strong snaps of Mount Gay Dark Rum tonight.

"Any one o' we have reason to kill that son-of-a-bitch!" Manny says. "We have cause."

"For years, now!" Sargeant says.

Manny and Sargeant are the only persons in the Selected Clienteles Room.

"Any one o' we."

The BBC Sunday night documentary programme *World War Two Round-Up*—a documentary on World War Two, already ended—comes on; and they stop talking, as they listen to the news of battles lost by the Allied forces in Sicily; of Allied ships sunk by German submarines in the North Atlantic, wreaking destruction upon merchant ships which pass through the West Indies, near Bimshire and continue in the ship lanes up North to England; and news of men drowned at sea.

Manny makes the sign of the Cross.

"The Axes bursting we arse, Sarge!"

"Licks leff-and-right."

"Licks like peas, we getting up in the European Theatres!"

"The Axes painting our arse, black-and-blue!" Manny says, when the news, which is now three minutes old, draws near the end.

"Bull-pistle lashes," Sargeant says.

"We lossing this War," Manny says.

"But I don't know if it is a *fete-accomplee*," Sargeant says.

The programme is over, now. Hymn singing follows the BBC *Round-Up* programme.

"I merely responding to a call. I don't know wha' happen up at the Great House. Perhaps she and Gertrude had a quarrel. Perhaps nothing ain't happen. Nuh cause, nuh act, nuh motive. I don't know."

There is no wind tonight. The air is heavy and tight; and it clutches the collar of Sargeant's tunic, as if it is a necktie that a criminal is pinning him down with, like a Boston crab choke-hold he had suffered at the hands of Boysie-Boys, the first murderer to escape from His Majesty's Glandairy Prison.

Sargeant's tunic has five silver buttons that run down his paunchy chest. The heaviness of the air and the fit of the tunic are making it difficult for him to breathe. Beads of perspiration forming on his forehead and under his neck pour from his smooth black skin, like small beads of pearl.

Still, he does not take his handkerchief from the sleeve of his tunic. He leaves the sweat on his face, as if it is a religious mark, a talisman, a spiritual reminder of faith, and experience.

Earlier on, he had been sitting in the sub-station, the white tunic of his daytime uniform draped over the back of an upright wooden chair with a cane bottom. His braces hung from his waist like the harness of a small parachute; and his grey flannel undershirt had changed to a darker shade than the colour from the perspiration that poured out of his body in the clutching humidity, like larva rising from the ground.

The Constable, his assistant, was sitting in a matching wooden chair, slouched in the same manner as Sargeant was, fanning himself with the four pages of the *Bimshire Daily Herald*, one of the Island's four newspapers, which he had folded into the shape of a Chinese fan. Naiman, the man who swept the yard and ran errands to the rum shop, who bought cigarettes and tins of Fray Bentos corn beef and hard round biscuits, and who did odd jobs around the sub-station, cleaning out the two cells, throwing Jays Fluid on the prisoners' urine to deaden its pungency, himself a former convict, this man Naiman, who also fetched Sargeant's and the Constable's home-cooked meals (food: made by a woman in the Village, off the passenger bus, at the appropriate hours—eleven in the morning, for lunch; and five o'clock in the evening, for dinner), sat with them, barefoot, in his workman's uniform of blue denim short-sleeved shirt and matching short pants, gasping instead of breathing, as if the humidity was about to choke him to death.

Then the telephone had rung, rousing them from their lethargy. Sargeant turned the BBC programme down. They were playing hymns from St. Martin's-in-the-Fields.

The telephone rang fifteen times.

It was Naiman who had risen from his chair first, slowly and half-dead, to answer it.

"His Majesty's Police Station! 'Strict D Sub-station! Naiman speaking . . ."

There was a pause.

You could hear the change in Naiman's breathing, the sudden intake of breath.

The time by the noisy, ticking clock on the wall is seven thirty-five. Sunday night. The clock is round, and has large black hands and hangs below a framed colour photograph of King George the Sixth.

Just as the three of them, Sargeant, the Constable and Naiman himself, could, at certain times of the afternoon, hear the waves in the sea, when there were no cars and buses speeding in front of the sub-station, so too, now, they could hear the weak waves touching the iron pipe and the crumbling foundation wall of the sub-station. And they could hear the leaves in the beach almond trees shake. And hear the rattle of the dried inedible fruits of the shack-shack tree.

"What you say? You had-better tell this to the Sargeant, your-self, ma'am," Naiman said into the telephone. "Miss Bellfeels, the Sargeant here . . . he here."

Naiman pointed the telephone at Sargeant. Sargeant moved slowly, taking fifteen seconds to reach Naiman's outstretched hand.

Some time passed in silence. Naiman and the Constable could hear Sargeant's breathing.

"Miss Mary-Mathilda? What you telling me? I don't want to hear it, if that is what you telling me, Miss Tilda. . . You sure you want me to hear this? Yes, ma'am . . . yes, please, ma'am . . . yes, ma'am. I will come to get a Statement . . . yes, yes . . . it is my duty as a police . . . I can keep a secret. Yes, please . . ."

Sargeant gave the telephone back to Naiman, who put it back on its hook.

"Constable," Sargeant said.

The Constable stood up.

"Get-dress. Put-on your night uniform. Quick. Something like it happen. You ain't got much time to change . . ."

The large, round noisy clock told them it was exactly thirty-seven minutes past seven o'clock. That was the time. Sargeant made a note of it. *"Thirty-seven minutes passed seven o'clock, PM, Sunday evening,"* he wrote in his small black notebook.

Sargeant had looked through the window in the sub-station, to-wards the Plantation Main House, and could see the cane fields that stretched for miles and miles, round the small three-roomed sub-station, cells, water closet and office-cum-dressing-and-sleeping-room, making it look and feel like a fishing boat marooned in a sea that had no waves and no current; and no wind blowing on its surface.

"Go up to the Great House," Sargeant told the Constable, "and see if you could pacify Miss Bellfeels, Mr. Bellfeels lady Miss Tilda, till I get there. And whilst you there, see if you could find out what the arse that woman mean 'bout intent and intending. Tek-down every word she tell you, in a prelimary Statement. Tell she I com-ing, soon-soon . . ."

"When I was a lil girl, I used to like to climb. Trees and rocks. Spe-cially trees. Ma said I reminded her of the brown-and-white goat we kept in the yard, to give milk. Goats don't climb trees, though; only rocks and hills. You know the clammy-cherry tree at the junc-tion of Highgates Commons and Reservoir Lane that the Villagers sit under and shade from the sun, when they're waiting for the bus to Town?"

"I know it!" the Constable says. "We uses clammy-cherries to stick kite paper on our kite frames, during kite-season, when we mekking kites. 'Specially at Easter. Yes! The clammy-cherry tree at the junction!"

"Things made from clammy-cherry last for generations. Tough and durable and rugged things. From clammy-cherry, the Plantation makes the handles of certain implements used in the fields. Like the handles for forks and hoes. And sickles that we cut Khus-Khus grass and Guinea grass with.

"The handle of the hoe I used for all those years in the North Field was made from the same clammy-cherry tree. Yes.

"Ma herself used the hoe she inherited from her mother, my gran. And it was there, on the day she died, leaning up in the yard, strong as anything, strong as the day the Plantation made it. This is the same hoe I inherited from Ma. Yes!

"And it is the handle of that hoe I have been polishing. Rubbing-it-down in oils. Night after night, for the past three months. And why three months? I can't find rhyme nor reason to explain it! Must be one of the *ironies* Wilberforce always talking about, constantly. . .

"I went one morning, when he wasn't too busy, to see Mr. Waldrond the Joiner and Cabinetmaker. Mr. Waldrond makes the most beautiful furnitures in this Village, in the whole Island, if you ask me! And I respectfully asked Mr. Waldrond for a drop of oil and a daub of the stain or polish he uses on mahogany. Mr. Waldrond look at me, and laughed. 'Never,' Mr. Waldrond say, 'in all my born-days, and during my time as joiner and cabinetmaker to this Plantation, plying my trade in this Village, have a girl, a woman, axe me to lend she the tools of my trade!'

"Heh-heh-heh! I had to laugh, too. I didn't tell Mr. Waldrond what I needed the stain and the oils for. But outta the goodness of his heart, and without cross-questioning me, Mr. Waldrond give me a few drops of linseed oil and some Hawes Lemon Oil and some homemade polish he uses for polishing mahogany.

"I took those three things, and from that day, I would sit down in a chair in the kitchen, evening after evening, whilst Gertrude would steal a glance at me, when she think I don't notice, wondering what I am doing rubbing and rubbing the handle of a hoe with linseed oil and Hawes Lemon Oil for, but there I would be, rubbing up and down, up and down; down and up, polishing till the handle start to shine, like Mr. Waldrond's mahogany furnitures.

"While Gertrude is washing the wares, or starching clothes, doing her housework, there I would be, polishing and polishing the clammy-cherry-tree handle.

"I then turned my attention to the blade. And I used a piece of sharpening-stone with oil on it. This I got from the blacksmith, who shoes the horses on the Plantation. The mules and the donkeys. If-only I had the strength to use a anvil, and was able to lift his hammer, I would have beaten-out a brand-new-brand blade for myself. And sharp as a Gillette razor! But I had to rely, every evening, on the sharpening-stone and the oil only. For three months.

"I had-got the oil off the chauffeur, Mr. Broomes, poor man, who drove the cane lorry the Saturday afternoon that he run-over the Bardrock fowl.

"Sometimes, in the heat of thinking of things to do, like making doilies for the furnitures, or preparing great-cakes for festivals and bank holidays, I would miss a evening of polishing and sharpening. But, as regular as I could, I would be at that kitchen table . . .

"But what was I polishing and sharpening for? What was my purpose spending all those hours on a hoe, in the kitchen of this Great House for? After so many years using the same hoe in the fields, retired from the fields, put into the Main House as a house-servant, eventually given certain favours in my upliftment . . . then turned into some man's kip-woman! To where I am now. Or was it that I am a dreamer?

"Ma always said, *'Girl, you is the biggest dreamer that I know. You's a born dreamer, Mary-girl!'*

"But there I was . . . not really knowing what destiny God had in mind to put my hoe to.

"And sometimes, as I sit in my kitchen with Gertrude and my hoe, Wilberforce would come in, and pour himself a drink, or take up a slice of sweetbread or steal a pork chop outta Gertrude's frying pan, and start telling us, Gertrude and me, of his travels.

"And *not once*, did it enter his head to ask me why I was polishing a old hoe? And sharpening the blade?

"And I would stop polishing and sharpening, and let Wilberforce words carry me on those journeys he describe. Wilberforce had travel all over Europe, after the War; and once, coming back from Italy, north of a lil town name Vincentia, and seeing the Dollarmites, near the Alps, caused him years later, to make the comment, about how he found the place so desolate; and at the same time, so pretty and appealing. The sharp points of the hills and the mountains, the steepness of the sides of hills forming themselves into gorges, down, down into the valleys, and the sides of those valleys, and how those valleys was so dramatic and frightening, harsh and lovely, painted in the strange colour of the Eyetalian light. Those wonderful colours, Wilberforce say, are to be found only in Italy. And Wilberforce conclude that this part of the world, the valleys of the Dollarmites— I think this is how you pronounce the word—the Dollarmites seemed to be a place where history ordain that a lot of killing and fighting had to take place. As if it was destiny. He told me it was the geography of the place that gave it that ironical meaning, and that history. A history of killing and fighting amongst those European tribes and clans.

"Once, to show me the meaning of words that Winston Churchill used, during the War, namely, *'Give we the tools, and we will do the rest,'* Wilberforce said those words were really a code.

"The women in my field gang, ordinary women, ascribed to weeding the North Field, I witnessed how some of them never took care of their hoes, the instruments they use daily, to make a living with—such as it was. So, their job and their labour was always more harduous. They had the tools, but not the sharpness in those tools to do the job well. And whenever their hoe hit a rock, their labour ended; and the rest of us women would bend over and laugh and laugh at that poor woman's expense. At her misfortune. Yes.

"When a hoe hits that rock-stone, it send zings of pain climbing right up your two arms. And it dullens the blade of your hope; and the hoe itself. Yes.

"But the history of a hoe hitting rocks and old roots, stumps of pigeon-pea trees and other trees planted generations ago, before this very Plantation was cut out of the land, trees such as the same tamarind tree which Clotelle used; the clammy-cherry tree whose berry is used for sticking paper to kite frames; or the cordear tree, the loveliest tree in the Island, with the sweetest flowers, according to smell and fragrance, but a flower, my God, with the shortest lifespan of existence, this accident of a woman's hoe hitting gainst a obstruction like the root of a tree hidden in the soil, was an every-day occurrence. Yes. Cause, from in the olden days, in the times of my great-gran, before Ma's time, this Plantation was nothing but virgin land. Yes.

"I must ask Wilberforce if the Plantation planted these trees after cutting up the land.

"But, going back to Churchill's code, *'give we the tools,'* my hoe was always ready. No rust. Always sharp. Sharp as the long knife Manny use for slaughtering animals. Sharp as a iron cane bill for cutting canes. Yes. And always shining. From the linseed oil and the Hawes Lemon Oil. And the sharpening-stone.

"But going back to Wilberforce and his memories of flying over the Dollarmites and the Alps, and how it reminded him of Churchill's code . . . that boy applies Churchill's codes to *every* part of life, even to his own practice in Tropical Medicines . . . by having tools that are always sharp and sharpened, instruments and surgeons' scalpels. If Wilberforce happen to be cutting-open a person's stomach, in search for the groins, or the pennicitis, or the liver, my God, and the implements are not sharp . . . and you happen to be the patient on that cot . . . my God! And you are at Wilberforce mercy! Yes! But Wilberforce believe in the right tools, as a man who needs them for his use, to cut-open living persons with . . .

"But he won't use them on me! Wilberforce will never cut-open me! Not me! And he is my son! You think I would let Wilberforce come near to me, with one of his scalpels?

"And all these years, I suffer silently, and in pain, from penni-citis? Still, do you think I would grant Wilberforce the right to come-near me, with a knife in his hand? No!

"And you know Wilberforce is one of the best surgeons in Bimshire! . . .

". . . but the code about tools applies to everyday life. Yes.

"Still, my question to myself is '*Why?*' Why-though, was I pol-ishing the handle and sharpening the blade of my hoe, all those evenings, after I wash my face-and-hands? What is the reason and motivation?

"Ma used to call me a crazy girl, along with saying I am a dreamer, when I was small.

"Yes! *Be prepared*. As they learned me in the Girl Guides, teach-ing me preparedness concerning the tools I worked with.

"If it wasn't so dark outside, I would ask you to look out that window, and let your eyes travel to the shed, near the stables now turned into a cottage . . . the shed is made outta coral stone . . . but the shed was originally an oven. We used to bake cassava bread in it. It is a relic from the slave days . . . you would see the hoe in question.

"No! I don't think it is there. The hoe is not there. I didn't put it back, I don't think, when I returned from the Main House. And, my God, I can't call-to-mind where I put it. The memory going, Constable. The mind slipping. But it got to be in this House, on this property, *somewhere*. The hoe is here. My hoe. Tonight, after I returned inside-here from the Main House, I realize tonight is the very first time, in all the years I inherited it from Ma, that my hoe hasn't slept within my reach.

"When I was carrying Wilberforce, after I lost his brother, William Henry, and his sister, Rachelle Sarah Prudence, soon after they born; after I start cohorting with Mr. Bellfeels . . . and God, you have to pardon me for that mistake . . . but life is life, and full of *ironies* . . . years and years afterwards; after cohorting, and I allowed Mr. Bellfeels to do what he wished with me, it suddenly hit me that I needed something to preoccupy myself with. Wilberforce was growing-away from me. Will married and move-out, someday. The crocheting was making my two eyes burn, and my eyesight bad. And three months ago, almost to the day, I took the hoe from its resting place under my bed, and start sharpening and polishing it. Sharpening and polishing in preparation for the right use to put my hoe to.

"So, I slept with my hoe. Underneat my four-poster bed with the Simmons mattress. And before I moved into this Great House, I slept with it, wherever my bed was, in whichever place I lay my head.

"I had an obsession about that hoe. And a identical one with the wishbone. That wishbone went with me wherever I went. I could hide it anywhere. But my hoe was too big to conceal. Still . . .

"The afternoon that I asked Mr. Waldrond for the oil and the stain, when he told me how strange it was for me, a woman, to be interested in his profession, as if I was invading his sacred territory, it made me think of the place of woman in this Island. That thought hit me, hard-hard. It made me see that in this Village, now and in bygone days, and in Ma's time, women were relegated.

"Women were allowed to be schoolteachers sometimes. A few that you could count on one hand made it to headmistress. A few more became nurses in the Bimshire General Hospital. But the vast-majority spent their lives as field hands, maids, cooks and nursemaids. The enterprising few was the group that left and went Away, overseas to Amurca, Englund and the Panama Canal Zone. Some who got their hands on Amurcan magazines, from places like the South and Brooklyn, start looking in those magazines at Technicolor pictures of coloured women, these women tried their hands in a follow-pattern way, at imitating black Amurcan women, at fixing hairdos, at hairdressing; and needlework. The most ambitious put up shingles and announce themselves as SEAMSTRESS WITHIN.

"Basically, not much more were women allowed to do, in this Island.

"We never had the education that women in Amurca—not counting-in the South!—and other parts of the outside-world were allowed to cumulate from book-learning and practical experience; and encouragement.

"But we were women who understood things; and we learned by listening and observing. So, even though I never had the education that could explain to me the reason and the motivation for polishing the handle of the hoe, and sharpening its blade, I knew that I had to keep-on doing it. And Be Prepared, religiously night after night, as the Girl Guides' motto says.

"I became overprepared. But I did not know who I was going to test the keenness of my preparation on. And while we're waiting on Sargeant to come, I cannot tell you that I knew what my real intention was, neither.

"There is a time when your past takes over you, and takes over your present; and if you stand and remain passive as Ma was in the Church Yard, that Sunday afternoon . . . when she stood there as if she had a sunstroke that rendered her parlyzed in speech; and all she could do was to watch how Mr. Bellfeels passed his riding-crop slow-slow, slow, over my body, as if he was telling Ma to her face, *Old woman, look, I don't need your wrinkle-up body no more. I have Mary-girl, this young, sweet delicious piece o' veal, to feast on, at my heart's delight.*

"That was done in times when a woman, with no education to speak of, didn't know the term 'feminine-suffrages.' We knew we were feminine-minded-women, though. That was driven into us, by instinct . . .

"There was no feminine-suffrages in my time, Constable. But we still knew what was happening to us, in this Island. As women, we didn't comport ourselves with the talk of English suffrages-women. But that voice was buried inside our hearts. And although we could not, dare not, shout-out a dirty word in Mr. Bellfeels face, or pick up a rock-stone and pelt it at Mr. Bellfeels, and break his arse . . . pardon my French! . . . and watch his head burst-open like a watermelon, and watch the blood spurt-out like the water from a water coconut, all those thoughts and buried acts, and stifled wishes concealed in our craw, were always near the top, near to erupting. We couldn't act like this modern generation of darkskin women I see walking-'bout this Village, in dresses of African print; and wearing their hair natural; uncomb. But the plot of defiant words and Africa was already hatching inside our heads. Yes.

"A woman of my generation could not even dare to think of poisoning a man like Mr. Bellfeels, with a few drops of Jays Fluid, put by accident in his gravy. A silent, and secretive poisoning. With a teaspoonful of glass-bottle grind-up fine-fine-fine and sprinkled-over his food, to conceal the act against detection.

"But, thank God, there was at least one feminine-suffrages woman living-'bout here. *One* woman, in the whole of Bimshire, with big-enough balls to confront a certain gentleman, who shall remain nameless . . . Yes.

"She poisoned him. A lil grind-up glass-bottle, fine-fine-fine, in appearance no difference from white pepper in a shaker, and just *a little pinch*, and sprinkled it with carefulness on the fresh parsley leaves he loved so much to have on his souse. And *out-goes-him!* . . . God rest his soul . . . Yes.

"But before Ma left this life . . . and may God rest *her* soul, too . . . she said to me, *'Mary-girl, you must never forget that Sunday afternoon in the Church Yard! And bear witness to how my mouth was stricken. But there is times when it is more better not to open your mouth, than to speak a word.'*

"Ma whispered those words, using her dying breath, to utter her last advice."

The Constable is getting tired.

Miss Mary-Mathilda is standing by the window, looking into the blackness of the night, towards the North Field, unidentifiable from the surrounding darkness of the night.

The Constable tries to recall details of a dream he had last night: Naiman was bringing him and Sargeant sixteen salt fish cakes in a

greasy brown paper bag, along with special rum, cured in prunes
and raisins and golden apples. He can taste the rum scorching his
throat as it goes down . . . But Miss Mary-Mathilda's voice keeps
following a path that is more fixed than his own dream, a path to
another kind of life lived in this Village, but which he knew nothing
of before tonight. It is a life he could not see from his distance down
the hill.

Tonight he has been sitting in a house, inside its cool, large,
shuttered doors, on a mahogany tub-chair, offered a drink of milk
with chocolate, from a crystal glass. The utensils in his home are all
made of tin. The tinsmith rivets a handle onto the empty "tot" that
contained condensed milk, imported from Englund. And on other
"tots" that once held green pigeon-peas, Canadian pears, Canadian
apricots, Canadian plums; and larger ones not round, nor cylindri-
cal, which came with pilchards, salmon and Fray Bentos corn beef,
with "Halifax" and "The Argentyne" marked on them, before they
got into the hands of the tinsmith. These utensils are the "crystals"
of the Villagers.

But his life down the hill was still a life. In his world, he was
happy; had been happy even without the acquaintance of this Great
House, this other world that was, for him, out of reach socially.
Now that he has seen the life Miss Mary-Mathilda lives, even under
the circumstances; now that he has entered her world, he can still
feel that what beckons him here, in this world shuttered against
hurricane and intruder, is not its size and comfort, more and more
unenticing; and not better than his existence in the sub-station;
nor better than in backyard palings sitting on a rock, eating pudding-
and-souse every Saturday afternoon, with the pleading eyes and
the hot breath of the neighbourhood's mongrels focused upon
his enamel plate; not better than pounding domino seeds under a
sea-grape tree, on Hastings Beach; and not better than just sit-
ting in his one-roomed, one-roofed chattel house, down the hill,
through the fruit trees and the royal palms, near the Pasture, near
the Rock Quarry, near the Church of the Nazarene, in the Village

of Sin-Davids which borders Flagstaff Village, reading detective magazines full of murders lent to him by Sargeant, sent by his daughter Ruby, from Brooklyn.

". . . and when I left this house, a few hours ago," she is telling the Constable, "there wasn't a shaving of a moon in the sky. It bring-back two things to me. Number one: as girls, Clotelle, Clotelle's sister, Cecily, who we called Sis, Gertrude my maid, although slightly younger, and Mr. Brannford's wife and me, we never played games at night, even beside our house, or in Clotelle's paling, unless it was a moonlight night. And we girls played with boys, in them days. Golbourne and Sargeant and Pounce and Naiman, before he went-off slightly in the head. The game we played the most was London Bridge."

And she recites the first verse:

"'London Bridge is falling down,
Falling down, falling down,
London Bridge is falling down,
My fair lady . . .'

"And after 'London Bridge,' the next popular was 'A Riddle, a Riddle, a Ree.'"

And again, her face transformed by the recollection of her children's games, and her voice strong but tender and sweet, she recites the first verse of this rhyme:

"'A riddle, a riddle, a-ree,
No one can solve this riddle but me!
What is long and tough and shiny
And have a smell, and a sharp
Shiny thing at the end, and . . .'"

"A hoe!" the Constable shouts. And immediately is embarrassed that his voice was raised, so he covers his mouth with his left hand to erase the words spoken, to draw them back into his mouth, to apologize for speaking out of turn.

She smiles with him. Her face becomes more beautiful, and youthful; and she is once again the young, frisky, little girl with the falsetto voice, keen as a knife, who laughed the loudest amongst her girlfriends and boyfriends, as they played London Bridge.

"Yes!" she says. Her face is beaming, beautiful and joyous. "A polished hoe."

"I like riddles bad-bad, ma'am," the Constable says, and wipes his eyes, and then sits erect.

"That's a good thing, specially for a policeman doing detective work.

"And the second thing about moonlight nights versus dark nights is a story of a woman who was two-timing her husband. I don't recall the details in full . . . My mind is not my own, tonight . . .

"Earlier this evening, heading to my destination, I deliberately walked in the middle of the road. Now that Crop-Season in full swing, and the canes cut, the ground animals and other pests are disturbed from their lairs and habitats in the canes, so it could be a lil dangerous to walk too close to the side or gutter, specially near a cane field; and that cautiousness made me walk in the middle of the road.

"Two motor-cars passed me like this. The first was the Vicar, late for Eveningsong-and-Service. He wave. And when he see who the body is, *bram!* he apply the brakes in the middle of the road and back-back the car to greet me.

"'Ma'am,' he say to me, 'where you going with that?' His two eyes rested on my two hands behind my back. He couldn't see what was in my hand, though.

"'Just stretching my two legs, Revern Dowd, sir,' I say. 'Tekking a lil stroll. Is such a lovely evening, though it dark!'

"And *blam!* he put the Morris Minor in first gear and roar off.

"'Church,' he say, holding his head out through the window. 'I late!'

"And the Pucker-Pucker disappear round the corner, in smoke and exhaust, thick-enough to choke me.

"The second car that pass was Manny.

"'Jesus Christ, Tilda!' Manny shout-out for everybody to hear, in case there was somebody listening. Manny's mouth doesn't have any cover. And knowing this, I kept the hoe behind my back. And succeeded. 'Where you going this time o' night, Miss Mary-Mathilda, ma'am? I could give you a lift?'

"'No thanks, Manny-boy!' Manny possess the eyes of a hawk.

"'I just stretching my two legs, Manny-boy!' I tell him. 'Just tekking a lil constitutional, boy, before it get more darker.' And before Manny move-off, he say, 'I went down Oistins Market for flying fish, but them fishermens so blasted thiefing! Sargeant dropping-round for a snap, later . . .' And like the Vicar, before him, Manny was gone!

"I continued my journey, slow; taking my time.

"If you have a weak heart, even on a moonlight night, the canes have a way of shaking themselves, and making noise in the wind, that could put the fear of God in your heart. And on a dark-night, like tonight, if your heart weak . . .

"But I was a woman of determination.

"The smell of bourgeanvillea flowers, even the crotons, and specially the lady-of-the-night, followed me all the way from here, to where I was heading.

"And over and above those scents, the smell of burnt canes and cane trash filling my nose. With cane fires occurring every other night, you bound to smell the smell of trash and burnt canes, raw-liquor and crack-liquor. And the syrup . . . and the canes themselves burning.

"No lorries were running this time of night, taking canes to the Factory, on a Sunday.

"You couldn't see no moon! I used to like moonlight nights so much, on a full moon; when I was a lil girl, oh-Lord! how Ma would take me and Clotelle and Golbourne and Sargeant and

Pounce for long walks! Sometimes two miles. Sometimes three. Oh-Lord! The times we used to have! Walking to the Factory, and seeing the steam from the engines, and the smoke climbing outta the chimneys, rising to touch the clouds up in the skies . . . Crop-Season, Constable, Crop-Season! Days of glory 'pon a Plantation! We thrildren would steal a piece of cane from a pile in the Yard; the sweetest cane that we called 'Juice-nine-tray-five' . . . and the juice running down the two sides of our mouth, oh-my-God . . . and later on in life, I now am a lil older, on nights like tonight, black-as-sin, that Mr. Bellfeels used to take me in the canes. In any field of canes. Just so it was out of hearing distance from the chattel house where me and Ma and Gran lived. I would hear Mr. Bellfeels motor-car, a lil red Vauxhall, and he would press the horn, *beep-beep*, soft-enough to alert me: not loud-enough to alarm Ma; and I would tell Ma I going to the Standpipe for a fresh bucket of water to wash my face-and-hands with. And once, in my excitement, I left the bucket in the house! But Ma knew. Ma did-know. Ma had to know. How couldn't she not know, when she-herself had to dream-up similar strategies to get away from her own mother?

"And through those encounters, mostly on dark-nights, I started to carry this lasting smell of mould; a smell with the tinge of sweet-ness; the smell like cane juice and burnt trash; this smell in the pores of my skin and on my clothes. But it is the smell of mould, that closeness to the soil, that can't be separated from natural things, nor from the stench of the soil itself. You understand what I saying?

"The closeness to the mould and the dung and the horseshit and the cane trash and the hard ground, and the soft muddy ground—in the rainy season—this closeness left their taint on my acts with Mr. Bellfeels, and on my clothes, on my skin, on my natural smell, on my mind. In my pores.

"That is what I am telling you, Constable. So, write it down *so*, please.

"Perhaps your age prevents you from handling the *ironies* of my life. But I am talking to you this way for a purpose, since I already decide that you are not too young to hear the ironies of life. It is better for you, as a young man, and a police Constable, to hear these things from the mouth of a woman old-enough to be your mother than from a woman more younger in age and attitude. Yes."

She looks up, and sees that the Constable is sleeping; and snoring mildly; and his face is serene; and he looks so innocent; and she ignores him, and goes on talking, as if he is not in the room with her; and she seems to gain confidence in talking these personal "woman-things," as Gertrude calls them; and it is as if she is really talking out aloud to herself.

"I remember the first night, oh-my-God, how I hurt and hurt. I think I had a lil blood flowing. Not from my menses . . . though, I hope this doesn't frighten nor embarrass you, a Constable and a man, to hear me talk this way. But you are sleeping, anyway . . ."

The Constable is still snoring.

"I have to give you a Statement, even although it is a preliminary Statement, keeping the pot warm till Sargeant come, more or less . . . certain things I have to state whilst I still have the memory . . . in case they are important.

"I do not mean to frighten nor embarrass you. You and me are bound by duty. And obligation. The same duty. The same obligation. Me to talk. And you to listen.

"Yes, I know that most men can't take such plain talk. Specially from a woman. They love women. Men say they do. Most men. Would even tell you that they like women. But they don't like to know too much of the close, personal 'woman-things' that make a woman a woman. Or what makes a woman tick.

"I am not dwelling on this to scare you. It is merely the *ironies* of my life. And life itself."

The Constable is still sleeping. A gentle snoring comes from him; and a smile paints his face.

"For no reason at all that I can find, right-now I am remembering how the cane blades would be biting into my skin as Mr. Bellfeels grinding and grinding himself into me. And you know, in spite of that, in spite of my present attitude about that, there was a certain niceness to those nights . . . a sweet taste. At the beginning.

"At the very beginning. I was a lil girl then. But I am not ashamed to say to you that I liked it. I liked giving myself to a man. Yes.

"At the beginning. In a way I enjoyed it. I was being made a woman of. And I knew the power of the man who was turning me into a force-ripe woman. I wasn't so young not to also know that the man fooping me by force was a man of means, and privilege, able to put me in a category which *not one* of the boys I grew up with, and who, later on as men, were after me, could: Golbourne, Pounce and Sargeant, Manny and even the Headmaster of Sin-Davids Elementary School. Not one of them could put me in a house. Not in the same category certainly as this Great House. Not on the same peg as Mr. Bellfeels could. And did. Not on their bottom-dollar!

"Sargeant? No.

"Golbourne? No.

"Pounce? Forget Pounce.

"The Headmaster of the Elementary School? He come closest . . .

"Your own father, Granville, before he met the accident, no.

"So, you see, Constable!

"Not one of them could lift me up outta the mud; outta the thick, black soil and the hot-sun that me and them lived in, and toiled so hard in, so long in, in the North Field, and in other jobs on this Plantation. Yes.

"Mr. Bellfeels made a woman of me. I was made a woman of. Not in the proper manner. Of matrimony. Family-life. And hearthside-bliss. Such as we learned in *Bible Stories for Little Christians*, taught by Miss Smith in Sunday School. Or that I started seeing in the *Illustrated London News* magazine. No!

"It was robbery.

"And you ask yourself, year after year, as I have, for years, *Why you let him do this to you? Why you let Mr. Bellfeels crawl-all-over you, Mary-girl? And only now, in the last three months, decide to take matters into your two hands?*

"You want to ask me that question?"

Just then the Constable wakes. He rubs his eyes, roused from a dream he was having, and not knowing where he is, he looks around stupid, for a moment. His eyes are bloodshot. But she is kind and sweet to him; for she likes him; and does nothing to make him more uncomfortable.

"Don't you want to ask me why am I talking so much about my life, and nothing-much about my act?" she says. "Don't you want to put that question to me?

"I would ask myself that question. Yes. And get this answer: 'I am talking this way because I am really talking aloud to myself, and nobody is present.' And even so, you are here and yet you are not here. Yes."

"I would like to axe you a question, ma'am," the Constable says. "Not as a means o' curiosity. But as part of your Statement. A different question altogether, ma'am, that Sargeant axe me to axe you, concerning the . . ."

"But where Sargeant is, though?" she says.

"Sargeant had to visit . . . had to visit . . ."

"The rum shop, I know. Manny told me. He's preparing flying fish . . ."

"The Selected Clienteles Room, ma'am."

"Today is a funny night!" she says. The Constable has a blank look on his face. "You ever heard that saying? *Today is a funny night?*"

"No, ma'am."

"*Today is a funny night* was used the first time by men who pull lighters . . . big-big boats the size of a barge . . . with foodstuffs from off merchant ships, which they on-loaded in the warehouse bonds; and also by "spidermen," men pushing wooden barrels of molasses, in metal-things the shape of a spider, working on the Wharf and the Interior Careenage. These is the men who played a big role in the Riots. Who started the 1938 Riots. Ordinary men and women of this Island, the first to seek freedom and political franchises. Later, full independence. The Riots of '38.

"A police, much like you or Sargeant, was the first to brand the statement I just used, *today is a funny night*, as a revolutionary statement, saying it contain a hidden code and meaning; swearing that *today is a funny night* contains threats against our rulers, people like Mr. Bellfeels, and the Vicar, and the Solicitor-General and the owners of Cave Shepherd & Sons, Haberdasheries, and the members of the Aquatic Club on Bay Street. And with that simple statement, which Wilberforce tell me is complete with bad grammar, you should have seen the throngs of men and women, who the rulers got the police and the volunteer-soldiers to shoot-down and kill; and lock-up for using incendary statements. So, I always guard against using incendary language, from that day in 1938. But the men and women came within *one* inch of burning-down the whole blasted Island, beginning with the stores in Town! Yes! What a beautiful sight it was to see, too. Yes! *Today is a funny night*."

"Sargeant should be here soon," the Constable says.

"Any minute."

"He soon here."

"You wanted to ask me a question."

"I can't remember the question now, ma'am."

"So young and losing your memory?"

"Is the police work, ma'am."

"Soon, Sargeant will be here. The lovely perfume from the lady-of-the-night, and there I was, walking along the track between the North Field and the South Field, flat for the most part, now that the canes' cut; and all that is growing now is young canes and plants, yams and eddoes and a few holes of eight-weeks sweet potatoes . . . and the Plantation Main House, with its lights on, like the lights on a steamer, coming through the darkness, facing me. The bright lights reflected from the white marl and loose gravel, back onto me, was like a big wave coming towards me, and rolling over my head; and the feeling of weakness and being impotent that came over me tonight was the same feeling that I remember had-consume me that first Sunday in the Church Yard, when the position of the sun and the height of the man looking down from the saddle at me, knocked me to one-side, as if indeed I was struggling with a powerful wave.

"That big powerful house, which hasn't lost its affect on me, and which to enter the driveway, and walk-up the white marl and loose gravel path, and approach the verandah, brought in my limbs that first trembling sensation. For a moment, I was exactly like Ma, turned into a pillar of salt.

"I remember thinking how the circumstances of my life had-change, since from the time I was a field hand . . .

"I grew up liking the Plantation Main House. And though time have passed, with no change of heart on my part, it is something I feel so shamed about still, that I can barely raise my head in certain circumstances, as I contemplate the change in my life."

Just at this moment, the ticking of a bicycle breaks in upon her words. Just then, they hear *cling-cling! cling-cling!*

"Is Sargeant," the Constable says.

"Is Sargeant!" she says.

"He come?"

"He come!"

"Let me look out, and see if . . ."

Sargeant sat looking at the first shot of rum that Manny had placed before him in a short, stubby, thick-skinned glass. The glass looked like a bullet from a .38 revolver, magnified a few times. It reminded Sargeant of the day after Mr. Bellfeels became manager of the Plantation, and as a symbol of his new authority, how Mr. Bellfeels rode through the fields, wearing a revolver in a brown, large holster tied like a harness across his back. He had shown the revolver to Sargeant one Monday morning, demonstrating how fast he could, like Gary Cooper, pull the revolver from his back, in a flash, like a magician, "quick-quick as shite!" he said, laughing, "more-quicker than any fecking police 'bout-here"; and so it seemed: faster than Sargeant himself could flick-on his searchlight.

"Like one-two-t'ree!" Mr. Bellfeels had told Sargeant, laughing. "More quicker than blasted that! I is more faster than *any* cowboy in any Western playing at the Empire Theatre! More faster than that!"

And Mr. Bellfeels then snapped his fingers, for greater emphasis, to demonstrate the speed with which he could "kill any son-of-a-bitch who think he going-thief the Plantation things, and get off Scotch-free!"

He had laughed some more. And Sargeant became more uncomfortable.

He and Mr. Bellfeels and Manny were in the Selected Clienteles Room late one night.

"I is the law, round-here, boy," he had said, putting his arm round Sargeant's shoulder, "and I intend to tek the law inside my two hands! I is the law round here, Sarge-boy."

"This-this," Sargeant had stammered, "this thing, this thing could blow off a man's head, Mr. Bellfeels!"

"Clean-be-Jesus-Christ, *clean!*" Bellfeels had agreed.

Sargeant did not, if he had been asked, know why all of a sudden, in this cozy, club-like Selected Clienteles Room, where he passed so many hours drinking and talking about his work, about discrimination in the Police Force, about the traps he laid for criminals, giving his drinking buddies confidential details about crime and criminals in the Island, and women's secrets; he could not explain why all of a sudden he should be thinking of that one time, when he and Manny listened to Mr. Bellfeels talking about his .38 revolver, which he had bought from the Commissioner of Police.

The shot glass now sat untouched before Sargeant. He knew he had to face duty and responsibility because of his rank and his oath, his service in the Royal Bimshire Constabulary Police Force, acknowledge his allegiance to the Governor, and beyond His Excellency, in his loyalty, stretching to His Imperial Majesty, he had to assume that whatever surprise, danger, deadly confrontation, whatever the night might throw up, he had to face it. It was duty and loyalty and Scout's honour. It was his duty.

He sat fully dressed in his night uniform, long after the telephone call from Mary-Mathilda had roused him from his lethargy; and here he is now, in black serge, thick as the Plantation's horse blankets, and as rough to the skin. Sargeant kept the neck of his tunic clasped shut at the throat, tight and almost choking him. He was a stickler for neatness and appearance, as he was fastidious about discipline and uniforms and duty. But tonight, he wished this cup of duty would be taken from him. Taken from his lips, and placed at someone else's.

He had sent the Constable to take the preliminary Statement, because he wanted the emergency to remain on the vine; and wait; and fall to the ground and be buried in the other heaps of untouched memories. He wanted to evade his duty. He knew he did not dispatch the Constable because he felt that his report, even preliminary, would be of much eventual help.

He had no taste for this case. It was tricky, and dangerous. And if it turned out to be what he thought he heard Miss Mary-Mathilda say on the telephone, a lot of people were going to have their feet stomped on; and their balls squeezed. And his own career could wither on the vine; and fall in ruin. "Best not to get involve in chicken fight, if you is a cockroach," his mother always warned him. He might have to start thinking about writing a letter to his daughter and ask her to sponsor him as an immigrant to Amurca, in case.

He had no stomach for this taste of reality, as Manny called it. He was sitting stationary; not moving any part of his body; giving the impression there was no life in it; so still that even Manny was becoming concerned. It worried Manny to see him just sitting there, as if he was waiting for some spirit to tell him to move. It was as if he was a mechanical toy whose spring needed rewinding to provide the semblance of movement and "life." Manny waited to see if this new life might bring his friend back to reason.

"Is a hell of a thing, nuh?" Manny says.

Manny moves from sitting at the unpainted deal-board table, and goes behind the counter. He is not looking at Sargeant. He is just staring ahead.

"All o' we was after Tilda, one time or the other, when she was more younger; from when she was a girl growing up," Sargeant says. "We uses to play together. Me and Mary-Tilda, you and Clotelle and the rest o' girls. Pounce. And Golbourne. Even Naiman, before he turn to crime. We all grow up together. Manny, good-Jesus-Christ, you know, man! You was there!"

"I was there," Manny says.

"Playing games! Hide-and-Hoop. London Bridge. Hobbina-Bobbina. And, Ship-Sail, Sail-Fast. One moonlight night, remember? We was sitting in a ling, in a ring, in Mary-Tilda paling, remember? And I was in the ling, and Mary-Tilda was in the ling, and she pointed at me, remember? And said the part in the Hide-and-Hoop game, you know . . . *'My mother and your mother was hanging out clothes; my mother give your mother, a cuff in her nose. What colour was the blood?'*

"You remember Hide-and-Hoop, don't you, Manny? And my God, Manny. Jesus Christ, I was only eight or nine at the time, and Mary-Tilda mustta been eleven or twelve. But when I tell you that at that moment when Mary-Tilda pointed the whip at me, and axe me, *'What colour was the blood?'* expecting me to say, *'Red!'*, and then spell-out the word, *red* . . . r-e-d, red . . . Good-Jesus-Christ, Manny, you remember don't you? I can still see Mary-Tilda eyes, and Mary-Tilda lil bubbies, her two breasts, and smell the way her body smell. And I can still smell the smell of the cologne Mary-Tilda had-on, a smell that is a mixture of seawater and Limacol. It was her mother's cologne that she was wearing that night."

"You wasn't the only boy smelling-round-behind Tilda, and getting-on like a ram-goat," Manny says. He takes the forty-ounce bottle from the counter. The bottle leaves a ring on the unpainted deal board. And Manny pours some of the contents into a snap-glass.

It is water. He holds his head back, and lets the water fall into his mouth. "Emmm!" he says, clearing his throat.

He then takes up the nip-bottle containing half pint of Mount Gay Rum. It leaves no mark on the table where it had stood in front of Sargeant more than thirty minutes. He pours a shot of rum from the nip-bottle, right up to the rim. And he holds back his head, and allows the dark, golden liquid to fall in an even flow into his mouth. He closes his eyes. He shakes his head, from left to right, in two quick jerks, as if he is in the sea, and seawater has entered his ears. He shakes his head in two more sharp, powerful quick jerks. "Emmm-emmm!" he says, in appreciation of the sting, and the strength of the rum. And then, he says, "Ahhh!"

"We was all after Mary-Tilda, in them days . . ."

"But she wasn't for we," Manny says. "She was already ear-mark for Bellfeels, that red-skin son-of-a-bitch! I think her mother make that decision. People like me and you can't offer Tilda nothing, whiching, when you think of it, is true as shite, Sarge."

"*Ear-mark* is not the word, Manny. Not ear-mark. Reared for. Given to. A burn-offering. For Bellfeels. That is the way I sees it. Mary-Tilda was too good for either o' we, for me, nor for you, neither. Her very mother as much as tell me so, down in Town one day. That's before I join the Force."

"I won't go suh-far, Sarge. I won't go so far in that direction. Is fate and destiny. Fate and destiny have a way of levelling-out things in our lives that we can't understand. But Tilda was one o' the most prettiest girls growing up in this Village. And Bellfeels get there first."

"And none o' we ain't get the chance to foop she first!" Sargeant says.

"None o' we didn't get tha' piece."

"Neither you, nor me, Manny."

"Neither you, nor me, Sarge."

"Bellfeels get there first."

"And look wha' happen to him!"

"*Wha' happen?* What happen to Bellfeels? What you mean?"

"What I mean is what I mean," Manny says.

"You mean something that you not telling me, Manny."

"What I mean is what I mean, man," Manny says. And then he adds, "Let we change the kiss-me-arse subject."

Sargeant fiddles with the stubby glass; crickets chirp in the darkness outside, and the singing of hymns from the BBC soothes the quiet night.

Then Sargeant begins talking, his voice rupturing the silence.

"It must o' been my first assignment as a detective, when I was sent to guard the Plantation Main House, and the grounds, 'cause thieves was making the chicken coops shite. Every morning, Bellfeels calling in reports of thefts and petty larcenies; and going over my head straight to the Commissioner o' Police. So, the Commissioner himself call-me-in and assign me to keep a' eye on the Plantation, and catch the blasted fowl-cock thieves. And I remember the Commissioner winking to me when he give me the assignment. I got my first stripe, Lance Corporal, for carrying out that 'vestigation for the Commissioner—successfully. I just remember that, and I don't know why."

"Bellfeels have been a pain in the arse, all this time!"

Manny again raised the shot glass to his lips, and flung his head back in a sudden jerk. When the rum hit his chest, it was as if a man had landed a hard punch to that part of his body. He then flung his head from one side to the other, just as an unlucky boxer, stung by a jab, would do, to shake the sting out and to recover his equilibrium. And when he was finished, when he was done with this ritual for drinking rum, when his eyes cleared, and he could feel his blood surging through to his face, he was livelier and looked younger; and ready to do battle, whether with the remaining bottle of Mount Gay Rum, or with the conversation he was having with his old, dear friend Sargeant.

"I never liked Bellfeels," Manny says.

"Me-neither!" Sargeant says.

"Bellfeels is such a avaricious, greedy man!" Manny says. "And whose secrets can't hide. Can't be hidden no more, in this Village. We can't go on excusing Bellfeels, no more."

Sargeant passes the index finger of his right hand round the rim of the short, stubby, ugly shot glass. It makes a deep sound, deep as the bass part Manny sings in Sin-Davids Anglican Church Choir.

"We sure not singing in the choir tonight!" Sargeant says.

"Not tonight," Manny says.

He drinks another shot of rum. He makes his body shiver as if he is taking a dip in the sea, early morning, when the water is chilly.

"Emmmm!" he says, making his body shudder.

"'. . . and with all thy soul, and with all thy mind. . . ,'" Sargeant is saying.

"'. . . and with all thy strength,'" Manny says, completing this section from the Eucharist.

"'This is the first and great Commandment,'" Sargeant says.

"'This is the first and great Commandment,'" Manny says.

"Was never a case o' Bellfeels loving his neighbour as he love himself."

"A woman walking by herself, at a certain time o' night, in the shadows, is a occurrence that does-happen in this place, all the time," Manny says. "And if you put two and two together, you know, for-sure, that that woman meeting a man, at a particular rendezvous. In a cane field. A woman walking by herself, at a certain time o' night, and on a Sunday night to-boot, and hiding something behind her back . . . I couldn't make-it-out in the darkness! Man, Jesus-Christ, Sarge, that is a horse of a different colour, altogether!"

"You saying something to me, Manny? You leaking evidence?"

"Jesus Christ, Sarge! Me and you know one another too long for you to bring this shite to me, man! Leaking evidence? You calling it that? Man, I only recounting something that, now we're talking, happen to me earlier this evening. I am trying to piece together and reconstruct certain strains, certain strands, to see what I come up with, in regards to my understanding how mankind does-act.

"Is a matter of loving thy neighbour. A matter of the first and great Commandment. Tonight is Sunday night. I should be in church in the Choir, but man, I had hell learning the bass-part to the '*Kyrie Eleison.*' Man, I make my house miserable, singing the bass-part all Friday and Saturday night, over and over again, until I thought I got it. 'Cause, is Lent. And as I tell you last weekend, I not hitting the bottle so heavy these days. Is Lent. I drinking less.

"But I trying like hell to remember the details of my meeting-up with Tilda tonight, as she was walking up the road, in a certain manner, like if she was on a mission. With something in her hand. I couldn't make it out. Tilda was heading in the direction of the Main House.

"I couldn't see it too-good, whatever it was she had in her hand. But I swear it wasn' a piece o' sugar cane. Nor even a stick, which a person sometimes would walk with, to chase dogs. Tilda didn't carrying a walking stick! Still, though . . . I don't really know."

"You giving me evidence, and at the same time, you holding-back evidence from me, Manny, man."

"I not giving you *shite*, Sarge! And I not holding-back one shite from you, neither, man! Me and you grow up in Flagstaff together. Me and you went-school together. Me and you play cricket together. Was in the Cubs and the Scouts together. You joined the Police, I emigraded to Cuba and Amurca, return-back here, and went in business-for-myself. I sells rum, be-Christ, and kills pigs! Together through thick and thin. Your life tek you one way. Mine a next way. But never have we stood in the way of one another path. Not even with regards to fooping the same woman. Or running after the same piece o' pussy. We is men, man! Men, Sarge! So, why at our fecking age, after forty-something years o' close friendships, would you come in my rum shop with this load o' shite, on a Sunday night? Why? Would I jeopardize our friendship? To save a son-of-a-bitch like Bellfeels?"

"Well . . ."

"Well-my-arse! . . . Or even to hold-back evidence from you, in regards to Miss Tilda, who stand a good chance of being suspected for doing something, just in case the thing she was carrying in her hand, was—"

Sargeant's hand strikes the truncated, stubby shot glass, knocking it over. The strong-smelling, rich brown liquid flows over the table, like a shy laughter, like an exhalation of wind and voice, and then dies as quickly as it had come out. The glass rolls in a kind of arc, a short, rough, clumsy movement that matches its ugliness.

Sargeant is now staring at Manny.

Manny stands with his own glass to his lips, not touching the glass, his lips not seeking to touch the glass; and all Sargeant can see are Manny's eyes fixed upon him.

Manny's eyes are bloodshot. His eyes are asking a question by their penetrating gaze and focus. At the same time his eyes are withholding the question they are eager to ask.

Sargeant continues looking at Manny. And then he fastens the thick brown leather belt with its silver buckle, with the Imperial Crown on it, round his waist. "Must cut down on my fats," he says to himself. "Got to follow Dr. Wilberforce orders."

His own concern with blood pressure, and his doctor's, passes through his mind like a sharp reminder, just like the cold touch of water from the public Standpipe for his bath in the wallaba tub, first thing in the morning.

"Well, I never thought," Sargeant says.

"How long you going-grieve over Tilda? And after all these years, you still smelling behind her?"

"What you trying to tell me, Manny?"

"How long you going grieve over Miss Bellfeels, alias Mary Gertrude Matilda?" Manny says. "Listen to the Gospel, man. Let the Gospel be your guide, Sargeant. You don't have to listen to me. Not now. Not ever. But you got to face the question, even if you can't find no answer.

"So, I put it to you, a second time. How long are you going to grieve over Mr. Bellfeels kip-woman?" Manny says. And for no reason, he starts to sing:

"'Mah-til-dah! Mah-til-dah!
Mah-til-dah, she tek muh money
And run Venezuela!"

"What you mean, Manny?"

"'Mah-til-dah . . .'" Manny sings.

"Manny, come right out and tell me what you mean."

"Is a serious thing, Sarge. And a serious thing must get serious consideration. You got to face facts. After you face facts, then you could plot your strategies, to get a piece offa Tilda, if that is what you want. Or to forget she. If it is what I think it is, she was carrying something in her hand. I am here to assist you. In anything. Be it legal, or un-legal. But as I tell you, when you meet a woman walking alone-by-herself, on a Sunday night, going in the direction opposite from where her Great House is, you have to consider two things. Number one, she looking for a man to foop; or, number two, she going to feck-up a man."

"Thanks, Manny. Good night."

"Good night, Sarge. Follow the Gospel."

"As man, Manny!"

"As man, Percy. As man! I here to help, legal, or un-legal!"

"You haven't call me Percy in years!" Sargeant says. "Why you calling me so, tonight?"

"A man should be address' by his proper name, once in a while."

"Thanks, Manny. As man!"

"Good night, Percy."

"Good night, Manny."

"'. . . *and the second is like unto this, that thou shalt love they n'igh-*
bour as thineself, 'cause on these two Commandments heng all the laws
and the prophets . . .'"

"Manny, you been tekking Communion on the sly?"

"*The laws and the prophets,* Sarge. *The laws and the prophets,* Percy
DaCosta Benjamin Stuart."

They could hear the ticking. Mary-Mathilda and the Constable
stopped talking.

"Yes," she said. "It gotta be Sargeant, this time."

"Is Sargeant now," the Constable said.

A smile came to his face. A smile of relief. He was free to leave
now, and go back to the sub-station; and the night was still not
too old; and change into mufti, khaki short pants, pink T-shirt and
leather thong slippers; and he would jump on his bicycle and ride
to the Church of the Nazarene, which was having its annual Rejoice
in Harvest services and Revival meetings; and he could sit on his
bicycle bar, in the darkness, just outside the span of sharp light
from the powerful acetylene lamp . . .

There was a soft tap on the door nearest where they were sit-
ting. The side door. The Constable had chosen this door, too. And
he was surprised, but glad, that Sargeant's tap was no louder than
his had been; and that Sargeant, too, had not chosen the front door.
It was Sargeant's respect for Miss Mary-Mathilda, and the symbol
of the Great House, that controlled these two actions of his. This
respect had also been bred into the Constable, as indelibly as the
custom of doffing his cloth hat to the Vicar; and as a little boy, to
the Headmaster of his elementary school; and now as a policeman,
tipping his cork hat, in the daytime, and his peak cap in the evening,
to Mr. Bellfeels, and to the Solicitor-General, and to the other
powerful men in the Village. Yes, the Constable knew the respect
he had to give both to this powerful Great House, and to its mis-
tress, Miss Mary-Mathilda, alias "Miss Bellfeels." Sargeant had ac-
cepted this, too, and it was his acknowledgment of power that

caused the respectable, soft rap on the side door from his knuckles.

It was so soft that the Constable could barely hear it.

The wind was high. The leaves of trees overhanging the roof of the Great House were scraping its red tile shingles; and the Constable thought he could hear the branches scratching those parts of the roof made of galvanized tin.

Mary-Mathilda remained in her chair.

She was now "Miss Bellfeels" to them.

For she, too, having been placed into this Great House for all these years, had got to know the value of her position.

Miss Mary-Mathilda remained in her straight-backed chair, while Gertrude went to the side door. When the door was opened, the cool air came in first; the Constable could feel the chill in the wind, and then see the rectangle of blackness painted by the opened door. And then he heard the scratching noise Sargeant's bicycle made as it was being leaned against the side of the house. Metal scratching stone.

"Sargeant, sir," Constable said, standing at attention. But before he could say more, Sargeant waved his hand to dismiss him, and also to denote thanks; thanks for taking the preliminary Statement.

Sargeant knew that if he made one blunder investigating this case, in the way he took the Statement from Miss Mary-Mathilda, whom he has known all his life, if he should question her in the wrong way, in spite of the circumstances, his job would be in jeopardy. And to make matters worse, he was about to take evidence from a woman he had loved all his life, from a distance.

His mind went back to those nights, long ago, but different from this night of such thick and velvety blackness, when the moon was shining brighter than even the most powerful electric bulb in any room on the Plantation; to nights when he and Golbourne, and Manny and Pounce, and Miss Mary-Mathilda herself, would sit in a ling and play Ship-Sail, Sail-Fast, and stand and jump and dance as they dramatized London Bridge . . . and how Tilda, now Miss Mary-Mathilda—or Miss Bellfeels, depending—always the love of his life, the girl he felt faint and helpless over whenever he looked at her; and whenever she looked at him; when she would say to him, "How you, boy?"; and his heart would melt; all this going on through the years they attended Sin-Davids Elementary School; she, for girls: he, for boys; and they both left school in Standard Seven . . . She was a brighter pupil than he . . . All these years now culminating into this night, ending in this black, moonless night, this Sunday night when he would have preferred to be in the Choir beside Manny, singing tenor; loving the descant in psalms. *Yea, though I walk through the valley of the shadow of death, I will fear no evil . . . ;* and hymns, his favourite hymns, all of which he liked better than the psalms, which he knew by heart.

The hymn the Vicar selected for tonight, Hymn 568, in *Hymns Ancient & Modern,* is his favourite. He even liked the title of the book—*Hymns Ancient & Modern, Standard Edition, and The Book of Common Prayer.*

"Lamb of God, I look to Thee,
Thou shalt my example be;
Thou art gentle, meek, and mild,
Thou wast once a little child."

He had sung this same hymn standing beside his mother, in the pew that engulfed him, and that reached his mother to her waist; holding his small hand with her hand soft and sticky from the humidity of the morning; and he had also sung this hymn in Assembly at school every morning; and then in Sunday School, so many times; and later, in the Choir, and at services-of-songs; and on Friday nights at the social evenings in his home, when he invited friends, and played the piano, and fed them cake and pudding and coconut bread and baked pork. So many times, and on so many occasions, had he sung this hymn that he knew all seven verses by heart. But he especially liked the tenor descant for which the choirmaster and organist Mr. Charles DeB. Straker, L.R.C.M. (London), a native of Bimshire, always chose him to demonstrate his voice, rich as the taste of molasses, clear as the bell that started labour on the Plantation; a voice announcing the end of labour, tidings of great joy and of Island disasters; singing at weddings and funerals.

Each time Sargeant sang the solo, he was overcome by a sensation he could not explain, nor describe.

His tenor voice sent chills through the body. Manny dubbed him "The Voice."

"*'Thou wast once a little child.'*"

He must pull himself together now. He is on duty. He is a Crown-Sargeant. And a detective. A member of the Island's loyal Police Force. The Royal Bimshire Constabulary Police Force, or as Wilberforce liked to tease him, "Sarge *ipso* of the Constabulary of the Island of Bimshire *facto!*" He is, in his mind, singing the descant of the seventh and last verse of this hymn, as he holds his hand out and takes Miss Mary-Mathilda's, as she welcomes him into her home; and he notes that her hand feels the same way as his mother's, soft and sticky from the humidity of the night; and it is "hot-hot" tonight, in more than one way, as he had told Manny earlier. . . . "Come in, come in, man. You seem so distant," she is telling him. "Come, Sargeant. Siddown, siddown, and . . ."

"I don't like imposing on your horspitality under these circumstances, Miss Mary-Mathilda," he says, "and I hope . . ."

". . . take the weight of the world off your feet, Sargeant."

"Thanks, Miss Mary-Mathil . . ."

"Come in, Sargeant."

"I hope we could get through with this . . ."

"As soon as we can," she tells him.

"*I shall then show forth Thy praise,*
Serve Thee all my happy days;
Then the world shall always see
Christ, the Holy Child, in me."

And only after this verse has passed entirely through his mind does Sargeant continue to speak with her.

"Good evening, Miss Mary-Mathilda. I hope you understand how I feel over this."

"Don't worry, Sargeant-boy," she tells him. "We can't-all-have all happy days."

He wonders if she is reading his mind.

This is one of the things that had attracted him to her, like the magnet the Village carpenter uses to find nails buried in the saw-dust on the floor of his shop . . . her knife-like perception.

From the time they were young, playing children's games, like Ship-Sail, Sail-Fast, she was always the one who won: always able to guess the correct number of kernels he held inside his closed fist, when she challenged him, "Hommany men on deck?" And he was equally happy when she knew the number, for that would give him the excuse to touch her, even though it was only touching her hand. But a touch was a touch. And touching Mary-Tilda's hand sent shivers through his entire body. It was a sensation he could not explain, nor describe.

Yes, Mary Gertrude Mathilda always had this effect upon him.

"Your Constable comported himself like a gentleman," she tells him.

"Well-train," Miss Mary-Mathilda, "well-train."

"I could see that."

"Well, Constable," Sargeant says; and nothing more. His voice is louder, and firmer than he intended. And the Constable reacts, suitably. He stands at attention; and then, at ease.

Sargeant can see and feel the power and magnificence of wealth that is in this room in which he is standing: the cut-glass vases and cups and plates; and the Berbice and tub-chairs, and settees and couches made out of mahogany and cherry wood; and the breeze, a new wind that has risen with his arrival at the Great House, sweeps now through the room, carrying with it the fragrance of roses growing in the gardens, bourgeanvillea, lady-of-the-night, and other flowers whose names he does not know . . . for that one moment, when he spoke to the Constable, Sargeant was transported back to the small patch of unpaved gravel, the Parade Square, at the front of the sub-station. The Parade Square is one-half the size of this front-house parlour in which he now stands, uncomfortable; with his police cap in his hand.

"Good night, then, Constable," he tells the Constable. The Constable snaps to attention again and salutes.

"Sir!" the Constable shouts.

"Carry on," Sargeant says. And then he tells the Constable, "At ease! Stand easy!"

The Constable salutes a second time, and rams his peak cap back on to his head.

Sargeant salutes the Constable with a gesture like brushing flies from his face. His own police cap is in his hand. He runs the fingers of his left hand over its sweatband. No one can see his fingers. The sweatband is slippery, and smooth.

"Well, good night, Constable," Sargeant says.

"Good night, sir!"

"You dismiss," Sargeant tells him.

"Good night, Mistress."

"Good night, young man."

And the Constable leaves.

"Nice young man," she says.

"Well-train," he says.

"Young-enough to be my third child, if I had any more boys."

"My right-hand," Sargeant says.

"Something to drink, Percy?"

"Should I, Miss Mary? Under the circumstances?"

"What circumstances, Percy? That would make it wrong for me to offer you a drink, Percy DaCosta Benjamin Stuart? Eh?"

He smiles. She smiles, too.

"Last time I hear my name call-out like that, Christian names and surname, in full, was when I was inducted into the Constabulary of this Island!"

"*Admitted!*" she says. "The *Herald* said you got the Baton of Honour for passing out at the top of your class. You came first, Percy!"

"When I was admitted in the Constabulary of this Island," he says.

"So, Percy, are we going to act like strangers the whole night, just-because of the circumstances, as you call it? Or, like two grown-up people?"

"Miss Mary-Mathilda," he says. In his discomfiture, he has turned his cap around, passing the fingers of his left hand along the sweatband.

She goes up to him and takes the cap from him and places it on the tub-chair the Constable had sat in.

"Still dark rum?"

"Still dark. Please."

"Private stock? Or ordinary?"

"Six o' one and half-dozen of the next."

"You have the choice. A man should always make his choice known! So, private stock? Or ordinary?"

"Well, ma'am . . ."

"Mr. Bellfeels has some private stock he cured himself. Bellfeels Special Stades White Rum, if you please! You want a whites? Your Constable drank milk," she says; and laughs. "What you say?"

"Private stock, please, if you don't mind."

"The times we lived through, Percy!"

"The times."

"Look at you! Seeing you stanning-up here in my house, for the first time, after all these years, for the first time . . . now, in what you call, under these circumstances, fidgeting with your cap, the same way as when you were a lil boy in Second Standard, fiddling with your school cap . . . look at you! . . . the lil boy who fell in love with me! Didn't you think I knew; or remember? Yes . . .

"Years-back-when," she says, "years-back, when we, you and me, Golbourne and Pounce and Courtenay Babb, father to the Constable . . . Naiman and Manny and Charles . . ."

"Charles? Charles Jurdan?"

"Charles Jurdan."

"What happen to him?"

"Amurca. He disappear to Amurca . . ."

"My God!"

". . . and Gordon and Randolph . . ."

"Gordon and Randolph! Didn't Randolph?"

"Leff and went to Panama . . ."

". . . to help build the Canal Zone?"

"Build the Canal."

"Yes, he did."

"The Panama Canal!"

". . . and Milton and Lionel?"

"Milton Mawn and Lionel Greenwich! What happen to them two brutes?"

"They were close always, like brothers, although they were only third-cousins. But they went to Englund on the same boat. I heard about it, through Mr. Bellfeels, that they dead within the same week. In the same manner, too. By the same means. Lick-down in traffics, by a London-Transport bus!"

"My God!" Sargeant says.

His amazement is not about her knowledge of all these boys and girls they grew up with, it is more to do with the way she speaks, using the Village dialect. Her voice sounds so musical. This is the first time he has had such a long conversation with her, as an adult. Her voice sounds so soft and beautiful. It takes him back, weakened now, in limb and heart, across the miles and years of adolescence.

"Good God!"

"But didn't they . . . now that you mention it . . . work for the same London-Transport?"

"That's the *irony* of life! And on their off-day, to-boot. Consecutive. One after the other. The two o' them was going to some place in London, called Piccadilly Circle . . ."

"You remember names that I forget, Miss Mary-Mathilda."

"What about Pearl? And Barbara, and Minta? Mignon and Elsie?"

"Pearl. Pearl Hunt! She married a man from one o' the Small Islands, didn't she? Sin-Lucia? And Barbara. Barbara Cheltenham! Barbara Cheltenham went to Englund to do nursing. Minta. Minta Whiteacre! Minta Whiteacre, what become of her?"

"Minta died."

"God rest her soul."

"May she rest in peace!"

"Mignon. Mignon . . . Mignon, Mignon Osbourne! And Elsie! I'll never forget Elsie. The prettiest girl . . . after you, of course, Miss Mary-Mathilda . . . who ever lived in Flagstaff."

"The prettiest, Percy! Elsie Pilgrim was *the* prettiest girl amongst all o' we!"

"All these boys and girls still living here? Or they emigrade? Except the ones who dead."

"Most. Most gone. One way, or the other. To the grave. Or Amurca. But this is the full list o' girls and boys who we used to play with."

"Most emigrade. I miss them, now that you mention their names. But I can't say that I did-remember all o' them, though."

"And Clotelle . . . remember Clotelle? You can't forget Clotelle. She went to an early grave. An early death. And a tragic death, to-boot! . . . and Mr. Courtenay Babb, father to the boy, the Constable, who was just here . . ."

"Courtenay Babb-the-first?"

"I wonder if he know that I knew his father?"

"He too young to know things, Miss Mary-Mathilda," Sargeant says.

". . . as children, we used to have summuch fun, on moonlight nights . . . Well, I had better call Gertrude and get something for you to drink . . ."

And she moves to the small heart-shaped, polished table; and she lifts the bell, a heavy, metal bell with a brown handle of darkened wood, to clang its tongue against its side; this same bell, the same size as that one, similar in manufacture, and used by the Headmistress of her school, and the Headmaster of his, to summon girls and boys to the platform for floggings, and for rewards; all these bells in Flagstaff Village being rung as if there was such an urgency to be called, to be halted, to be roused from the bed, from the dead, from the cane field, to be always on time. And always "summonsed," as Miss Mary-Mathilda says to Gertrude.

Mary-Mathilda lifts the bell from the table and rings it, with a quick flick of her wrist, two times. Sargeant sees this bell as a miniature of the bell of Sin-Davids Anglican Church that tolls at six every evening, that sounds the alarms of hurricanes and cane-fires, for ships in danger on the sea; the sea that is everywhere, visible from every corner of the Island, that bell that tolls for the dead, in slow step with the fall of black shoes on the macadam road, polished to a blinding indulgence, slow to match the march of pallbearers and the reduced speed of the dead, always loud and mournful, from the tall steeple of the Anglican Church.

The bell in this Great House has a hollow sound. As if there is a crack in its small girth. But perhaps this kind of a bell, manufactured intentionally to "summonse" servants, may be able to sustain this hollowness in its ring, and still be used, deliberately and daily, to "summonse" Gertrude from the large, dark, smoky kitchen, with its pleasing tingle, much unlike the rebellious, violent, loud and ear-shattering *cuh-lang-cuh-lang-cuh-lang clang-cuh-lang-cuh-lang* of the bell in the Plantation Yard. That bell is nailed onto a piece of wood, onto the limb of a strong tree, the tamarind tree, and a thick short length of rope is attached to its tongue and knotted at the end so that any hand, the hand of the Plantation's children, the hand of Mr. Bellfeels, or his wife, but the hand of someone with privilege, might reach it easily just above the head, and hold the knot of the rope which is like an extended tongue itself, and send the tongue of iron *cuh-lang*ing against the steel of the thick-girded bell. The bell was fired in cast-steel in England.

Sargeant shakes his head, as if indeed there is seawater in his ear; and is once more paying attention to the beautiful things surrounding him: chairs, tables, settees, pictures on the walls; and ornaments of glass and China and clay, all in the shape of animals, leopards, crocodiles and lions and tigers which he has never seen —he knows only horses and jackasses and mules and cows and sheep and goats and dogs, yes dogs, Alsatians and Doberman-Pincers, and stray cats, mongrels and bitches—but all these animals, the leopards and the tigers, in lifelike permanence, are now surrounding him in the front-house of this Great House.

From a room within the large house, noiselessly along a hallway, comes Gertrude walking like a cat; silently; dressed in maid's uniform of black poplin, without the starched white cap, without the starched white apron that goes with the uniform; but informal in a black dress that is long to her calves, and blacker than its natural blackness against the heavy black complexion of her sturdy smooth skin. And she walks in her bare feet, bold and secure; and after Sargeant sees her enter, he is fascinated how her feet, black on the instep, and pink and thick round the heels, touch the Persian carpets on the brown-stained, shining hardwood floor; and make no noise.

"Evening, sir," Gertrude says.

"Evening, Gertrude. You getting on, all right, Gertrude?" he asks her.

"Yes, sir."

"Gertie-dear," Miss Mary-Mathilda says, "Sargeant Stuart is a bit thirsty. What we have in the house to slacken his thirst?"

"Something soft, Mistress?" Gertrude says; pauses, and adds, "Or something hard?" She manages to send a glance in Sargeant's direction, quick and furtive. Sargeant gives no indication that he has noticed.

"What you think, Gertie-dear? You be the judge. You think Sargeant Stuart should have something *hard*? Or something *soft*?"

She is not looking at Gertrude as she says this.

"Something hard," Gertrude says, putting the stress on "hard." And Sargeant does not, still, give any reaction. "Something hard, Mistress."

"Do we have it?"

"We have everything, Mistress! We have the twenty-year dark rum Mr. Bellfeels bring back from the Rum Bond. We have some Mount Gay Special. We have something that Master Wilberforce bring back from his last trip, from . . ."

"Israel."

"Jerusalem, it was, Mistress. The bottle say 'Made in Jerusalem.'"

"Thanks, Gertie-dear. You know more about this House than me. The mind, Sargeant, the mind . . . not good any more. But, Israel-Jerusalem, or Jerusalem-Israel, that boy o' mine goes all over the world! What he trying to find in Israel?"

". . . and we have our usual private stock, Bellfeels Private Stades White Rum. And there's some brandy, Mistress. We also have the Wincarnis Wine that Master Wilberforce buy for the house, plus the dry Australia sherry that Master Wilberforce bring back from down in Demerara . . . and don't forget the wine that Master Wilberforce bring us from over in Italy and Europe. We stock-up good, Mistress."

Mary-Mathilda smiles at Gertrude's litany of drinks.

"What you would like?" she says.

She is aware that Gertrude is playing a game with Sargeant. But she does not let on she is aware of this. This is the first time this evening that she feels safe.

Gertrude and Sargeant's game relaxes her. But she feels herself in control knowing the power she has, and has become accustomed to having, which she wields over her servants—excepting Gertrude, who is closest to her in the Great House—she feels this power and authority swell inside her body, and take over her disposition; and re-siding once more within her is her characteristically bold, indepen-dent and carefree "temperriment," the frame of mind she said she had when earlier tonight, she walked to the Plantation Main House.

Now, as "mistress" of the Great House, it is time to have some refreshments.

She does so every Sunday evening at this hour. By herself. Sometimes, she would invite Gertrude to sit with her; and they would drink their rum in silence, as the BBC played hymns from St. Martin's-in-the-Fields. Sometimes, she and Wilberforce would sit together. So, why be different tonight? Even "*under the circumstances*"?

But still, she is a little saddened to see this little game she knows they are playing about the drinks come to an end.

"A lil Mount Gay won't kill, Miss Mary-Mathilda, please," Sargeant says.

"Make it two."

"Yes, Mistress," Gertrude says.

And when Sargeant hears Gertrude speak these words, in this strange, big, beautiful Great House, and knows that in all the years he has known her, he has never heard her talk like this, if he could put form and construction now to her words, Gertrude, by her own words, would have created some delicate and valuable token, some expression of love, of loyalty, of devotion, some demonstration of her closeness to Miss Mary-Mathilda. And this could be called quite frankly a small, short, beautiful curtsey.

"How you want yours?"

"Lil ice water on the side," Sargeant answers.

"Soda in mine, Gertie-girl."

And when Gertrude has served the refreshments, she leaves in the same silence as she had entered. In the same fading silence like the picture in a magic lantern, going out of focus and then completely disappearing. And then is forgotten.

And at this time, on a Sunday night, normally Sargeant would be in the Choir; and she, sitting by the window, where her chair is now, her arms spread on the windowsill, her chin placed on her arms, listening to the broadcast of church service on the Voice of

Bimshire Radio Station. And when the local Church service is not broadcast because of "a technical difficulty"—she got to know that this meant the Chief Technician was drunk—she would listen to religious music, hymns and sacred songs from Sin-Martin's-in-the-Fields, from the Mother Country, from in Englund. Yes, from Englund!

She has never visited Englund. But she knows Englund "by heart," as she always says. She knows its best radio, the BBC; its best magazines; its best education, through Wilberforce's success; its best music; and its best, proper accents of speech.

She looks through the *London Illustrated News* regularly as they arrive "by surface mail," into the Island of Bimshire.

Every Sunday, she hears her own Vicar, Reverend Mr. M. R. P. P. Dowd, M.Th. (Dunelmn) Third-Class Honours, as he stands in the pulpit, tall like the water tower in the Plantation Yard, talking about sin and the poor. "*They shall inherit the kingdom . . .*" Yes, listening on a Sunday night like tonight, "but under different circumstances"; she is, through her closeness to the singing coming through the radio speaker, and her closeness to the songs and hymns themselves, able to imagine that these songs and hymns were coming from across the knoll, over the green Pasture, and the green fields of sugar canes just a few yards from her Great House. That the music is born out of the burnt grass and old rocks and stones, the walked-over gravel in the Church Yard, beside the graveyard of the Church. She does not have to look farther than this tall structure of coral stone and mortar, of stained-glass windows showing birth and death; defeat and conquest; crucifixion and resurrection in its paints and colours which come to palpable life in the sun, and bleed; yes, thick red blood, red as wine, comes pouring down, as if the tree and the spear and the diadem of thorns, and the voices of abuse and submission that the afternoon sun blazoned forth from the stained windows that give this history is being witnessed by her, and takes place, in its full pageantry and panoply of history, in the yard of the Plantation Main House.

And in addition to this pageantry taken from the Old Testament in her Bible is her own saga, which began in this very Church Yard so many years ago, also on a Sunday.

But tonight, life is under different circumstances. The radio is turned off. She cannot remember having listened to it at all today.

Missing the voices in the radio does not upset her, nor cause her to think long upon it. But in the short space of time, like the tightening of a muscle in the calf, she can hear the words of her favourite hymn. Hymn 332. "There Is a Green Hill Far Away." But it is the second-last verse she likes:

There was no other good enough,
To pay the price of sin,
He only could unlock the gate
Of Heav'n, and let us in.

It is a hymn written for her moods, to reflect her day when it has been a good one, when the running of this Great House is smooth; when Gertrude is not complaining about "the hard-work you putting on me"; when Master Wilberforce comes home late to luncheon; and in the same day, early to dinner; and brings five friends; when he and his friends eat Gertrude's "sweet-sweet" food, and smile, pat her on her shoulder and leave in their roaring cars, kicking-up pebbles and dust against the large panes of glass windows—and into the front-house parlour she had just cleaned —when the French doors are open; after her coconut bread comes out well, and "cloiding" and delicious, the smell that brings Master Wilberforce and his friends into the kitchen, large as the galley on an ocean liner bringing "them cheap-ass, tight-ass English tourisses" to "feck-up *my* fecking Island!"; when Wilberforce and his friends would break off chunks of the warm coconut bread; and disappear, in clouds of dust.

She never sat at table with Master Wilberforce and his friends. And she did not sit with him when he dined at home alone. She sat always in the kitchen, at a smaller table Gertrude set formally, with silvers, butter knife, main course knife, dessert knife; soup spoon, salad spoon, dessert spoon, two forks, one for the main dish, the other for dessert; and a small spoon placed at right angles to the other implements—even when she was taking only split-pea soup, for luncheon. And a warm, white, damask napkin folded in three, in a long rectangular shape, in the middle of the three white plates bordered in royal blue. Each crystal glass, and each plate and the tips of the handle of each implement bears the coat of arms of the Plantation: two sugar canes with their tops attached, crossed vertical on a shield. *Triumph* is written in gouged-out letters, under the shield.

She and Gertrude prepared meals together, sitting at the unpainted deal-board table, cutting the pork and seasoning it; gutting the chickens, leaving on the head and the "feets"; "leave on the feets, Mistress, the sweetest parts"; kneading the dough for the coconut bread; laughing in spite of the smokiness in the kitchen; eating dunks and ackees and golden apples, in season; and suggesting how the food might have tasted better, if they had added "just a lil more o' tumbrick," or "a piece-more salt-beef," or a "lil-less water in the rice, Gertie-girl!"; talking about everything that went on, over at the Plantation Main House, that week; at Harrison College and the schools; at the Vicarage, and in the Selected Clienteles Room of the Harlem Bar & Grill, down the hill, in the Village.

Gertrude fed Miss Mary-Mathilda with the gossip and scandal of the Village; and Miss Mary-Mathilda regaled Gertrude with the "wirthlessness you behold mongst the rich." With this information exchanged between the two women, Miss Mary-Mathilda learned a lot about Sargeant from Gertrude's lips; and she invented the rest; and during the day, alone in her bedroom, Mary-Mathilda trained a powerful spying glass on the front door of Sargeant's house, focused it on the shield made of tinning that showed the name of the company that insured his house; even picked out his chickens moving round outside his house; yes; and she got to know Sargeant in recent years from this distance, through her telescopic lens; and Gertrude learned "how many nights when you in your warm bed sleeping, and I up here, can't sleep for the screaming and the shouting coming from the direction of that Main House, girl; like two people fighting . . ."

Miss Mary-Mathilda drank at each meal, except breakfast, a snap of dark rum, with a glass of chipped ice on the side. Sometimes, she drank three snaps. Gertrude drank dark rum with chips of ice in a half-pint crystal glass, drowned in fresh coconut water— with each meal, including breakfast, especially when Miss Mary-Mathilda did not come into the kitchen.

Master Wilberforce had stopped eating a breakfast of two fried pork chops, three strips of fried plantain, two bakes, sliced cucumber with lime juice, fresh parsley, white vinegar, salt and nigger-peppers—he called this cucumber dish, "prickle"—and two large cups of strong Jamaica Blue Mountain Coffee. In recent days, he was now eating his breakfast standing up ("I got to fly this morning, Gertzie-love!"): one slice of brown toast spread thick with home-made sweet butter and gooseberry jam, and a small amount of coffee, in a very tiny coffee cup, which Gertrude called a "semi-glass," holding less than a gill, of very strong coffee from overseas.

"*Expresso!*" Gertrude reported to Miss Mary-Mathilda, the first morning.

"Expresso?" Miss Mary-Mathilda asked.

"*Expresso!*" Gertrude repeated to her mistress. "A Eyetalian habit he say he pick-up in Italy. And him a big man, Miss Mary-Mathilda, and a doctor, to-boot, who should know more better! Forsaking the breakfast that I prepare for him, a real Bimshire breakfast! And telling me he having a Continental breakfast instead! *Expresso*, Mistress? And eating stanning-up! For the food to lodge in his ankles and his two feets? Mistress, you could tell me what so special about this Continental breakfast that consist of only *expresso* coffee?"

"Well, when he get run-down, we will see. He will revert-back to eating real food!"

"I really hope so, Mistress. I like Mister Wilberforce too good for this tragedy to befall him."

"Civilization, Gertie-girl. Civilization . . ."

Gertrude had turned away, hurt; and she left behind her, as an indication of the injury to her status in the kitchen, which Wilberforce had compromised with his European habits, a vexatious stewpsing of her mouth: when she sucked her teeth in disgust, it came out as *stewwwwwpsse*.

Gertrude was off usually at three o' clock in the afternoon, every Sunday, except when Easter and Christmas fell on a Sunday. On normal Sundays, Miss Mary did the cooking herself.

The meal is served at twelve-thirty, after Church, whether she had attended or not. She feels she is a better cook than Gertrude: but she will never tell her so.

And when she has a bad day; when she would stand alone in her bedroom, and look towards the largest house on the Planta-tion estate, the Main House, which stands on a hill, a quarter-mile through the fruit trees that seem to guard it, she would think of her life, of her days at school, ended in Standard Seven, too soon; without being able to take up the scholarship to St. Michael's School, if she had sat the Secondary-to-Second-Grade examina-tion, which she would have passed, and landed her in a secondary school for girls only; paid for by the Social Committee of the Vestry. But she could not, because she had to work in the fields and help the household, consisting of Ma, and Ma's mother, Gran; and her; and because women were not encouraged to pursue higher learning beyond elementary school (learning to read and write, and the Ten Commandments, was sufficient); so, when she had a bad day, she would stand for hours in her large bedroom in the Great House, and look at the Main House, and at Sargeant's small chattel house; and see the brightness of day taken over by the sombreness of gold and thickening, rich, heavy colours, the sun touching the sea, the coming on of dusk. The approaching blackness of the end of the day. She would become enveloped in this engulfing sad, veloured house; and her thoughts would wander over the unending fields . . . of the nights, after she had washed her face-and-hands; when the shine on the long handle of the hoe did not satisfy her, did not shine bright enough; when she passed the middle finger of her right hand over the blade of the hoe, to test it, she knew easily that it was razor sharp, because it left a line of red, thin as the thickness of a page, on her finger. Her hoe had to have the same sharpness of any knife-blade in her kitchen.

> *There was no other good enough*
> *To pay the price of sin . . .*

She awakes from her dreaming as Gertrude brings the drinks in on a tray made of mahogany. A tall bottle that once held Gordon's Dry Gin, with no label, and now containing ice water, is sweating down its sides. There is a soda syphon, and two crystal glasses.

There are two kinds of rum. One, in a tall crystal decanter that is square and thick-skinned, contains special rum, cured in raisins, currants, orange and grapefruit peel, and gooseberries. The other is kept in a jimmy-john for six weeks, and then poured into a round crystal decanter. This is the ordinary rum.

Gertrude pours this ordinary rum religiously only for the postman, and for the sanitary inspector who checks once in a fortnight, for "larvees" in the buckets and tanks of water used for drinking, for bathing and for cooking.

Gertrude pours two drinks of the special rum. She knows the size and strength of her Mistress's drink. She pours hers first.

She hesitates before she pours Sargeant's drink. She does not want to ask him, "Heavy on the rum? Or heavy on the water?" And she does not want her Mistress to know that she has previously served drinks to Sargeant. She has done it, in fact, many times in her house, when her children are not home.

Sargeant understands her hesitation, and comes to her rescue.

"Light on the rum," he says. "And heavy on the water."

Gertrude smiles, and is about to leave the parlour, when Miss Mary-Mathilda says, "I won't need you no more, Gertie-dear. We'll fix ourselves, if need be . . ."

Gertrude moves silently over the thick carpets, and pads the floor in her bare feet, like a cat.

Miss Mary-Mathilda takes the same chair as before, and waits until Sargeant sits before she takes a sip of her drink.

"Normally, I would have brandy, but I already had one brandy for the night, when the Constable was here."

She shifts in her chair, fidgets a little, touches the cover of a large Bible, moving it two inches to the right, on the heart shaped tabletop; then, two inches to the left; and then passing her palm over it, she dusts it, although it had been dusted by Gertrude on Saturday morning, when she herself had passed her hands over it, each time she passed beside the table. Her fidgeting settles her nervousness. She touches things she does not even know she has touched: the coconut palm leaf, in the shape of a cross, that she received from the hand of Vicar Dowd last Good Friday; touches the porcelain crocodiles and lions on the mantelpiece; touching all these things that have lived with her, things that give her balance and calm.

"Why we don't start the Statement, Percy?" she says.

"How you want we to start, Miss Mary-Mathilda?"

"From the beginning, and work towards . . ."

"From the beginning, then."

". . . towards the end."

"That way . . ."

"We'll hear the whole story."

"But Miss Mary, you don't need to tell the full story. You don't have to tell me. It is my duty to hear it, but I don't really want to hear it. The powers-that-be don't. The public don't. And the Village don't. I not telling you what anybody down in the Police Commissioner office tell me to say. Nor am I 'sinuating that I got orders to-don't take a Statement from offa you. But I telling you what I know the situation is, under the circumstances, namely that *nobody*, not the Plantation, the Vicar, the Solicitor-General, nor the Commissioner o' Police himself, going-raise a hand against you, for whatever it is that you say you do. Not the Police. Not the Church. Not the Mothers Union. Nor the Church itself, meaning Revern Dowd. Not the School Systems, meaning the Headmaster and the Headmistress of the two Elementary Schools. And not a member of the Board o' Governances will want to raise a finger and vote 'gainst you, for whatever it is that you do. And I don't want to know what your act is, neither. You haven't tell me what is the act, and I don't want to know.

"And I don't know if I am in the right frame o' mind to take a Statement offa you, Miss Mary Gertrude Mathilda, to use your full name as I have to do in all official legal circumstances, seeing as how you and me grow up together, though separate. You is a person of great repuke. People follow your lead. People swear by you. People love you. And respect you. In ways that they don't respect nor follow the Plantation nor the Plantation's jurisdiction, if you following me.

"So, this is the predicament I see myself inside."

"But Percy . . ." She takes a sip of her drink. She places the glass daintily upon the doily on the heart-shaped mahogany side table. The light in the crystal glass, and the light from the top of the table, flash; and collide. She cannot decide which of these objects, crystal glass or mahogany polish, gives off the sharper and more pure reflection. "But Percy, I still have to tell the story.

"For as I said to the Constable, I still have to leave the history for Wilberforce, and one to be left back to the people of this Village, and people coming after me so they would know what happened. And I still have to save my soul."

"Save your soul, Miss Mary? What you mean by that?"

"From the fires of Purgatory. Seek redeeming mercy."

"Purgatory, Miss Mary? Redeemings?"

"A legacy of words behind me so people will know. Not that it was wrong. Or was right. I don't want people to see my act in such a simple way. In such black-and-whiteness. But if I don't leave something behind, *anybody*, anytime . . . tomorrow, next year, in the future and in the generations to come . . . will only know what happened from word of mouth, and from the *Bimshire Daily Herald*; and the words from the lips of Village gossip. There won't be nobody to tell the pure history of my act . . ."

"I sorry to interrupt you, Miss Mary-Mathilda."

"That is my meaning to '*save my soul*.' To save my soul from the various interpretations."

"Nobody in their right mind would put a wrong interpretation to . . ."

"Thank you, Percy, for saying so."

" . . . your act. That ain't nothing at all. And if these circumstances wasn't such as they are, I would say that your position doesn't take any skin offa my teet'. If you are following me, Miss Mary. You know what I mean?"

"I know what you mean."

"But you called me and I had to come."

"Police response. Yes."

"As hurtful as it is."

"Duty is duty."

"I had to respond."

"You have that duty. And I have a duty to give you the history of my situation."

"You want to begin now?"

"When you ready."

"I think this drink going to my head."

"You was never so light-headed, Percy."

"This drink working 'pon me already."

"When you are ready for another one, help yourself, Percy. And before I start my Statement, I want to say how glad it is that it is you I giving it to."

"Is my honour."

"It could be worse. Although I am made aware of how I stand in this Village, I do not intend taking any privileges with the Village. Or with you. I giving it to you. The way it happen. Whiching is the way I intended it to happen. Because I am not talking only about one single, isolated night. Or one act. Something that my body, that only my limbs carried out, physically. And that my mind didn't play a role in that act.

"I am talking, about more than that one act. I am talking about history. About the reason my body took it physically upon itself, with the assistance of my head and my mind . . . my soul . . . I am thinking now about the code that a coloured Amurcan from the South stood by; a code that he invented, and nailed-up above the doorpost of a one-room schoolhouse he was headmaster of; and later displayed and distributed this code on other buildings, workshops and sleeping quarters where the coloured people lived and studied and did practical work, like in apprenticeships, for woodwork, carpentry, joinering and making furnitures; and learning the meaning of drainage, crops, cycles o' planting and agriculture. That coloured Amurcan man's code was *Head. Heart. Hand.*

"It is this code I use to guide the footsteps of my life. I used it to drill common sense inside Wilberforce head; and plant a sense o' duty . . .

"And Percy, I don't have to tell you, a man who sings tenor in the Choir, and takes Communion every first Sunday, that there is something to this act of mine being perpetrated on this sacred day. Sunday.

"All these years, people from the surrounding villages would visit our Village, take part in Mothers Union meetings, social gatherings, and play cricket against our team; even attend our church festivals; walk in processions, through every road and alley in this Village, with our choir, in praise and in acknowledgment; and anybody, from here and from elsewhere would envy the life I was leading all these years.

"But they would envy me because they see only the outside of my life. The shell. The husk. The skin and the peel.

"Nobody would believe that the life I lead in this Great House caused the act that put an end to that very life.

"I haven't explained it too well. But what I want to tell you is that my act brought a end to its history. To my history.

"So, Percy, first I have to show you my hoe. There . . . would it be still leaning-up outside, beside the front door?

"After tonight, I may not have any more use for it. After tonight, its sharpness and its shininess won't be *ironical* no more!

"All those years, I must have been waiting for a sign. A sign, yes.

"A sign to tell me the correct time had come, counting week, day, daytime or nighttime, hour and down to the minute. Yes.

"Right down to the second. To the fraction of a second! Yes.

"And in all of that time, I really could not understand the meaning of my hoe!

"My hoe, that I used in the North Field; weeding young canes; weeding potato slips; yams; eddoes; just plain weeding; and starting-out as a common field hand, on this Plantation, I was a girl sprouting two bubbies, a spring in my backside, the prey of any bookkeeper, driver, overseer or manager to take advantage of. And they could. And did. Take advantage of this girl. The only body who didn't stir his spoon in the pot, God bless him, was the Revern. But the rest? I was there. To have, and to discard. To have, at a whim and a will. But, I still had some pleasure to go along with it.

"For there was little acknowledgment of the advantage-taking: but a acknowledgment, nevertheless. By the Plantation, by the bookkeeper, the overseer and the manager, that I was a damn good labourer. Yes.

"Damn good in the fields, and damn good in trash heaps, and damn good in bed. Yes.

"I gave the bastard a son and heir, didn't I? Yes.

"And damn good in other ways, too!

"But my claim to fame, for what it worth, is, I was a damn good labourer.

"What labourer, though? *Field hand!*

"I am talking about a time, when any one of them, driver, over-seer, bookkeeper, manager, any one of the four o' them, even the man-leader of a field gang, anybody in the scheme of things, in a more higher position, could grab your hand, and lead you in a cane field; pull down your bloomers, put you to lay-down on a pile o' cane trash; and after he unbutton his fly, and pull out his dickey, pardon my French, Sarge-boy, he could lay down 'pon top o' you, *bam-bam-bam!*, and jerk off. And that was that. Yes.

"That is the history of life on a Plantation. In this Island. On *any* Plantation in Bimshire! I am not talking fiction, Sargeant."

"No, you're not, Miss Mary-Mathilda!" he says. "I have heard such. But not in this abundance."

"So, my hoe, in its other history, has served me well. And still, in those nights, listening to the BBC programme *Calling the Wessindies;* or playing the Victrola grammaphone; or else tuning-in to the Voice of Bimshire, I would sit here and listen; or I would turn on the 'private-set,' and pick-up Latin-Amurca, Caracas, Brazil, Montevideo, Valparaiso, the Argentyne . . . yes.

"Even Trinidad, I would get sometimes. All those foreign coun-tries! With their languages and different ways of behaving. Yes, you could find me here, late-late-late, any night turning into morning, with the music from those foreign countries keeping my company.

"Listening to foreign music is natural to me, because I live in a island. And because the water surrounding we, the Carbean Sea, is the same water flowing here from the oceans of the world, one being the Atlantic, everything that that Atlantic Ocean brings in, with the currents, touches the way we live in this Island; and in any other island in the Wessindies. And I just love to listen to the way foreigners talk, although I don't understand one damn thing they're saying.

"But still, their language is so sweet to listen to. *Brabba-rabba-brabba-rabba, sennorita*—if they're speaking Spanish. And if it is Eyetalian, *ciao-ciao, bonna-days, bonna-days, mangiamo, grazzias* and *ciao*. Yes.

"Foreign talk, foreign language and foreign rhythms and foreign music! And once, by mistake, the 'private-set' pick-up Germany. Oh my God! *Heine, mine, zee Deutch-zee-Deutch, spraken, racken, nine, nine, nine!* And in the midst of the War, to-boot. Whilst the bombs was still falling.

"And all the time that I am listening, I am running my hand over the handle of my hoe, feeling the bumps where the smaller branches were cut from; and I would praise God, that I, Mary Gertrude Mathilda, a simple woman, living so far from what Wilberforce calls the centre of the world, the axis of civilization, is still filled with the spirit of God, to be able to listen to these small wonders.

"I don't see eye-to-eye with Wilberforce in all things. I think that right-here, rightfully-so in Bimshire, we have things and we do things, that qualify we, that qualifies us, right here in the Wessindies, to be as much important as *any* country in Europe, or Germany, or Italy or France—not to mention Englund—as being a similar axis, and a similar centre of civilized things, too.

"And it is God. In the lateness of the hour, and in the darkest hour, as Mr. Winston Churchill calls those late-late nights of tragedy, I have to be thankful only to God, for maintaining the handle of my hoe so strong and so long-lasting.

"Things made from the fustic tree are everlasting in their lastingness. Strength and lastingness. I am sure that the handle of my hoe comes from one of the fustic trees growing on this Plantation. But it could equally-be-from a tamarind tree, too.

"And still, with all that polishing and sharpening, I still couldn't pinpoint what use I was going to put it to. Or, what act destiny and fate had in mind for me to perform, using it.

"But I knew, from the very beginning, yes, that there was an act ordained for me to perform. Yes.

"One Saturday night, late-late, as I was tuned-in to Latin-Amurca, and was listening to Latin-Amurcan mambos and tangos, and parangs, on my 'private-set,' I heard a discussion in English, about the hardness of woods. It surprised me to hear English spoken.

"As you know, they have lots of forests in that part of the world. Take British Guiana, or Demerara, for an instant. In those jungles, there're woods from trees that are famous for their hardness and prettiness; lasting wood that never rots, that we use in furnitures. Look round this room. You will see what I mean. That couch, with the white pillows. And the two matching Berbice chairs. The tea trolley. They are made from Demerara red wood.

"But coming back to the hoe . . ."

"So, Miss Mary-Mathilda," Sargeant says, "you telling me that you don't have intent nor intention. Are you stating what we in legal terminology calls 'no malice aforethought'? In quotation marks. Eh, Mary? I mean, Miss Mary. Miss Mary-Mathilda."

"Nothing in the way of malice aforethought," she says.

"That is a big difference."

"How much of a difference?"

"Well, it is a difference. A big difference. I don't know how to simplify these legalistical matters in plain English for you to understand, Miss Mary-Mathilda, but, um, is a big difference."

"Because if there is such a difference, and a big one at that, after all those nights polishing and sharpening, I did not consciously know, how the hoe would feature. I hope you consider that in your calculation of the differences."

"I consider that, already, Miss Mary. I already consider that."

"Because, I don't really understand what you're saying. And I don't mean this with malice aforethought. The Law is a strange thing."

"The Law is a strange beast, Miss Mary."

"*Malice aforethought*! But isn't it a pretty way to say things! English, boy!"

"English."

"The English language! No language, under the sun, even those from Latin-Amurca, comes close to English, in beauty. 'No malice aforethought.' In quotation marks, as you say. It is a nice way of saying things, as if it comes from the Bible."

"Is the Law, Miss Mary-Mathilda. The Law. And the Law have a way of talking with words of seriousness."

"You sure it isn't from the Old Testament? One of the biblical prophets?"

"Malice aforethought? Is pure Law! Pure jurisprudence, Miss Mary-Mathilda! No connection at-all, at-all, to the Old Testament! None, whatsoever. Far's I remember, my Torts and my Comma-Law from Police Training School, *malice aforethought* is nothing but a legal terminology!"

"With this in mind, I going-begin from the beginning, then."

"As aforementioned."

"It is always better to begin from the very beginning.

"And my beginning starts, and ends with the hoe that I used to use round this very House where I now living. I was assign, as a lil girl, to weed only the flower beds, beginning from the age o' eight or nine; and when I reached my teens, I was sent to work in the North Field using the same hoe.

"Round the yard here, I use it to weed the beds of the kitchen garden, the small tomatoes, for making gravy; and large beef-steak tomatoes; string beans, christophenes, squash, cucumbers, lima beans, pigeon-peas and punkin-vines, all from the kitchen-garden.

"And in the afternoons, when there is a lil relief from the sun and the humidity, I turned from the kitchen-garden to the flower beds, cleaning and weeding the rose of Sharon, daisies, pansies, bourganvillea, flowers . . . to help-them-along more faster.

"You could see the lovely flowers round the property, as you ride-up the path of white marl and loose gravel, if it wasn't so difficult in the darkness to see the flowers?"

"I see flowers all the time, Miss Mary-Mathilda, even on a dark night. Flowers don't mean that-much, to me, though," Sargeant says. "They grow and I passes them; and sometimes I don't see them at all. But I know they are there."

"I-too. I'm not much for flowers, neither. No.

"But to give Satan his due, Mr. Bellfeels was. Is. A master at growing flowers. Specially roses. He even grafted a new rose and named it after my daughter, Rachelle Sarah Prudence, who did not live long, my only girl, who didn't survive two months after birth. God rest her poor soul! Sweet child . . ."

She makes the sign of the Cross.

Sargeant makes the sign of the Cross, imitating her.

"The Rachelle Rose. Named after my late daughter. You can see it better when the sun come up . . . in the morning . . ."

"I see it once, one day long ago when I had to pass here," he says.

"And Wilberforce take after Mr. Bellfeels, in regards to having a green-thumb. And Gertrude. Now-and-then. Gertrude's two hands are green thumbs. But she is sometime-ish, even although anything she touch, turns to gold. Anything I plant, drops-down-dead by the second day. My *fortay* lies in the use of my hoe, with regards to tending and cultivating the ground, the hard, thick, musty, smelly ground, that black soil. The soil that is so cruel, when you come to know it. When you clear a field of trees and tree-roots, or even turn a fallow field, once full o' canes, into a field for planting potatoes, or even yams and eddoes, my-Christ, Sargeant, the number of forty-legs, *centipees* that appear at your two feet, up to your ankles, thick as if you are walking through mud! The droves of centipees crawling outta that ground the same colour as the soil, that fresh ground, that they call virgin soil! My God-in-heaven, Sargeant, centipees in such countless, numberless numbers! . . . So, all you could do was just stand there, dumb-struck. And you would think that what it is, was the earth, the ground itself, moving and wringling, swelling and contracting like the bellows of a concertina.

"Sargeant, pray to God that one of those bastards don't crawl-up your trousers leg, oh Christ, man! The sting they could put in your you-know-what! Or, in your behind. Takes days and days to bring-down the swelling, and ease the sting and release the pus and the venom!

"Jesus Christ, Percy. You must remember Golbourne? And the pain? And the sorrow Golbourne went through, when that centipee crawled slow-slow from under his bed, one night, and walk all over Golbourne face, as if it was vestigating his entire anatomy, and then how it slip-into his mouth . . . Golbourne still sleeps with his mouth wide-open . . . and the bastard crawl-back-through Golbourne nose-hole, his nostril? Jesus-Christ-in heaven! Yes!

"I shake, I shake with, with disgust. . . my stomach quiver, and get into knots, even to this day, whenever I think of it. Golbourne was how old when that happen? Five?"

"Six!"

"Six? You sure? Yes. But he wasn't quite-six, yet, Sargeant. He wasn't yet in Primer Standard at Sin-Davids Elementary, although he start late. Nor in Kinter-garden, neither."

"Not quite six. Five, then?"

"Yes. Five! Golbourne was five when that centipee crawled-through his two nostrils, from the inside out."

"My God!" Sargeant says.

And he pulls a large white handkerchief from the sleeve of his black serge tunic. He pulls it out like a conjurer performing tricks. And when the handkerchief eventually comes out, like a long white snake, he wipes his face with it. The buttons at the front of his black tunic are buttoned. Up to his neck. The buttons are silver and shining. His face is large, and strong. And black. Like ebony. A happy face. A face you normally would confuse with honesty, if not with unsophistication and jewelled naivety. No, not quite that kind of a face. It is, in its smooth roundness, a face with no trace of compli-catedness and complexity, shaven with such regular care that it looks as if hair has not yet sprouted from it. The face of a boy. Yes, that is Sargeant's face. It is an honest, boy-like face.

"My God!" he says.

And this time, he shivers. He shivers and hopes it tells her that his skin crawls, too, to hear about Golbourne; that he, too, can feel pain, and can recoil at the disgustedness, same as hers, at the sight of a centipede coming back out through a child's nostril.

The sudden and uncontrolled movements his body goes through, are larger and more dramatic than normal.

"And you call yourself a detective, Percy! Haven't you seen worse things? A lil thing, like a centipee crawling-through a child's two nostrils makes you shake and shudder and squirm like that? You look as if nothing tragic ever stared you in your face! You remember the plight of Clotelle? You remember Pounce's lot?"

"Just the thought, Miss Mary, just the thought."

"It wasn't pleasant."

"Being a Crown-Sargeant in the Force, I see certain things which a normal person isn't privilege to see; and don't see. And when my two eyes sees such things, it don't mean that my constitution is so toughened-up by my job that I loss all sense o' compassion and feelings . . ."

"You have any compassion and feelings for me, in my present circumstances?"

"I know, Miss Mary, that . . ."

"You have a job to do. I have a job to make your job more easier. Not making statements to com-promise you."

"You already do," he says. "Making my job more easier."

"What you mean?"

"Making my life easier? I mean, sitting here with you in your front-house, on a Sunday evening, talking to me as if you are really not Miss Mary-Mathilda, Miss Bellfeels of the Great House, as we call you, and what that mean, but sitting here, you is still, some-how, the girl who I went-school with. And who uses to play London

Bridge and Ship-Sail with me. And as if I is not a police come to take your Statement.

"This is the very first time that I have the honour to grace a seat in your front-house. Except years ago, the time Mr. Bellfeels bring me here, on his horse, before you was living in this house, and make me stand-up in the kitchen, as he question you and axe you to swear that I steal the Plantation mangoes . . ."

"Yes! Bellfeels scared you like hell. Threatened to give you five years in Dodd's Reformatory!"

"Yes. And he hold me by my two ears, and turn-me-round, and lifted me up in the air, offa the red tiles on the kitchen floor . . . I'll never forget the colour of the tiles in the kitchen . . . and twist my ears, whilst forcing you to swear um was me who climb the mango tree. No, you were not living in this Great House yet. You was your mother's helper in the kitchen, hero in this Great House."

"What a brute! Bellfeels. Is. And was. Treating you like a harden criminal.

"And when you count the number of mango trees we have on this Plantation, mangoes like peas! Pah-wees, common-mango, the Trinidadian version; mangoes from Sin-Lucia; and see the number o' mangoes, ripe ones, green ones, and young mangoes, that fall outta the tree, and leff on the ground to rot . . .

"Or, to feed to the stocks!

"Bellfeels was itching to tar your backside, that afternoon. And if I didn't lie . . . with Ma touching my back to do it . . . and intervene in your behalf, Jesus-Christ, Percy-boy, you wouldda gone up. Straight to Dodd's. Over *one* mango!"

"One mango. From that day forth . . . I pee my pants that day Mr. Bellfeels hold-me-on on the hard leather saddle of his horse, tight . . . from that day, and years afterwards, every time I see Mr. Bellfeels, I wet my pants, again. And for years afterwards, like a thing that Mr. Wilberforce call a cause-and-effect, the mere thought of that day in the kitchen, on the red tiles, makes my bladder burn and I want to pee . . . excuse me for talking so plain. But that day, I also make a vow to be a police. So that nobody-else could ever take advantage o' me. This burning bladder and wanting to pee bad went on till a year or two before I joined the Force. The peeing of my pants, in times of emergency, I mean."

"The man is a savage," she says.

"Was like a savage he treated me," Sargeant says. "But that is over."

"Thank God for that!"

"Thank God."

"That part of him is still alive. That in-born nastiness don't ever die. It is round-here, somewhere. Perhaps, in the fields. Or in habi-tation in the Plantation Main House itself. For sure, I know it is still inhabiting this Great House with me. And I regret that it still resides inside this place, with Wilberforce living here. But my days here, are numbered, and . . ."

"What you mean by 'numbered'? Nobody isn't counting your remaining days, Miss Mary-Mathilda."

"I mean death. When I dead-and-gone, this Great House may go to Wilberforce. I hope that if he inherit it, first thing he will do, is give it a thorough going-through. Purge it."

"Oh!" he says, "you had me scared, there!"

"Mr. Bellfeels start talking to the owners of the Plantation up in Englund, to let me live in this Great House, the day after he was promoted from overseer of the field gang. As gang leader, he looked after the horses, and the mules, and the donkeys. And the pens. Head of the stables and stable boys. He got a quick promo-tion from being head of the stables, to be assistant overseer. Then, overseer. Then, bookkeeper assistant. Then, full bookkeeper. It was as bookkeeper that this Great House was put at his disposal.

"Mr. Bellfeels, as white as he looks today, is really not pure white. He mixed. He doesn't like to be in the sun too long. And he never bathes in the sea. Saltwater, he used to tell me, tans the skin, and turns you too black. Isn't that man a foolish son-of-a-bitch! Pardon my French, Sargeant.

"Then, he was made manager-acting. And from manager-acting to his present position. Manager of this Plantation.

"The Main House, as you know, is the biggest house on this estate. It is just the distance of a four-hundred-and-forty-yard race, from this Great House. But with the fruit trees and the fields and the turns in the road, you can't see it from here, and it look more farther from where we are. The Plantation Main House is the power on the estate.

"Yes! So, he was eventually made Manager, and it take exactly the number of years Wilberforce born for Mr. Bellfeels to rule this Plantation.

"But that taste I was talking about. That taste, that taint, that mouldiness like the soil of the North Field; that sickening smell of dirt and wet dust, reminding you of something that is dead, perpetually rotting . . . I suppose our bodies go through that kind of disfiguration, 'earth to earth: duss to duss'; the mould carrying in its smell, the smell of a million centipees crawling in one thick, never-ending dark-brown wave of nastiness and stinging disgustedness, disgusting to people, all people, not only infants and boys like Golbourne. Disgusting to animals, too. That smell of wet, black soil, is his smell, is Mr. Bellfeels smell. Yes.

"And it will always be lingering-'bout here; inside this house; on these curtains and blinds; inside the wallpaper; on the pictures and picture frames; in this front-house parlour where me and you sitting on this Sunday evening, in question. It is lingering in the kitchen with Gertrude, poor soul, as she does her housework; in all the rooms upstairs, my dressing room, Wilberforce bedroom and his study; and even after all these years, in my bedroom.

"Don't even mention in my bed, or inside the mattress. It is like the rot that grows from dampness. Regardless of the amount o' Jays Fluid, blue soap, white-head bush, bleach and kerosene oil that you pour over certain stains, that kind o' spot will never come out. Will never leave delicate material, like muslim or sea-island cotton, which it has stained with its stubbornness.

"My boy, Wilberforce, a doctor of Tropical Medicines, calls this kind o' stain, indellable. Indellable."

"Indellable," Sargeant says, with a smile on his face. "Like the ink we have to use in the writing-up of Confidential Reports and Statements! And in our promotion examinations."

"Like that."

"Like Quink Ink, Royal Blue in colour."

"Like Royal Blue Quink Ink. We used it in Penmanship classes at Sin-Davids Elementary School for Girls."

"We still uses it in Reports and Statements, that is official. And in our promotion examinations."

"I have seen Mr. Bellfeels use that same ink to write in his ledgers; and he would try over and over to wipe out certain fig- ures, before he felt safe-enough to present them to the owners up in Englund, his superiors; before he could justify his personal statements of how the Plantation money was handled; yes, to the Board of Governors living in Bimshire, and the overseas owners, up in Englund. I have seen Mr. Bellfeels struggle many a night, sweat and perspiration pouring down his face, lose his temper, curse stink-stink, '. . . these fecking Limey-bastards! They think all o' we in Bimshire is slaves?'; having the nerves and anxious moments, shortening-tempers, as he struggled to change a hundred- Pounds loss, into a seven-hundred-Pounds loss; and pocket the difference struggling to make his figures written down, coincide with his verbal statements, in telephone conversations to the local Board of Governors; and with the cablegrams he sent overseas to the owners in Englund.

"So, I know about Quink Ink. The Royal Blue tints and tinc- tures, as Mr. Bellfeels himself was in the habit of calling it by."

"But what a lovely ink, though!" Sargeant says. His face is beaming. Perhaps it is the perspiration on his cheeks. "I have a Watermans fountain pen that the Commissioner o' Police give me, the day I made Crown-Sargeant. And I won't be caught dead without my Water- mans, always full o' Royal Blue Quink ink. I even got it with me, now!

"Once in Standard Four, a afternoon, round half-pass two, we was doing Penmanship; and the Teacher was telling we how to write the *t* more shorter than the *h*; and he show we on the black-board . . . blackboards in them days not only was to write on, but they was used as dividers of one class from the next. Behind our blackboard was Standard Five. On our blackboard, though, the Teacher was writing, *Manners Maketh Man*. The Teacher went to the blackboard to show us how to write; and he had a pretty-pretty writing-hand; and every time he write a *g*, the chalk make a shrieking sound like a squeak; and the boys would laugh. I was the only boy to get catched laughing. And the Teacher screeled at me, '*Stuart! One mark off! For cackling like a hen in class! Lines!*' And I start crying. And the rest of the boys start laughing. '*You will write out* Manners Maketh Man, *fifty times. In your English Grammar Exercise Book! In Quink Ink, Stuart! Quink Ink.*' That is why my writing-hand is so good today.

"I know 'bout Quink Ink. And fountain pens. I carries my Watermans clip-on in my inside-pocket, whether it is this uni-form, or the shirts I knocks around the house in; whatever I am wearing. My Watermans is in my black suit I wears to weddings, funerals and Services-o'-Songs. My Watermans! Or in the inside-pocket of any suit I wear to church, when I singing tenor in the Choir.

"I don't leave home without it. Not my Watermans. It travels with me, wherever I go."

"I know. I know it. And I have seen you wearing it, too. In a short-sleeve sports shirt, one Saturday afternoon, watching cricket on the Pasture. Just like my wishbone."

"Your wishbone?"

"Yes. My wishbone."

"This is something I should take-down and add-on to your Statement? It may be something extenniating."

"You can get it from the Constable. Me and him talked enough already about that wishbone, a wishbone I carried around for years, the same way you carry around your Watermans pen. But mine was like a talisman, a word I hear Wilberforce use."

"I would not know that word, Miss Mary-Mathilda. *Talisman?*"

"You are a Crown-Sargeant in the Royal Constabulary of the Island of Bimshire, and you should know the word, Percy DaCosta Benjamin Stuart?"

"Well . . . well, I have my thoughts . . ."

"On Friday nights over their fried dolphin steaks and dry-peas and rice, Percy Stuart, what you think they does-talk about? The crops? The thrildren? Church? Or even school? For one thing, they don't talk nothing about education, cause the majority of them didn't get too far in school!

"They talk about you. Not meaning you, personally. But, about you. In broad terms. And me. The labourers. The maids. The cooks. The messengers. The men who tend the stocks and the stables. Cane cutters. Lorry drivers. And the women they foop and rape, on the Plantation. And breed.

"They lambast politicians who they don't like. And *everybody* coloured, or that black. Yes.

"And they talk about taking their next Home-Leave, in Englund. They all born *here*, mind you! But home is still Englund. So, every year, they head straight to Englund. You see what that mean? Yes.

"They hate all o' we. Me. You. Gertrude, out there in the kitchen. Everybody.

"Regardless to colour and complexion. So long as we are not white like them, and belongst to a Plantation.

"Percy Stuart, I have served and I have listened, and pretended I didn't hear nothing that pass their lips in their condemnation of the black people of this Island.

"I watch them iamming fried dolphin steaks, and fulling their mouths with dry-peas and rice, wash-away in thick, brown gravy; and I smile to myself. But I listen with my two ears prick.

"I have washed their plates, their cups, their glasses and their silvers; and I have listened. And I would pretend not to hear, nor be interested in hearing their stories; have no concern with nothing; aside from concentrating on the sting of the blue soap in the water, and the tightness from the detergents clogging-up my veins as I wash their clothes.

"In my mind was nothing but the sound of the washing.

"I have washed their clothes, yes. I have washed their drawers, their shifts and their panties, their underwears and their monthly-rags, and I have seen their stains, and blots and blood; and I have not pointed a finger at, nor singled-out a, the owner of those stains or blots or blood, in judgment.

"Nothing but the sound of washing took my attention, as my two hands rub the clothes on the jucking-board.

"I have cleaned their rooms. Their bathrooms, their bedrooms, their beds, under their beds, seen the stuffing of their mattress, where I have come face-to-face with their true colours: the things they have left, the mess and the messages. And I have closed my two eyes against all temptation to broadcast that evidence. I have cleaned their topsies, their bedpans and chamberpots when they are laid up; and when they are poorly, at death's door.

"But I always knew the day would come. I lived always with the hope that *my* day would come. When my knowledge of that evidence was seen by me, I knew then that my knowledge of their ways, their behaviour, and their secrets, would be my education and my deliverance.

"We, to them, are all labourers, Percy. You, me, Manny, Golbourne, the Constable. The Headmaster and the Headmistress of the elementary schools. Gertrude. All o' we. Common, low-class workers. Discardable, Percy. They talk about how to keep you and me in our place. Constantly. And the fact that I have a son, fathered by one of them, Mr. Bellfeels; plus the fact that he treats Wilberforce no different from the way he treats his two girl-thrildren, the inside-thrildren, Miss Euralie Bellfeels, who I call 'the Duchess,' and Miss Emonie Bellfeels, 'the Lady'——not to mention the other lady, his wife, Mistress Bellfeels, formerly Miss Dora

Blanche Spence—it still don't mean that Mr. Bellfeels carries any respect in his heart for me. Does Mr. Bellfeels respect Wilberforce? Perhaps. Because he is a doctor of Tropical Medicines. Does Mr. Bellfeels respect me, the mother of his son-and-heir? Not on your blasted bottom-dollar! *Never!*

"There is a distinct difference in the way Mr. Bellfeels see me, and the way he was brought up to see me, from the way he see Mistress Dora Blanche Spence Bellfeels. Yes.

"One is wife. The other is harlot. One is Mistress. The other is the whore. One was. . . "

"Did you say *whore*, Miss Mary?"

"Is there a difference, Percy?"

"Are you referring to your hoe?"

"They are both the same, and sound the same."

"Well, one is a thing; and the other . . ."

"So, at those Friday night dinner parties, I got to know more about you than you could ever imagine. And the strange thing about this kind of information is that I know more about you as a thing that you stand for in their minds, than as a person. Than as a man. A full person who plays his piano on Friday nights, and takes a snap regularly, as anybody else, at the Harlem Bar & Grill, in the Selected Clienteles Room. You understand now, what I mean?"

"You know *all* this 'bout me, Miss Mary?"

"You understand now, the difference between how you see yourself, and how somebody else who don't know you, or like you, see you?"

"I understand. But the source of your knowledge of me, frightens me! This is dangerous knowledge that you are in possession of, Miss Mary-Mathilda."

"I was telling the Constable about the music Mr. Bellfeels used to play in this House. It was like a Victorian parlour in the olden days. Like the ones in the *London Illustrated News*. And like the Friday night magic lanterns that the Department of Social Development and Culture put on, that always had pictures of drawing rooms up in London-Englund, with pictures of the King, George-the-Fiff, sitting in a wing-back chair, playing with a dog, listening to music, on His Master's Voice.

"But I don't encourage the dog inside the house!"

"But, Mary-girl," Sargeant says, in a burst of exuberance followed by contrition. "I don't mean to be so personal. But, Miss Mary. You mean to tell me that in all these years, as a woman, you was so interested in my tinklellings of Do-re-me-fa-sol-la-tee-do? Well, God bless my eyesight, this Sunday evening! What I am hearing at all, though?"

"Some things are things that don't bear repeating two times. One time is enough. So, one chance is all I am offering you, Percy."

"I tekking that one chance."

"In a short time from now, in the circumstances, I may not be able to talk to you no more. This is the last time, maybe, we'll be in the same room."

"I hope not, Miss Mary-Mathilda. I know you are in possession of certain knowledge that will never come my way. Regardless to my rank."

"This is a case of the possession of knowledge, and having that knowledge conceal from me. Unless you come to my aid, Miss Mary-Mathilda, this is one case I will never crack. So, I have to listen to you, with both o' my two ears wide open.

"But I have to axe you *one* question, first. What caused you to say, a minute ago, and I quote, *'This is the last time, maybe, we'll be in the same room'?"*

"There was always dangerous talk going-on round me," she says, ignoring his question. "From the time I was a ignored eyewitness and listener till the time they trusted my presence amongst them, they trusted me to listen. But not to talk. Never. Nor repeat secrets. Not if I value my life. Secrets, scandals and plottings. You don't know what goes on in this little Island of Bimshire!

"Ma would put me to siddown, and regardless to who happened to be in our house, at the time, Ma always allow me my contribution in their conversation. I raised Wilberforce with identical guidance. You know, of course, that Mr. Bellfeels never put Ma in a house, like this one. Although he had his full of Ma.

"Mr. Bellfeels had his full with me. He had ownership and control over me. And I am the first to admit it.

"But he faced the price and the penalty of my ownership. I made him pay. I made him pay. I made that son-of-a-bitch pay. Pardon me, Sargeant, I losing control over my emotions. I am not like this. Pardon my French . . .

"But I don't have to tell you, a man trained and schooled in the art of listening to people talk, gathering-up conversations and talk, and putting them in a legal fashion, to be constructed as evidence, that a lot of the things I heard, I cannot repeat to you. Some of them dealt with family secrets and Island secrets, that scared me, and made my blood crawl, even to think about them now; or want to remember them, after they were pronounce round the dinner table. I knew exactly what I heard in whispers in Ma's presence round Mr. Bellfeels dinner table over at the Main House, and later, here in the Great House when Mr. Bellfeels was a regular visitor . . . visitor, or courter? Courter, yes! With his invited guesses, Revern Dowd, the Solicitor-General, and the other two leading barsters-at-Law in the Island.

"I try, all these years, not to remember those things; and certainly not to repeat them. Not the real good secrets and scandals. Like the one of a woman, who lives in this Village, who poisoned a Governor of this Island. Yes. She was the Governor's outside-woman, or 'kip-miss.' Every Saturday afternoon, punctual at three o'clock, regular as a bowel movement, regular as God send—you could set your clock by His Excellency's arrival; yes—the Governor would tie-up the horse-and-buggy outside that woman house. To a ackee tree. In full view for the neighbours, the Marrish and the Parrish, to see! Yes. Horse-and-buggy tie-up outside her house. This went on every Saturday, for months and months, turning into a year and a half. On the dot of three o'clock. You would see His

Excellency, dress-off sparkling in white drill suit, white shirt, grey plaid tie, white cork hat and white socks and white patient-leather shoes cleaned by Blanco four times a week, by his batman. Mr. Bellfeels told me all this. Yes. And the Governor would walk in through the front door. And the second he cross her threshold, and step inside, and siddown in the best-polish Morris-chair, *bram!* the window-blinds drop. Drawn. Jalousies shut down tight-tight . . ."

"My God!" Sargeant says. "I heard 'bout this, but I didn't know that it really happen! I thought it was a myth, like a 'nancy story! My God! Miss Mary-Mathilda, what you telling me?"

"And the poor man . . ."

"The poor Governor? His Excellency?"

"Not the blasted Governor, Percy-man! The husband! That poor man. That poppit. She had him like a loopey-dog. Send-him-out in the yard; stanning-up beside the pigpen, under the puh-paw tree, in the shade, where he had to wait there, till the Governor do-his-business. And eat his belly full. And that man, her poor, legal wed-ded poppit husband, could not move a inch, nor come back inside his own house, the poppit; could not cross the threshold of that one-roof house he build with his own two hands, till His Lordship the Governor was first satisfied. And had-eat what he wanted!"

"My God, Miss Mary! Things like them, didn't happen in this Island, man! Couldn't!"

"And in case the husband wasn't home when His Excellency come for his stuff, the pudding-and-souse, she used to send the husband a signal. With music. The moment Sir Stanley parted the pink cotton blinds and step-in her front-house, the wife would put-on a record 'pon the grammaphone. 'A Tisket, a Tasket,' by Ella Fitzgerald. "'A Tisket, a Tasket.'"

"'A Tisket, a Tasket,' Miss Mary?" Sargeant says, singing the tune. *'My brown-and-yellow basket'?"*

"And when the husband hear the music, he would walk *back* out Flagstaff Road, to the corner, siddown on the embankment, on the rock beside the Standpipe; and watch the General Company passenger buses, and lorries from the estates carrying canes to the Factory to grind, pass; the poppit; and private cars, donkey-carts and mule-carts passing him sitting down 'pon the rock, laden-down with goods for the peddling shops that sell mainly salt fish and flour; and lumber. The husband sitting and watching and amusing himself by memorizing the licents-plates on all these traf-ficks travelling-past, going up into the country, passing Sin-Davids Anglican Church, Upton Hill, Lower Estate, Frere Pilgrim, Kent Great House, all them places and plantations. And that man *dare not* move from that rock. Balls cut off! It was like . . . he was all of a sudden . . . turned into a statue cut outta rock-stone. Or a watchman.

"The husband stood there, till the horse-and-buggy carrying the Governor pass-back, and . . ."

"I wouldda kill she!"

"And something else used to take place."

"What more could take place?"

"One of the most hurtful things a woman could do to a man."

"What used to happen, Mary-Mathilda?" Sargeant says. "I mean, what *more* could happen, Miss Mary-Mathilda?"

"Percy, as a man, it would make your heart bleed, just to hear how that woman treat her poppit-husband."

"What-so, that could be, Miss Mary?"

"The husband had to stann-up, at attention . . ."

"No! Noooo!"

". . . with his hat in his hand. His brown felt hat. Resting at the top pocket of his khaki suit, short pants and short-sleeve shirt. He was a gardener. At the Aquatic Club down in Town. Hat touching his heart. You must have seen pictures of Amurcans, how they does rest their hand on their heart as they stand and sing 'The Star-Spangled Banner'? And *salute*. He had to salute the buggy-and-horse carrying the Governor from his house. The husband couldn't move a inch till that horse-and-buggy, conveying the Governor, get out o' sight. Stiff, at attention, like an Amurcan, until the horse-

and-buggy went round the corner, through the Pine Plantation and the fields o' green sugar canes growing as pretty as anything, like waves in the sea, going towards Guvvament House."

"Miss Mary-Mathilda, tell me the truth. It wasn't *that* bad in the olden days, was it? My mother and my gran-mother always talking 'bout them days as the good-old days. But was it *that* bad, in the good olden days, in this Village?"

"In *this* Village? In this Island, you mean! You shouldda seen Mr. Brannford! Stanning-up at attention. Straight as a arrow. A arrow from a cane stalk. Like the arrows growing outside my window. Brown felt hat in hand. Resting at his top pocket. On his breast. Near his heart. And bowing. Whilst the horse-and-buggy pass. And dare not lift his eyes, nor move, till that horse-and-buggy reach the intersection of Highgates Commons and Reservoir Lane to take His Excellency back out to Guvvament House."

"What a piece of Island history!"

"What a Island!"

"And not more than thirty-forty years ago, since these things happen, you say ? These occurrences occur so recent in the history of this Island?"

"His Excellency, Sir Stanley."

"A governor Englund send down here to govern we!"

"Cuddear!"

"Sir Stanley and Mr. Brannford."

"And Mistress Rosa Mary Antoinette Brannford, his wife. She made everybody stranger and acquaintance alike, call her by all-four of her names. Particularly, if she thought you were lower than her, in social status. The curly-hair, curly-hair . . . *bitch!* Pardon my French."

"'A tisket, a tasket,'" Sargeant says.

"And it seem as if the horse had real horse-sense. Every time that horse got near to where Mr. Brannford was stann-ing up, on the rock, it would drop a line o' shit, *plop, plop, plop, plop* . . .

plop, just before it reached the corner, and until it rounded the corner . . . in Mr. Brannford's face!"

"'A tisket, a tasket,'" Sargeant says.

"'My brown-and-yellow basket'!" Mary-Mathilda says.

"'A tisket, a tasket,'" Sargeant says.

"And one Saturday evening, after Sir Stanley had had his full, and had dined on her pudding-and-souse . . . and I have to admit, that Rosa Mary Antoinette Brannford made the best pudding-and-souse in the whole Village, if not the Island . . . this particular afternoon in question, after Mr. Brannford stann-up in his stiff, starch-and-ironed khaki suit, with his brown felt hat resting at his heart, like an Amurcan; standing this way, in salute to Sir Stanley, and as per-usual, Sir Stanley would wave his whip, to the husband, in acknowledgment, the horse would shit, as if in punctuation, *plop, plop, plop, plop . . . plop . . .* Percy, it was not ten minutes later that the next person to visit Mistress Rosa Mary Antoinette Brannford to pick up her order, six cents in pudding-and-souse, that person being none other than Ma, my mother . . . Ten minutes after the Governor had-left, Ma found the corpse! Mistress Rosa Mary Antoinette Brannford. Leaning over the wooden platter that contained the lengths o' black pudding, the *black* black pudding which the Villagers prefer; whereas the Plantation-people prefers the *white* black pudding . . . there she was, according to Ma, with her throat *slit*. From ear to ear. With the same knife she had-use to slice the black pudding with, into servings. Yes."

"Jesus Christ, Miss Mary-Mathilda!"

"And not one day! Not one day, did Mr. Brannford spend in His Majesty's Glandairy Prison, for her!"

"You mean, scotch-free?"

"Scotch-free. Simply because the Plantation-people and the Solicitor-General, and them-so, had-wanted Englund to make one o' their-own, Governor—as promise by the Colonial Office."

". . . the name o' the Father, and the Son, and the Holy Ghost!" Sargeant says, making the sign of the Cross.

"And for murder! And not a day in Glandairy! And why? Because the Plantation-people and the Solicitor-General didn't like Sir Stanley!

"And a good thing about the Governor. Just before Mr. Brannford, poor soul, kill she, Sir Stanley had-start paying a carpenter to add-on another roof to their house."

Mary-Mathilda gets up from the straight-backed chair in which she has been sitting, all evening.

The chair creaks a little. It is relieved of her weight. She is not a large woman. But her body is solid. Her build tells you she is a strong woman, in good health, with good stamina, very beautiful, still desirable.

Her strength and sturdiness that you can see in her physical appearance, the way she stands, erect, and the way she walks, with a determination that sometimes makes you feel she is pounding the floorboards out of annoyance, all these, you might surmise and conclude, are the result of years working in hot sun, digging into the black soil with her hoe; weeding; and lifting bundles of canes that would break the back of the average man.

She is a beautiful woman.

"No sooner than the Governor reach-back, went upstairs to take a shower before dinner with the Legislative Council, leaving the six members in the drawing room drinking rum punch after rum punch, and eating parched nuts; and waiting on the Governor to join them, and waiting to get at the food on the dining table, roast pork, baked rabbits, a whole dolphin steam with the head still on, and dry-peas and rice . . . waiting, waiting . . . when finally, one of the members decides to call the batman. And when the batman came back, he went up to the same member of the Legislative Council, and whisper something in his ear . . . and immediately each of the guesses put down their rum punch, glance at the table laden down with all this food, and with whizzy-whizzying, walk soft over the thick carpets, down the red runner on the stairs, cussing the blasted Governor for spoiling their dinner . . . the batman had found Sir Stanley, naked as he born, in the shower, slump to the tiles, with the cold water coming down like a waterfall. Dead. The Legislative Council and the *Bimshire Daily Herald* said he dead from heart attack. A blasted lie! But the attopsy declared, '*Slow poisoning, using the agent of glass-bottle ground fine as flour and administer with the Bimshire cultural delicacy, to wit, 'black pudding-and-souse.'*" Yes.

"My God!" Sargeant says. He is overcome by the story.

She stands now, beside the heart-shaped mahogany table, on which the maid had placed the decanter of Bellfeels Special Stades White Rum; and the glass jug that contains the milk the Constable had drunk from; and the decanter that contains brandy. She lifts the decanter. Immediately the light from the electric bulb touches the decanter and shows to greater effect the lead and the magnificent workmanship in its design. It is a design of diamonds and of a swirl like the symbol for wild strong winds blowing in hurricanes over the Carbean Sea, making typhoons, and ending in whirlpools; and some of the workmanship in the design is like the shoots of sugar canes with their silken arrows that point upward to the short fat strong neck of the decanter.

"Another taste, Percy?" she says, without turning to him.

She is not using her words to make him feel they are intended for him. She is just talking. As if she is trying out her voice to make certain that it still sounds like the voice of Mary Gertrude Mathilda; using her voice to say words that are like traps to catch a fly. She wants him to be able to dig beneath her words for meaning, to detect her sexual interest in him, which she hides inside her words, tricky as a spider's web. Her seducing voice. A strong voice. A distinctive voice. Sometimes a mellow voice. Capable once upon a time of prising Wilberforce and his friends from their game of cricket beside the House, too close to the vegetable garden and the Rachelle Rose, and the glass in the French doors; or scattering the neighbourhood kids who rambled on to the Plantation grounds; and boys from down in Hastings, from stealing her mangoes; a voice that was once capable of making Mr. Bellfeels' tool get harder and rise to horizontal prowess and expectation; of softening his heart; years ago; a voice even now, still strong enough to raise the dead from the grave. A strong voice. A sure voice. But used mostly now, not with that strength of vocal chastisement, but as a soothing reminder of youth, and playfulness; and with guile. And love.

"A taste, yes, please," he says, "just a taste, Miss Mary. Please."

"'A tisket, a tasket,'" she says now, looking directly at Sargeant, her voice speaking, and not exactly singing. "What in the name of hell is a *tisket*, Percy?"

"A tisket?"

"Amurcans are funny people with the English language."

"But it is a lovely song," he tells her.

She does not pour the brandy for Percy. She replaces the decanter back on to its doily, after she has poured her own drink. And she goes to the end of the room, far away from him, and for a moment stands beside the large window whose thick glass is divided into four equal parts, and with outside wooden flaps like two heavy eyelids, even though they are latched back away from the frame. The wooden flaps are perpendicular. And in this light, not the light of a moonlight night, or the light thrown by an acetylene lamp; in this new light, Sargeant looks at her in the same slow, sensual, scrutinizing and undressing focus with which his eyes had travelled over Gertrude's body earlier; just as he had stripped Gertrude's clothes off her with his eyes: the white, starch-stiffened maid's cap; her detachable collar; her pleated, white starched apron that covers her breasts, and that winds around her entire body, tied at the back in a bow; and her black muslin maid's dress; and my God, Sargeant had now to pause, to catch his breath, although he has been doing this for years, every week, every two days in every week in cane field and in bedroom; and admire the round, soft, dark brown skin on her belly; and then the black stockings, after unlatching the clips that secure them to her corset; and her corset is a soft corset; for it does not have the stiffness and the bones of her Sunday-go-to-meeting corsets which she wears to the Pilgrim Holiness Church; and at the sight, and touch, of her dark brown belly, and brown pubic hairs, short and stubby and stubborn, looking at her compelling nakedness, this holiness brings about a lurch of emotion, each time he undresses her. He would handle her too roughly, in that moment, and too hastily, always; as if someone was about to enter the safe, thick canes, and see them like this: he with only two buttons of his fly unbuttoned, on the thick, brown trash; but going over Gertrude's body in his mind, in this large front-house parlour of this Great House, he can feel her skin, soft and cool against the back of his hand, made rough as sandpaper by the growth of hair, as if it is between her legs; for this is no fantasy; he has undressed her so many times that it is like himself dressing into his special uniform, for parades on the Garrison Savannah Pasture, on the piece of land, grass, gravel, tarred surface, set aside for regimental parades. He is celebrating, with spit and polish, and erect posture, and stiffness; with precision, and unsmiling visage and countenance, this year's King-George-the-Fiff's Birthday Parade . . .

"*Eyeeessssssss, right!*"

"*Eeee-eyessss, front!*"

"*Roy-yall, Sah-lute, Preeeee-zent . . . arms!*"

You can hear, from one hundred yards, the sound of sweaty palms hitting the barrel and butt of guns fired in the Boer War; and hear with clearer echo the snap of palms hitting the "board rifles" made by the school carpenters of the Island, for the three companies of the Island's Cadet Corps. "*Mock-soldiers,*" Wilberforce, who was a Harrison College cadet, calls them. "*Carrying mock-guns, and mekking mock-sport!*"

And the Royal Bimshire Police Constabulary Band plays "I Vow to Thee, My Country"; and the rich announcement of tuba and trombone curdles his blood and makes him feel important; and then "God Save the King," and the Band Master, a native of the Island, sneaks a jazz riff in amongst the stiff military Sousa-like music, a musical dipsy-doodle; and for that moment, as the reverberation comes over the tall mahogany trees and the royal palms, you think you are listening to a foxtrot, played by the Percy Greene Orchestra, fifteen black men born in Bimshire.

His eyes leave Gertrude's body, moving out of focus, departing from his exertion, from the falling of the light in the middle of the cane field, in the North Field, and the colour of the cane blades, and the brown colour of the cane trash, and the blueness of the skies getting deeper; he can no longer see her body in such fierce, desirable sharpness. She never took off her shoes in the cane field. She always wore her black canvas shoes, pumps, on her feet; and she would wrap her legs tight around his black, thick, tickly, serge policeman's uniform. She wore her black canvas shoes on every rendezvous with him, in the cane trash of the North Field; and stomped them against the noisy trash, to announce her coming. Her black canvas shoes were cleaned with Nugget Shoe Polish. Jet Black. Noir.

And his eyes comes now into this new focus, into this shocking realization that in this stiffer atmosphere, grandfather clock ticking in a suppressed voice of consideration for their words; the white, ironed doilies on the backs of all the chairs, Berbice, straight-backed, rocking and tub-chairs; settees; the animals from all the countries in the world, in diminutive stature, like Lilliputians . . . not a single animal amongst this collection, he has seen running round this Village, or this Island . . . the pictures on the walls, pictures in watercolour and pen and ink; all of English countrysides; landscapes, fields and puffs of smoke from chimneys and burning brush, and animals lying on their bellies; and their sides; and half-asleep . . . unlike the ones in this Island, who sleep standing up, and with their eyes open . . . workers in the fields, carrying brambles and hay, but no sugar canes or Khus-Khus grass; scenes she identifies with, and claims to be part of, and that are just an extension of her beloved Bimshire; yes, watercolours, pen and ink, oils; these

paintings and pictures he lumps into one. To him, they are "pic-
tures." But it is the formality of this front-house parlour that shows
him the distance he has come, from his rendezvous in the trash
of the sugar-cane field, of the North Field, with Gertrude. And
he hopes that he would not have to go back there, and lie on his back,
on the damp cane trash, some night, and pretend that he is in his
heaven.

He must do everything not to let Miss Mary-Mathilda know
about his knowledge of the North Field, with Gertrude.

He has already, gladly, transferred his old preference for that
tumbling trash, and of that loud, raucous room in the back of a
rum shop, even when it is filled with Selected Clienteles, sacri-
ficed and transferred them to this sedate, quiet, quiet, cool front-
house room, with this woman, slightly older than himself—as if
there is air-conditioning that comes silently throughout the house,
quiet as how Gertrude walks barefoot into a room . . . he has lost
the hesitancy that delayed his arrival; and now that he is here,
under these circumstances, he likes being here, although he hates
the circumstances.

For the first time, and with the passing of all this time taking her
Statement, he really sees her, no longer as a matriarch, as "Bellfeels
child-mother," but as a woman. As a woman, in her own sexual
right. With a burning desire of lust and sexual pleasure in his mind
for her that began in childhood; in limber wonder. Now, in adult-
hood, stiff; tom-pigeon has turned to dickey, to wood, at this first
meeting. And in this moment, painful as a sudden stomach ache,
frightening as a shudder that tragedy will fall over his path, he sees
her as a woman he can still love, and want to foop right now; and
this madness of desire transforms her, and makes her desirable,
even younger and more satisfying than Gertrude; younger also
than when he first entered her House a short while ago.

In this moment of speculation and equal confusion, Sargeant,
a man who has more confidence in his behaviour if it deals with
emotion and feeling and violence, than if it demands the analysing

of thought and rational action—which can, after all, contribute to the expenditure of unnecessary energy from the brain and the mind—Sargeant sees this confrontation with Mary-Mathilda as facing the truth; her new truth, and his, in terms of light, the light reflected in the pictures surrounding him.

The very light in the colours he sees in these pictures, is the light he places her in. Pictures that are strange and foreign and inexplicable to him. But he likes the colours, nevertheless.

The colours he sees, and the colours he paints her in, in his mind, are those same colours which were used by painters whom her son, Wilberforce, had told her about. European painters, Wilberforce called them. And he called them Renaissance Men. And Impressionist Men. And Surrealist Men. And Men from various Schools, and Periods. He told her they all lived in Europe. And Europe became to her, at that powerful moment of knowledge about colours and drawing pictures, a place she wanted to see, to visit, to live in, at least for one week, before she died.

But in spite of her son's guidance and his suggestions to help her appreciate this art, she was more interested in the audacity, and marvelled at it, how these European men of the Renaissance, of the Impressionist Group, of the various Schools and Periods of red and white and blue—she giggled the first time Wilberforce showed her a figure of a man drawn entirely in blue; even although he reassured, that "It's his Blue Period"; to which she had said, "It's a blasted ghost. The colour of death. And ashes." It still did not make sense to her that human flesh and human features, hair and fingernails and eyes, should be drawn with blue paint; or with blue chalk.

All blue?

"It's his Blue Period, Mother!"

All blue?

"Nobody with a brain in his head would draw human flesh in blue is my answer. Human flesh is either black or white. Pink, if you so desire. Blue is death!"

No. She could not figure out what gave these Europeans whom Wilberforce was teaching her so much about, the liberty to draw figures of European women to look like Bimshire men, whose bodies rippled with muscles and sweat; these Europeans who drew females to look like the bodies of Bimshire men who lift weights; and "pelt iron" in small backyards paled-round with galvanize, grunting and breathing hard, noises gasped to heighten their concentration, add strength in order to lift the huge iron bar of heavy metal, lead and iron and "metal"; screaming, straining and cleaning-and-jerking, as they raised the avoirdupois above their heads, their bodies shaking from side to side, in uncertainty, until they can stand motionless, for three seconds, before they hear the sound of victory, and see the flag of legitimacy.

Why? How *could* they draw pictures of women painted entirely in blue? What gave them this right, this bravery of art and creation, to draw nudes of the female body, and to manipulate the colours of blue, white and red, and to legitimate memberships in Schools? The women they drew do not resemble those women she sees walking about the lanes and narrow roads, passageways and back alleys off Suttle Street, down in Town, in the prostituting district, where the light that points you on your way to short-lived satisfaction and victory is always red. Those Suttle Street whores are not the women she is accustomed to seeing in her Village. But the European women drawn by European men from the Blue Period and various Schools bear a more striking resemblance to those women in Town, than to those in pictures of English women she has been seeing for years, in the *London Illustrated News* and in other English magazines which Mr. Bellfeels read in the Lounge for Gentlemen, at the Aquatic Club down in Town; and afterwards pushed into the deep pockets of his khaki tunic; and took with him, from the premises. Some of the magazines, like *Boys' Own,* and some children's books, like *Tom Brown's School Days,* were read by men from the various Plantations, who lay on their backs, stretched out in canvas chairs, guffawing in the restricted men-only lounge; and these periodicals and books were sometimes handed down to Mr. Bellfeels, by the manager of the Club himself, for Little Wilberforce.

Sargeant, who knows nothing about art except the drawings of donkey carts and of women with huge pads on their heads to relieve the weight and discomfort of heavy trays of yams, potatoes that they carry: "yuh breadfruit, yuh sweet-cassava!"; and galvanize cans of cool mauby; and sketches of fishermen throwing nets into the sea which does not look like the same sea he bathes in every morning at five o'clock but more like a field of blue, molten lead, without waves, because they are drawn in watery colours; no, Sargeant has never seen drawings of the sea that he would call art. The sea that is drawn by the local artists is a sea whose colour he does not recognize; a sea sometimes with the colour of blood; and not the deep blue-green waves he bathes in, just after dawn. The colour of the sea the Bimshire painters draw is a sea he has never seen.

Yes, this heaviness of limbs and eyes and lips and features, in the paintings, do not remind her of the women in the Village, and the women working on the Plantation; and these portraits bring back her own memories of back-stiffening labour in the North Field.

"What was I about to . . ."

And before she finishes her words, she closes the two louvres, and the light changes, and her beauty is outlined both in the shadows that have crept into the room, and from the light from the two electric bulbs. The bulbs each hang on a single strand of plaited electrical cord, like the tits of a cow. In the changing light, it looks also like two strands of her hair, plaited in three streams with two ornaments at each end. Her hair which was once black and thick and long, is now black, streaked with silver and white.

The number of years these electrical cords have been hanging here, holding the single naked bulb, has caused the original black colour to change, also through age; and the habitation of flies and mosquitoes and moths; and from paint leaked onto them, when the ceiling was painted white, now a colour similar to tints in her hair.

She passes her hand, the left hand, through her hair; and then she uses her right hand to remove a strand of hair from the ruffles in the design of her white dress. And when she is sure that she has picked up the strand of hair, almost invisible against the whiteness of her dress that reaches to the floor, she flicks the hair off, and it falls unseen on the carpet. Wilberforce calls her hair salt-and-pepper.

She moves her neck and her shoulders the way people do, to take stiffness from their joints; and as if this jerking of her neck has succeeded in removing the kinks, she moves with a sprightlier gait to the large Victrola grammaphone, and fits the crank-handle into the hole, to wind it. The brown rich leather of her laced-up boots is seen from the ankle to the sole, and then is afterwards covered by the fall of her dress.

Sargeant watches her shoulder stiffening against the tension of the cranking; as she turns the handle, as her entire body moves; and he can see how the flow of her long dress catches the laces in her leather boots that expose the richnesss of the leather, up to her ankles. He can count the "eyelits," as he calls them, in each boot.

She turns the handle, now more easily and with greater smoothness. She does this in the same way he imagines how, on a Saturday afternoon, she would turn coarsely ground yellow Indian meal-corn in a pot with water, made greenish and slimy from ripe, fresh okras in which it is being boiled; how she turns and turns and changes the yellow blobs into an appetizing paste, into cou-cou, rich and mellow and slippery in the throat: now a yellow substance speckled with green pieces of okras; and he imagines sweat from her face, the sign of her labour and her carefulness in the turning of the cou-cou, falling into the pot with the slowly bubbling Indian meal-corn, like a gentle geyser, to add to its taste. He imagines that his hand is touching hers, relieving her of her fatigue in the turning and the turning and the turning; resting on her wrists. For cou-cou, like the making of a glide, a stroke in cricket to fine leg, or the landing of a stinging jab, all these activities in sport that demand the expenditure of sweat, require even before that expenditure the knowledge that it is the wrist which adds subtle power to the natural expression of beauty in the cricket stroke, in the deadliness of the jab, and also to the turning meal-corn in order to make the mellowest cou-cou.

His hand moves from her hands, and travels all that nervous, trembling distance up from her wrists to her shoulders, over the white sleeves of her dress. This approach takes place in his imagination. He evades through his nervousness, even in his fantasy, touching her breasts. He feels, however, that to touch her breasts, without forethought and foreplay, might awaken a hurricane of passion and sex he might not know how to deal with; so, he moves his hand away from her breasts, as her breasts move with her breathing, beneath the demure cut of her bodice.

Yes, his hand moves from her hand holding the cou-cou stick, all its trembling slow progress up her arms, over the carefully laundered sleeves until at last, they reach her shoulders.

The emotion this touch of her body causes, like an explosion, brings with it the caution of pause. But then, his hand takes a detour and moves under her armpits. He can feel the stutter of his blood. The loss of breath. Then the regaining of breath and grown confidence. The warmth of her flesh. And he feels also the dampness of her armpits. The scent of Johnson's Baby Powder rises suddenly to his nostrils, from under her armpits, and this gives his hand greater courage, and adds force and roughness to his caresses. When she moves away from him, she leaves a different perfume behind her. The scent that fills the room, is the smell of Eau de Cologne No. 4711 . . . He has smelled this cologne before, merely once, in a bottle with a gold and green label, in the Perfume and Fragrances Department at Cave Shepherd & Sons, Haberdasheries, in Town. He had blinked his eyes in disbelief, when he saw the price; and a woman, "the clerkess," seeing his unease, and understanding his interest in the perfume—it was the week before Christmas—came to his rescue; and when he saw her coming towards him, he raised his arms above his head, as men do, who want to confess, or to surrender . . . He was in his policeman's uniform.

He was a private . . . and then he smiled; and the woman smiled with him, and said, "Constable, hold your hand out, nuh." And he had held his hand out; and received the squirt; and his eyes started to burn; and he held his hand out a second time, this time palm-up; and received another spurt of vapour; and his mind went wild, for he was smelling the cologne in the bottle, and the fragrance of lust that lay heavily in the woman's eyes, and in her hands as she passed them softly, slowly over his hands; and hours later, he held this same hand out, his left hand, in the barracks in Central Police Station, on Coleridge Street in Town, where he was stationed, across one narrow street from Cave Shepherd & Sons, Harberdashers; and he thought of the blue veins in the woman's hand that held the bottle of Eau de Cologne No. 4711.

He did not wash that hand, his left hand, for three days.

Miss P. Wilkinson was printed on a small rectangle of metal that looked like gold, that was pinned above her right breast. Her nipples came clear through her salmon-coloured jersey to his eyes.

Yes, it is Eau de Cologne No. 4711. And the room is turning, slowly; spinning like the revolutions of the grammaphone record when the song has ended. His hands are travelling, as his breathing is racing. Now, they have stopped for breath above her breasts; and his fingers, the thumb, index and second fingers on each hand wander to and feel the softness of her nipples; and a shudder comes through his body, weakening him. He is stiff as a piece of iron. His hands now stray farther afield, to find the richer, the sweeter, the more churning and turbulent downward climb in his travelling, to the heat between her thighs. And then, he hears the voice of a woman.

It is the voice of the singer, saying: "'. . . *My brown-and-yellow basket . . .*'"

"You haven't heard a word I been saying to you for the last five minutes, haven't you, Percy?"

This is her voice. Not the voice he thinks he is hearing. The grammaphone is playing; and the other voice is the voice of Miss Ella Fitzgerald.

"I was going over things," he says.

"Sometimes I sit here, and my eyes would travel over the canes, and I would imagine that the canes are the waves in the sea, or the Atlantic Ocean; and I am travelling over all that saltwater; and the currents leading me away from Bimshire, this Island; and I am one of the tourisses, visiting those places that Wilberforce is always ranting about. Countries. Cities. Civilizations. Places where they speak different languages from me and you. Englund. Germany. Sicily. Austria. Italy. Sicily."

"You mention Sicily two times."

"Yes? Sicily. Rome. London-Englund. And Paris! Oh boy! Paris! The things I have heard about Paris! And seen! In magazines knocking-around this house!

"If I could only choose. Percy, if I only had the power of choice to change my life, even at this late stage, under the present circumstances, Paris would be the destination in my first-and-only overseas-European-travel.

"Yes. Going overseas to Europe! Going away!"

"Yes. But gimme Amurca! Any day! The bigness of Amurca. And the money of Amurca. The cars and the clothes of Amurca. And the idea that a man, if he don't like going to work in the daytime, could choose his working hours to night. And tek the night shift. That is a pretty thing, Miss Mary-Mathilda, a thing of freedom. Just to hear about. It is a thing that we don't have in this Island. Not yet. But we need to learn to work at night. Yuh got to be big, big-minded, to give a fellar that choice. Between day-work and tekking the night shift? A fellow who lived in both Amurca and in Englund tell me that they haven't arrived at that big-mindedness yet neither, in Englund. The night shift. Known also in Amurcan vernacular, as the graveyard. Even the words, *night shift*, sound so pretty. You don't think so, Miss Mary?"

"You haven't listened to one word of Miss Ella Fitzgerald song!"

"I was travelling with my thoughts."

"Travelling overseas. Gimme Paris, any morning . . ."

"You don't mind winding the Victrola again, do you, Miss Mary? And playing 'A Tisket, a Tasket' a second time? If you don't mind, please?"

She winds the grammaphone, until the handle gives a slight kick back, warning her that the spring is tight; and she takes the thick vinyl record off the turntable, and passes it in a circular motion over her left hand, and then she places it closer to her face and blows upon it. It is a loud, strong, exhaling of wind. And she goes back to sit in her chair just in time, as Miss Ella Fitzgerald, who has been waiting for the opening notes of the orchestra, begins "A Tisket, a Tasket."

"What really is a *tisket*, Percy?"

"A *tisket*?"

"You ever come across one?"

"Not to my knowledge, Miss Mary."

"My boy would know. If he was home, I would ask him."

"Yes, Mr. Wilberforce would know. We should axe Mr. Wilberforce."

"I should ask him. And *tasket*? Could that be a *tisket* with a *a*?"

"Your son would know."

She takes the heavy arm off the record, and the weight of the arm, tricky in her own hand and unexpectedly heavy, drops too early on the black record and misses the groove, and the sound of the scrape that results reminds Sargeant of the noise of brakes late at night, at the intersection of the two roads, Highgates Commons and Reservoir Lane, which meet close to his house.

But this noise is a sweeter noise. And less jarring upon his nerves. This noise brings peace and a desire to travel, to walk, to stroll, loll about the narrow tree-lined lanes of the Village, winding around clusters of mahogany trees, of Guinea grass and Khus-Khus grass, cut out by the passage of time, and of bare feet, between fields of sugar cane. The lane he takes to lead Gertrude deeper into the green night, to lie on the padded brown trash. He can see the cane field from where he is sitting in a chair with a white doily

draped over its back so that the heavy Vaseline grease for grooming
his hair cut to suit a policeman, does not touch the rich, expensive
velour material of the chair. He knows that the back of the chair is
filled with horsehair. A strand of its stiff stuffing shows through in
two places near his neck, like whiskers left two days on the chin.
Sargeant travels over the land that surrounds him now, in thick
green silence, as he listens more attentively to the words of the
American woman coming through the speaker of the Victrola
grammaphone. The speaker is in the shape of a large horn, a cornu-
copia, attached to the body of the grammaphone.

And his mind, and his body with it, go back over the years,
searching as he had turned the pages of those out-of-date magazines
in the equipment room of the Garrison Savannah Lawn Tennis
Club, sitting amongst the long, black rubber hose for watering the
lawns, the noisy lawn mower, and old, damp, stinking tennis shirts
and shorts of the male members; going back over time, until it had
rested on that Monday, a bank holiday, Easter bank holiday, when
the sea was calm and the sand on the beach was fresh as if the waves
had come in during the long black night and had used its quieter
current to comb the sand clean of pieces of dried bramble, of flot-
sam and jetsam, empty Trumpeter cigarette boxes, and empty Swan
Vesta wooden matchboxes, "the smoker's match" . . . Sargeant
knew these beaches and the sand on them, so often resembling
a dump where the Villagers threw their garbage. Empty tots that
once contained condensed milk, and young water coconuts, some
still green on the outside, and used by small boys as cricket balls;
and some riper coconuts chopped into two, exposing where the
skin was left on the brutally chopped shell, and thrown away on a
mounting pile of rot; and still some other water coconuts chopped
into half or as near to half as hungry, impatient hands could perform
the trick; and pieces of stick and twigs, blackened by age and the
constant pounding of the waves. And Sheik french leathers.

Whenever he was on night patrol on this same beach, usually after
midnight, which hour he assumed was best for catching criminals,

he would find himself looking up into the darkened sky, always at this time, painted in blackness; and he would try to count the stars, and name the constellations; and sometimes the skies would be without stars; at least he could not see them, and could not count them; he was always uneasy when he looked at the skies without stars; but there was always enough light for him to see the coconut trees growing tall to almost touch the skies. This is why the Villagers called them "mile trees." He always was in wonder at the guts it took for a thief to climb these "mile trees" in the blackness of night to pick the coconut from the highest branch of these majestic trees that grew almost straight as a cane arrow; and getting away from the watchman stalking him, invisible in the black night by means of his dress, the uniform of his profession: black jacket, black discarded policeman's serge trousers—with the two two-inch red seams at the sides, removed—and barefoot. The night watchman in his tracking of the thief, had already discarded the pair of policeman's black boots he had been given by Sargeant, because their creaking might reveal his presence and expose him to the thief; and his own black skin, the mark of his rank, the qualification insisted upon by the Plantation, the Solicitor-General, the leading barristers-at-Law, before anyone who needed a night watchman, would hire one, his black skin was discussed as the desirable testimonial for being "taken on" for this dangerous job. *Night watchman.* Flagstaff Village has more night watchmen than teachers, policemen and needleworkers put together. It is as if the Village has within its boundaries, valuables and trinkets and priceless jewels stored in safes in locked bedrooms, and in caves and in underground tunnels, that these have to be watched during the day, and continually and "vigilled-over" especially during the night. *Nighht waaatchman* . . . the Sin-Davids Anglican Church Annual Outing and Picnic, held this Easter Monday bank holiday on the beach at the Crane Beach Hotel, where the breakers were sometimes as tall as the night watchman himself; where the sand moves like a waltz along the beach, in places fifty yards in depth; where the pure, clean sand is the colour of a conch shell; and is swept by the hotel gardeners with brooms made from the spine of the leaves from the coconut palm, in preparation for the outing.

The gardeners had been given strict instructions by the manager of the hotel.

"I want the blasted beach sweep clean-clean-clean, *so* clean that any son-of-a-bitch could pick up a chicken foot offa the sand and eat it! You hear me?" he had told them.

Mr. Bellfeels, the manager of the Plantation; the Reverend Mr. M. R. P. P. Dowd, Vicar of Sin-Davids Anglican Church; the Commissioner of Police; the Headmaster of Harrison College; and the Headmistress of Queen's College, "Harsun College sister-school"; the Solicitor-General of the Island; the two leading barristers-at-Law in the Island, Mr. E. Wharton-Barr, KC, and Mr. G. Herbert-Addis, KC; and the Member of the Legislative Council of Bimshire would be present. With them would be their wives. And families. And dozens and dozens of the Villagers, bearing chairs with heavy invalids in them; pushing perambulators over the tricky, shifting sand of the beach, near the waves which come in at high tide, during the early afternoon, like small climbing hurricanes, to make the men scream at their maids fearing for the safety of their women and their children, "Oh Jesus Christ! Not suh-close to the blasted waves, girl! You want to commit murder this nice bank holiday? Not so blasted close! You can't see the tide coming in?"; with toddlers in them; and on this Monday bank holiday years ago, Mary Gertrude Mathilda—Tilda to the Village boys—young and with her well-nourished body bursting through her thin, cotton white dress that reached one inch below her knees; thirteen years old; and her hair combed and plaited in long rows that were then woven back into the rest of her hair, giving her hair the overall effect of rows of ploughed sweet-potatoes, or like terraces on an Italian mountainside; and he remembered how her legs looked: sturdy and

shiny and soft as velvet from the coconut oil with which they were
rubbed and bathed, and greased; and she was smelling sweet, with
that smell which he did not know the name of then, not before he
had found himself standing in the Perfume and Fragrances Depart-
ment of Cave Shepherd & Sons, Haberdasheries; and he, a young boy
then, having just completed Standard Five, was at the time of this
church picnic, apprenticed to the Garrison Savannah Tennis Club,
as an Assistant Gardener and Chief Water Boy; and his job which
paid him one shilling and sixpence per week, every Friday at two
o'clock, with two changes of blue denim suits, short-sleeved shirt,
short pants, no cap or hat, no shoes—not even canvas pumps—was
the most happy and exciting days of his young adolescence; and he
grew accustomed to seeing women's legs and to witnessing flashes
of their "knockie" and pubic hair, dark brown and red, blond and
fuzzy; and once, there was no hair there at all; swift like visions, in
lightning speed as if these exposures were matching the backhand
shots played by the women in doubles; and in this fast time, he
would see these private parts that the short white cotton panties
could not conceal completely from his wandering eyes that loitered
on legs, whenever a backhand shot was smashed against the tape
on the net and dribbled "out!"; or when the woman player slipped
on the freshly watered grass surface, and her body was slammed
against the tall green-painted fence that kept the balls inside the
grounds, and out of the hands of the Village boys who watched;
eyes and heads moving back and forth, wishing that their eyeballs
were magnets; hoping that a ball struck with spin and pace would
climb the ten-foot green-painted fence; and they would pocket it in
a flash, pocket it in delight and with equal lightning speed "take off"
with the tennis ball, for their game of "hopping-ball cricket"; and
this very sight and sudden showing of legs within the safety of the
club, safe from the wandering, fast, flashing eyes of the young men
and boys who pressed their faces against the green fence to see the
direction the ball would take when it crashed against racquet, the
sound it made announcing that it is hit, the unrhythmic sound, close

to that of leather hitting skin, in random accuracy; or to the sound of a broken string: *plop . . . plop . . . plop; plop . . . plop . . . plop . . . plop, plop, plop-plop . . .*

"Well-played, I say!"

"Good shot that!"

"Ball! Ball! Boy! *Ball-boy!*"

It is the hysterical, high-pitched voice of the man partnering the woman who has just struck the ball, who has now fallen on the green grass in her white shorts, who has exposed the entire area taken up by her "knockie," by accident; she had made a commitment before she was ready, had made an unforced error, had hit the ball by chance, *in casu*; an act; a stroke similar to putting too much spin on the backhand shot; this high-pitched feminine voice coming from the man playing with her always shouted orders at Sargeant, as if the voice was asking a question, incapable of giving an order, not knowing how to "be a man," as it were; as if the man talking was wondering aloud whether the tennis ball was really a ball or a green golden apple.

"Ball?" he shouts. *"Boy? Boy?"*

Sargeant is still taken in by the strange colour of this woman's pubic hairs and the colour of her panties, and her flesh, turning pink from exhaustion in the tennis game and exposure to the sun which beats down savagely just before three o'clock in the afternoon; taken in by her sadness at being beaten by the two players across the net, as much as by the humidity; and so he does not hear the high-pitched voice of the man ordering him to get the *"bloody ball!"*; Sargeant's eyes have taken in too much for his ears to function now to hear the warning falsetto cries that leave the woman's male partner's mouth in threatening . . .

"Boy?"

. . . and Sargeant is blinded by what his eyes have chanced upon, and is insensitive to orders; cannot obey; is motionless, incapable of seeing danger, and cannot reach for the ball and throw it back into play, in to the woman who still holds service.

"Boy?"

And the voice comes at him again, speaking with a heavy English accent.

"What the dickens, boy? Boy!"

The voice is shrieking now. The voice wants to rouse the staring black eyes from their examination of this young beautiful girl's private parts. To protect her. To remind the "boy" that this is a closeness, this staring, which is *infra dig*; this is an assault, this is a kind of rape by eyes and staring, that his brothers, yes, his type, those boys standing at the ten-foot fence painted green, with their faces pressed against the fence with its fine mesh, which has left its design imprinted, like embossed fine English stationery, on their concentrating faces; yes, his brothers, the voice seems to say, as it would contain in its anxiety and anger, some knowledge of this kind of staring, by this type, by this kind of boy, similar in his desire to Emmett Till's, "up in Amerrica where this kind of thing," these kinds of staring boys are lynched for . . . She puts on a grammaphone record; and in his mind, Sargeant dances with her, and can feel the softness of her body, and can touch her body, clear and as real as that bank holiday afternoon when for the first time, he saw her body through the fabric of her dress. She was dressed in a frilly white sea-island cotton dress . . .

"We didn't get the answer," she tells him.

"Which answer?"

"To 'A Tisket.'" Her body had developed all of a sudden, before his eyes, on one other occasion he had seen her, with her hoe, standing with other women, much older than herself; she was nine then; in the North Field; and he thought the gang of women looked like soldiers, standing erect, with their hands resting on their hoe handles, just as he had seen soldiers and policemen do, when they were ordered by the Drill-Sargeant, to "Stand easy!"; and he had seen her, the other times, in church, at Matins; and now on this Easter Monday, in white dress, with white patent-leather shoes, and white anklets and with a white silk ribbon in her hair, which she always wore the same way: plaited in "cornrows," and the short end of the plaits bound together with the white silk ribbon tied into a bow; or, instead of the ribbon, an ornament, a heart, made from polished tortoiseshell.

He could see her body as if it had been developing right in front of his eyes, her breasts getting larger, and their nipples standing erect, and her breathing increasing its beat and rhythm, and making her chest rise, and heave in expectation, like the muscles of weightlifters rise when they address the iron bar, preparing for the clean-and-jerk; and her eyes, clear and bright, with dark brown pupils, white eyeballs round the pupils, as white as the clouds overhead are always white on Easter Monday; and her fingers, moving, perhaps against her wish, expressing her nervousness, the pent-up emotion, which cannot at her young age be put into the correct words; and his manhood, his little tom-pigeon in his khaki pants, his "lil pen," gets harder and harder and just a little larger; and he does not even know, fully, what he is going through. But he had known, nevertheless, that with the female tennis player whom he was being scolded for watching; screamed at for being unable to turn his head, and turn his eyes away from her body, where they remained on the same blond spot with the blond hairs, for exactly three shotgun seconds, three fast bullets of time—in case the woman's partner, or anyone else, had owned a stopwatch and had been inclined to measure that staring time—he had known deep down, as part of his experience, as the character of his life, circumscribed by myth and ritual, that he could never get close to this fallen, frightened woman; close enough to touch her. And now, seeing her at his feet, bruised against the green-painted fence, he dared not extend a hand to help her up. The reason behind her partner's high-pitched thin voice was that very hysterial warning about touching. *Do not touch.* Yes, he could not touch her. "Look; but don't kiss-me-arse touch, hear! Looking is one thing, boy: it harmless; but touching is something-else-altogether-different!"

Time would unroll, and Sargeant would be able to draw a conclusion from the similarity of that afternoon in the Garrison Savannah Lawn Tennis Club, about the warning *Do NOT Touch*, along with the notices nailed to huge wooden gates, with wickets cut into the gates, in black capital letters on pieces of tinning painted white, warning DO NOT ENTER. DOGS. Alsatians. Bloodhounds. Doberman-Pincers. Vicious dogs about which Sargeant, years later, joking amongst the "selected clienteles," would chuckle and say, "They have dogs in this Island, 'specially trained to put a bite in a black-man arse!"

And because it was delivered as a joke, all the men laughed.

The Headmaster of Sin-Davids Elementary School for Boys laughed. The Senior Assistant Sanitary Inspector laughed. The civil servant who worked in His Majesty's Customs and Excise Department laughed. Manny laughed. And Sargeant, who had given the joke, laughed as if it was a joke.

Each one of these men, at some time in their growing up, had suffered from the viciousness of dogs owned by estates and plantations throughout Bimshire. And down in Hastings; in Belleville, and in Strathclyde, which Ma said was as "serrigated" as the South in Amurca, "'cause in Strathclyde, in the middle o' the road, a iron-rail keeps black from crossing over into white, I swear to God! Except you is a servant."

And still these men laughed; and laughed; and laughed. And then poured themselves another shot of strong, dark Mount Gay Rum, and laughed as they said, in chorus, "*Down the hatch!*"

"*As man, man!*"

"*As man!*"

And Sargeant, still reflecting, knew too, on that Easter Monday, that when he saw little Mary Gertrude Mathilda, Tilda, with her developing body, that he could not dance with her, could not ask her for the honour, would not get permission from Ma, to dance to "Evening Shadows Make Me Blue." No. Not in the presence of the entire outing crowd. In the open air. Sargeant, like all the other boys and growing men in the Village, knew that he dared not ask Mr. Bellfeels for permission to dance with his servant girl, little beautiful Mary Gertrude Mathilda.

Word had just started to travel from that Sunday in the Church Yard, and had gathered strength, like a hurricane, through repetition, throughout the Village, and through the rows of eddoe plants that rolled and rollicked like waves painted green and that stretched for acres and acres in the North Field, that it was Mr. Bellfeels who "*was pushing along Mary's physical development*"; that it was Mr. Bellfeels who was "*force-ripening her*"; that it was Mr. Bellfeels who was "*tekking the sweets*"; that "*is Bellfeels, that son-of-a-bitch, who licking-cork with that girl*"; that it was Mr. Bellfeels who "*committing statuary rape, by fooping a child!*" Oh, Mary, Mary, Mary!

Yes, but was it really Bellfeels?

Yes, it was Bellfeels!"

"*Yes!*"

"*Is Bellfeels who guiding Mary-Mathilda into this beautiful pulchritudinous ripening pubescence,*" the Headmaster of the boys' Elementary School said, raising his snap-glass to take a sip. And to propose a toast. And to damn Bellfeels. "*Between me, you, the doorpost, and the wall in this illustrious Harlem social institution of levity and grace, our beloved Harlem Bar & Grill, associated in culture with that other Harlem in Amurca, before that, Haarlem in Holland-Europe . . . between me and you, my friends, and the four walls, in strictest confidence, and amongst Manny selected clienteles, Bellfeels can't be accused of ever having had a brain-cell in his head. He didn't get-past Standard Four in my school! Down the hatch! As man!*"

Mary Gertrude Mathilda was thirteen that year of the first Easter Monday when Sargeant *saw* her for the first time; noticed her existence; could smell the ram goat in his mannishness, as the Villagers say; and for each year that followed, his lust grew with his limbs and with the size of his tom-pigeon, which now began fluttering each time he saw her, from across the street, or passing like the wind, in the front seat of the Plantation's car, beside the chauffeur clad in stiff khaki, during the day; dressed in black, during the evening. But he remained even farther removed from any closeness . . .

But now, he is in her house. This Great House, the second largest on the Plantation's estate, a symbol of her privilege and status, which the Villagers knew was given by Mr. Bellfeels to her for her son Wilberforce to live in.

The Headmaster and the other "clienteles" said openly, in the Harlem Bar & Grill, that the Great House she lived in, was the "cost-price payment for the pussy!"

The men, including Sargeant, roared with laughter, and said, "As man!" and downed the next round of rum.

Sargeant is close to her, now. And he recognizes that his presence here, is a gesture of fate, a stroke of luck, the circumstances of the present notwithstanding. But he feels shame and contrition for all the bad things he has said, and thought of her.

He is in the Great House. He is able, if this is his desire, to put his arms round her waist; now that he has already walked his hands over her arms and round her neck and across her shoulder—in his imagination; and had stopped at the thought of touching her breasts; but had done so, anyhow—he feels he can bring her body close to him, real and in the flesh, and give himself the bodily satisfaction similar to dancing with her, similar to what he gives Gertrude.

His heart has imagined this lust for more than thirty years now.

He was ten years old that first Easter Monday. Mary-Mathilda was thirteen. Mr. Bellfeels, an old man to them, was forty.

Now, Sargeant has the same desire. Age and maturity, and "knocking 'bout as a police," as Manny says, has transformed Sargeant's respectable desire, into "raw, animal-raw luss!"

This time, this Sunday evening, his desire is that of a man who sees for the first time, in his bed, the woman he had been painting from fantasy, but who—it seems to him—now is the one changing the portrait of that fantasy, to willingness; and his mind in turn, paints her body before him, outstretched and willing, more real than in life, in the tableau of his imagination, more real even than the furious fantasies drawn in Quink Ink on blank pages of school exercise books, and in double-lined ledger-size policeman's Evidence Books, on sleepless interminable, wet-dreaming nights. No amount of imagining or the drawing of clouds could ever get her sitting willingly beside him, like this. Not even after he had dreamed that she was walking beside him up the long chilly marble aisle in Sin-Davids Anglican Church, while the choir sang "The Wedding March," and witnesses flung congratulating rice grains into their faces.

He is listening to the song that Miss Ella Fitzgerald is singing. The words in the song do not make sense to him. No one in the Village speaks this way. No one in the Island of Bimshire. Nor in this part of the world.

And he is surprised now, as he always was surprised, years ago, whenever he heard "A Tisket, a Tasket" being played, that the words in the song were jibberish. "A tisket, a tasket." But he had never put his surprise into words, until this evening. He is surprised that he does not know what the words mean, what they are supposed to convey to him.

He has sung this song and has whistled this song, and has danced to this song, like many other boys growing up in the Village. And he has stood under the front window of a neighbour's house, and heard each word in the song, after the neighbour had placed the speaker of the Voice of Bimshire Radio, a little farther onto the window ledge to make it easier for him to listen; and one Friday night, as he was standing under the front window of Manny's house, at a time when Manny was learning to be the Village butcher, before he had opened the Harlem Bar & Grill, Sargeant heard his own name announced in the stillness of the dark night; and it frightened him. To hear his address called out on the programme heard throughout the Island; and followed by the name of the song he had requested to be played. "A Tisket, A Tasket". . . . *"Ladies-and-gentlemen-out-there-in-Radioland, our next request comes-from-a-young-man whose heart is quivering from-his-love-of-a-young-lady he dreams about every-night-when-the-sun-goes-down, and wishes-to-marry some day . . . we cannot-tell-you-the-name-of-the-lucky-lady, his beloved . . . the young man did-not-give-us-the-lady's-name . . . but it is our-pleasure-and-great-happiness, ladies-and-gentlemen-out-there in Radioland, to say that our next request goes out to . . . none-other-than Percy . . . Mr. Percy . . . to Percy DaCosta Stuart residing in Flagstaff Village, in-the-parish-of-Sin-Michaels, the Island of Bimshire, in-the-British-Wessindies, the Carrobean . . . So, on this Friday evening, without-any-further-a-dew! . . . Ladies-and-gentlemen invisible-out-there in Radioland, with-your eyes-glued-to-your radio . . . for Percy of Flagstaff Village, here's El-laaaaaah, in 'A Tiss-kit, A Tassss-kit!' Take-it-ah-waaay, Ella!"*

The words of the announcer remain with Sargeant all these years, and they come back to him now, with the same surge of deep love as the sea and the first wave in the morning that comes in and covers the beach; comes in, wave after wave, with the same freshening power; after all these years; and now as he hears her voice say a second time, just like the wave, that she shall play "A Tisket, a Tasket," a second time, he is no longer under a neighbour's window. He is in Miss Mary-Mathilda's front-house parlour.

On this Sunday evening, his excitement and sense of pride and of importance blows up equal to that Friday night, years ago, when the announcer called out his name.

And time went on, and the announcer left Bimshire for the Canal Zone, in Panama, with hundreds of men from the Island, on a work crew, contracted for five years, to help build the Panama Canal. And never came back.

Yes, as time went on, Sargeant got to know the announcer of the hit parade programme; and would see him at dances; and once, in the Stationery Department of Cave Shepherd & Sons, Haber-dasheries, in Town, reading advertisements for songs he wanted to compose; and looking through Amurcan magazines that told him how to have his songs, so far unwritten, put music to; and pub-lished; and other magazines about how to become an Amurcan announcer. And Sargeant wondered then, even at that tender age of ten, or eleven, why the announcer spoke with an Amurcan accent even before he emigrated to Amurca. Perhaps, he figured, because Miss Ella Fitzgerald and "A Tisket, a Tasket" were both Amurcan . . .

On that Easter Monday the skies were blue; not the deep blue that they are, sometimes, early in the morning; but blue as the sea always is when the skies are reflected on its surface; and that day, the sun was behind one white cloud, and the bathers were saved from the brutal humidity which at three o'clock in the Island, together with the afternoon sun, can clutch you at the throat, burn your skin and make it difficult for you to breathe; and the children of the various households in which Sargeant's and Manny's and Golbourne's parents and cousins worked, and Mary Gertrude Mathilda's mother, Ma, worked; households belonging to the Plantation, to the Church, to the two leading barristers-at-Law, and to the Solicitor-General, with those households, were the children of the workers in those households, screaming and "skinning cuffings," thrashing about and dancing in the warm waves. And laughing. The waves were blue, and warm and kind and clear; and they reached most of the children only up to their knees; and for some, up to their waists.

When the waves came in like a hand about to embrace the children, the children screamed; and some of them tried to jump higher than the welcoming waves, and succeeded; and some jumped and fell into the waves; and some still, jumped higher than the peaceable waves, seeking to, and succeeding, in getting out of the way of the rising wave; and did not succeed. The waves knocked them over, and buried them from view, for just one moment.

Some of these children were not too young to remember what the waves can do to a man. Or to a woman. They knew of cousins and friends and a few fathers who were fishermen, and who were carried away, far-far-far out to the horizon where the rainbow is

born, where the large boats climb over the horizon and the surface
of the waves sailing for Englund and Amurca, and were drowned.

They knew the moods of the waves.

And the accommodating wave came in, on this joyful after-
noon of Easter Monday, like a touch, like a pat, like a kind hand
laid for a moment upon their bodies; and then it went farther away
from them, into the sand where each advance and retreat of the
sleeping blue water marked its line of progress and of retreat, like
the boundary of a country.

Here, on the beach, the sand is clean.

The sand has remained clean from the sweeping it received at
daybreak, by the yard boys of the Crane Beach Hotel, clean as the
front and backyards of the homes, wall-houses, estates, plantation
houses of the women who now are sprawled out on the swept sand,
as if they are lying on a carpet in their parlours; or on grass on their
lawns, under umbrellas.

Some of these women are lying on their stomachs, hiding the
bulge of their gigantic breasts, and their stomachs which are now
heavy and a little sagging from too much leisure, from too many
times of childbirth, from no exercise, from too much rich food.

Some of these women are lying on their sides, those whose
breasts did not attract the eyes of the men and the lust of the young
boys, because of their small size.

One daring woman, the wife of the Solicitor-General, a woman
born in Englund, is lying flat on her back, her eyes closed, her arms
spread as if the area of the wet sand she is occupying is a cross; and
she is smoking a cigarette without ever taking it out of her mouth
once, to flick the ash into the waves . . . when the smooth calculating
wave reaches these women, the blue in the skies seems to take on a
softer hue, and the wind coming from the lighthouse, from the
west, rises just a little, and some sand flies a little distance from
the large blue-bordered bath towels on which the women are re-
clining, crawl over their bodies, but not too much, just like a whis-
per; but still, the wind is strong enough, farther along the beach to

make the air spotted with the dried leaves of the beach-grape trees which it holds in its puny power.

These beach-grape trees are low and thick. Their branches grow in many different directions, like vines more than like trees. The grapes are still green, and young. And most of them have been picked off the deep-green trees. And eaten. By everyone who can reach them.

Under these trees, which from a certain angle look like wounded soldiers, deformed, their arms and legs amputated by explosions and cannon shot and mines and hand grenades, under these trees lie the men, the husbands of the women lying on the sand, washed by the waves. The men are telling dirty stories about women. Their stories cover their women and their wives, at the edge of the water, oblivious to everything but their children. These men are not the men of the Village. They are not men like Percy or Manny or Golbourne or Pounce. These men are the leaders of the Island. The big men. The Vicar and the two leading barristers-at-Law, Messrs. E. Wharton-Barr, KC, and G. Herbert-Addis, KC, the Plantation manager Mr. Bellfeels, the Solicitor-General, the manager of Cave Shepherd & Sons, Haberdasheries, in Town, the Commissioner of Police, the Organist and Choirmaster of Sin-Davids Anglican Church; and the ADC to Sir Stanley, the Governor; men who play tennis at the Garrison Savannah Lawn Tennis Club, and who sail yachts that set out from the marina of the Aquatic Club. Big men.

And there are the other children. The girl-children. Daughters of the women who work in the North Field, of women who are schoolteachers, of the women who are nursemaids; and of those who work at various jobs in the Plantation Main House; and daughters of women who, like Mistress Rosa Mary Antoinette Brannford, take in washing for the big houses, and who "try their hand" on the side, "doing a lil picking," at needlework; and prepare black pudding-and-souse; white sugar cakes, brown sugar cakes, pink sugar cakes . . . "no brown sugar cakes, please!"; and "coconut-bread," for sale, on Saturdays; and the children of the few Village women who are housewives. These women and their children are gathered together, in small clumps and both from the lolling women at the edge of the water, and from the men sheltering from the sun, under the beach-grape trees.

These women, with some help from their children, are transforming the beach into a kitchen, like those built in camps, by the soldiers in the Bimshire Volunteer Regiment and Brigade; or by Girl Guides and Boy Scouts in their annual camps during the long vacation, on this very same beach.

The boys, sons of the workers and sons of the men under the beach-grape trees, are playing a game of beach cricket, with a hopping ball from the Tennis Club . . . Percy is watching Mary Gertrude Mathilda; and the gust of wind dies down, and the black pieces of leaves from the beach-grape tree are now settling on the sand; and these black dots make the sand look as if it is littered with dead, rotting cobblers, those black cousins of the sweet-tasting sea eggs; and Percy sees Mary Gertrude Mathilda again, after a short time, while the leaves and the small black dots are settling down on the sand, from flying through the air; and here she is, coming out of this clearing, as if she is emerging from clouds, from light shining behind her, as if she is a figure of adoration, in a story in *Bible Stories for Children;* and with the light on the beach, she is emerging in just that state of frightening glory, as if mauve velour curtains are being parted, and time is still; is halted; in order to allow her the space and the breath and the air her appearance demands; but Percy is too small to know these things, to see this holy angelic association with Mary; with Mary Gertrude Mathilda; he sees her only as a little innocent girl, a virgin he loves; and he follows her with his eyes, as she moves as if without legs, going farther up the beach, approaching the cluster of beach-grape trees and the men under them; reaches the end of the trees and passes the clump of men; and approaches the rise of rock that juts out from the evenness of the sand, the beginning of a wall, like a breakwater; and here she is, alongside the spot where the cooks and the maids and Mistress

Rosa Mary Antoinette Brannford have chosen for the makeshift kitchen and the place for serving lunch. The women engaged in this occupation are all members of the Mothers Union. Slabs of three-ply wood are already placed on "horses," to be made into tables; and the men are driving nails, with huge galvanized heads, into the plywood, into the "horses"; and white linen tablecloths are ready to be spread on them.

The tables are long. Each one is large enough for twelve to sit at, which reminds Percy of that table in *Bible Stories for Children*, from Sunday School, of the Last Supper. And they are also similar to the Altar in Sin-Davids, especially on the first Sunday of the month, when Holy Communion is served by Vicar Dowd.

On these Sunday mornings, the altar top is covered with a rich, white brocade cloth, embroidered with angels and crosses and swords and fire rampaging across the plains of its landscape, white as snow. Sargeant knows that his mother—when she was alive— and Golbourne's mother, and Mistress Rosa Mary Antoinette Brannford, all the mothers in the Mothers Union knit these scenes of religious history, and turn them into altar cloths, and religious banners for Festival processions.

And when the light is coming through the stained-glass windows to the east, behind the altar, just as the sun this afternoon is coming through the shivering deep-green leaves of the beach-grape trees, it makes the makeshift dining tables on the beach, in this picnic, appear to be more sturdy and resemble that part of the chancel in the Church where Communion is served.

The cooks and the maids are now taking out the glass jars of rum punch, and jars of punch without rum for the children; and the glasses; and the bread for making sandwiches; and the chicken, fried and roasted and baked; and chicken boiled-down in Indian curry; and pork chops, thick and with the skin keeping the oiliness in, fried in butter from Australia; and a joint of roasted pork, as large as half the size of an ordinary pig, that part of the pig cut just under the head and including the highest ridge of ribs, succulent, deep brown and crackling, with the oil; and the heads of whole cloves, pieces of black pepper kernels dotting the skin, jutting through the skin like broken glass-bottle in the street; and the green of onions. And a huge crystal bowl, which contains the gravy.

These eatables are being taken from boxes that previously contained loose-leaf tea, covered by white linen cloths, and placed, in the order for their eating, upon the tables. The bright, white brocade tablecloths make the tables shine in the sun, and give off a glare.

Huge pots of steamed white rice are cooked with green pigeon-peas. And pieces of sweet potato pone and cassava pone are cut into large rectangles. They look like bars of gold. Ma places a large crystal vase in the centre of the two huge tables. And into each vase, she places a bunch of flowers. Dragon lily and bird of paradise.

Percy does not know the name of these flowers. Although he sees them every day growing around him; and passes them in the front garden of the Plantation Main House; in the grounds of the Garrison Savannah Lawn Tennis Club where he fields tennis balls and waters the gardens and mows the lawns, and still, he does not know their names. Flowers, to him, are to be looked at; and picked. Not to be known by name, regardless of where they spring up. And some of them spring up round the rum shop, which was at this time, owned and operated by Cyril Mandeville White, Mannny's father; and called simply, Manny's Rum Shop.

It is at this time, this exact moment when Ma arranges the beautiful red and yellow flowers evenly into the vases, that Percy first rests his eyes on Mary Gertrude Mathilda; when she appears as in an Annunciation, like the one illustrated in *Bible Stories for Children*.

He sees her come from behind a boulder, by the rock that served as a wall and a breakwater, and walk over the sand, moving as if she is really not walking, as if the sand, the grains of sand are small engines, ball-bearing contraptions that provide her motion.

And Percy can feel the wind as it touches his face, and cools his excitement; the same gust, the same wind which had come up earlier, and had distributed the dried beach-grape leaves, and a few hats along the swept beach.

It is this same gust of wind that lifts Mary Gertrude Mathilda's white dress just that much above her knees, so that Percy can see the shape of her knees. The colour of her legs is "light-skin," two or three tones lighter than her arms. Four or five tones lighter than his own black skin.

And a pinch of a muscle, like a blow caused from the sudden pumping from his own blood, comes into his chest as he watches Mary Gertrude Mathilda move away from Ma, from the other women, and from Mistress Rosa Mary Antoinette Brannford, as they go on preparing lunch.

It is when she passes the two dining tables—one to seat the husbands, one to seat their wives and children: the servants will sit on the warm sand, and on rocks on the beach—and is approaching the three short fat-limbed beach-grape trees, under which the husbands are sitting, only now does Percy first notice the water jug that she is carrying.

It contains something. Rum punch, perhaps. Or freshly made lemonade, sweetened with white granulated sugar, and made from the limes on trees that grow wild like flowers, around the kitchen-gardens of the Plantation.

She carries the jug in her left hand; and he can see that clearly; and he can see that she is carrying only one glass; and the glass is in her right hand—he thought she was right-handed—and she is holding it like an object of disgust, with the daintiness of touch, and held by her fingers, making it seem also that the object has a smell; an offensive smell; a strong smell. He wonders if she is left-handed. And he wonders why.

There are ten men sitting under the three beach-grape trees, talking and laughing, and they make sure the thick green leaves will muffle their jokes about women from reaching the ears of the women lolling at the edge of the water.

Percy sees Mary Gertrude Mathilda walk past these men. Some
nod to her. Some wave to her. Some turn their heads towards her.
Every one of the men know her, through her mother. And some of
them call to her by name.

"Hello, Mary!"

"Hello, Mary-girl!"

"Hello, Mary-Mathilda!"

"Hello, Tilda-girl!"

And some wave, and smile.

Sargeant sees how her body stiffens as it reacts to the differ-
ences in their greetings.

The wind, always a companion, rises just a little more strongly
and it lifts the hem of her dress a second time, a little higher, one
inch more, and shows her legs and thighs; and she moves on and
passes a second cluster of beach-grape trees, past the cave cut out
by the wind and rain, and by the perpetual pounding of the waves
laden with salt, at high tide, that corrodes it; and as she moves
round the last rise of rocks, like an embankment, there is a solitary
beach-grape tree. Under it, Mr. Bellfeels is waiting . . . and
Percy can remember as if it was today, how his chest became tight,
and the tightening of his chest was taken up by the stiffening of
his tom-pigeon; and his desperation took a hold of him, telling
him about actions taken; insults endured; challenges made; things
that warriors did for chivalry; of warriors he had read about in a
book, *English Social History for Infants*; acts of brave men like
Richard the Lion-Hearted, and Lord Oliver Cromwell and St.
George who killed not only men but ferocious beasts, like drag-
ons; of men like Charlemange and Napoleon and all the Czars of
Russia; of men who had fought duels for the women they loved,
and died doing it; men like a man named Pushkin who wrote
poems; and of men who killed for the honour they had given those
women, and for the insult that men, complete strangers, some
bastards, had made, that some, sons of bitches, had thrown upon
the character of those worthy women, ladies all; and Percy

ignores the chastising voice of his own mother . . . Percy is ignoring the cries of his friends calling him to play Lilliputian cricket; ignoring Clotelle who is challenging him to a race along the wet sand . . . Percy walks far from the men sitting under the beach-grape trees, sheltering, talking, joking, hiding from the sun; and he follows in her footsteps, rough and large and deep like the footsteps of the man in history books named Friday, whom Mr. Edwards, his teacher, told him, walked this same stretch of beach to fetch water for "his master, that son-of-a-bitch Robinson Crusoe, the sex-molester"; he could still see the marks made by the heels of her white shoes, and the flatter indentation of her soles, and the shape in the sand that her speeding footsteps had left, elongated prints in the thick, white, clean sand. He is walking and looking into her footprints as if his eyes are not sufficient to give him direction to follow her.

He came to the last cluster of three beach-grape trees. Then, to the pile of rocks. And to the cave built into the larger formation of rock. And then, to the clean, swept expanse of sand, pure as coral, shimmering with small almost invisible crabs, scurrying in no fixed or single direction, in flight, from the sudden appearance of a human being.

On this stretch of sand and beach which dipped back into the sea—he came face-to-face—for the last twenty yards he has been walking in seawater, making it impossible for him to hop out of the way of the incoming waves—to the place, under a large tree, that gives shade and security and safety and the lack of detection. Privacy. And he knew. He knew what it meant. Even though he was only ten years old; a boy; he knew that such security, safety, such protection from the mouths of gossip, had been built up over years, by practice and by those times when there was no protection and no safety, and the two of them stood in danger of being heard and seen and detected; and that is why, now, today, Easter bank holiday, in the presence—even though they are farther down the beach—

of all these ladies and gentlemen, the Vicar, the Solicitor-General, the two leading barristers-at-Law, the Headmaster and the Headmistress, they, the two of them, could be here. He and she. Mr. Bellfeels and Mary Gertrude Mathilda.

The two of them in their cave, are safe and secure and not seen, or even thought of, by any of the others, servants, mothers and their husbands, on this happy food-clogged Easter Monday, attending Sin-Davids Anglican Church Annual Outing and Picnic.

In the cave that custom and history had made, Percy could see the coconut fronds on the ground, and the softer leaves piled thick and comfortable as the Khus-Khus grass which Ma beat into sudden softness to make the mattress of her bed feel as if it were stuffed with the feathers of the peacock. And two stones. The two stones to serve as chairs. Or, as pillows. Depending upon how much time they had to spend, on how much secret time they could spend, on how much time they were wanting to spend in their retreat, in their cave.

Percy reached their cave after "*it*" had started.

He heard Mr. Bellfeels' voice. It was the voice of a man who tried to talk while running, tremulous and emotional.

He heard Mary's voice. Her voice was tender, soft, like a soprano. It was a frightened voice; frightened as if it was coming out of the throat of a fawn; and who was trying to speak; and who knew that its throat would be cut.

And when he was near the mouth of the cave, he heard Mary Gertrude Mathilda cry out. Perhaps, he imagined hearing her cry for help . . .

He was not sure if her voice was a warning. If it was a cry of pain. Or a cry of surrender. Or of ecstasy. And if it were any of these, warning, pain, surrender, or ecstasy, he knew all of a sudden that he could not transfer the bravery and chivalry he had read in storybooks, to this sun-beaten portion of the beach. A black bird came from farther inland, and sailed close to him, and disappeared down the beach where the women were sitting in the lapping waves.

And in his confusion—fear and anger—into his mind comes the sagas of bravery and chivalry, Richard the Lion-Hearted, Hercules, Charles Atlas; his mind sending these bouts of bravery to his heart, and to his limbs; and he was now rushing from the waves that reached only to his ankles, to the mouth of the cave, water and sand spurting in his assault on the cave; and he grabbed Mr. Bellfeels by his neck and held on tight, but the bigger man's body was too much for him; and even though this unfairness of body and might against his puny strength reminded him of the Bible story of David and Goliath, Percy could find no reason to prolong his defence of little Mary's honour. The task was too epic for him.

So, he walked back down the beach, looking at the sand, kicking old skeletons of crabs out of his way, counting the pebbles, trying to memorize the number of her footsteps stamped into the sand that he had followed, and that were now shifting under the weight of his weight.

On this return journey, the sand was cleaner and more beautiful; and it had the shimmer of the inside of a conch shell, that colour of light pink and pearl.

This has always been the colour of sand on all the beaches he remembers having walked on; and especially on this beach at the Crane Beach Hotel, that afternoon returning from Mary's cave, when he held the conch shell up to the full blast of the sun; when he made an attempt to put the conch shell to his lips, to blow it, like a trumpet, to send the sound that fishermen made along the beach, when there was a tragedy at sea, into the ears of all. When a man had drowned . . .

Mary has now taken the crank out of its hole. And is placing it on the blue felt cloth that lines the inside of the Victrola grammaphone; and she places the thick black disc to her face, inspecting it as if she is short-sighted, like a woman who wears glasses of thick magnification. And she moves her face ever so gently in a small circle, in the exact way, almost, as she does every morning when she gets out of bed religiously early, at five o'clock, even on Sundays; as she washes out her mouth with warm water with salt in it; turning the water round in her mouth, bulged like Dizzy Gillespie playing his trumpet—as if she is hiding two small balloons inside her mouth—as if a "centipee" had stung him there . . . She moves her face round and round the disc, as if she is whispering to it. But all she is doing is blowing the dust off the black circle. And then she places the disc on the turntable.

The years she has had this record, and the number of times she has played it and played it for Wilberforce, even when he was a man; and the shorter number of times she played it for William Henry and for Rachelle Sarah Prudence, to their memory; and the times it has been dropped, through carelessness, or too much brandy, by mistake, on the hardwood floor not covered by the thick Persian carpets, in this section of the parlour.

The scratch the needle makes on the disc sounds like a nail moving over glass; and it makes his skin crawl; and it also marks off all those years when he passed near this Great House, and from a distance, heard this music being played on the grammaphone, coming through the open windows and the French doors. That was years ago, when he could only imagine what the inside of this Great House looked like. He and Manny and Golbourne and Pounce knew, in their bones, in their blood, that they dared not go too near to this House. It was an edict, unspoken and unwritten. But an edict, nevertheless. Mr. Bellfeels' edict. Sargeant knew that before tonight he could not cross this threshold; even on police business.

"Percy would know more better," Mr. Bellfeels had said. He was not really talking to Mary-Mathilda, or to Wilberforce, when this threat was first uttered, but rather to the entire land; to everyone, even those who did not live on the Plantation. "He and the rest o' them, Manny and Pounce, those little black bastards, would know more better than to think o' crossing this blasted threshold. Not if he and them value their kiss-me-arse life!"

Neither Mary-Mathilda nor Wilberforce understood the depth of Mr. Bellfeels' anger; nor the cause of it. To their knowledge, Sargeant had never visited the Great House. The threat began when Sargeant was a boy, and lasted until he was a man.

"I don't give one shite if he is a police!" Mr. Bellfeels said, years later. "I would-blow his fecking brains out!"

Mr. Bellfeels continued threatening, snapping his riding crop against the brown, shining, leather riding boot.

The sun hit the boot as sharp as the whip cracked against it; and the rich leather, made redder in the sunlight, gave off blinding flashes.

"He could be a Corporal, a Lance-Corporal, Sargeant, or Crown-Sargeant, be-Jesus-Christ even-if he was the fecking Commissioner o' Police . . . 'cause I don't trust no fecking man with my property, with what is mine! Tha's why I gotting-on so. I protekking my property as *any* man who is a man would do. So let him fecking try!"

In this large front-house parlour, containing so many beautiful objects: the grand piano; the mahogany Victrola grammaphone with His Master's Voice and the sitting dog printed on the horn-shaped speaker; the upright mahogany chairs, sofas, armchairs and settees made by Mr. Waldrond the Joiner; and the walls covered with pictures and paintings and photographs framed in dark-stained wood, in the shapes of squares and ovals and circles; and the clean white-knitted cloths, doilies, thrown on to their arms and on their backs, and on the surfaces of the centre tables and the side tables; these objects outside his reach, kept hidden from him, like clues of an unsolved crime; or like ordinary clues that he and his Constable, Manny, Golbourne and Pounce had always felt could give the answer to the differences existing between Mr. Bellfeels, the Vicar and the Solicitor-General—*"them"*; and people like him, Constable, Golbourne and Pounce—*"we."*

"Them" always had: and "we" never got.

"Come," she is saying to him now. "Come."

But he is still walking on the beach, with his head down, hold-
ing the conch shell, counting pebbles washed smooth as marbles
by the waves; and seashells over which he walks, while his foot-
prints crush hers, and bury them beneath his larger feet.

"Come," she says again.

He is still on the journey back, beside the cluster of beach-grape
trees under which the men are sitting and talking. He can hear their
laughter, the sound of their guffaws; and see some of them roll over
in the sand, holding their bellies as they shake with uncontrollable
laughter.

". . . and, me-too, Jesus Christ! I would take a piece offa she, too!"

"Statuary rape," Percy hears another man say, and then this man breaks
out into raucous laughter.

It is the man who the Village calls the Solicitor-General. Percy does not
know the word statuary; had never heard it used. But he is wise enough to
know that it means something serious. It comes from a serious man. The
Solicitor-General of the Island.

"But learned counsel," the first man says, now howling with laughter
and holding his belly, "learned counsel, you-yourself would have to senn-
he-up to His Majesty's Prison at Glandairy, for a few years, nuh!"

"He gone!" the Solicitor-General says.

"All sport aside, now," another man says. "But the child suh-young!
How Bellfeels have the stomach to stomach pussy so young, though?"

"The soil," the Solicitor-General says, no longer laughing.

"What soil?" the first man says.

Percy is now abreast of the group. He doffs his cloth hat to the men.
And the men wave to him, in acknowledgment of his good manners.

"What soil?" the man asks again.

"Working with his hands in the soil! Anybody working so close to the
soil, with his hands in the soil, day and night, week after week, have to
behave so! Ipso facto. A man working with his hand in the soil is a different
man from a man selling silk handkerchieves down in Cave Shepherd store!"

"All that girl have to do," another man says, *"is call the police."*

"But the kiss-me-arse Commissioner right here!" a man says.

"Oh shite!

"Or call she mother."

"You mean Ma?"

"Mary-Mathilda's mother."

"Bellfeels fooping the mother, too."

"The man have a big fecking appetite!"

And Percy walks on, kicking the sand, and making small low clouds with each kick, until he reaches the group of women, who are still sitting at the edge of the waves.

At this point, he breaks into tears. And he gallops down the beach; and the sand is shifting under his feet; and spurts around him, in his sadness; and he thinks he will stumble, and fall; and he whispers, to the sea and the waves, and the women who are lolling in the waves, *"I hate Mary, I hate Mary, I hate Mary . . ."*

"You haven' heard me, Percy. I am telling you to come and dance, Percy," she says.

He looks up, pulled from his daydreaming. He sees Mary-Mathilda before him. Her eyes are fixed upon him. Her arms are extended in welcome, inviting him to her; and her fingers are moving inwards to her palms, beckoning him.

"Come, Percy."

"Come?"

"Come."

"Okay, Miss Mary."

"I have put on 'A Tisket, a Tasket.' We're going to dance, Percy. Me and you. So, let us dance." And then she says, "May I have the honour of this dance, sir?"

"Of course, Miss Mary-Mathilda," he says.

He goes to her.

"Let us dance, sir!"

He takes her in his arms. The same feeling of sudden weakness, like a physical incapacity, comes over his body, just as it had done so many years ago on that first Easter Monday.

He can smell the perfume she is wearing. He knows it well. He has smelled it before, many times; but from a farther distance: he smells it on Sundays, at Matins, when he passes beside her standing in her pew, with her name on it, on a brass plate; she standing alone in the pew reserved for four for William Henry, for Rachelle Sarah, for Wilberforce and for herself, at the end to the aisle, able to hear the choristers as they walk singing and slow in procession; passing her, close; but out of reach; and he has smelled her fragrance when she leaves her pew, when she leaves the church, and leaves behind her, the rustle of her starched white dress, the soft creaking of her black laced-up boots, and the fragrance of her perfume. Eau de Cologne No. 4711.

He is nervous. His hand in her right hand is sweaty. Her hand on his shoulder is light and loving; and he can still feel the grip of her fingers touching his muscles.

He wonders if his armpits are smelling.

He cannot remember if he patted his armpits with a dab of Limacol just before he left the sub-station when he got dressed. He keeps the bottle of Limacol in the top drawer of his desk. *"The freshness of a breeze in a bottle,"* the advertisement on the Limacol bottle says.

In the same top drawer, with the Limacol, he keeps his bottle of Mount Gay Rum. Twenty-six ounces of it.

He does not remember if he had dabbed his armpits, with the Limacol, as he does before leaving the station on emergencies.

He tries to inhale deeply, trying not to let her know what he is doing, making an over-elaborate move to follow the rhythm of the music, at the same time; and in this exaggerated move, he tries to smell his two armpits.

He cannot smell his armpits.

There is a gold pin on her chest. It is larger than the saftey pin his mother used to secure his handkerchief with, daubed with Chanel No. 5, Paris, in a miniature vial, which she took from her employer's cabinet.

He is still trembling; and he can hardly follow the beat of the music; he can hardly follow her as she leads him in and out of Miss Ella Fitzgerald's powerful voice. Ella's voice is as lyrical and strong as his nightly snap of Mount Gay Rum. If he had his bottle now, he could put it to his lips, in place of her face so beautiful and so suddenly close to his. Now, with this closeness, he is less exultant than his fantasies about this moment had painted and had anticipated.

Her face is touching his. This face, which shows not one wrinkle, as his own face does. The nightly snaps of Mount Gay Rum could help him now to regain his equanimity. His balance. Could help him recover his composure and help him to put his attention on the music.

He must learn to move with her, as he must learn to listen to her. Move in more harmony with her views, her advice and her strong guiding lead.

She is the man. He is the woman, being led.

This is more than a dance.

She closes her eyes. He becomes alarmed, and more nervous.

He takes this opportunity to remove his head from hers, lean over and put his nostrils closer to his armpits. He cannot reach his armpits, to smell them.

He wishes to smell nice for her. And he wants her to feel that he does. He wishes her to like him. To feel that he is worthwhile; and acceptable.

He wishes tonight had come on another night, in different circumstances.

He knows he has to go back to asking her questions; must go back to taking her Statement, and not let her continue giving statements to take him off his track.

He knows what he has to do. But he knows that he does not want to do it. Under the present circumstances.

But it is the perfume, more than the force of duty, that overpowers him. It tingles the nostrils with its tantalizing, sensual fragrance.

Sargeant does not realize that the music has stopped.

"A Tisket, a Tasket" has come to its end.

She is still holding his right arm, a little distance from her breast; and his left hand is resting on her shoulder. Her right hand is on his back, in the middle of his back. She can feel the dampness of perspiration, and imagine the smell of his body. The grammaphone record begins to scratch, and it is at this point that she releases him. It is at this moment, too, that he awakes from the reverie the music and her arms had held him in.

She now guides him to an upright mahogany chair. It has a cane bottom. From this position, he has a better view of the room.

"Thank you for the dance, sir," she says; and curtseys.

"Thank you, too, Miss Mary-Mathilda," he says, returning the curtsey, with an exaggerated bow.

In other circumstances, it would have been he who would have escorted her, at the conclusion of the dance, back to her chair.

He takes in the pictures and the paintings—making no distinction in his mind between the two—that hang at the level of his eye.

He knows, as if the words are being whispered into his ear, that he will leave this Great House a different man from how he entered it. The voice in which the words are spoken in a whisper is telling him that in one way, he will never leave this house. Perhaps.

The first picture he passes he recognizes. He has seen it many times. In books. And he has seen it most often in *Bible Stories for Children* when he was a child. Now, here is the same picture, larger and more lifelike than in the children's book.

Here, on this wall, it is in a dark brown frame of mahogany wood. *St. George and the Dragon.* He guesses that this frame, like the others, is made by Mr. Waldrond, from the same wood.

He inspects the painting of *St. George and the Dragon*. The name is printed at the bottom.

He looks closely at the white horse, and at St. George in black armour, holding a brownish red spear in his right hand; and then at the Dragon, painted in the shape and fierceness of a dog, like the Alsatian dogs in Hastings District where the Solicitor-General and the two leading barristers-at-Law live, near where the Hastings Salon for Modern & Classical Dance, Madame Glorie, Instructoress, is situated.

The scenery surrounding this struggle to the death, between St. George and the Dragon, is similar to the vegetation and the surroundings of Hastings Rocks, where the Bimshire Police Band plays popular classics, and Sousa marches, every Wednesday evening, in the bandshell shaped like a gazebo.

The scenery is of rocks, polished by the perpetual pounding and washing by the waves at the foot of the bandshell. There are trees. They look like the local trees of the Island. Like clammy-cherry trees. And dunks trees. Like beach-grape trees. And tamarind trees. In the painting of St. George and the Dragon, the trees are short and stumpy and fierce-looking, as if their branches are ready for a fight; to join in allegiance with St. George and help him to defeat the Dragon. There is a woman praying at the side of a road. And in the background, there are two buildings like towers, tall and dignified and powerful like the water tower in the Plantation's yard. Or like the Factory that groans and clanks at the start of the Crop-Season, grinding canes.

The painting is done by a man named Raphael. No one in this Village was ever christened Raphael. Sargeant knows no one by this name.

"Ralph, in a foreign language," she says. "I can't remember which one, Eyetalian, or Spanish."

"Is a strange way to write 'Ralph,'" he tells her. Perhaps, the man writing his name this way, or the man who sold the first original print of this *St. George and the Dragon* painting, could not spell properly.

Or, perhaps, it is a name common to other parts of the world.

The woman at the side of the road is praying for something: for the happy outcome of the struggle between St. George and the Dragon.

In this Island of Bimshire, there is a Church by the name St. George. The St. George's Anglican Church, which has the best Choir, and the best Organist in the Island. And there is a parish named St. George. People in the Island laugh at people who come from the parish of St. George, because St. George lies in the middle of this small Island, and still is not touched by the sea. The Georgians of St. George, as "serrigated" from the sea; and therefore stupid, the Villagers say.

There are no Dragons in the parish of St. George. Or in the Island. Just the Alsatian dogs and the Doberman-Pincers that the rich people keep. Dogs that can tear your guts out, and your heart out, if they catch you on the wrong side of the road, at the wrong time, in their district. Dogs that are trained, so Manny swears, to rip out the hearts of the poor Islanders, meaning black people.

St. George's Dragon looks no more frightening than a Hastings District Alsatian dog. And now that Sargeant sees St. George's Dragon close up, and in the flesh, so to speak, he is not frightened for Dragons, or for Alsatians; and he feels that the bravery people bestowed upon St. George, and showered him with, and talked about in storybooks for children, and in bedtime stories, the bravery for killing the Dragon, has the same truth and the same history, as *The Man Who Jumped Over the Moon.* Or *Little Red Riding Hood.*

This Dragon fighting with St. George is nothing but a big Alsatian dog snarling at the mouth, at the wicket gate of the homes of rich white people in Hastings District, in the Island of Bimshire, in the Wessindies, in the Carbean. In the "New Whirl," as Wilberforce calls it.

Even its teeth, the teeth of this St. George Dragon, snarling, and covered with thick white foam, is nothing different from the scare Sargeant has spent his whole life living through, every day of the week when he had to cross the white road, to go about his business, Personal, or Police; this Hastings Road, called the white road, because of its white marl and the angle of the fierce sun shining on it, whitening it; white, too, because no one, no other black person, but he—small, scared boy; or big man, police Crown-Sargeant, but still frightened to death, to be in this Hastings District—was passing along on it; its loneliness and the fear the loneliness instilled, always made him regard it as a white road.

And when the teeth sank into his soft black sweet flesh, in the softest part of his behind which has no muscles, and the blood spurted out from the punctures made by the teeth, teeth longer and whiter than these drawn in the mouth of this Dragon by this man named Raphael—a name no more important than Ralph in this Village, in this Island of Bimshire, in this part of the New Whirl—for the first moment, all Sargeant could feel, was aware of, could experience, was the exhilaration of fear, and the excitement of the contest, of the duel like the one he experienced in his imagination of locked horns with Mr. Bellfeels that Easter bank holiday; now it was he against Alsatian. Sarge against the Alsatian. St. Sarge and the Alsatian. Nigger against Rover. They called all their dogs *Rover*. They called Sargeant *nigger*. And they called all their servants and labourers in the fields *nih-ger*, to rhyme with *chigger*. And he didn't have even a clammy-cherry stick in his hand, or a limb from the ackee tree, or even a piece of the coconut frond— with which he swept the grounds and the yard and the tennis courts of the Garrison Savannah Lawn Tennis Club—to protect him from the Alsatian, and ward him off, until the owner came reluctantly, with the white smear of a smile on his face; and said, *"Here, Rover! Here!"* And when the wicket gate was closed, he could read, more clearly now, in spite of smudges of someone's hand attempting to erase the message, this warning, painted in black stencilled letters: NO DOGS, NIGGORS & JEWS ALLOWED.

And here now, in the safety of thick paint, is this big man, in armour, dressed in cloth of mail; iron, painted black; mounted on a horse, a white horse, and holding a spear or a lance—or is it a sword? He must go back and take a second, longer look at St. George's picture—in such a puny, overblown struggle of gigantic, mortal proportion. He must go back and take a second look. They have now passed St. George and his dog-faced Dragon, and are standing in front of the framed head of a woman. All this protection and armaments, lance, sword, armour, steed, just to kill an animal no bigger than a Bimshire dog, an Alsatian; and still have his name sent down to the Island, in history, in school books and in Bible stories for educating children, all the way from Europe to teach him and a million other Bimshire boys in this sleepy corner of the tropical New Whirl, a lesson in strength and in daring and in big-heartedness; and in fortitude.

And in moral bravery?

And chivalry?

The painting she is showing him now is of a head. The head is the head of a woman. At the bottom of the painting, it is written that this head is *Head of the Madonna*. It is done by someone named Boltraffio.

"Boltraffio," she says. She pronounces it as if she were born speaking those names. "My boy who spend time in Rome-Italy brought back this with him. And he teached me, taught me, the right way to say the name Boltraffio.

"Bolt-raffio," Sarge says.

Here is another strange name, Sargeant thinks. Here in this Island, the names that name people are names that show and paint and reflect who the people are: or, at least, part of what they are. Here in Bimshire, names are names you understand; Sarge, Constable, the Revern, Manny, Naiman, Mary-Tilda; names you can pronounce easily; and remember. But the name of this painter. And this *Madonna*. Madame, he knows. He has heard that name used many times. As a matter of fact, he was thinking of her a few moments ago. Madame Glorie, the Instructoress of the Hastings Salon for Modern & Classical Dance. Madame Glorie, he knows. Donna, he understands. There are lots of whores down in Town, in Suttle Street, with the name Donna, Nelson Street, famous also for whores, is crawling with Donnas and sailors off English ships, and native pimps; and Donnas-to-burn, too. He came across a Donna once, who said she is a writer, not a giver of pleasure . . .

Yes, they come to Nelson Street down in Town, in droves, both during the height of the War and in the hushed safety of Armistice; and then, the quiet of peacetime. Pre-War, and post-War. Yes. He knows about Donnas. But the larger name, *Ma-donna. My-dear-donna. Muh-dear-donna. Muh-donna. Ma-donna.* Perhaps, in a foreign language, *Madonna* means something different. He surmises that this could be a European name for the Virgin Mary.

The name is foreign. But the features of the person with the foreign name are local, are native, are peculiar to this Island of Bimshire. Are Bimshirean. He knows women, black and white, and those mixed with black blood and with white blood, who could be this woman's mother, or sister, or aunt, or child, so strong is the resemblance.

Head of the Madonna.

He likes *Head of the Madonna.* He likes the native women whom this *Head of the Madonna* reminds him of: he has seen her walking in Town, coming from Cave Shepherd & Sons, Haberdasheries, after she has purchased her vial of Eau de Cologne No. 4711; and he has seen her changing from dress to sporting whites, quick, in fumbling speed, frantic; in a rush to evade his eyes, as he passes behind the green-painted CHANGING ROOM: LADIES ONLY sign at the Garrison Savannah Lawn Tennis Club; and he sees this face, part of *Head of the Madonna*, as the face of the woman playing tennis, as she tosses her head backwards in a sharp violent movement, to settle her straying hair, and keep it out of her eyes, before she serves, from blinding her from seeing the returned ball coming at her from across the net, like a bullet; and when her hair is controlled, he sees the face in *Head of the Madonna*, calm, controlled, confident and beautiful, as she begins tying her long brown hair into a bun, into a knot, in this same shape shown in these European colours on this shimmering painting, rectangled in the dark brown mahogany frame that he is looking at, that Mr. Waldrond made. She and this woman are the same *Madonna*.

When he moves a little to his right, he is still face-to-face with the head of *Head of the Madonna*. Her eyes are following him. He has seen eyes like these. Eyes that follow him, eyes of a thief, a shoplifter, working amongst the thick crowds of Easter and Christmas shoppers in Cave Shepherd & Sons, Haberdasheries, down in Town. He sees eyes that give off this compelling dare, this occular defiance, this attaching glare, this magnetized stare, this piercing, convicting stare, whenever on his beat he passes along Nelson Street in Town, when the Careenage in Carlisle Bay is filled with ships that fly the Union Jack; during the War; and then, afterwards, in peacetime, when English tourisses replaced the English sailors.

He moves to his left, and the stare remains as piercing and focused upon him. He moves to the right, and the eyes are pinned upon him, still.

The stare of the head of *Head of the Madonna* frightens him.

He is glad that Mary Gertrude Mathilda is now holding his arm, his left arm, her hand resting just under the three silver stripes under the large silver-and-red Imperial Crown, resplendent in what it stands for, "a Crown-Sargeant" in the Royal Bimshire Constabulary Police Force; and she moves him, just as when she was still gliding him through the words and riffs of "A Tisket, a Tasket"; and they stand, with her hand still touching his arm, in front of another picture. *Pietà*—the Madonna with the dead Christ.

The person who drew this picture has a foreign name, too. A man named Sebastiano del Piombo. He too comes from Away, overseas; from Europe. But this name is not so foreign to Sargeant's ears as the other two. He knows many black boys living in this Island named Sebastian. The *o* at the end is merely for style, he feels, to distinguish between a black boy playing cricket on the beach at the Crane Beach Hotel and another boy from Away, overseas, from Europe, who is playing tennis at Wimbleton, Rumbleton . . .

or cricket, probably in a Test Match, at Lord's; or probably playing soccer in Estrada di Vicenza Italy; or in Sydney Australia . . .

What game could a white European boy of this same age be playing at? Not cricket. What would this European Sebastiano be playing at? Swords. Duelling with swords. Playing to be a soldier, like St. George. Learning to fight and to kill, and to spill blood, just as they . . . Sebastiano's father and Sebastiano's uncle did years ago in their history of cruel culture . . . in this very Island of Bimshire, and in Trinidad farther to the south, and in Demerara buried amongst bush and jungle and drenched with rivers and waterfalls; and in Brazil, in the Argentyne, in the Canal Zone of Panama where men and women drowned in mud and escavations; and all of South America. A game of blood.

Blood. And swords. And trees trampled. And no knowledge of, and less liking for the local, native horticulture, the native vegetation, the native forestry. And not enough willow trees in their crunching, destructive path, from which, he has been made to understand, the very best, effectively functional, longest-lasting cricket bats are made.

"It is strange, you know. Very strange."

It takes him a while to realize that it is the woman holding him by the arm, just below the insignia of his rank and status and Imperial Crown, who is talking to him. It is Mary Gertrude Mathilda, and not *Pietà*; or *Madonna*.

His mind is still on the games taught to Sebastiano the European kid when he was growing up Away, overseas, in Europe; in Portugal, in Holland, in Spain and in Liverpool-Englund; at the same time and age as the barefoot boy born in this Island of Bimshire, drenched in sunlight and painted green in sugar canes, and beautified by the native horticulture, the native vegetation, the native forestry, flowers and the green fields growing, young yams and sweet potatoes and the pastures of Khus-Khus grass now brown and ripe for sickles and for sheep, and the majestic glory of the tall casuarina trees that reach and, in his imagination, surpass the dizzying height of the deep blue skies; the colour of sand on the beaches the tinge of the conch shell . . . all this majesty, all this beauty, wasted for years, for childhoods, before this moment, when he faces a painting drawn by a man with a European name . . . all this Island majesty . . .

"It is my boy, Wilberforce," she is telling him, "who first intro-duce me to these things. Showing me this European Culture, as he say they call it over-there. But when I look at these drawings, these things, they only are pictures, to me. I don't see no European Cul-ture in them. Meaning that by the seeing of something European in them, that they are superior to what I see in my own backyard, when I look at the cane fields and the breadfruit trees around me, by virtue of the fact, because they come from Europe? I don't see the superiority Wilberforce say they have in them; or over us. I see Bimshire. When I look at them, I see the Island of Bimshire, in which I was bred-and-born, in all their colours, Blue Period and Red Period, and all their Schools. I see the Island of Bimshire. Plain and simple. I see this Village. Flagstaff Village. I see the Plantation. I see the Plantation Main House, the biggest, most powerful house on the face of this earth, this Island. This Planta-tion. I see this Great House, in which I happen to live. And I see my own life. And I see the other houses of an in-between size and importance to the Plantation Main House and this Great House where we are; and the houses that house the labourers.

"Take this one, this *Pietà* drawing. What you think *Pietà* stands for?"

"Is a woman's name?"

"No."

"A man?"

"You serious, Sargeant?"

"I am serious, Miss Mary-Mathilda. Let me think . . . *Pietà, Pee-eta* . . . *Pee-ate-ah, Pee-aa, Pee-ate-her. Pietà.* Not a man. Not a woman. I have heard this word, this name, before. Don't we have this name in one o' the carols and songs we sings in Church on special occasions, on festivals, and certain liturgies? Not a woman's name. Well, Jesus Christ! . . . pardon my French, Mary-Mathilda. . . *Pietà* could only mean one thing! *Pity!*"

"Course! And the reason it take you so long is because *pity* is written in a foreign language! And we are educated to believe that anything from Over-and-Away is either more difficult to imitate or is superior to anything we have in this Island."

"Imagine! *Pity is* the real meaning!"

"And if you see this picture as a example for pity that people in the outside-world make so much fuss over, I ask you, as a educated man, you don't see more better examples of pity right here in this Island? This Sunday evening? In this village? In this Atmosphere . . ."

"You mean, Hemisphere?"

"Thanks. Hemisphere," she says. And then there is silence. The two of them seem to lose interest in the paintings; as if they were never on the wall of the front-house.

"Clotelle," she says after a while. "I am remembering Clotelle. Who comes into my mind, all of a sudden. If somebody had-had the time and the paint and the colours and the right time o' day, and if the rain wasn't falling so hard the last few days, and if the person doing the painting had the inclination, such a person, with a touch o' talent, couldda drawn a more authentic picture of Pity, which would be a close-up image of Clotelle's face. And Clotelle's body. And Clotelle's life.

"Even before the tragedy."

"Even before the tragedy."

"Before Clotelle was found tie-up, and henging from the tamarind tree."

"Dead."

"Yes, dead. Before they tek-she-down."

"'*Who tie-she-up
And feck-she-up,
Could tek-she-down!*'"

Sargeant closes his eyes while Mary-Mathilda sings the calypso. "Dead," he says.

"So, Europe can't teach we *nothing* about Pity! Even if they call it by a different name, '*pee-a-tuh*'!"

"*Pee*," Sargeant says, intent upon finding the meaning of the word from its root and deconstruction. "*Pee. Pee . . . ate . . . ah. Pee-ate-ah*? Or, *pee-ate-her*?"

"Or, even piety! You ever thought of piety? It could, in its foreign-language meaning, stand more for piety than for pity."

"I think I prefer piety to pity."

"Me too."

"*Pee-ate-her.* And piety."

"You see the man laying-down there on that white sheet? And you see how he is dressed? With nothing more covering his nakedess than a bare piece o' cloth? My Wilberforce calls it a lion-cloth."

"A lion-cloth?"

"Did I say a lion-cloth? What am I saying? I mean *loin*! Loin as in a piece o' pork . . . pork-loin, loin-pork that Manny would cut for you on a Saturday, when he kills a pig."

"Oh!"

"With nothing more covering his nakedness than a loincloth? And you see the woman there, praying? Wonder what she is praying for? But whatever it is that she is calling-on on God for, I had to tell Wilberforce when he was introducing me to this *Pietà*-thing and European Culture, that it is always the role, the turn and responsibility of the woman to do the praying. Regardless to what she is praying for. The man do the action: the woman has to pray to correct that action. And regardless to where the woman come from."

"But this woman has a resemblance to you, though, Miss Mary-Mathilda! She features you."

"Do I look so white to you?"

"Not from the point o' view of colour and complexion, I mean from the point o' view of manners and attitudes. And the praying; and the way her body look as she is praying."

"You see the shawl she is wearing on her head?"

"Perhaps it is the shawl that make me say she look like you, although I never really saw you wearing a shawl over your head, nor praying. Sometimes, on Sundays in Church, from my seat in the Choir up in the chancel, I would catch a glimpse of you in your pew, but from that distance I could not tell if you was praying, or not . . ."

"What a funny thing to say! But you already noticed the shawl on this poor woman's head. But what puzzled me and Wilberforce is what is this woman doing sitting on a cloud, when she is supposed to be praying? And, to-boot, what is she doing, sitting on a *black* cloud? A cloud that is almost touching the ground. Is this what they mean by European Culture?"

"Sitting on a black cloud that is touching the ground! That is somthing, now that you mention it!"

"Many nights, particular those nights when Wilberforce isn't out drinking and dancing, either at the Marine Hotel or the Aquatic Club, or down at the Savannah Tennis Club where he plays tennis with his doctor-friends, for, as you know, the various committees are always holding social-hops, those informal dances; and parties; well, on Fridays and Saturday nights when Wilberforce stays home, he and me spend the time right here. And he tells me things that he witnessed and observed in the outside-world. And always, as sure as a cent, he wants me to believe that the things he sees, and have observe in that outside-world, are better than anything we could ever see in this Island.

"I was born-and-raise here. Wilberforce was educated as well as born-and-raise here. You would think that a young man like him would have more love and loyalty in his birthright. Is that the word for it? In his roots. In his origins. In his birthplace!

"And when he talks to me so, about being educated through travelling, and the education it brings, I always have to remind Wilberforce that education is not the same thing as learning.

"A person could be well-educated. Educated to the hilt. To the very heights. Like Wilberforce himself. Educated at Harrison College. Educated up in Englund, first at Oxford doing Philosophy, Politics and Economics; then Law. Then, educated at Cambridge University, over-and-above-that. Wilberforce studied Laws for two years first; at Oxford; then turn-round and went to Cambridge and the Imperial College of London, to take up Tropical Medicines, for a further four years, because . . . listen to this! . . . in the Laws concerning Criminalities, all you do in the briefs they give you is to defend murderers; and murderers don't have the money to pay you when you don't got-them-off. No money to retain a good barster-at-Law that Wilberforce would have become.

"But he could afford to waste all those years studying, for three reasons. Number one, his father Mr. Bellfeels had the money to throw-way on him. Number two, Wilberforce is the only son Mr. Bellfeels have. And number three, I drove it in Wilberforce head that *learning, learn-n*ing, not merely education but *learn-ning*, will deliver him from whatever chains and shackles Mankind or Life, or all-two-both, have in store for him, or have conspired to place in his path.

"Get your education /*first*, I tell Wilberforce, even before you start thinking of breeding woman. Or considering marrieing one o' the young-girls round-here.

"But what did my words of wisdom fall on? The bare ground. A rock-stone. On arid, barren soil.

"At least, he ain't breed one o' them, yet! I knock on wood.

"Sometimes, though, when I look at Wilberforce, I have to wonder if, with all the book-learning his father paid for, Wilberforce isn't still one of the single most stupidest men walking this earth! Stupider even than Mr. Bellfeels, then. And nobody never accuse Mr. Bellfeels of having tummuch sense!

"Stupid still, with all that English education.

"But it is learning, I tell him. Learning. Give me a learned man anytime.

"Mr. Bellfeels was kind of a educated man. Semi-educated. And therefore, semi-literate. I hope that Wilberforce, my only surviving child, hasn' inherited those genes from Mr. Bellfeels, in this regards. Even though Wilberforce is a doctor, 'cause these things, like genes, could be delayed, you know what I mean? Buried . . . but not dead."

She leads Sargeant to a chair. It is the tall, straight-backed mahogany chair with a cane bottom and with a heart carved into the design in its back, the chair he had béen sitting in before.

She leads him to this chair as if she is exhausted, worn out by her talking.

She draws a white lace handkerchief from her left sleeve, and it comes out slow, tantalizingly slow, and beautiful as a snake made of cloth. She passes the handkerchief across her brow, and the smell of her perfume wafts to his nostrils.

He closes his eyes, and breathes in the fragrance. Deep.

In this moment, she is more beautiful to his eyes. And the years that have rolled by so fast, and which had pitched him at such an untouchable distance from her: only seeing her at church, on first Sundays in the month, for Communion; only seeing her, from a distance, in her vegetable garden at the back of this Great House; only seeing her at the annual Church outings, in later years, at the Crane Beach Hotel, but surrounded always by all the children who lived in the Plantation grounds, in the estates, and in Hastings District, including the two daughters of Mr. Bellfeels, Miss Euralie and Miss Emonie; and those of the Solicitor-General, greying now, and made Lord Chief Justice; and the children of the two leading barristers-at-Law in the Island; she was never alone, for him to talk to.

In all those years that he saw her, she was unapproachable.

And now, he and she, alone in this parlour of the Great House, are really very unhappy, uncomfortable and on edge, in their privacy and closeness; and even without the presence of her son, Wilberforce, they still feel and behave as if they are chaperoned; and not alone. Yes.

Yes. It is difficult for them, especially for Sargeant, to relax: he is aware of her son's presence in the room. Her boy, her son, the apple of her eye, Wilberforce, "my boy-child," she calls him; "Mr. Bellfeels the Doctor," the Village calls him; or "Tilda boy," to the Vicar and to his closest friends—Wilberforce, Sargeant's doctor.

Always in those years, after that first Easter Monday bank holiday, at the Church outing, at the Crane Beach Hotel, when he saw her from a distance, she had remained beautiful, and desirable. Sometimes, the distance was a few feet, as she walked up the aisle on Sundays, with Wilberforce beside her.

Sometimes, the distance was even shorter, more painful, more dramatic, when she sat near the aisle, in the next row of seats occupied by the Plantation Main House; at the annual cricket match between the Village First Eleven and the Plantation's team, she would sit beside Wilberforce, not far from the men who ran the Village and the Plantation and the Church and the haberdasheries, and the private clubs in the Island. At other times, still, that distance was the one row of seats, at the annual Gymkhana of the Bimshire Volunteer Regiment and Brigade, performed on the Garrison Savannah Pasture, near the green fence of the Tennis Club, on the other side of the iron cannons, guns now relics, brought over by ship from the fields of the Boer War as symbols of English bravery and military supremacy.

There was always this distance. Small in its nature, gigantic in its social significance. But always uncrossable in all its other meanings.

Here now, in this house that bears just a trace of the smell of burnt sugar cane, from the cane fire that raged many hours earlier on this Sunday, which the wind blows in from the fields; and with

the smell of lady-of-the-night, but more of burnt trash . . . per-
haps, it is because he can see through the windows, in the distance,
the red smouldering cane fires near the North Field; and on his
way here, on his bicycle, still some distance from the burnt-out
cane-field fire, the illumination from the distant fire reflected in
the skies made Sargeant feel closer to the fire, and caused him
to start wondering who had committed this arson; he can see the
golden, sparkling flames so clearly, and hear the crackling of the
canes, that he can easily smell cane juice being burnt; and can taste
the burnt sugar-cane juice.

It is the wind that results in this breeze coming strong from the
Factory, half a mile from the Plantation House, in the short dis-
tance away. The Factory is grinding canes. It grinds the canes
tonight, and every night, as it will do right through the night until
daybreak; and start up again, perpetually, without turning off the
machinery; and the breath of the wind coming from a farther dis-
tance, from the sea, is the scent that he is smelling. And he is
smelling the night. Just the night. A smell that is the mixture of all
the smells of the day, combined into the sensual, thick, passionate
smell of the lady-of-the-night. And at this time of year, the smell of
the raw cane juice, which the Villagers call "crack-liquor."

And then, suddenly, he hears the whistle of the Factory. The
sound is thin, and like a wail; and it makes his skin crawl; it does
not add to his comfortableness in this room, and sets his nerves on
edge. The sound of this whistle rattles him, each time it goes off.

It goes off now, to signal a change of shift. New men arrive at all
hours of the night, during Crop-Season only, to feed the crushing
machinery and engines with canes. The whistle signals the depar-
ture of worn-out men and tired women, every three hours, and up
to midnight. And others who live in houses that surround the Fac-
tory and the Plantation. And when the whistle goes, it is also the
signal that corresponds to the time for food; and the hour to bring
food; or make food.

Food. Something to eat: to put into the belly.

All the inhabitants of the Village call it by this name. Food. In spite of the time of day or night, when it is served. In any other part of the outside-world, it is called breakfast, lunch or dinner.

So, when the shrill whistle is blown, from inside some part of the Factory, and the spurt of steam comes out, and the noise inhabits the entire Village, and covers all the land, and all the roads, and all the back-alleys, and the laneways, and the pastures, with its shrieking high pitch that unsettles the nerves, the women know automatically that it is time to take food to their men. They know what time it is.

"Time to tek this lil bittle to that man," they tell one another. "The man wukking hard, so he hungry, child!"

And just as suddenly, as if it has heard the voices of the women, the whistle stops blowing. The whistle stops blowing. And in the silence which comes as sudden as the wailing had begun, the night goes back to its former sleepiness. And lounges in its soft fragrant, discreet darkness, as if somone has poured a bottle of Eau de Cologne No. 4711 gently, and evenly, over the entire land.

"Did you know that I saw Amurca?" she says. Her voice, and her words, what they are telling him, are as surprising as the sudden turning-off of the Factory whistle. "Yes. Once. Amurca. Yes! Amurca! And every time I hear the Factory-whistle blow, I remember my journey to Amurca. And how that train whistle was blowing to announce stations and towns. And destinations.

"It was Buffalo. The Factory-whistle remind me of Buffalo. It remind me of the train, every time I hear it blow. What a trip!

"Mr. Bellfeels had to see some machineries and engines, equipments and parts for the Factory, and he had to go up to Buffalo. It was during the times that things between the two o' we was still sweet. I remember those good times. How he uses to come over here, to this Great House, at six o'clock in the evening, just as the sun going down below the hill there; and he would take off his riding boots, and lay-down on the floor, on the hardwood floor, bare and by itself; and pore-over magazines with coloured pictures in them, like *English Country Life* and the *London Illustrated News*, and the brochures that Wilberforce subscribed to, with such lovely pictures in them in Technicolor; pictures of machines and machinery made in Amurca; and heavy equipment; and I think one magazine was named *Heavy Engineering and Equipment*. And one afternoon, it was a Saturday, he decided all of a sudden to invite me to go up to Buffalo with him. To Amurca. Just like that. He up and say, not ask me, nor request of me, he just say, 'I tekking you to Amurca. Get some clothes ready. We tekking a plane to Miami-Florida. And train to Buffalo. I got business up in there. Machines for this fecking Factory. The fecking Factory always brekking-down.'

"Sargeant-boy, I didn't know one damn thing about Amurca. Nothing at all. Except what I hear on the BBC news. Or sometimes, on the private-set coming in from Latin-Amurca, the Argentyne, Brazil, Panama sometimes. And from a few magazines and books that Wilberforce leff-'bout-the-place. Along with some that Mr. Bellfeels himself steal from the Aquatic Club, or the Marine Hotel, and leave-'bout here. But Amurca? Amurca?

"Amurca was always a place that frighten me. With its bigness. Its badness. Its richness. But after Mr. Bellfeels extend the invitation, I started to listen more careful, to the radio. The BBC. And the private-set. And I pick up everything that I could. I got to know about this place, Amurca. Yes.

"I learned myself the ins-and-outs concerning Amurca.

"I was damn frighten, though, when that plane take off. My heart was in my mouth. I don't think a word ever issue or pass my two lips. From the time the plane run down the runway of Seawell Airport, like a . . . like a thunderbolt. And all that time, up in the air, during the flight, I didn't have the heart to hold over and look out the window and take a peep, to see what a lovely beautiful landscape my Island of Bimshire is from the air. My son, Wilberforce, and his father, Mr. Bellfeels, would always, being more frequent travellers than me, say how pretty this Isle o' Bimshire is from overhead.

"Bimshire is the most beautiful scenery from the air. As if they really mean to imply that Bimshire is the worst scenery from the ground! Or that when you're on the ground, in Bimshire, it is the worst place imaginable in the world. Heh-heh-heh!

"Well, boy, yes! In the plane. In the air. I didn't breathe easy, wasn't myself, didn't feel normal, wasn' regular, nothing. No. Not a word, not a iota passed my two lips, till that plane eventually touch-down and land at the airport in Miami-Florida.

"I don't remember nothing about Miami-Florida. But the heat. The humidities. My God, the heat? Hot? Well, I thought Bimshire was hot. I used to walk-'bout here and complain; miserable and with my face set-up like rain, with vexatiousness. I does-get angry whenever you see August come around, and the heat and the humidity hit we, and this Island turn into a oven. But Miami-Florida? Christ, Sargeant, when I step-off the stairs leading down from the lil small plane that had one engine, and was taking the steps down, and the stairs moving and shaking, as if they were about to capsize me, my-God-in-heaven, Sargeant-boy! Yes!

"When my two feet touched that tarmac, or whatever the word is, Christ-have-His-mercy! The Miami-Florida humidities clutch me by my neck, and nearly kill me right-there-and-then, on the spot. *Heat?* And the humidities?

"But apart from that. From the little I was able to see from the window of the motor-car that picked we up from on the tarmac, on the runway of the airport in Miami-Florida, Miami-Florida is not a bad place. The coconut trees. And the mango trees. The oranges. Grapefruits in the grapefruit trees ripening on the trees, things I never see, nor imagined in all my born days. All these things growing before my two eyes, and I don't have to rely on seeing them in a picture in a book, to know that they exist. Things of prettiness just a few hours' journey from where I live. Not from Europe. From *here*! From right here! In my own backyard. Isn't that something? Pretty things. And the land, Sargeant! Oh-my-God-in-Heaven, the land! The land!

"I understand now why over the years there's been labour schemes on which they have always been men, young men, middle-age men who is husbands, but men only, only men leaving this Island willingly, heading to Amurca, to Miami-Florida to cut canes in that broiling Miami-Florida hot-sun and humidity. With all those snakes!

"Because. The place is too pretty. Damn pretty, if yuh ask me! God's country. And close-close in climate to here. What a expanse o' land! If I had it in me to travel, or if my fate and fortune had-o'-held travel in it, I would pick Miami-Florida over any place in Europe. And after Miami-Florida, any other place in Amurca. You think you would catch me harkening after Europe? I used to think of Paris, but no more. Placing Europe in the status and preferences that that overeducated boy I gave birth to, Wilberforce, tell me I must do? Europe is too old for me. And miserable. And cruel. And violent. And thiefing, thieving. Slaves, minerals, raw materials and silver. And they already kill-off all the Indians in this part of the world, where we live.

"You could only like Europe maybe if you didn't have a grain o' history in your blood, and inside your head. Or if you-yourself was another European.

"I have it from my son, who has visited Europe and lived in Europe, and those other foreign strange places, that this same Europe that he worships-so is the cause to the sufferations of the black race.

"I already mention the Indian tribes of this part of the world.

"'S'matter of fact, the white races, too! And don't talk 'bout the brown races! Those people who found this-very Island of Bimshire. And those other brown people who live in Latin-Amurca. Brazil and the Argentyne. Cuba, too! The Canal Zone.

"The Europeans do whatever they like. Filled their greed and wishes with anything that they could lift and car-way, found in these parts of the world. Lay-claim to it. And anything they could put their two hands on, anything that was light-enough for them to lift and haul-way, they steal. Yes!

"This is my definition of a European.

"Wilberforce always refer to this part of the world where we live as the 'New-Whirl.'"

"So, gimme the New Whirl, over the Old World, any day! Miami-Florida! Then, any-other part of Amurca, anytime! But that train ride I was telling you about . . .

"And the stations the train stopped at, like Stations of the Cross on Good Friday! And the land, again. The land. Passing through towns. Passing through cities. Through neighbourhoods. And through communities. Passing through fields. Pasing herds o' cows. Passing horses. Their bodies shining in the sun, in all colours of grey, dark-grey, brown, brown-that-is-like-red and a few black-black horses, reminding me of a racehorse Mr. Bellfeels had-own. Man o' War! Yes.

"Passing wild boars and wild animals that you see in cowboy movies and in the magic lantern shows the Department of Social Development and Culture put-on in the Village; and wild animals like they shoot for sport on safaris, in Africa, big-game hunting. Passing whole stretches o' land where nothing grows, laying barren, places more bigger than the whole of this entire Island. And in all this time, travelling by now hundreds and hundreds o' miles, Mr. Bellfeels is seated in a different section of the train, invisible to me, and separated from me. Mr. Bellfeels is sitting in one section, a reserved compartment of the train, a sleeper. And I in a next section they called third-class, sitting-up, my back hurting me, all throughout this journey north.

"And when I finally notice that something wasn't setting too good with me, that something was not normal, at first, I could ony shake my head.

"I was *serrigated* from Mr. Bellfeels.

"I was travelling through serrigated country!

"It hit me in the pit o' my guts. Like a sledgehammer.

"I am sitting with *all coloured and black people only*. You hear me? And with me, is all these coloured people; and they are talking

in such a pretty language; as if they have molasses, or sling, cane
syrup, on their tongues; but in a language nevertheless that sound
like English, but wasn't really English, but that was more sweeter
than English, sweeter than the English that we speak in this Island;
and the words coming outta their mouths were sounding more
like what Ma told me my great-gran used to speak. Like African.

"I didn't understand one iota of this African language they were
using! In a journey that take-up sommany hours. They're speak-
ing amongst themselves; and once in a while, they would turn a eye
towards me, and smile; and one started talking to me; and I couldn't
understand one blasted word she was saying! I not shame to tell
you. But I was shame as hell to let on that I didn't understand a
damn thing of this African-sounding language they were speaking.
Or hardly anything.

"But then, my mind tell me that it couldn't be African they
were speaking. They were dress like Amurcans. They were not
wearing African robes, or nothing so.

"Then, it occurred to me it was a different language.

"They spoke something that sounded like Spanish. I recognize
it as Spanish . . ."

"Spanish?" Sargeant says. "Do you speak Spanish, Miss Mary?"

"Not that I know Spanish to speak it, Sargeant. I know Spanish
only in the way that I recognize it as Spanish when anybody speak
it. Or when I hear it on the 'private-set,' in a programme on the
Voice of the Andes. No, I do not know how to speak the brrrrrrabba-
rrrrabba of the Spanish language.

"The people on the train with me, was most of the same com-
plexion. Negro people. Some a lil more lighter than others. Some
more darker. But all with a lovely smooth-skin complexion.
Coloured people. And I felt so happy to be amongst them. To be in
the company of these Amurcans.

"And the train passing big buildings. Buildings touching the
sky. Building after building. One that looked like a tower. A small
tower. Painted red. Reddish. With one window. Later, after we

reach Buffalo, our destination, Mr. Bellfeels would tell me that that tall reddish brown building with the one window was a silo-granary. For holding wheat. I even seen wheat growing, with my own two eyes!

"We are passing cornfields, now. Fields o' Indian corn. Fields as big as from one end of this Island, Sin-Lucy in the North, and you drive straight-straight down South, passing the hotels for tourisses on the West Coast, and come, come, come-right-down to the other end of the Island, the South Coast, to Oistins Town, in Christ Church. I never knew such bigness before! Couldn't contemplate that bigness. In anything. In the fields. In the size of the cows. The cattles. Or in the land. That a field of Indian corn could be more bigger, seen from a train, than the whole o' Bimshire! My God-in-heaven, Percy! Amurca is such a pretty place. Such a lovely place—"

"Not meaning to interrupt you, Miss Mary, but what the time is?"

"Check the hour gainst the grandfather clock there, Percy."

"Nine."

"Nine? Only nine?"

"I have to keep an eye on the clock."

"I know, Sargeant. But we just sat down."

"I still have the Statement, and my report to . . ."

"We have time, Percy, we have time."

"I know we have time, Miss Mary-Mathilda, we have time. Not that I rushing you . . ."

"Nine o' clock, though!"

"And I listening . . ."

"So, going north, now . . ."

"From Miami-Florida?"

". . . and we stop at a place called Atlantic. No, not Atlantic. Atlanta! Atlanta-Georgia. I knew Georgia. I knew about Georgia. From the title of a Negro spiritual, I think it is. But I didn't know Atlanta. Georgia is also the place where they had the most

slaves. And the worst slaveholders and slave-drivers, Wilberforce
studied that in the History of the Laws of Slavery, at Oxford. In all
the years he went-school at Harrison College, one of the most
reputed and best institutionals in the British Empire, not one
Master who teached him ever mentioned to him a word about
this History of the Laws of Slavery! He left without knowing the
history of . . . what-you-call-it? . . . the history of himself.

"But getting back to Georgia. And Wilberforce. His name,
Wilberforce, you may or may not know, is a historical name.

"And it was the history in his name that cause him-himself, he
told me, after he went up to Oxford, to vestigate his name in rela-
tion to history and slavery and the Laws of Slavery. Yes.

"But when that train was passing through Georgia, all I could
think of was the refrain that we used to sing almost every Saturday
night, right here in this front-house, when Mr. Bellfeels played the
piano. 'Georgia.'

"We would sing that song, sometimes in the presence of Mr.
Bellfeels and his friends, like the Solicitor-General, the Vicar,
Revern Dowd and them-so, when they visited, to gamble and
drink rum; and to see how Wilberforce was progressing, prior to
his going-away. And sometimes, Mr. Bellfeels sang 'Georgia'
along with we.

"All those years, and all those times, me and Wilberforce put
on that performance for Mr. Bellfeels and his friends without
knowing what the hell we was really doing. Yes.

"It is only then. Travelling through Georgia, Atlanta-Georgia,
on a train, on that serrigated train, that I knew, then-and-there,
what the hell that song mean.

"And the history of that song.

"For the first time.

"And a funny thing happen. All the people in the part o' the train
with me . . . Mr. Bellfeels by now comfortable, in the part of the
train called the Private Car, by himself. But I didn't mind that,
cause it was a place where the smoke from the Cuban cigars those

men were smoking was thick-enough to choke a hog . . . the coloureds, as I got to know was how they were addressed. Yes. Coloureds. All the people in the comportment, compartment of the train with me . . . I was very happy to be numbered with these coloured people who spoke as if it was Spanish coming from out their mouth.

"And as I said, a funny thing happened. No, not a funny thing. It was not funny. These things aren't funny. Even in appearances. Or even after they happened to happen.

"A announcement came over the thing in the top of the roof . . . the loudspeaker in the ceiling of the train . . . informing us sitting in that comport, compartment, that the car with food was now open and available. Down the aisle of the train where I was, sitting with all the coloured people, of black and fair-skin complexions, sudden-so, there came so many, so-many-people in droves, that I didn't even know one train could hold summuch, hundreds o' passengers! Droves and droves of people. Yes.

"And all these people coming down the aisle of the train into our compartment—the compartment of the coloureds—with me, now numbered amongst them, cause by that sociation, I was classified suddenly as a coloured-Amurcan—the hordes o' people marching-through, was *white*. Yes, boy.

"Boy, I was classified through sheer sitting-commodation as a coloured-Amurcan. Yes, man! You hear me?

"One of the white-gents looked at a woman in the seat ahead o' me, and says to her, 'Jane, y'all sure enjoying your first trip Nawth, now, ain't you now, girl?'

"Or so it sounded to me. The white-gent was using the *same* language o' speech as the coloured lady!

"As if he was talking in a foreign language. In Spanish. And this Jane . . . when I tell you a pretty woman? A pretty, fair-skin woman of about forty years, well, Jane just held her head down, as if she was searching for something important in her lap. Yes. In pure embarrassment.

"I couldn't figure it out no better than that. Nor, no plainer than that. The other people on the train, in the comportment of the coloureds, in the compartment with me, they-all just kept quiet. Quiet-quiet. While this troop of white-gents passed. Yes.

"And not one woman who was white passed. Not one white woman walked with the troops o' white-gentlemen! Isn't that something!

"Right down the middle of the aisle of our compartment, these white-gentlemen marched on their way to the Club Car. Such a strange thing! And such a strange place! This Georgia. This Amurca.

"And the last white man passed. And quick-so. Afterwards. As if they was acting in a play. Reacting to stage directions. Brown paper bags. Plastic bags. And hand towels of blue-and-white cloth, and red and white, like dishtowels. Started coming out. Yes.

"And the smell! A smell like you never smelled in your whole life before. The smell of chicken. I learned afterwards that those coloured ladies have a special way of fixing chicken. That only former slaves in the Amurcan South, places like Atlanta-Georgia and Alabama could make it. *Southern-fry chicken*. Southern-fry chicken, yes!

"This lovely smell took us straight north, north straight outta Georgia, until the conductor-man announce that we were entering North Carolina.

"But he didn't pronounce it as North Carolina. He said something like '*Naaaawthcarlie-nah! Nawthcarlie-nah!*' Sweet-sweet, so!

"God, how I like to hear Amurcans talk! All shades.

"Having just passed through Savannah. Another sweet name. *'Charlessss-ton! Charleston! Next stop, Charlessss-ton!'* Charleston. That sent me back to the dance. Doing the Charleston. You know that dance, don't you, Sargeant? The Charleston?

"It was my first trip on a train. And my last. But what a trip! Charleston–South-Carolina. And before I knew it, the conductor-fellow announce Williamsburg-Virginia. And then, the biggest shock.

"The biggest shock I ever had in my born-days.

"'*Lynchburg! Lynchburg, next! Next stop, Lynchburg!*' the conductor-man announce.

"And when the conductor announce, '*Lynchburg!*' I found myself looking at this Amurcan coloured woman sitting-cross the aisle from me. Watching her close. I watched her close-close to see her reaction whilst the conductor-fellow coming down the aisle announcing, '*Lynchburg next! Lynchburg! Next stop, Lynchburg!*'

"I don't know what I was expecting. Whether I was expecting that all the coloured Amurcans were going to stand up and walk straight to the door and step down the metal step, and get off, jump off, at Lynchburg. Or, if they were going to stand their ground. To protest against retaining a name awful as that. *Lynchburg.*

"Can you imagine those Amurcans, of any stripe, and complexion, living-through that history, while white Amurcans, like the white-gents who marched down the aisle . . . and listening to that name, naming a town on a train line, a train station *Lynchburg? Lynchburg?* After all the lynchings that goes on in Amurca? My God-in-heaven!

"It is the same thing as naming a residential district in Israel Auschwitz Boulevard, in these present times, now that we know more about the Nazzies and the Jews. You don't think so? It is a ironical thing to do. As if somebody is making a joke. Yes.

"*Lynchburg!*

"After that, I lost interest in watching the places we were passing in that train journey. And in Amurca.

"So I took out my Bible, at *Philippians,* and read . . .

"'. . . *whatsoever things are true,*
Whatsoever things are honest
Whatsoever things are just . . .'

"Fields fly-past, and I didn't notice them; nor like them; and I didn't pay them no mind. Field after field of Indian corn. And other things that I didn't know the names thereof. And all I could think of was Lynchburg. And the coloured Amurcans sitting in the coach with me, in the compartment of the coloureds, eating their delicious Southern-fry chicken, in a serrigated train.

"But at last. Buffalo! Our final destination. The final solution to Mr. Bellfeels problems! Buffalo, where Mr. Bellfeels had come to buy second-hand Amurcan equipment for the Factory. And machineries. And cane-grinding engines.

"And it was in Buffalo, a pretty little town, near the Falls of Niagara, that I tasted my first Buffalo wings."

"A buffalo don't have wings, Miss Mary!"

"Try them!"

"Buffalo wings? A buffalo don't have wings, Miss Mary. A buffalo is a animal!

"They are named after the City of Buffalo. The wings, that is. Nor after water buffaloes, Percy. Chicken wings!

"Oh!"

"You eat them . . ."

PART TWO

"THAT EASTER MONDAY, twenty years ago . . . twenty years ago? . . . when I noticed you noticing me, my right hand had-in a water jug I was carrying, on orders from Ma to Mr. Bellfeels. The jug had-in rum. Bellfeels Special Stades White Rum. My closeness to him, through Ma, and later as he started to have me, first as house servant, and then as kip-miss, this closeness to him came with a smell, and a taintedness. It came strong from him, and became my own. I started to smell like him.

"All these years, from servant passing into kip-miss, I brought him his waters, at the dot of three o'clock. Cocktail hour. A saying he picked up in Buffalo.

"This smell of white rum. Yes.

"Wasn't long-after that first Sunday, when I looked upon the face of that man that looked so tall, with the sun shining in my face, facing Mr. Bellfeels; looking up, looking up to the top of the water tank, as if I was looking to trace the plight of a kite caught in a tree.

"Kite-season was times of love and niceness, colours and the humming of kite-tongues, laments of joy and fear. The kite-season was the first act to the tragedies of the hurricane season. The hurricane season. With a different humming sound. Not the kite-tongues this time. A greater humming. The humming of the wind. And the licking of the lightning, fork-lightning lighting-up the skies, and coming at you like a knife aiming for your throat. Death and murder. Misery and loss.

"In the kite-season, a poor boy loss a kite. And he break down in tears. A simple, cheap penny-kite, made from shop-paper. But to that poor boy, a priceless jewel.

"In storms and hurricanes, the loss is much more greater. Life. Deaths. Stragedies. I mean, tragedies. Water and wind. Winds and water turning into floods covering the land, covering the fields, the North Field of canes just planted; eddoes, yams and sweet potatoes, and the South Field planted up in corn, Indian corn, washed-away.

"The water was like in the Great Flood. When God was vex with this world. This time, God was vex with Bimshire. A deep layer of death and misery and drowning. It started on the Friday afternoon, just as the labourers had come in from the fields, and were lining-up in the Plantation Yard, under the tamarind tree, waiting to hear their names call-out to get their wages. Waiting for the bookkeeper to call-out their names. And a flash, Percy. When I tell you a flash? Of lightning. Like a sword. The Sword of Damocles henging over Bimshire. That was the first sign of dreadful things to come. Then, all o' we stanning-up under the tamarind tree . . . one wondering if the Shop have mackerel from Canada in stock, as promised; another woman wondering if her child-father coming round this weekend with any money; the third woman, poor soul, just wondering, wondering where the hell she going-get the balance of the money for her rent. It overdue three weeks now. Yes. We were there, lining-up for wages, with our minds on other things. What storm? What hurricane? Life this Friday afternoon is no different from other Friday goings-on, as per usual. Then, Percy, when I tell you without warning, a clap o' thunder! It shake the earth. The big tamarind tree in the Plantation Yard shudder. As if it was going to uproot itself, by itself. The half-ripe tamarinds start falling outta the tree. The labourers start to scatter, not waiting for their wages they were so frightened. And the rain came down in buckets-o'-drops. Men and women scamper for safety under the verandah of the Plantation Main House the minute the bookkeeper, scared as everybody-else, drop the few coppers in their hand. And then, they beat it cross the gap; cross the fields; for those who the fields was a shortcut to their house, and would take them home more faster; cross the long road of loose marl and gravel, heading for the tenements, and the junction of Highgates Commons and Reservoir Lane, bounding home. For shelter and safety. And that was the moment when the men and the women fleeing in all directions, like ants, that was the moment when the deluge of rain poured down upon our heads.

"In those days, they didn't give names to hurricanes and storms. But we, those of we who survive the three days and three nights of horror, we christen this one with a man's name. And pick Darnley, to call it by. Using one of Mr. Bellfeels Christian-names. Darnley the Hurricane. Or Hurricane Darnley. We christen it Darnley the Hurricane, the day after it ended.

"But you should have seen that man, Mr. Bellfeels. Like most of his type, he had-join the Sea Scouts as a boy, the First Bimshire Sea Scouts, despising as his clan does the other scout troops, namely the Land Scouts, as we used to call them. Being a Sea Scout at this hour of need came in handy and saved us.

"The lightning flashed. Like a knife. *Whhhhhhh!* Three seconds later. You could have count-off the time with a watch. *Blam-blam!* Over the North Field. *Whhhhhh! Whhhhh!* The lightning turn-into fork-lightning. The skies light-up. People bawling. Scared. *Blam, blam, blam! Blam!* The drops of rain so thick, coming down like a curtain o' lead, can't see two feet in front o' you.

"'Come-come! Come!' I hear the voice, and I couldn't move. Percy, when I hear the voice, I had to look round to make sure the voice addressing me. I thought it was the heavens talking to me. In times of natural disasters and fear, the very times become supernatural, like in the Bible.

"I look-round. And there is Mr. Bellfeels. On his horse. Holding-down, waiting, to grabble-me-up and put me in front o' him, on the saddle. 'Come-come! Come! I tekking you home to your mother. This blasted rain is a night-rain. A hurricane coming.' Well, when the next thunderclap came after the flash o' lightning, *whhhhh*, I was on that horse, my two legs straddling the saddle like any man. And through the downpour Mr. Bellfeels take me galloping, splatter-up water in the road, and deposited me at my front door. Ma was already home. I can't remember why; but she was home when Mr. Bellfeels deposited me, sliding down offa the horse, making my alighting more easier; and he put me down on the coral stone step.

"'I checking on the people,' he tell me. 'I have to see that the blasted labourers, nobody, don't drown 'pon the Plantation property. Tell your mother, if things go all right, I stopping-off when I pass-back. You hear me, girl?'

"I was either fourteen or fifteen.

"I had-barely step-in the house before the wind slam-back the door, luckily keeping me inside the house, before a limb from the mango tree growing at the side snap; and when I tell you, *brugguh-down*! It slam against the very front door, nailing the door shut, and me inside it, safe. Yes.

"The hurricane raged all night; and there was Ma and me, inside shivering through fright; and Ma holding the Bible in her hand, Gran sitting by the table, with her head in her hands, eyes closed, shaking her head from one side to the next, and mumbling words which I couldn't understand. Ma it was who told me later that it was her native language Gran was talking in, asking the spirits for mercy; and all the time Gran pleading to her African gods in her African dialect, Ma whispering, *'By Sin-Peter, and by Sin-Paul . . . by Sin-Peter, and by Sin-Paul, don't let this storm bury we alive in this house. Don't let this house be our grave in this Flood, please Lord, and overcome we . . .'*; and holding the Bible in her two hands, shut.

"Ma it was who filled-me-in, after Mr. Bellfeels deposit me on the step. And when he bound-off, I had to say that he reminded me of that coloured man in Amurcan History that Wilberforce tell me

about, who had-ride for miles and miles in weather that was not
clement, through hurricane and storm, enemy fire, gunpowder
and mortal danger to bring a message to the troops fighting in the
Amurcan War of Slavery and Independence, to liberate Amurca
from having to pay taxes on tea that was mannifactured in Englund
and which Englund unfaired them with, making them buy this tea
at outrageous prices. Yes! Mr. Bellfeels holding-over the horse-
mane with his body synchronize with the body of the horse; rider
and horse blended into one piece of machinery, driving through
the heavy downpour of rain, now for all intents and purposes a hur-
ricane, Hurricane Darnley; and traversing the Pasture, the fields,
every house in Plantation Tenantry, ducking from wallaba shingles
falling off roofs; galvanize-roofs sailing through the black night like
submarines, fast and just as deadly; even coconut trees falling like
pins in a game of bowling. And Mr. Bellfeels, according to Ma, who
had a soft spot still for that bastard, inside her heart, giving me,
after the third day and the third night, a running commentary of
the way he behave brave like a hero. During the performance of
Hurricane Darnley, Ma was reduce to silence, like the silence in
the Church Yard that Sunday after Church; holding her Bible, pray-
ing to God, with the pages shut. Ma. Poor Ma.

"Every house in the Tenantry was brought low-low-low by
Darnley the Hurricane. It reminded me, as Ma continued giving
me the commentary of Mr. Bellfeels exploits, not because he was
acting like a real Sea Scout for three days and three nights only, but
she was giving me details more as a means of softening the hard-
ness she knew I carried in my heart for that bastard. Yes.

"But anyhow, every house was lay-waste; brought low; at one
with the earth; roofs lick-off; whole sides of houses in the Ten-
antry blow-way, as they were all built with board, deal board
mainly; wood; now reduced to piles o' matchsticks; the mission-
houses that were opened to serve God, stripped bare to nothing,
back to the ground, to the land. It reminded me of the words in a
Christmas carol we used to sing in school . . . the hurricane hit we

in December, when people had-start varnishing and stripping and painting furnitures for the holidays; the ingreasements for the Christmas cake already soaking in jimmy-johns with raisins and rum, yes; that's why the hurricane remind me of the Christmas carol 'O Holy Night.'

'People on your knees, await your deliverance . . .'

"And I think another part of the same carol goes something like this:

"'Long lay the world in sin and error pining . . .
Fall on your knees, oh hear the angel voices.' Yes!
'Fall on your knees . . .'

"We certainly did fall on our two knees those three days and three nights of Darnley. The only buildings that was left standing when it was over, were the two elementary schools, the Church, the police sub-station and any wall-house made with cement and coral stone. Everything-else gone! At one stage, it was unsafe for anybody to stay in their house, so Mr. Bellfeels made a human chain with the people holding one another's hands, and he guided them, with him on the horse, from throughout the Tenantry, going from door to door, and led them to safety in the two Elementary Schools now without roofs; and who couldn't fit in the schools were guided to the Church, Sin-Davids Anglican Church.

"The other Churches in the Village, the Pilgrim Holiness, the Church of the Nazarene, the First Baptist and the First Congregation of the Shakers of Bimshire that people like the field hands and labourers, and people-so worship at, were all reduced to piles of matchstick. Raze to the ground. All. Gone. Yes.

"God in his wrath spared the dwellings of the mighty, the rich and the powerful. And reduce-to-rubbles the habitations of the humble, the meek and the poor. I asked God, as young as I was, *'Why?'* Why this vengeance visited upon the heads of the poor, the same poor which He said could go through a eye of a needle, and will inherit the earth? Why? Why, God? God, why?

"The answer is clear. We had sinned.

"We had sinned in our actions, in our lives, in our dealings with people living amongst us, with the truth.

"But, praise God, not a life was lost. Not a living-soul of this Village lost his life.

"But the slaughter of the stocks, the sheeps, the goats, the cows, horses, mules and donkeys—not to mention the fowls, the ducks and the turkeys—pure carnage. Bodies swell-up, bloated, eyes staring at you like the visages of mad people, but dead; bare circles, dead eyes that look like glass instead of pupils.

"And the stench that rose over the entire Village when the flood waters drain off, through the gullies, down the hills on their journey to the sea; the trail of destruction and desolation that was disclosed in their wake, my-God-in-heaven, it was as if the entire Flagstaff Village was transform into a huge abattoir of dead and rotting animals. A battlefield of the fallen, at the end of a fight. Something like in the Bible. That was the work of Darnley the Hurricane.

"But that is not all. Mr. Bellfeels. After he shepherd the other Villagers from their houses into the Elementary Schools and the Anglican Church, to safety, he came back for Ma and Gran and me. He take the three of us round to the back of the Main House, which faces the gully that looks out over the North Field, and surrounding fields, from where you could see the back of Guvvament House, where His Excellency Sir Stanley live; and into a shed which I think I told the Constable was built originally as a Dutch oven, to bake bread and cassava-hats in, but now was converted into a cottage. It was one large room, with four windows with shutters, with walls of raw cement, not painted, nor plastered too good; and the floor was the same raw cement as the walls, that wasn't treated. Two cots against one wall, and separating what look like the space for a bedroom from the rest of the room was a blind made out of a crocus bag, henging on a string made of herringbone twine. A one-burner stove, a wooden table, two upright chairs and nothing more. I felt, over the years, that Mr. Bellfeels had-bring us to the place where the cows that were with calf, and nearing birth, were tied before delivery. Or-else, the place where Watchie, the night watchman, changed. But it was safe. And it was clean. And dry, but with a touch o' dampness. The four walls were as thick as the walls of a fort or a castle, thick as the walls in a underground tunnel that runs underneat this Great House, thick as the walls of His Majesty's Glandairy Prison, then. Or Sin-Michaels Lighthouse, at Needhams Point.

"Mr. Bellfeels delivered us there. Safe. But drowning-wet, like three rats. To the skin. Thank God for small mercies! Yes.

"And I being only fourteen or fifteen—I can't remember which—but in more than a minute's-time sleep overtake me, and I collapse on one of the cots which Ma moved from the bedroom-area, out into the other space, probably to give herself some privacy. Gran scotch-off, meanwhile, on the same cot, with me . . .

". . . and drifting off to sleep, with the rumbling of the thunder no longer so close, and in my eardrums, but far off in the distance, over the West Coast, and the lightning flashing just as much as earlier, but no longer like a knife, sleep overtook me. In two-twos, both Gran and me were in another world. Yes.

"I don't know why. To this day, so many years after Darnley the Hurricane, I don't know why. I can't find the answer. And I don't know if it is my imagination; I don't know if it is what I saw with my two eyes; I don't know if it is what I wanted to see and to happen, and that I wished it in my recollection of that terrible Sunday night of the hurricane. But I swear that as the light of the dawning of the new day peeped through the shutters, the Monday—the hurricane had-begin on the Friday evening, and raged through the Friday night, Saturday morning into Saturday night, and was at its worst before it fizzed out, tired and exhausted, on the Sunday night—but with the first rays of the breaking morning, Monday, the start of a new week, the wood-doves didn't even start to coo yet, stupid-me, thinking that I was still home in our house, opened

my two eyes, stretched, break wind and got up, not noticing that it
was Gran side-o'-me, in the narrow white canvas cot. I headed in
the direction of what I thought was the back door leading to the
paling of our house, to wee-wee in the yard . . . I found myself in
the next room. Partitioned from me and Gran by the crocus bag
blind . . . there, on the cot was Ma. With Mr. Bellfeels on top of
her. Yes.

"Transfix by thus seeing my mother, Ma, underneat Mr.
Bellfeels, all I heard after this vision was '*Huhn, huhn, huhn, huhn,
huhn*,' coming from Mr. Bellfeels, muffling his voice, as if he didn't
want who was in the next room, Gran and me, to hear; and Ma
shaking her head, as if each *huhn* was a knife driving-in her heart.
'*Huhn, huhn, huhn, huhn, huhn* . . .'

"You remember that I begin this Statement by telling you that
when the hurricane petered-out, Mr. Bellfeels was so exhausted
that he sleep-through the Monday morning, the Monday night, the
Tuesday morning through the Tuesday night, and didn't wake up
nor come-to until the third day, the Wednesday?

"Well, this is how I know! Yes."

The room is quiet. From the BBC *Overseas* programme come the
voices of the choirboys of St. Martin's-in-the-Fields. Mary-
Mathilda holds her hands in her lap, and her eyes are fixed on them,
as if she is inspecting them for cleanliness; but she is picturing her-
self in Church, at Sin-Davids Anglican Church, instead of sitting
here, talking about a hurricane. Sargeant looks like a man numbed;
overcome by some drug, the effect of the story of Hurricane Darnley
on his mind; and he thinks of the mercilessness of the hurricane
which brutalized the Village; and he tries to recall his own experi-
ence of the three nights and three days of blackness and rain and
thunder and lightning which descended upon the land. His mind
does not go back over those years to pinpoint his own experience
of that tragedy. And this is what causes the expression of numbness
upon his countenance. He cannot recall many details of Hurricane
Darnley.

The Choir of St. Martin's-in-the-Fields is now singing Hymn 126. They have now reached the fourth verse. Sargeant knows this hymn by heart; and so, silently and to himself, he sings along with the voices coming through the speaker in such beautiful pronunciation and musical perfection. He sings the tenor part, along with the Choir, to this verse

> "'The pains of hell are loosed at last
> The days of mourning now are past.'"

and wishes for the second time tonight that he was in the Choir of Sin-Davids Anglican Church, and away from this Great House, in spite of its seductive pull upon his heart and his body, a pull he is trying both to accept and to reject.

She surprises him, by singing the last two lines of the fourth verse:

> "'An angel robed in light hath said,
> "The Lord is risen from the dead."'"

"Thirty-six hours ago," she says. Sargeant does not pay any attention to her. He is still thinking about Hurricane Darnley. "Thirty-six hours before this," she says again, "I was a different person."

"That is how life is," he says without interest.

"Yes! And thirty-six hours later, I am here."

The silence falls upon the room. She and Sargeant go back to listening to the Choir from St. Martin's-in-the-Fields.

"In police-work," he says, "'specially when you're on a 'vestigation, some of the strangest things does come into your mind, Miss Mary. Some o' the strangest things. With me, it is the fear that the man I tracking-down going-play a trick on me and get away. But not many have get-away from my paws. Not many. If I had one-hand only, I could count the number o' escapees on half the fingers on that one-hand who escape. But according to what you just said, in regards to the differences that time bestow, I, many a time stand-in-awe and tremble when it get dark, like tonight; and I not 'shamed to tell you that I fears that the man that I am tracking-down, could, if he get the chance, kill me before I nab him. Or kill *him*. But not one, so far, get that chance.

"The last murder in this Island, tek-place five years ago; and I was in-charge-of-the-'vestigation; spending many a dark night tracking-down that son-of-a-bitch—pardon my French, Miss Mary . . ."

"Boysie-Boys, you mean! Boysie-Boys terrorize the whole Island . . ."

". . . many a night tracking-down Boysie-Boys in the canes, in the gullies, in the caves back o' this very Plantation, in the woods; under cellars, and every step I take in the darkness, I imagine that Boysie-Boy have a knife to my throat. I could even feel the cold-ness of the steel in the blade of the knife in the crux of my neck. And taste my own blood.

"But I tell you, Miss Mary-Mathilda, God was with me. The very next night, I see-heem, crouching under a cluster o' pigeon-pea trees. I hold-on-more-tighter on my bull-pistle. All eighteen inches of it. And I creep-up-on-heem. Slow-slow. And quiet as a micey. And I measure-he-off, with regards to the distance he was from me, and the length o' my bull-pistle, plus the length of my hand holding the pistle. *Whapppp!* Miss Mary, when I drive the first lash in Boysie-Boys arse, he tremble. And then he shake. And then he stann-up. Straight-straight-straight as a arrow. And *whapppp!* Jesus Christ, when the second blow hit heem, Miss Mary, pardon my language, but when the second-one-hit-heem, and the bull-pistle land *whhhapps!* in Boysie-Boy's arse, excuse my . . ."

"He was terrorizing the whole Island!" she says.

"When the third lash hit-heem, I-myself was sorry for him!"

"Good-God! But still!"

"That was the last murder that tek-place in this Island.

"I sometimes does-think that some of the crimes I read-'bout in magazines that my daughter send-down from Amurca, dealing with murders and crimes in the Canadian North, and 'pon the Prairies, where the snow does be ten feet deep, and white-white-white, falling ten months outta twelve, and the Mounties and the RCMPees tracking-down criminals and serial killers, on foot and sometimes on horseback, when I read about them crimes, I does imagine that I am facing the same breed o' criminals and mass murderers, in this Island.

"In a magazine, I read about a fellar who kill thirty-five women in three months . . . in Canada."

"Thirty-five murders? And *all* women?"

"At the ratio of thirty-five murders to three months, that comes out to seven killings every month, or one every twenty-eight, or thirty-one days, as thirty days hath September, April, June and November, all the rest have thirty-one days, excepting February alone, which hath . . ."

". . . but twenty-eight . . ."

". . . and twenty-nine in each leap year."

"God-have-His-mercy!"

"I sometimes think that the level o' crimes and criminals that I reads about that is part of Amurcan life, and life in the Canadian North, will one day reach these peaceable shores of Bimshire. But I pray to God, and hope not."

"Oh, North Amurca!" she says. "I told you that I visited Amurca? I did. Didn't I? But thinking about it now, I don't even know what I related as a experience undertaken by me actually might not've been something that I undertaken. You know what I mean?

"It could be that I was relating a story I read in a book. It don't matter if I remember actually going to Miami-Florida. If I was actually on that train going north. It is not those facts that I claiming to be true. The story itself is the thing. That experience of living through the story. Wilberforce tell me that you could pick up so much knowledge from travelling, that the more you travel the less you sometimes know exactly where it is that you travel to.

"I see things when I sit-down in my chair, and I am studying. And I see things when I dream. And I cannot make a distinction between living-out a story, and reading a story.

"I think that is how the journey to Amurca happened. It was the story that I wanted to give to you. I may not have visited Amurca. And then-again, I may-have-in-fact visited Amurca.

"But I know that those coloured ladies eating Southern-fry chicken out of paper bags, on the train, is one and the same thing in real life, as in my imagination. It is the fact, and it is the story.

"Also, the Buffalo wings . . . Yes.

"The Buffalo wings. And the eighty-one-year-old woman who I heard singing the blues."

"Amurcans are real singers!"

"The best in the world!"

"If you don't mind me putting this to you," he says, "what we are going do with him?"

"With who?"

"Bellfeels."

"*Mr.* Bellfeels, you mean!" she corrects him.

"Mr. Bellfeels. Sorry. What we going to do about Mr. Bellfeels? We can't sit down here all night and not face facts, Miss Mary. We got to face facts. What are we going do with Mr. Bellfeels?"

"In the matter of this case?"

"In the matter of this case," he says. "And in tekking the evidence that belongst to this case."

"In the taking of the evidence."

"And from who?"

"Who from?"

"Witnesses. From supporting witnesses. 'Leviating circumstances, with evidence in support; and things-so. And it is getting late, although the time is moving in slow motion, like in a magic lantern."

She remains still; "studying," as she calls thinking; and the night seems to stand still, too: crickets are chirping; fireflies that were drops and flickers of light, like starlights seen from a distance, disappear altogether; or else are dropping dead, falling off into nothing; the nothing that the night becomes: thick, heavy, shining with blackness; a blackness like death.

"Wilberforce coming into my thoughts," she says, "with such a heaviness of soul and spirit. Why, at a time like this?

"Very often Wilberforce would be in this same room, sitting down just where you are, and not one word would pass between him and me. And then-again, he and me would be in this room, and would be talking and chatting and laughing our head off. Wilberforce playing the piano, and me singing along. Or else, just listening . . .

"I bet you that the wife of the Solicitor-General, or the wife of Revern Dowd or the wife of either of the two leading barsters-at-Law, even the wife of the Headmaster of the Elementary School, are all women schooled in the ways of appreciating music. And that they could tell you everything about music and art. And beautiful things. Things like the pictures on this wall that we were trying to figure out. We got some answers right. But we didn't pass the exam, though. Even a simple thing like the meaning of *tisket*. These simple things that are so hard. And being such, being schooled in these better things of life, even in this Plantation life, is the explanation of their not-ever giving me a invitation into their fronthouses, to have tea with them. Or to dinner. Saturday night after Saturday night will come and pass, and you will find me here, watching the stars and the tops of the canes. Watching the four walls, as the saying goes. A invitement from one o' them bitches to dinner in their home? I would dead waiting for one! Not even for a cucumber sangwich . . . not that their cooking is anything to make your mouth water! So tasteless; and without salt. And don't talk about no pepper! Yes . . .

"It is not that they are prejudice, and serrigating me. I don't think they have a dislike for my colour. They just couldn't be so prejudice and serrigating!

"They are not, after all, Amurcans. No,

"Not in this regards

"Or am I fooling myself?"

"I don't know, Miss Mary. You are more closer to white people, than me. To-besides, the only white people I know is the ones round-here, that I grow up with. And sometimes I don't know them at all. But the real white? The only ones I know is the woman who missed the ball and fall-down and hit the paling at the Savannah Lawn Tennis Club; and the clerkess, Miss P. Weatherhead from the Perfumes and Fragrances Department at Cave Shepherd & Sons, Haberdasheries, who one day in Town showed me a bottle o' Eau de Cologne No. 4711; and rubbed some on my hand. A perfume like your perfume. On my left hand. On the back. Plus, the Commissioner o' Police. But I won't call them bosom-friends."

"And the Revern," she tells him; and he nods, agreeing; and she adds, "And what about the Solicitor-General and the Headmaster of Harrison?"

"You didn't tell me to name-off all the white people that exist in this Island!"

"And how you see *these* local white people?"

"These white people that I name-off, that born here? They're not just white people. They are Bimshire-people. Like me and you. Regardless to what they say. Or feel. But Amurcans, on the other hand . . ."

"And the English?"

"I don't make no exceptions between the two o' them two races. The Amurcans and the English to me is one-and-the-same. Six o' one, and half dozen of the next!"

"I couldn't be fooling myself, all these years, you think so? . . . I feel that it is education, and knowing things, like the meaning of a *tisket* and a *tasket*, the real meaning of 'The Ride of the Valkyries' and understanding *Head of the Madonna*. Things so; and certain other words, and things, like being able to play 'The Ride of the Valkyries' on a violin, or the piano; and be able to explain the history behind 'The Ride of the Valkyries.' Knowing these things is what separates the wife of the Solicitor-General, or the Commissioner wife, from me."

"You really think so, Miss Mary?"

"Take 'The Ride of the Valkyries.' I have heard it so many times that every time I hear it, I learn something more about Mr. Bellfeels. And the Solicitor-General. But moreso about the Solicitor-General, because he is a Englishman. A pure European. Mr. Bellfeels, on the other hand, is a Bimshire-white, with mix-blood, the same don't apply . . .

"You remember the calypso we used to sing 'bout-here, the one they made on Clotelle? And you remember how all o' we knew the words, by-heart? Well, that was our way of celebrating Clotelle, even though it was a tragedy. That made it, therefore, a damn-strange kind o' celebration.

"Well, it was no celebration at all. No. It was a memorial. Like a wake. And it was our way, the Village way of telling the whole Island, the world, everybody, people living and people not born yet, but who, when they hear the calypso, would know that Clotelle existed in a certain time, lived in that time and met her death in that time, by certain means. Our singing the calypso on Clotelle was our way of saying these things to the world.

"That calypso was therefore something like a history, or like a myth. I got that word, *myth*, from Wilberforce. We were building-up a myth over Clotelle. It is something like a shrine, then. Yes?

"That is the word! Maybe that is the word!

"But whether-or-not, you know what I mean. Clotelle is a local shrine, a myth.

"'The Ride of the Valkyries,' played on that piano by Wilberforce, all these years that I have sit and listened to him playing it, is the same thing. A shrine. Or a myth. Yes.

"The least it is, is a story about Europeans from that part of the world, just north of the Eyetalian mountains, the Eyetalian Alps. The Dollaramites. I am smart-enough to know that.

"It tells me what a cruel race o' people they were. With all the killing they executed over the ages. Both there. And down-here. There first. Then, with Columbus and all o' them, Drake, Hawkins, Newton, Bligh and Lord Horatio Nelson, turned their affection to down-here. The only exception, so far, in present times, is Winston Churchill, the leader of the Allieds . . . and we still have to watch him.

"The killings by Europeans appears plain-plain-plain in their music. . . .

"I wish, though, and I would give anything to find out, that I could know the name of the man who compose this piece o' music, 'The Ride of the Valkyries.' And what was-going-through his mind when he was putting those notes, breves and semi-breves, quavers and semi-quavers, 'pon paper. What he was thinking?"

"That is easy, Miss Mary. The name of the composer is written-down on the front page of the music-sheet."

"Really?"

"Always. You know where the music-sheet to 'The Valkyries' is?"

"Well, you know something? Perhaps this is why. There is no music-sheet. There never was a music-sheet."

"There-gotta-be!"

"When Wilberforce was learning the piano, the music-sheets were the property of his teacher, Miss Smith; and when the lesson done, Miss Smith took-up the music-sheets, put them inside her leather portfolio and gone! And that, ironically, is what made Wilberforce into such a good piano player. He had to memorize every note by heart."

"With that kind o' memory for music, Mr. Wilberforce should have take-up the concert stage! That is how the most brilliant piano players in the world, like Artur Rubinstein, become stars on the international concert stage. That is what virtuosos are made out of!

"Wilberforce took up the next best thing. So far as memory and memorization is concerned."

"What that is?"

"Tropical Medicines!"

"Course! Though I never look at it that way. But I suppose now that you make me think of it, that it take even more greater memory and memorizing to be a doctor. To have to remember all the various parts inside of a human body; all the proscriptions you have to write; all the insides, the lungs, the heart, the liver, the spleens, the veins, the blood, and the various calesterols contained in the blood . . .

"I watches him and I pay attention when he tends to other patients, when I'm in his Surgery, or in the Casualty at the hospital, with a suspect. And sometimes watching Mr. Wilberforce, I does-wish I was a doctor. But I didn't even went to high school, although I took private lessons after school, to get into Combermere."

"Wilberforce tell me that Mr. Edwards, the teacher you had at Sin-Davids Elementary, tried his very best with you, with private tuitions in Latin and History, for the scholarship-exam, the bursary, to get-you-in Combermere School for Boys free. Wilberforce tell me what a hard struggle Mr. Edwards had with you with Latin. But you were very good in History. Is a pity you didn't come twenty-fourth, 'stead-of twenty-fiff, just *one* more, and you would have had a scholarship. Free high-school education, to prepare you for one of the professions. Wilberforce say your teacher tried his best with you. Wilberforce was much more younger than you when the same teacher, Mr. Edwards, gave him private tuitions. But Wilberforce was always bright for his age."

"History I could take. But not the Latin."

"Latin is a hard language."

"Latin is a old, dead language. The language the Romans and, later, the Eyetalians used to speak. I could never understand why a dead language had to be so hard to learn."

"The people who used to speak it are now dead . . ."

"My teacher, Mr. Edwards, used to tell me that wasn't it funny that the people who spake those dead languages are the people we still worship today, as being the people who civilized the whole world! Dead people.

"Dead people could civilize any world? You mekking sport! Miss Mary, I used to think, before Mr. Edwards showed me this strange thing about human nature and human civilization, that if the people of a certain part of the world who had a certain civilization die-off, therefore the civilization that they had would consequently dead with them, too. That don't make sense to you? It mekking sense to me. But it was my elementary schoolteacher, Mr. Edwards, who-first made me understand that certain civilizations live on and on, even after all the people of those civilizations was dead. Like the Latin and Greek civilizations.

"But one afternoon, years later, soon after Mr. Wilberforce had just come back from studying up in Oxford, Mr. Edwards was reminding me of those pre-historic, ancient times . . ."

"*And* Cambridge! Don't leff-out Cambridge. Wilberforce studied both in Oxford and Cambridge. Mr. Bellfeels see to that."

". . . and at Cambridge, when he was telling me and Mr. Edwards about his time up in Englund, and about the British Empire, because the year I took the scholarship exam, one of the questions in the General Knowledge Examination paper was, What are the things that the British Empire, meaning in other words Englund, what are the natural resources of Englund? Well, Miss Mary, I'm not ashame to tell you . . ."

"I know. Wilberforce came in, laughing-his-head-off!"

"I didn't know I was such a fool to have-give the British Empire *so much* credit and so much know-how in the lines of their ownership of natural resources from which they were producing products."

"Exports," she says.

"Exports? What do you mean by exports?"

"You were mixing-up exports with products."

"Mr. Edwards axe me one day, 'Percy, name one thing that Englund produces.'

"'One thing?' I axe him.

"'One thing.'

"'Iron, sir,' I tell Mr. Edwards. 'Englund produces iron.'

"'Good, Percy,' he tell me. 'Name another product that Englund produces.'"

"I heard all about it," she says. "Not that Mr. Edwards was bringing tales outta school!"

"At the time, Miss Mary, it wasn't no laughing matter."

She goes to the Victrola grammaphone, and searches in the box which holds the records, for one to play.

"'Frenesi,'" she says.

"Artie Shaw!" he says. "And his orchestra!"

"Big-band music, boy!" she says. "The times I danced to 'Frenesi'! But you were telling me about the things that Englund produces."

"Yes. All those things that I had-come across, with 'Made in Englund,' and 'Mannifactured in Englund,' and 'English-made' stamp on them. Consequently I conclude as a result that from English natural resources, they were mannifactured into English products, native to Englund. And I gave him examples: chocolates; tea biscuits by McVitie & Price, makers of the finest quality biscuits, in Edinburgh and London and in Manchester . . . and teas, like Red Rose Tea, and Typhoo Tea; and candies. All these things I said were grown up in Englund and mannifactured in Englund, as natural resources."

"Red Rose Tea?" she says. "Isn't that Canadian?"

"Still the British Empire!"

"The things we read in the *Illustrated London News*!"

"And other magazines."

"Those magazines are like Nazzi-time!"

"The Windsor Chair."

"And William Kent bureaux."

"And Louis the Sixteen cabinets."

"They're French."

"In name only. But they are mannifactured in Englund."

"And Sheraton chairs. I have one in this front-house. You see it, there, under the window that looks out on the North Field?

"That chair is my favourite chair. The chair in which I sit and do my studying in, where I listen to the sounds of the night . . . crickets and blind-bats flying through the house when they get lost, smelling the flowers . . . my studying chair."

"And Brown Windsor Soap."

"A Roberts Original."

"Why do we know all these things?"

"From books the people in Englund make us read in school."

"But the question about English mannifactures didn't turn up on the General Knowledge paper. I left the exam room early after that, from nervousness and my palms sweating," Sargeant says. "Do you remember Bronnley fine English soaps? My mother used to steal it from the hotel where she was a servant. I grew up bathing in Bronnley fine English soap, in a wallaba tub of cold water, six o'clock every morning, with mint leaves thrown into the water. The smell of Bronnley would cling to me all day. Anyway, I left the examination room early, from nervousness and my two palms sweating, and therefore didn't obtain a Vestry so I could attend Combermere School for Boys free. Consequently-hence, my lack o' secondary education. And not being able to be a doctor, or a barster-at-Law. But I still make Crown-Sargeant!"

"We're talking too much, Percy. Why we don't listen to some music, to take our mind off the circumstances? My nerves need settling. Let me play-over 'Frenesi,' for you. I even love the name of this song! 'Frenesi.' It must be a word from the Spanish language. You think so? Or is it from the Eyetalian language? Which you think?"

"Spanish. But it could be from the Eyetalian."

"Much of a muchness."

"I bet you that 'Frenesi,' whether it is Spanish or Eyetalian, have the same meaning. I bet you."

"How we would know whether you win, or me?"

"Wilberforce."

"Yes, Wilberforce would know."

"Wilberforce knows everything."

"Yes. Wilberforce. He knows anything."

"Wilberforce should know!" she says. "Never a minute without his head inside a book."

She says it in such a way as to let Sargeant understand that everyone else in the Village is aware that her son knows everything, or almost everything, about anything . . .

"Let we listen to 'Frenesi' a second time, then."

"'Frenesi' by Artie Shaw. Big-band music, boy! The best music you could ever dance to and listen to! Artie Shaw! Once upon a time, there was no big-band orchestra music more sweeter to listen to than Artie Shaw. Not even Duke Ellington. But the thing with Duke Ellington, and him not regarded as a more better big-band musicianer than Artie Shaw, was the simple fact that they never played much Duke Ellington music on the radio; and we never get the chance to hear nothing-much by Duke Ellington. But when the first records was heard, either through somebody coming back from the War, or from cutting canes in Florida, or even from the Panama Canal, that was the moment we start hearing Duke Ellington. Real swing-band music! And Duke Ellington became the true-true king of Swing.

"But for a time there, it look as if Artie Shaw would rule the waves forever. With 'Frenesi.'"

"It was the foreign name! People in this Island are lovers of foreign names, and foreign things, and foreign places. As such, you would agree that 'Frenesi' is a prettier name than 'Take the A Train'! Although when you hear Duke Ellington music, versus Artie Shaw, it is a horse of a different colour."

"Chalk-and-cheese!"

"So, let we listen to the music, then," she says. "But Sargeant," she adds, "you play the piano, so why you don't play 'Frenesi' for me? Or any other piece of big-band dance music. 'Frenesi' was the rave when we used to go to dances. Although you and me never went to the same dance. Nor never danced together.

"You and me went together mainly to Church outings and picnics. You went with the men, to the 'brams,' mainly where men mostly congregate. Like the Shed, in Queen's Park. Constable say that you really like to play the piano for your bosom-friends on a Friday night. Isn't that the piano I hear your daughter send-down from Amurca, by boat?"

"The first girl!"

"Ruby, then!"

"Ruby, the first-daughter."

"In domestic work, isn't she?"

"Domestic work."

"You ever see the mother?"

"The mother left for Demerara sixteen months after Ruby born."

"And never looked back?"

"Never look backwards to see what happen to her own thrildren."

"And the second child?"

"Pass-away."

"Lord-have-His-mercy . . . may she rest . . ."

". . . in peace . . ."

"Domestic work up in Brooklyn, eh?"

"Engineering is what they calls it by, in Brooklyn. Domestic engineering."

"Domestic engineer."

"Nevertheless."

"Nevertheless."

"'Whatsoever things are pure
Whatsoever things are lovely . . .'"

"Is that from the Bible?" he asks.

"She's a treasure!" she says.

"That piano must keep you company better than any woman. And please you, too."

"I tickles the ivories, now and then! And learn to bang-out a few things . . . mostly popular pieces. I hear a tune on the radio, or listen to it on a grammaphone record, and the next thing I know, I start picking, and picking, and quick-so, I learn the tune. Not all the parts, mind you. Just the bottom line. The basic melody. Until when the postman pass and deliver the sheet-music, or the song-book that I happen to axe Ruby to send-down for me, come."

"The Thirties! The years of the best dance music!" she says. "Though 'Frenesi' came out in 1940."

"A year after 'Moonlight Serenade,' then."

"By the same Artie Shaw."

"No! No, Miss Mary! I sorry, but I have to disagree. 'Frenesi' did, in-true-and-in-fact, come out in 1940. But in 1939, the year before 1940, it wasn't Artie Shaw who compose 'Moonlight Sere-nade.' It was Glenn Miller."

"Didn't he give us 'In the Mood'?"

"Yes. But he also gave we 'Moonlight Sonata' . . . I mean, 'Ser-enade.' It was in 1940 that again Artie Shaw gave we 'Stardust.'"

"'Frenesi'?"

"Nineteen forty."

"'I Can't Get Started'?"

"Thirty-seven!"

"Who by?"

"Bunny Berigan and His Orchestra."

"'Dipsy Doodle'?"

"Tommy Dorsey and His Orchestra."

"Year?"

"I can't remember the year."

"Yuh slipping."

"The mind, Miss Mary, the mind."

"And 'Moonlight Sonata' . . . 'Moonlight Serenade,' as you said?"

"Nineteen thirty-nine!"

"And Glenn Miller and His Orchestra?"

"We covered everything, far's the big bands. With one exception."

"Who?"

"Duke Ellington!"

"No! Don't let we forget Count Basie! And Billy Eckstine! And Cab Calloway! And the one-and-only Louis Jourdan! And Fat Swaller!"

"And Les Brown?"

"Yes. Les Brown. And his Band of Renown! A funny name for a big band."

"'Stardust'! Still my favourite. 'Specially when I hear Nat King Cole sing it. Is a hard tune to learn how to play. All them changes, and the flats and the minor keys. But I pick and pick till I mastered it, though."

"We'll turn off the grammaphone, and listen to you play 'Stardust.' I can do even better than that. I can give you the sheet-music . . ."

She chooses the chair with the high back, a kind of rocking chair made from mahogany, with its back covered in a piece of brocade cloth, with flowers in its pattern. This brocade is draped over the back, covering it like a man's jacket, tight-fitting, following the outline of the back of the chair, which is as strong and defined as a man's chest. The chair is close to the window. Sargeant follows her with his eyes, as she chooses her place. And behind her head, through the opened window, he can imagine the canes, now clothed in a dark, dark green hue. The light that this Sunday evening gives them unwillingly, and sparingly, is not good to see in; but he can still imagine that he can see the sugar-cane fields around him, wide as the sea; and the waves of the canes; and although there is no wind and no breeze at this moment, he imagines them moving, as they do in the daytime; and their white silk arrows, silk even in the night light, but white only in the light of a hot sunny day, touching the tops of the canes that surround him in their cruel, skin-cutting fierceness, just like the sea, on that afternoon years ago: around four o'clock when the sun is fiercest, when he slipped from the side, when he was sitting on the gunwale of the fishing boat HMS *Barracuda* that belonged to Manny's father, too far out in the sea, fishing for kingfish, when he dropped fast and definite into the churning waves, and disappeared, in the twinkling of an eye, before Manny's eyes, and before Manny's father's unbelieving eyes. *"Jesus Christ, the boy gone! Percy? Percy, you gone? Man-overboard! Jesus Christ! Man overboard! Quick, Manny! Quick-quick!"* And they tossed the anchor overboard after him because they had no inner tube which served as a lifesaver; and Sargeant's weight, heavy for his age, was making him sink faster than the makeshift anchor Manny's father had fashioned out of the rim of the wheel of the tire of a motorcar, could sink; down-down like the anchor of HMS *Barracuda* itself into the green slimy sea . . . . Looking at this thick dark greenness now, he feels safer, more comfortable; at ease now, as if he is used to the tranquility of this house, as if he is a regular visitor to this Great House, and the big houses on the Plantation estate, and the Plantation Main House, as if he is, at last, getting even with Mr. Bellfeels; dispossessing him.

The smell from the bushes, and from the thick, prickly, studded trees round the House, under the windows, comes up full into his nostrils. Although he cannot memorize the names of the smells, does not know the names of bush, tree, vine or stalk, he knows there is beauty in the night, on this black, moonless Sunday evening; and love; and that there can be love making.

If he ever had the good fortune to sit in this House, on an ordinary day, earlier, just after the huge, fiery sun was touching the skim of wave and water far out where the German submarine had met the HMS *Cornwallis*, he would have been able to see the riot of colours, the drama of trees pushing against one another, the arrogant, supercilious disregarding casuarina trees that border the limit, boundary and ownership of the Plantation. He would have been able to see colour and colours. But the Plantation is limitless.

Now, all he can see, and he is not even certain that he is not imagining these tints and hues, as he had earlier imagined the violence and had fantasized the desperate criminal coming through the North Field, towards him; all he can see now, is the unending sweep of dark green, like a sheet of water, big as the sea, big and dark as the sea that night, when he fell from the gunwale of HMS *Barracuda* . . . There was something beautiful, something inexplainable, something almost religious about the thickness of his fear and fantasy, earlier, as he had stood foolishly with his Raleigh bicycle leaned against his body; and he, a Crown-Sargeant, useless beside it . . . But he is not useless now. He is inside. Inside the front-house of this Great House. And the size, and the grandeur, and the smell, of furniture and of cleanliness, of flowers cut from the gardens that are below the huge windows, all this, this quiet, this silence, this tranquility, makes him brave and confident . . . She finds the sheet-music, just before he reaches the piano bench; and she takes it out, passes it over the skirt of her dress, cleaning the dust off, and then she places it on the music stand that comes up over the keys. The built-in music stand conceals the name of the manufacturer of the piano, printed in Italic Script.

He flings the lid of the grand piano back with a flourish he had never been capable of imitating before.

He is surprised that the lid does not cry out when it touches its acquainting rich, expensive wood from which it is made. The ivories do not sigh, even.

He has never before sat at a piano of such beauty and magnificence. He can see his face in its polish. He can see his eyes in the sheen of the black keys. And his hands begin to shake.

He is incapable of going further, of imagining his life further from this first touch of gentility and graciousness; this is like a journey into the unknown; through a cave; a challenge to embark upon this journey that he somehow knows he cannot take on. It is more than an ordinary moving of fingers over keys, of touching pedals, of travelling through notes over a landscape of such great, tragic foreignness, for any great distance . . . The pages of the sheet-music do not remain flat. She holds her hand on the pages, and then thinking better of it, takes from the pocket of her dress a long wooden clothespin. She affixes this clothespin onto the pages. The pages sit obediently, open, in the full reflection of the light in the room. She closes the book of sheet-music, just for one moment, to check that the cover bears the name of the song. The name is printed on the cover. There is a design. The design is a circle, with the name of the song inside it. The design shows something, specks of something rising. Of dust? Of stardust? Of sand that is like dust on the beach at the Crane Beach Hotel? But she has never seen any other dust but the white, fine powder that rises from the roads whenever a bus or a lorry or a motor-car speeds along the Front Road, the highway where it meets at Highgates Commons and Reservoir Lane.

"You ready?" she asks him.

"I am ready."

"'Stardust,'" she says.

"'Stardust,'"he says.

But he cannot play it. The surroundings are too overwhelming.

The window is open, and he suddenly becomes afraid, frightened that he is on HMS *Barracuda*; and he is drowning.

His earlier confidence slips away from him. Leaves his power, just as the cane juice slips out of his mouth when he sucks a piece of Juice-nine-tray-five sugar cane.

She rises from her rocking chair, and she goes and sits on the piano bench, beside him.

She places her hands over his. And as if she is a kindergarten teacher guiding him in the first curves of learning Penmanship, controlling his handwriting; she guides his hand over the keys; and he looks up at her; into her eyes; and she gives him back the look; and he closes his eyes because he knows the music by heart; and she locks her eyes onto his closed eyes, and continues to guide his hands over the keys.

His hands look blacker as they touch the white keys. Her hands, lighter by three or four shades, stand out against his. She removes her hands. He allows his hands to rest on the keys they were covering.

No sound rises from the keyboard.

The white ivories and the black ivories are like the conch shell which is discarded on the beach, without the benefit of a pair of lips placed to it to force a tune from it. No noise. No music. No sound.

He leaves his hands on the keys.

He remembers how another hand touched his hands, shaking and exploring, frightened and daring; and regarded them as ignorant hands, stupid hands; hands that bore the anxiety and the drama of defeat in learning Penmanship years ago in Sin-Davids Elementary School for Boys . . . It was about two in the afternoon; and the room was hot. Humid. Sweat—which the Headmaster called "spirsperration"—was running irrepressible and unrestrained, down his face in two small, slow streams; and he could feel their stickiness and their warmth as they dropped upon his sea-island cotton shirt; and this white shirt he had worn to Church the day before, for his regular school shirt, made of thick, cheap, raw khaki, was still wet from the rain that had fallen all Sunday afternoon, Sunday night and right into early Monday morning.

The blackboard was lined; and they were double lines; and the lines were drawn into the thick blackboard with a nail; and the slate in his hand was black like the blackboard; and lined; and it had a wooden frame; and someone had drawn those double lines even before he was born. Generations before.

The slate in his hand had been scratched on and disfigured in the calculation of the nine-times table; the three-times table; and simple arithmetic, by his own father.

"Manners maketh man," his teacher, Mr. Edwards, is saying. "What manners maketh?" he asks his class. There are fifteen boys in his class. His class is Standard Five.

"What manners maketh?"

"Manners maketh man, sir!" they shout, rivalling one another for loud-
ness . . .

"Louder!" Mr. Edwards yells at them.

And they scream, even louder, that the entire school can hear them,
"Manners maketh . . ."

The school is one large room, divided by the placing of black-
boards which spin around on a pin, in certain positions, to form
walls; to form classes or "standards."

There are seven "standards," excluding Low-Primer and High-
Primer, in the one-roomed school.

Boys "graddiated" from elementary school, in Standard Seven.
Some went on to Combermere School for Boys, a secondary Gov-
ernment school. Others entered various apprenticeships. Or they
fielded tennis balls in the afternoons, at the Garrison Savannah
Lawn Tennis Club, as Sargeant got to do. Or watered the flower
gardens of the rich who lived in Belleville Avenue, in Hastings, in
the Married Women's Quarters in the Garrison. Or they joined
the gangs of labourers in the North Field of the Plantation. Some
became fishermen. Some became carpenters. Some became thieves.
Some became gamblers throwing dice. "Dice don't nick five! Dice
don't nick five, man! Six cents the dice don't nick five! Mek it
seven!"; playing rummy and jacks, all day on the Pasture. Many never
worked. Some died without ever having worked one day in their
lives. All were black. Black boys with beautiful physiques and erect
posture, all "graddiates" or "school-leavers" of Sin-Davids Elemen-
tary School for Boys. Three from Sargeant's days went to Englund
to fight in the Second World War; some before that, in the First
World War. In Sargeant's time, two were killed by a mine, some-
where in France. One returned as a Private, First Class; with no
medals. And ten went to Amurca. Four got their letters addressed
"in care of Ancon Post Office" in the Canal Zone, in Panama, in
Central Amurca, before they disappeared. Some swept the large
front yards and grounds of those rich people who lived in Hastings.

Like Sargeant, a few qualified for admission to the Bimshire Constabulary as recruits. And more than that number became grooms, and bathed racehorses in the strong currents of the sea, at Gravesend Beach, near the Aquatic Club, near the Garrison Race Course, which the Villagers called the Race Pasture, every morning of the week, at five o'clock, just before most of the regular population arrived at the beach to take a dip. Manny went into his father's business. Selling rum and killing pigs. Yes, of the hundreds of boys who "graddiated" from Standard Seven, *not one*, over the years, ever ended up sitting in a front-house like this one, unless he was a servant. Not even as a visitor. And certainly not, as Sargeant is allowing his imagination to roam, as a suitor.

He is aware of where he is. Yes . . . And her hands are no longer touching his. They are placed in her lap. In the rich, white folds of her muslin dress.

Her hands are not moving. In his mind, he goes back to that humid afternoon, when Mr. Edwards, his teacher, screamed the instruction, *"Wunnuh going write out 'Manners maketh man' fifty times! Wunnuh hear? Wunnuh hear?"*

The teacher had grabbed the thick tamarind rod from the shelf on the easel of the blackboard where the white chalk is kept.

"Wunnuh hear?"

"Yes, sir!" they scream.

"What manners maketh?"

"Man, sir!"

"Again!"

"Man, sir!"

"What manners maketh, class?"

"Manners maketh man, sir!"

"Good."

That same afternoon, at three-thirty, he has to meet Mr. Edwards for his private tuition lessons.

They are going to talk about the things produced in Englund, from Englund's natural resources. English products. It is on this

afternoon that Sargeant learns about the fine biscuits and choco-
lates and pipe tobacco, and cigarettes and toiletries and soaps and
teas that Englund produce. . . .

"*Ten-sixty-six?*"

"*The Battle of Hastings, Mr. Edwards.*"

"*Good. The Battle of Bannockburn?*"

"*Twelve-fifteen? Twelve . . . sixteen?*"

"*Signing of the Magna Carta?*"

And Sargeant knows this; and screams, "Twelve-fifteen!"

"*When Cromwell take-over Parliament?*"

And he knows this, too.

"*Battle of the Roses?*"

He knows this, too.

"*Cranmer? When Cranmer get kill?*"

Sargeant hesitates.

"*Executed?*"

Sargeant hesitates.

"*Beheaded?*"

Sargeant remembers this.

"*You going win a scholarship, boy! You going win a Secondary-to-
Second-grade, for-true!*"

And Sargeant takes the Secondary-to-Second-Grade Examina-
tion, which is held at the Drill Hall, the lecture room of the
Bimshire Volunteer Regiment and Brigade; and the examination
lasts all morning; and Sargeant is sweating; for the questions on the
examination paper are questions Mr. Edwards had rehearsed him
in, Friday after Friday, Saturday after Saturday, for one full year;
and on Wednesdays, Fridays *and* Saturdays, two weeks before the
examination; but the heat in the room, from his own anxiety and
that of one hundred other boys, from all over the Island, makes his
hands sweaty, his palms sticky, increases his need to pee, to have to
ask for a "step-out"—"*Please, sir, may I have a step-out? I have to pass
water, bad, sir!*"—to make the Watermans fountain pen leak; and
mark his fingers black; and blot the paper on which he writes his

answers, many of them incorrect; and then, two months later, the results of the Secondary-to-Second-Grade come back from the examiners and are published Island-wide in the *Bimshire Daily Herald*; and Sargeant, listed officially and formally as STUART, P. DaC. B., comes *twenty-fifth*.

There are twenty-four places.

"Be-Christ!" Mr. Edwards says the Saturday morning, holding the *Bimshire Daily Herald* crushed violently in his right hand, pointing the newspaper and the hand at Sargeant, as if it is a tamarind rod, with the Official Results crushed in his grip, reading them off to Sargeant. "Let we pray that a boy, *any* one of the twenty-four that come before you, dead. Just-drop-down dead! So you could squeeze-through. Some boy. Any fecking boy . . ."

"*Manners maketh man.*"

. . . Yes, his hands are placed in the exact position, this Sunday evening, in this tranquil Great House, as they had been placed, poised, on his black slate, double-lined by a nail, when he was being coached by Mr. Edwards in the rudiments of Penmanship.

"*Penmanship is next to Godliness!*" Mr. Edwards had shouted many times. "*What is Penmanship next to?*"

"*Godliness, sir!*"

This time, there is more affection in the instruction he is being given; or that he is about to receive from Mary-Mathilda.

Her hands are soft. And they smell of perfume. And they are not sweaty. And they do not have the veneer of dust from the chalk on them. And they do not have thick, black hairs. And their nails do not have a line of black dirt underneath them. And they do not smell of tobacco. And they do not have knuckles that make the hands look deformed and swollen at the joints. And her fingers do not have the marks left by the kitchen knife, as Gertrude's have.

Her hands are soft, and shapely; with long delicate fingers, clean fingernails and nails shaped like the bottom of a heart. And natural. Without the colour of nail polish.

Her nails have half moons on each finger.

A ring with a shield as its design is on her finger. The initials MGMB are marked deep into the yellow rich gold, as if the owner, the wearer, wants the world to see her identity clearly. Sargeant looks at the signet ring, sees the initials as a blur of interlocking letters, pays no regard to the initials themselves and is satisfied only to say that it is a pretty ring. To himself. The gold ring is on the third finger of her right hand. The way Europeans wear wedding rings, Wilberforce told her. He had bought it for her in Demerara, and had got the initials cut out by the Indian jeweller, when he spent one week there, attending a medical conference on Fixing Tropical Diseases with European Facilities.

"This is real gold, Mother," he had told her. "Them Demerara jewellers have the best real gold in the world. Two times as many karats as these Bimshire jewelry-thieves who import semi-gold from Europe . . ."

"Hommany karats in this, son?"

"Forty-eight," he had told her.

"Many's these?"

"Forty-eight, Mother."

She had smiled in her heart when he insisted. She did not believe him. All the gold around her on the fingers of the men who came to her home with Mr. Bellfeels was good gold, pure gold, true-true gold. And none was forty-eight karats.

This gold ring on the finger beside her little finger of her right hand that rests on Sargeant's hand is the deepest, richest colour of gold that he has ever seen. And the colour of the gold in the ring attracts him now, with deeper interest.

MGMB. He goes back in his mind, over all those years when he heard her name called out, in Sunday School, and at picnics when the teacher was making sure that everyone was present and accounted for, to go back on the long trip through the hills of Bimshire, Bathsheba, Horse Hill and Mount Zion Hill, to the Village of Flagstaff; in the classes for the Confirmation of young Christians, learning the Catechism and the Nicene Creed; and

then years later, on the radio when the name Wilberforce Alexander
Darnley Bellfeels—her son's name—was announced as the win-
ner of the Bimshire Scholarship for that year, for coming first out of
every boy attending Harrison College and the Lodge School, in
Classics: Latin, Greek, Ancient History of Greece and of Rome
and Religious Knowledge—which is what he took—in the
Oxford and Cambridge Joint Board Higher School Certificate
Examination.

First in the Island in Latin Prose.

First in Greek Prose.

First in Latin Distinction Prose.

First in Greek Distinction Prose.

First in Latin Unseen.

First in Greek Unseen.

First in Distinction Latin Unseen.

First in Distinction Greek Unseen.

First in Latin Translation, both at Pass Level and at Distinction
Level.

First in Greek Translation, both at Pass Level and at Distinction
Level.

First in Roman Ancient History.

First in Greek Ancient History.

Third in the Island of Bimshire in Religious Knowledge.

"Jesus Christ, he let-we-down! Jesus Christ, he let-down the
entire blasted Parish!" the Reverend Mr. M. R. P. P. Dowd, M.Th.
—Masters in Theology—(Dunelmn)—Durham University, the
Vicar of Sin-Davids Anglican Church, where Wilberforce was a
Sunday School teacher, screamed in mock horror. "You mean, he
couldn't come any more blasted higher in a simple subject like
Scripture? Religious Knowledge is nothing but Scripture. Reading
the blasted Bible! And understanding the Sermon 'pon the Mount.
Anybody could understand the Sermon 'pon the Mount! Jesus
Christ! Wilberforce is a disgrace to this Christian community of
Flagstaff! And to this whole Parish."

Winning the scholarship was the cause for great rejoicing in the entire Village. Mr. Bellfeels and the other big men of the Island gathered the night previous, in the restricted private rooms of the Aquatic Club, away from wives, away from their servants, away from the Village, where they spent the night drinking champagne; and then eating well-done beefsteaks, washed down with turtle soup and Bellfeels Special Stades White Rum. This gathering was the second celebration; and Mr. Bellfeels was smiling, proud as a rum punch; and had invited everyone, regardless of social status or money, to join in the rum-drinking celebrations. Wilberforce was not invited to this second round, either, because, at sixteen, he was too young.

So, Manny and Sargeant and the Solicitor-General and the Headmaster of the Elementary School, and Mr. Edwards who had tutored Wilberforce when he attended Sin-Davids Elementary School, and Mr. Bellfeels, Constable and Naiman and Revern Dowd were drunk and merry and hugging one another, and singing hymns and calypsoes, in the Harlem Bar & Grill.

They were gathered this night in public, in the Selected Clienteles Room; and the curious eyes of the Village were on them.

"One o' the only things, the few things that this scion of my, of my loins, loins, is that he make me, make me proud of him, tonight, so I tip my glass to Bellfeels, W. A. R., Bimshire Scholar, in *Classics*, be-Christ! Wunnuh know what that mean? Virgil! Caesar! Homer! *The Aeneid*, gorblummuh, Euripperdees and *The Illiad*! Jesus Christ, the Classics, boy! *Amo, amas, amat*. The venerable Classics! My boy. The only son of Darnley Alexander Randall Bellfeels! Gentleman, so I raise my glass. A toast. Down the hatch!" Mr. Bellfeels said. And then he added, "As man!"

"Down the hatch!" Manny said.

"To Wilber . . . Wil . . . berforce Alexander Alex . . . xander . . . Ran . . . Randall Bellfeels," the Vicar, Wilberforce's godfather, said.

"Down the hatch!" the Solicitor-General, Wilberforce's second godfather, said.

"Down the hatch!" the Headmaster of the Elementary School said.

"Down the hatch!" Sargeant, a police Constable of ten years, said.

"*Haec apud Romanos consul,*" the Solicitor-General said, quoting from Livy, *Book XXI,* Hannibal's decision to let his Gallic captives fight in single combat for the prize of freedom,

> *Wilberforcus rebus prius quam verbis adhortandos milites ratus,*
> *circumdato ad spectaculum exercitu, captivos montanos vinctos in*
> *medio statuit, armisque Gallicis ante pedes eorum proiectis, inter-*
> *rogare interpretem iussit, ecquis, si vinculis levaretur armaque et*
> *equum victor acciperet ferro vellet.*

"The Classics!" Mr. Bellfeels screamed with admiration, although he did not know the translation. "The fecking Classics, boy!"

And the other men, who, except perhaps the Vicar and the Headmaster, did not know their Latin, screamed their delight at the Solicitor-General's oratory; and this encouraged the Headmaster to join in the declamations.

> "'*Glamis thou art, and Cawdor; and shalt be*
> '*What thou art promis'd. Yet do I fear thy nature;*
> '*It is too full of the milk of human kindness*
> '*To catch the nearest way. . . ,*'" Headmaster said, quoting from *Macbeth.*

The men screamed their delight again.

"Words, words!" Naiman said; and got a little carried away, and said, "Jesus Christ, words!" And then he softened it, and said, "Here-here!"

"Here-here!" the Constable, who was not yet a policeman, said.

So, when the announcement was made that Friday night on the radio, for every inhabitant in Bimshire to hear, the name of

Wilberforce's mother was called out first. And then Mr. Bellfeels' name, with all his Christian names.

Sargeant cannot remember if the announcer had said, "Mary Gertrude Mathilda Bellfeels." Or if he said, "This year's Bimshire Scholar is Bellfeels, W. A. R., son of Mr. D. A. R. Bellfeels of Flagstaff Plantation, and a student in the Classical Sixth at Harrison College, also the son of Miss Mary Gertrude Mathilda."

The four initials, *MGMB*, on the shield of the gold ring intrigue him; but they do not file his memory to the point of sharper recollection.

He moves his attention from her initials on the ring, and places it instead, and with greater concentration, upon the softness of her fingers.

Her fingers are like five boughs taken from the silken arrows that grow out from the tops of the sugar cane; and these silken boughs are touching his hand. Their lightness tickles his hand. It is a sensation he has never suffered through before.

She looks into his eyes. And remains silent. And the force of her gaze, her brown eyes piercing into him, causes him to lower his gaze, to close his eyes, to turn his face away.

Her grip on his hand is firmer now. He can feel the strength of her fingers digging into his flesh. Abruptly, she gets up from the piano bench and goes to the window, the one through which he had been looking at the waves of sugar canes; and she stands there. And hums.

He buttons the silver button on which is the Imperial Crown of Englund, embossed in raised figures and letters, at his neck. It is the top button. And he throws his legs over the piano bench, with his back to the keys; and sits erect, facing her, as she continues to hum "Stardust."

And when her humming is over . . . she has hummed long enough to have covered only the first two verses . . . she remains standing by the window.

"You are a man of the world, Percy. Can I address you as Percy, instead of Sargeant? You know things . . ."

She stops; and then she hums another line which he takes to be from the third verse of "Stardust."

"You are a man of the world. A detective. You can read people's minds. Or should be able to.

"And I don't have to guess, Percy, that you understand what nearly happened, just now.

"But we are big-people. A big man and big woman. Even under the circumstances."

"Under the present circumstances, Mary-Mathilda."

"Yes, Percy, under the present circumstances."

"These circumstances which bring you and me together, at a time like this."

"I find myself, a woman my age, here with thoughts that I haven't entertain in years. Which I always wondered about. But couldn't entertain having, because of the circumstances.

"Thinking now of back-then, and these thoughts, these new thoughts that I am having . . . but back-then, the only people who would have-have these thoughts . . ."

"What we talking-'bout, Mary-Mathilda?"

"You are a wise man. And I think, also, a sensible . . . a sensitive . . . man. Please, don't let me have to spell-it-out, Percy. Spare me that embarrassment."

"I spare you, Mary-Mathilda. I spare you. But I don't really know what you getting at."

"I am getting at you, Percy."

"Me?"

"And me, Percy."

"You-got-me-there!"

"How do you see me, Percy?"

"As Wilberforce mother . . ."

"That's obvious."

". . . and as Miss Bellfeels, Mr. Bellfeels . . . as the Mistress of this Great House."

"How do you *really* see me?"

"I see you as the lady-of-the-house. As a person close to Mr. Bellfeels. As a important woman of this n'ighbourhood. People in this n'ighbourhood feel you is the best person living on the Plantation. Only today! Well-yes! A lil earlier this evening, I happen to be exchanging a few thoughts with Manny at the Harlem Bar & Grill, over a snap; and Manny had to remind me—not that I did-need reminding!—but Manny remind me of the time, during one Crop-Season, when tomatoes was really plentiful, more plentiful than anybody did-know what to do with them; they were so plentiful that they were rotting on the vines; and Mr. Bellfeels wanted to sell them at the usual price, as when they was scarce, and it was you who put your two feet down and make Mr. Bellfeels give-them-way. Practically. For next-to-nothing. People in this Village respect you for things like this. And this happen ten years ago. They loves you for this kind o' thing. That is how I, and a lot o' people in Flagstaff, sees you."

"You see me as a woman?"

"Course! You's a woman, not a man. You's Wilberforce mother! I must, as a consequence, see you as a woman, therefore."

"A mother?"

"Yes. You born Wilberforce."

"Or a woman?"

"That, too. A little o' all-two-both!"

"Any-other-way?"

"As a person. A lady. Who goes to Church every Sunday, almost. And who would do anything for anybody."

"Thank you, Sargeant. But I was wondering how they see me . . . more, as a woman. As a woman, Percy. How *you-yourself* see me . . ."

She still has her back towards him. Between the space of her right arm and the right side of the large window, he can see into the black night, into the distant greenness. She turns around and faces him. And stares at him. But says nothing.

And he remains sitting on the piano bench, with his back to the keyboard, looking at her; but when she looks him in the eye, he turns his face and evades her eyes.

Her eyes are brown and are like magnets.

He knows the things the powerful persons in the Village have said about her. The Solicitor-General. The two leading barristers-at-Law in the Island. The Headmaster of Sin-Davids Elementary School; and the Headmistress. Mistress Bellfeels and the other wives. And Mr. Bellfeels himself. All, except the Vicar.

And Manny. And he himself, if he is honest.

He added his two farthings to their portrayal of her, and it was not always in the most polite language. He joined in because the same circumstances which placed her outside his scope also provided him with the cover of undetection, for statements of his nastiness could not get back to her. He did not speak them in Gertrude's presence. But he was as nasty as the others, because he was jealous. All this "bad-mouth" history he knew about her. His history of her. But he did not repeat the oral narrative of the Village's history of her.

Part of it is the narrative of his own history.

Here she is on this Sunday night, asking him things he dare not admit that he understands. For the hand of Mr. Bellfeels' vengeance, his hand that dealt brutality and violence—a savagery that touched men . . . Remember Golbourne and Pounce, and even women who were in his way. That hand is still able to flex its muscles and smash him into the soft black mud, the soil of fields, as he himself would crush a centipede. Out of fear. And out of hatred. Despised beyond redemption. That hand that Mr. Bellfeels and his friends called "justice" was able to spawn the white road that marked the Plantation Main House off from the rows of chattel houses, cross the width of this Maginot Line, and crush a man like Sargeant, even though he was the Law, a Crown-Sargeant.

Mr. Bellfeels and "them" had their own Law. *What does he think of her?* He thinks he wants to throw her down, right now, and push himself into her, hard, on this settee, or this couch, or on this hard-wood floor with the imported carpets . . . and he goes on thinking these thoughts about her, and living them, and making them real, as he had done on that Easter Monday bank holiday at the Church outing and picnic, on the swept sand of the beach at the Crane Beach Hotel, when he followed her, walked in her footsteps, right up to her rendezvous with Mr. Bellfeels, carrying the glass jug in her hand . . .

How do I think of him? she asks herself. And she answers her own question: I am frightened to face the thoughts that are going through my head. And through my body.

I am frightened of him.

A woman my age: with these thoughts; and at a time like this. This is madness. This is lunatic-madness. And it must be the mad-ness of a woman who lives by herself, without a man, even to inhale his stale breath in a bed not used for love; a woman getting old; alone; this madness of the cornered quartered animal, driven into a box; blocked, and with no hole for escape and redemption . . . *and what can he think of me, under these circumstances?* A woman used. A woman handled by another man. Man-handled. A woman "a-bruised" by another man. And now, in her release from that bondage, by an act she herself cannot face, cannot swear if it is not imagination and not from "temperriment," an act intended to bring about her release, but which has so far brought about only this meeting between me and him, this conversation between me and him. How pure then is my body to take this communion? And my mind? Have I achieved salvation and release? Am I able to bring about my full release with my own hands? Am I a woman tainted by her experiences?

What he could be thinking of me? she asks herself.

What she thinking about? he asks himself.

She wishes she could ask him openly; just get right up, cross the few yards separating them, rest her hand on his shoulder and just ask him. Put the question to him.

But ask him what? Has she already formed the words in her mind? Are they on the tip of her tongue? Breathing hard, and desperate to be spoken, putting voice to the imprisonment of her true feeling? Can she tell him the secrets of her life that she has buried all these years?

Has she also formed the words he would speak to her, in his own head, in anticipation of rejection, or of approval; and if the answer is not what she expects, how then shall she conceal the shock from herself, the wound sinking into dignity, her womanhood, her age, her attractiveness, her desirability, the withholding of her true age from herself, and faded beauty from her lips, and her breasts, and her hips, then . . .

When last have you found yourself even contemplating these thoughts? These thoughts of youth and lasciviousness? And you with one foot in the grave?

And let us say that what you think you have done, what you wanted to do, and dreamed that you did it, and it is true, your other foot rests on the rim of the platform of a gallows. Fate and destiny.

"I must have been sixteen when Ma, trying her best to bring a change in my life, to take me from being too expose to things on this Plantation, learning too fast, too much of its nastiness, Ma thought I would have a better chance in life, working in one of those small cloth stores that sells dress-lengths.

"Ma chose a store own by a Indian-man that she knew, who had a place in Swan Street, down in Town, a one-door peddling-store that sold and that still sells dry goods and haberdasheries, silk and cotton, in dress-lengths; a cloth store; and when I tell you inside that store was dark? Dark-dark-dark. And with a smell always of incense burning in a brass jar, or vase, with a thin neck.

"I don't know how the place never got burned down. With all that cloth piled up high, almost touching the rafters. And the incense always light, and burning.

"Ma chose that place for me to work at, to try my hand at being self-employed, being my own woman—strange as that may sound—a saleswoman to be trained into a businesswoman; but really meant for me to try my hand at something more better than forking ground, weeding potato slips and hoeing young plants and being a object for Mr. Bellfeels daily wishes. And for me, as Ma say, to have hands like Mistress Bellfeels, his wife, the soft hands of a white lady.

"To work in this cloth store meant bathing every morning, before five o'clock, in cold water that made your teeth chatter; getting dress in the dark, sometimes with a kerosene lamp; and walking half the distance from here to down in Town, since buses in those days didn't start at such a early hour; and the chance of getting a lift by some good Samaritan wasn't so good.

"But the Monday morning Ma delivered me to Mr. Patel, the owner of the peddling cloth store in Swan Street, I could hardly see Mr. Patel in the chair sitting in the small dark space between the counter and the wall. And not a window in the place. Incense and lights of the dimmest voltage . . . watts, or brightness, were on; and it turn out they were always left burning. And Mr. Patel, invisible almost, because his complexion of brown was identical and matching the colour of the wallpaper on the walls and the shade of light in the store, I could barely make him out.

"Mr. Patel looked at me with his eyes, as if his eyes were two knives, all the time that Ma was telling him how bright a young woman I is; well-brought-up; won't give him no trouble; and all the time that Ma is going through my testimonials and recommen-dation, Mr. Patel's two eyes penetrating through my body, boring holes in my dress, from my two bubbies down, all over my belly, between my two legs, undressing me, naked, naked, naked, although he never as much as touched my dress with his hairy hand . . .

"I start to get frighten, and start trembling; and although it was sickening to listen to Ma giving Mr. Patel a ritual of my good points, and good behaviour, I still didn't want Ma to stop talking, because I knew that the moment Ma turn her back, and left the store, before she reach the corner of Swan Street and Broad Street, leaving me to Mr. Patel's mercies, Mr. Patel would have his hand down the front of my dress. Mr. Patel would be all over me.

"I knew this, because Clotelle when I first met her, working in the kitchen here at the Plantation, had-previously worked for a Mr. Boobilal, in the same Swan Street, in a almost identical one-door store, selling dress-lengths and cloth.

"Clotelle tell me that Mr. Boobilal pass his hand all over her body the first morning she start work. By midday he had begged her two times please for a foop; threatening if she didn't, he calling the police and saying that she steal money from the till.

"And every day, punctual at midday, Mr. Boobilal wife coming with his food, curry and curry and curry, with split peas cooked soft-soft, and soft drink; and the moment the wife, Mistress Boobilal, left, Mr. Boobilal trying to get in Clotelle bloomers. And the threats. Because what could poor Clotelle do? Call a police?

"So I was forewarned through Clotelle's personal experience; in confidence.

"And Mr. Patel did come on to me. If I had-scream-out, Ma would-have-hear my plea, Mr. Patel made his move so fast. Ma couldda-heard my cries, if I had open my mouth, in resistance against Mr. Patel's attempt to take advantage of me, a young woman, not knowing the ways of Town, me, a girl from up in the country.

"You remember how the soldiers in the Volunteer Regiment and Brigade used to train on the Garrison Savannah Pasture, doing their exercises and other drills they learn from the War, and from being overseas? Things like ju-jitsu? How you could throw a man two times your size in weight and strength flat on his backside and nearly cripple him. Yes!

"Well, I was always a fast learner. And I would watch, and laugh, and see how those soldiers used to toss-'bout men twice their size in weight, in practice.

"Mr. Patel seeing me, a girl still in her teens, decide that I was a woman he could subdue. And when he make his first move, rubbing his smelly-self against me, ready now to grab-hold o' me round my waist, with his left hand, and forcing his hand up my two legs, which I had-squeezed tight, well, with Patel trying to separate my two legs, while his hands were occupied thus, Christ! Percy, I remember-just-in-time how I see a soldier-fellow of the Volunteer Regiment and Brigade throw a kick, one kick. *Bram!* Full between Mr. Patel two legs, smack in his two stones . . ."

"Oh-Christ, Mary-G! . . . Miss Mary . . . It was you? You? That do that to Patel, causing him to walk with a slight limp and a bend?"

"I see him, once-in-a-blue-moon, if I am in Town shopping at Cave Shepherd, or at Goddard's Ice House; and when Patel see me, he would look-off, pass me and not a word leave his lips, as if I am a invisible woman. Yes! Up to this day!"

"You? You, Mary Gertrude Mathilda, do that to the powerful Patel? As you know, it was never reported. You were lucky."

"You call it luck? I call it justice. And guts. To kick Mr. Patel full in his two testicles!

"Life, Percy-boy, that is life! I wanted you to know what life was like for a woman growing up in this Island, in them days, the nineteens and the early twenties, with all these wolves in the road, in the sea, in the Church, in the school, in Sunday School. In the cane fields. And in the stores in Town. In all stores where men are in positions to hire young girls and women. In jewelry stores, drugstores, the shoe stores. Even the Lumber Yard. And don't talk 'bout the big food stores. All o' them wanted a piece.

"In those days, coloured people didn't particular own stores like the ones I talking about. A few peddling stores selling salt fish, rice and potatoes, that's all. And *not one* coloured-owned haberdashery! But if they had-own one, would it be any different?

"It was as if we were like lil fish swimming-round inside a big-big oil drum full o' barracudas.

"Well, as I heard from fishermen who should know, we wouldda stand a more better chance had we been swimming in the sea surrounded by a school o' sharks. Sharks, at least, would spare your life, if their belly full, and they had-loss their appetite. A barracuda would eat you, just for spite."

"I didn't realize that a barr'cuda is such a dangerous species, Mary-Mathilda!"

"A bar'rcuda, as you call it . . . is no different from some men I know in this Village."

She no longer is interested in saying more. Her expression changes, and she is like a woman who has seen an object, a ghost that comes upon her without warning; she is a woman who has seen something she does not want revealed at the moment.

She wonders if she should go right up to him now, this minute, this second, and say, *Percy, I don't have much time. Why are we wasting time, then? Take me in the bedroom, please. My bedroom. It is upstairs. Along the hall, last door on the left. Lead the way. Or let me take you myself, into my bed. Upstairs. Please.*

But he would never do that. Percy does not have the balls. Percy is too much of a believer in right and wrong. Has never used his position in the Village and in the Police Force to put a half bushel of sweet potatoes or a few chickens in a crocus bag and take them home for Sunday dinner. Percy is too decent. Too Christian-minded. "Like church tummuch"; and singing in the Choir even more than that. "Butter won't melt in Percy mout'."

"You were talking about Patel a minute ago," Sargeant says.

"Yes! Mr. Patel," she says. "I was telling you about him . . . All through the day, I would see Mr. Patel wink at a certain customer, a woman. She would come in, look-round, go into the WC, come-back-out and never-once buy a inch o' cloth. But as the day wore on, and the store got empty, the woman-customer would put in a second appearance, and Mr. Patel would disappear behind a cloth blind henging in front the door leading to the WC, and I would hear the latch scrape against the metal and the door lock. If I listen good, especially when the incense was still burning, I would hear Mr. Patel panting, as if he was climbing a hill or running a race; blowing hard. His breathing rushed. And then, silence. The silence. And for some reason, the incense always seem to burn more stronger during this silence; and smell sweeter. But never a peep outta the woman. And when she left, Mr. Patel always gave her a parcel already wrap-up in nice wrapping paper and tied with ribbon, in a bow."

"Did I ever tell you that I went down in Trinidad once, to 'vestigate Patel?" Sargeant says. "It was from Trinidad that Mr. Patel originated from.

"It was a few years after you must o' left working for Patel. I was a police cadet, training at the District A Bimshire Constabulary Police Training School, when this big case break. And the Commissioner axe the Training School Sargeant why not send-'long some recruits to get the experience. Our Constabulary was more professional, and with more seasoned police than the Trinidad and Tobago Police Constabulary. So that is how-come I happened to went to Trinidad.

"In Trinidad you might as well be in India. *Indians?* Everybody look like a Patel.

"Anyhow, years later we get a call. With a Constable and a Lance-Corporal, they included me on the 'vestigating team. And we gone-cross Swan Street that Friday afternoon, in a police car, with sireens blaring, fast-fast, and flying as if we're going to a fire, and every damn building in danger of a conflammation, when the call came through.

"We bound in this cloth store, pushing-pass women that blocking the door, pushing-pass the reporters and the photographers from the three local newspapers, the *Advocate News*, the *Observer,* and our own *Bimshire Daily Herald,* till we get to the back o' the store. As I had never went in one o' these cloth stores before, not being a woman and needing dress-lengths, it amaze me that the place was so blasted dark, as a place of employment. No lights to speak of. And it was midday.

"We push-pass to the very back. The blind made outta cloth, as you mention. The newspapers on the floor. The water, urine or overflow from the tank on the floor. In there, damp. And dark. And smelling. I holding my nose. A handkerchief close to my nose. And the minute the Lance-Corporal fling-back the blind and pull-open the door, brekking the latch from the outside, Jesus Christ! . . . Can I have that drink now, Miss Mary?"

"Have a taste-more."

"After all these years, the thing still have this effect on me. It must be twenty, twenty-something years now.

"When the Lance-Corporal fling-back the blind and break-open the door, the body of a woman fall forward and land full in my hands!"

"Take a more stronger shot."

"Thanks. We went in Trinidad after we piece-together certain evidence, but nothing didn't point to Patel. It was a matter of only what we calls, in Law, circumstantial evidence. Nothing but circumstantial evidence. The premises was owned or occupied by Patel. The woman was trace-back to being a girlfriend of Patel. Patel had went back to Trinidad, staying in a place outside Port-o'-Spain, in Toonapoona, to find a wife; and it was put down, at the conclusion of our 'vestigation, to being a act of jealousy, inflicted by the victim. The woman put a dress-length round her neck and attempted to suffocate herself, but she faint whilst attempting suicide, in the wc, whilst waiting for Patel to give her the regular parcel containing zippers, snaps and dress-lengths. The parcel was there, tied with a bow, wrap in very pretty wrapping paper. The knot was red. But Patel never came back from the Purity Bakery, which had recently open a store round the corner from Patel Cloth Merchants, where he went to purchase six turnovers. The evidence in our 'vestigation brought out this."

"The woman in question was a needleworker?"

"Yes, Trinidad! What a pretty country, though! Meaning the different kinds of religions and religious people, and different dress and looks, and people of all colour-schemes; and my God, the food! The food, Mary-Mathilda! Roti. Curry. Callaloo-and-crab. Chocho. And dasheen.

"We stayed near the place where we find out that Patel was from. Toonapoona. Up a hill, at its highest elevation, you could see mango trees and the other fruit trees native to Trinidad. And from top that hill, almost a mountain, was a monastery full o' monks and holy men, chanting prayers in Hindu."

"So, that is where Patel and all the other Patels hail from!" she says. "So, that is where he got his habit of burning incense in the store . . . and ringing bells . . ."

". . . and our 'vestigation, which covered every inch o' that mountain in Toonapoona, and all the surrounding land round it, San Juan, Mount Sin-Augustines, Petit Bourg, Arima and places so; the house Patel born in; where he raise-up; the east-coast road where he walk, or ride a bicycle; the school he went to . . . he was a first-class student, liking the arts and paintings and music on Indian instruments . . . and we discovered that right there in Toonapoona, below the Sin-Augustines Mountains, was the sweetest mangoes in Trinidad to be found, in a place name Petit Bourg . . ."

"You learn summuch about Trinidad in such a short space o' time, Percy?"

"Patel had-intend to come back to Trinidad, but business wasn't good; and then there was the lil thing in regards to a fire in Swan Street, when four buildings to the right of Patel, butting and bounding, and one on his left, burn-down-to-the-ground; reduce to ashes; and as I say, one to the left, and Patel cloth store in the middle, left untouch.

"Another thing we discover was that Trinidadian women prefers men from Barbados, 'specially professional men, like policemen.

"The women in Trinidad! Of Trinidad! Indians. Like Patel,
Chinee. Syrian. Whiching we don't have none in Bimshire.
Porchageeze people. The locals. The *douglahs*. People like me and
you. And the rest."

"You mean the whites?"

"You-said-it!"

"Talking about Mr. Patel, and hearing you talk about the differ-
ent colours of people you meet down in Trinidad, living together
in harmony and peace, and not like the tribes 'bout-here, the
question came into my head. Who is responsible for the popula-
tion that we have?"

"The Colonial Office."

"The *who!?*"

"A *colony*! A colony o' people. The people who run colonies."

"Isn't the three o' them the same thing?"

"Colonialism is the way things are done, the means. But if you
want to know how we, as inhabitants, are arranged the way we
are, black on one side, and white on the next side, with no Chinee,
Indian, Porchageeze nor Syrians in-between, not even a *douglah*,
ask the Colonial Office."

"I wouldda thought it had to do with slavery and the slave ships
and the people who pick we off those slave ships and divide-we-up
between the various plantations and cotton fields . . ."

"Mary-G, where you hear this from? You talking about the his-
tory of Bimshire? Or the history of slavery? I don't know if there
ever was slavery here, on the same level as Amurca. You're telling
me so, now. I never would have *think* that you was the person to
know this. But then-again, you is the mother of a very learned man.
And you hears things round your dinner table, from the mouths of
men with power, and who travels."

"I appreciate the compliment, if it is a compliment, Percy. But
everything leaving my mouth that makes sense doesn't come first
from Wilberforce mouth. It is true that Wilberforce opened my
two eyes to certain things . . . to 'The Ride of the Valkyries,' to the

English and the Eyetalians; the social things of this Island. But there is certain things that nobody can't teach you. You pick up those things by yourself. From a library book. Though I never entered the Bimshire Public Library.

"But when Wilberforce finish reading his library books and leave them on a table, I would turn a page and find myself reading one. The pictures, if it had some, was what first attracted my attention to books.

"I would sit down, specially at night, alone-by-myself, and look at pictures in Wilberforce library books, to pass the time; and as time pass, I found myself looking more and more at more than the pictures and the photographs. Finally, I was reading the texes, until I started to enjoy the entire book. Over the years, and many years it is, I picked up the things I told you about slavery. From books that happen to be laying-round the house.

"Wilberforce library books. And the *London Illustrated News* that Mr. Bellfeels steals from the Aquatic Club.

"I would read those things. And those things would make me scared. Those things would frighten me with the knowledge that I was gaining knowledge. Those things would tell me first of anything else, how little I already know. And what is worse, there was nobody, until now, to share the knowledge with.

"A little learning, they say, is a dangerous thing. I can add to that parable, and say, having learning and not having nobody to share that learning with is even more of a dangerous thing. Yes!

"But you continue. Tell me more about Trinidad and the Trinidadian women."

"Well, we went down on a two-mast schooner, captained by a man who later end up in politics." He settles himself in his chair. She settles herself comfortably in her chair. She pulls her shawl tighter round her shoulders. "I remember the Sunday evening," he says, "that we sail-out from the Careenage, down by the Sugar Bond and warehouses, smooth as silk round the Pierhead, slowly out to sea. I had a feeling that Columbus and Sir Francis Drake and

Lord Nelson, whose statute decorates the Square in the Upper Green, mustta had the same feeling when they was sailing the high seas. A feeling that I was on top, that I was conquering something or somebody. That I was moving along. Just moving along. From one place to a next.

"So, we turned the end of the Pierhead moving along from the Careenage; and although, as they say, we wasn't under sails, meaning that the schooner we was travelling in, although it have two masts, no sails was unfurl yet, and it was only a lil schooner without even a inboard motor of the smallest horsepower. But it was the same sensation as sailing over the high seas in this schooner.

"I am sure that Sir Francis Drake and Lord Nelson, and those other sea dogs, must have had the same feeling of the power of moving along.

"We wasn't going to discover Trinidad. Nor any o' them lil Wessindian islands that we have scatter-'bout in the Carbean Sea. We were only going down there to help their police force work-out the 'vestigation problems they were facing in regards to the sudden disappearance from the Bimshire jurisdiction of Patel, aforementioned; and if there was any 'corborating' evidence that we could pick up. Plus, the sudden coincidence of death resulting from attempted strangulation of the needleworker woman, found at the scene.

"As I tell you, Patel had-went home to Toonapoona-Trinidad, to find a Indian-girl, a *doulahin* to married, *primer-facially* speaking.

"Or, in other words, he couldn't get enough woman 'bout-here in Bimshire, amongst the local women, like the needleworker, so he went back to his own, to try his luck. Simple as that.

"Yes. If we were train' like the FBI in Amurca, or the RCMPees in Canada, or even Interpool, we would have known that taking the religious beliefs that Patel hold, in mind, plus his propensities for his own people, meaning *doulahin* and Indian culture, a man would do the things that we only find out after the expense of sea transportation, putting up in a guest house, inland travel by pirate taxis, food subsistencies, sport, and . . ."

"Did you play cricket against the Trinidad police whilst in Trinidad?"

"No," he says. "If we had been train' by Interpool, the RCMPees, or the FBI; and if our 'vestigations was conducted scientifically, we could have solve the blasted Patel case without leaving the shores of Bimshire on a two-mast schooner that nearly sink two times, be-Christ, between here and the Gulf o' Paria, near Trinidad. Pardon my French, Miss Mary-Mathilda."

"But did you play cricket at all down there?"

"No, not that kind, Miss Mary. I am talking about the cost that the Bimshire Constabulary had to foot as entertainment for we . . . things like beers and rotis. Trinidad rum was so bad and inferior to Mount Gay, we didn't touch none of their Vat-19 . . . and the price of a ticket to see a movie on Charlotte Street! Lord-Lord. Some o' the fellars went to nightclubs looking for women, and to dance, offa our Entertainment Allowance. We didn't play any cricket against the Trinidad police team.

"The minute we get out beyond where the fishing boats does-go, to catch shark and cavalleys, kingfish, barr'cuda and flying fish, and we look back and could see Bimshire disappearing, like it was falling in the sea, it was then that this feeling, like the feeling that Sir Francis Drake and Lord Nelson mustta had, came over me.

"My daughter tell me that going into Amurca by boat, and entering New York Harbor, the first thing you does-see is the Stature of Liberty. It is a feeling, she tell me, like no other feeling on earth.

"I compare seeing Bimshire falling slowly below the surface of the waves, going down slow-slow-slow to match the distance we was sailing away from she, I regard that as a sentiment similar to what my daughter describe of the Stature of Liberty, my oldest daughter, the domestic engineer up in Brooklyn. The other one went to Englund to be a nurse, where she passed-away. But leaving Bimshire, that Sunday afternoon . . . and we sing 'For Ole Lange Syne,' too!

"We sing the national anthem of sailors and mariners, sea dogs and buccaneers, of people leaving one port, challenging the high seas, to get to another port.

"And apart from seeing the Island itself slipping slowly into the sea, as we disappeared out o' sight of land, the last monument I saw with my two eyes, was Lord Nelson stanning-up there, in the Public Square in Town, in the Upper Green, shining in the afternoon sun, with his right . . . right or left? . . . arm in his blasted jacket pocket, concealing the fact that somebody had cut-off that hand. *Oney!* Alias Lord Nelson. And that caused me to remember Napoleon Bonnaparte, a man, a Eyetalian who became Emperor of France, who is more closer to we down here in the Wessindies than Nelson ever could, from a family-point-of-view, namely and because of the fact that the woman he choose to married-to as his wife was one o' we. A Wessindian woman. Josephine. From down in Haiti, or that-other Frenchified island, Sin-Lucia."

"Martinique," she tells him. "Martinique. Yes, Josephine! I came-across Josephine in a library book."

"Land disappear. The sea start getting more choppy, and rougher; the fellars, meaning the police amongst the passengers, the sailors and the regular-paying passengers, including the captain who was also the navigator, start one pewking all o' them, be-Christ, as if by pre-arrangements. Every man run from below, walk over ropes on the slippery deck, and rush to the gunwales and, with his head holding-over the side, start pewking pewk into the waves.

"It is the worst feeling a man, or a woman, could experience. Seasickness. I sometimes wondered during that trip to Trinidad if seasickness amongst the ship's crew wasn't the cause of the mutiny on the HMS *Bounty*? You ever come across the Mutiny on the *Bounty* in one o' your library books?"

"Once. In a library book."

"Everything that I had-eat that Sunday, straight from Church— as I had to sing the descant of the carol, in the Choir before leaving for Trinidad—*everything*. I didn't really want to keep my two eyes open whilst I was vomiting, but I couldn't close them because I couldn't help admiring the birds that followed we out to sea, far-far from land; so pretty; and the fishes and porpusses coming up outta the sea, and disappearing even before you could see them plain-plain; and a big-big boat to our left, moving like silk over the water.

"The HMS *Cornwallis* came into my mind. And in the waves, not so rough yet, I counted the grains o' white rice, the pieces o' sweet potato, the individual peas from the pigeon-peas I had-cook with the white rice to give it flavour, even the pieces of pig snout that I had boil-down in the rice . . ."

"You didn't chew your food properly, Percy. Forty-six times before you swallow a mouthful, Wilberforce say you have to chew your food."

"I probably had-eat too fast that Sunday in-true, since I had to travel overseas on the Patel 'Vestigation."

"You eat too fast."

"Then I see this big ship following us. Nobody in my group didn't have binoculars nor a spying glass. And I couldn't borrow the captain own. This ship couldda been a enemy ship following us on the horizon, later to intercept us, and *bram!*, when you hear the shout, a torpedo in our arse! Like they do to the HMS *Cornwallis* . . . pardon my language. . . .

"'Oh shite!' I say to myself. Pardon my French, Miss Mary. I conclude that they could be Nazzies in these waters. This is the route that ships, merchant ships and others, with Bimshire men on board, working as deckhands and in the boiler rooms, tending the engines, throwing coal on them big turbines, does be on. Ships bound for Europe and the various theatres o' war. And ships coming from Chaguaramas in Trinidad; and the British Navy tekking men and ammonitions and things to the Allieds up in Europe, to the Ardennes, Calais, Tripoli, to Desert Fox up in the great African desert of the Sahara, to Sabastopool, them places in Europe, in Bremen, Frankfurt and Poland, and the Darnelles, places I come-across in books, to fight in the various axes and theatres of war, as Churchill define them in speeches 'pon the BBC. And I say to my-self, as I am holding over the side of the gunwale of this two-mast schooner, bringing up my Sunday dinner, 'Lord, don't let a Nazzie submarine pass this way! Not now!'

"At night, we was in thick blackness. Lights turn off. And men, the crews and the passengers alike, talking in whispers, in case a Nazzie submarine lurking in the vicinity, and they pick up the noise of our talking, and the voices we are talking in, on their high-power radio transmissions, and find out that we are English, and not speaking the Spanish language and from places like the Argentyne or from Brazil, places that the Nazzies like to hide out in, and use for refuelling in.

"Quiet-quiet-so, we travelling in total darkness, darkness more thicker than the darkest dark-night on this Plantation, where we are tonight. And I discovered something from that experience of travel.

"The darkness that fall over land is nothing compared to the darkness that does-fall over the high seas and the ocean. In particu-lar, a big ocean like the Atlantic, the one we was travelling on, even though it was just at the edge, and not in the great, real deep-ness, as if we was taking a passage from Bimshire up to Englund or a Lady-boat to Canada, by sea. But it was the same darkness.

"Then it was that I start to get frighten and wonder if the Cap-tain, only a local fellar that I would see many times coming out of a rum shop in Nelson Street, if he had-remember the things he learn in Navigational School. Or, if he even went to Navigational School at all, to learn how to be a navigator of a big-big inter-island schooner with two masts.

"They don't have no road signs on the high seas to tell a man tek this turn, this is Swan Street you entering; or that if you tek the next left, you nearing Baxters Road or Broad Street. Not when you out there in the darkness of the deep, yuh! And a compass is round in shape, and in circumference. It is like a circle. A point in navigation is therefore nothing more than a point. If the compass tell you that you pointing nor'-nor-wess, to use navigational language, the language of the deep, and of mariners and sea dogs, and if that compass was to shake a *lil*, just a pivvy, and that point get off mark, Jesus Christ, Miss Mary, we could have end up in the Argentyne, or in Brazil, in Saw-Paulo, or Buenos-Airs. Even in Caracas-Venezuela then, whiching, as you know from your library books, is only a skip-hop-and-a-jump from Trinidad, 'cross the Gulf of Paria.

"Matter o' fact, whilst involve in the Patel 'Vestigation, up in Toonapoona, we discovered a monastery full o' monks, as I told you about. But the biggest discovery, as I also tell you, was these real sweet mangoes . . ."

"Give me the Julie-mango anytime!"

"The Julie is only one! We eat mangoes like they was going outta style! Julie-mangoes, mango-veer, turpentine mangoes, zabecou, calabash, or hog-mangoes, and the one that I like best, mango-Rochelle."

"Still, give me a Julie-mango!"

"But if the captain had fallen off-course, just a fraction of a point, a pivvy, from the course the compass and the sextant—is it a sextant, or a quadrant?—had given him, we could have ended up down in the Argentyne, and I would now be speaking to you in Spanish, with the rest o' them Nazzies. Don't laugh!

"During the War, as a member of the Police Force, we had to engage in certain important kinds of espionage. Undercover work. With risses. Cloak-and-dagger. Things like making sure lights-out is observe. Blackouts. Pasting strips o' black paper over your motor-car headlights. Observing people that behave strange. Like listening too long to radios. Particular, radios with a short-wave band. *Private-sets.* They could be spies. And a lotta them was suspected spies. A lot o' them 'bout-here, in a small place like Bimshire, *was* spies. Senning vital information. To the enemy. Axes and Fascist sympathizers. Secrets. Disclosing Top-Secret secrets. Nazzies and barr'cudas. So, we spend a lotta time sitting down. Sitting down

on a hill, like Flagstaff Hill in Clapham, or Brittons Hill hill, below
Flagstaff. And those of us assign to the Special Branch, down in
Town, had to siddown night after night, in the darkness o' night,
with the dew falling, and in the cold, as if we were really up in
Europe in the theatres o' War, in the Darnelles, Tripoli, Sabastopool,
Poland and Calais, in the First Whirl War, watching the horizon for
perriscopes, in case a submarine flying the Swastika or the colours
of the German Axes, was to surface for air and to take on water, or
to blow up another merchant ship. Our superiors in the War Room
Office in Central Police Station down in Town, which was out o'
bounds to ordinary policemen, told us what German submarines
does do. We were on the lookout for German submarines, using
our bare eyes. We have good eyesight in this Island. Proper vision.
In this Island, we does see good-good-good. Twenty-twenty vision.
And so, the minute we spot a perriscope, or any enemy activity
at all, quick-quick-so, we raise the alarm! By blowing our whistle.
I blow my whistle, and a next man, engage in similar espionage,
yards away, hear me blow my whistle. And he blow his whistle.
And so on, down the line. Down the line of the chain o' command.
And that way, in no time at all, our message is transmuted in code,
and reach Espionage Headquarters, in the Special Branch. The
information is then uncoded. Next, is put in our dispatches into a
new, next code and transmuted by Morse code, *dit-dit, dot-dot-dot,
da, da, da, da, da* . . . that is Morse code.

"Morse code! It save the Allieds.

"And we, as ordinary police from Bimshire, played our part in
those two great undertakings of military endeavour, the First
Whirl War and the Second Whirl War.

"'*Englund expect every man to do his duty.*'

"So, Trinidad was a relief, a kind of reward for we hard-working
members of the Special Branch, on the Police Force, which they
assign me to, as a recruit.

"And the women. Well, as you would expect, I survive the
crossing, and the seasickness, and when Trinidad loom up outta the

morning mist—you always arrive by sea, into a new island, in the morning. You leave the place of setting out from, in the evening. Those are the laws and etiquettes of sea-travel by boat. The rituals of the deep.

"Trinidad! And Trinidadian women! For a minute, and with my vision of Trinidadian women, I forgot the mission we was on.

"Women like peas, Miss Mary-Mathilda, if I say so myself, in all good respects to you, being a woman yourself; and if I may say so, under the present circumstances, namely the cause of my presence this Sunday evening, and the more obvious fact that you is still a woman, a woman of substance, a woman that look still good; good-good-good, if you don't mind me saying so . . . that I have looked upon you, since we was small thrildren growing up together . . . and you will have to forgive me, Miss Mary-Mathilda, for talking so plain in the presence of a lady, whiching you are. But the truth is the truth. And you will . . ."

"Continue, Percy."

"Continuing . . ." he says.

"Continue, Percy."

". . . continuing. You's a woman that my eyes have looked kindly and soft on, from the time that Saturday morning, in the company of your mother, Ma, when she brought you to Manny's father yard, to get the piece o' pork she had engage. I was helping Manny's father clean-out the belly. And wash-down the blood from the table where the pig was cut up. You was dressed in a blue dress, part of your school uniform. And your hair had in a blue ribbon. Normally, you would wear the white blouse under the uniform part . . . the tunic, you call it? No, the tank! Anyhow, this was a Saturday, and you was allowed to wear just the tunic. The tunic! That's the right name for it, the *tunic*. You were wearing your tunic that Saturday afternoon. And a ordinary plain white bodice underneat'. It was a hot morning, that day.

"'*This is my Mary*,' your mother tell Manny father. '*My lil girl, Mary*.'

"'*So, this is Mary! Little Mary-had-a-little-lamb, Mary?*'" And Manny father laugh, as he does always laugh when he talk; and say things like this.

"And your mother say, '*Say morning to Mr. Biscombe, Mary-girl.*' And you say, '*How-dee-do, Mr. Biscombe? Good morning, sir.*'

"And Manny's father say, '*So, this is lil Mary, who is pretty-pretty-pretty as the Little Lamb in the storybook! Pretty as a butterfly. I hear that Mary bright-bright as a new shilling!*' he tell your mother. '*And I hear that this child bright-enough to be and shouldda be going-school at Queens College next term, to say nothing o' Sin-Michaels Girls School. If things was different with your pocketbook. You know what I mean.*'

"'*Yes,*' your mother tell Manny father. '*We have to creep before we walk.*'

"'*That is the Gospel, girl! How you mean?*' Manny father tell your mother.

"And he give your mother the piece o' pork she engaged. Half-pung o' harslick. And a pung-and-a-half o' pork, a piece near the ribs. For pork chops."

"You have a good memory, Percy."

"The detective-work. Detective-work sharpen my memory . . ."

"No wonder!"

"Cause I was watching you all the time. How you was holding your head down, as if you were shy.

"All this transpired in the presence o' me. Although it was big-people talking and my presence was invisible to big-people's company.

"From that Saturday morning I had eyes that followed your life, wherever possible. Eyes for you. You was in my mind. And in my body. I can say this now. Cause, we are big-people ourselves, and we have to face facts. Sometime-in-our-lives.

"I facing them facts, now. Tonight."

"Facing facts," she says.

"I may be outta order. Under the circumstances that find me here, meaning my position in the Constabulary of Bimshire, I might be outta place. But I am here not only as a police, Mary-Mathilda.

"I wish I was man-enough . . .

"I wish I could be able to face you, as a man . . .

"And see you as a woman.

"And if I am talking outta turn, as I may be, tell me. And as a man, I would take your reprimands. Put on my hat, button-up my tunic neck and leave. Vacate your premises.

"But that Saturday morning," he goes on to say, "in the yard of Manny father rum shop, when Manny father tell you about how you should be going to Queens College on the strength of your brains and brightness, but couldn't, on account of being poor, your mother uttered something which I will always remember.

"Your mother tell Manny father, *'Thank you, Mr. Biscombe, for your words in kind regards to my daughter's potentials. I am acknowledging your words in my daughter behalf. I know what you are saying. I know she deserve a place in Queens College. Mary deserve a place at Sin-Michaels Girls School, to say the least. But if she don't get there, she will get some-where else, praise God. She wants to take up needlework. And I promise her that I will try-my-best to buy a Singer sewing machine for her, 'pon time. Before I dead. One o' these days, this lil girl, this Mary Gertrude Mathilda, Mary-girl, as I calls her, that you see stanning-up here this Saturday morn-ing, well, one day, she will be living in one of the biggest houses in this Village, even on that Plantation! Even in the Great House, over there, then! Why not? She can dream, can't she? Mark my word!'*

"*'What a day that going to be!'* Manny father say. *'What a blasted good day!'*

"I live to see that prediction come to pass. I see the words your mother uttered that Saturday come true. Your mother, Ma, saw into the future, Miss Mary Gertrude Mathilda.

"And now, here I am, too; with you. In this Great House. For the first time in my life, I sitting down in a real front-house! And though the circumstances isn't what they could or should be, and isn't the right ones I would have desired, they happen to be the cir-cumstances the two o' we are faced with. And a man have to throw the dice that are pass to him to play with . . . *vap! nick! Throw a seven on the first throw, or crap out!*"

The large front-house is quiet now. Only her breathing can be heard. The smell of canes burnt in fires Saturday night rises stronger now that the wind comes from the direction of the North Field. There is also the fragrance of the lady-of-the-night and the smell of the furniture and the polish used by Gertrude on the mahogany chairs and tables.

And the smell of food cooking.

Sargeant tries to imagine what it is that Gertrude is cooking so late at night. And for whom. It could be roast pork. Or pork chops, dipped in meal-corn flour and seasoned deeply with fresh broad-leaf thyme, and cloves, frying in lard oil. Gertrude's cooking cries out in the sizzling iron saucepan.

He inhales and tries to distinguish the smell.

It is chicken being fricasseed.

It could be pork chops frying.

It could be a joint o' pork baking.

It could be stew, Bimshire Stew, a mixture of fresh beef and fresh pork and fresh fine-leaf thyme, being boiled in the same pot, with onions . . . to be served with meal-corn cou-cou. But this is Sunday, and cou-cou is cooked and eaten piping-hot, on Saturday afternoons only . . . *"You staying for dinner?"* . . . his mind goes back to that Saturday in Manny's father's yard, with him in his khaki short pants patched in the seat in so many places with different colours and materials, so that it was difficult to know which colour or which material was the original the pants were made from, by the Village tailor; his legs stained with traces of pig's blood; and his bare feet covered with the black shiny hairs that had been scalded off the body of the eighty-pound pig, with pails of boiling water; and then scraped off with a stone. It was a boar-hog . . . *"Are you staying for dinner?"*

"I was trying to guess what your maid could be cooking, that smell so sweet?"

"Well, why don't you call her and find out?"

"Me?"

"Touch the bell, and she will come."

"So, this is how."

"I wonder when Wilberforce coming back?"

"What the time is?" he says.

"It getting late."

Sargeant rings the bell. It reminds him of that bell the Headmaster of his Elementary School rang at nine o'clock every morning to "summonse" the boys from their games in the schoolyard beside the Church wall that has graves behind it; and again, at eleven, to announce "ten minutes," a break for water from the pipe in the schoolyard; or to pass water in the WC; and again at one minute to twelve noon, for lunch; and for the fourth time, at two in the afternoon, to announce the names of boys allowed to leave early to field tennis balls at the Garrison Savannah Lawn Tennis Club; or to water the flower gardens of the rich; and at three o'clock, the fifth and last time, when the afternoon is tired and humid, now to announce *"Singing!"*

The entire school stands at attention. "Rule Britannia!" It is the end of the day. The last bell.

All pupils are admonished to go straight home. *"Now, go straight home, boys!"* To doff their caps to strangers and adults. To make no noise on the way home. And the boys scamper out of the school like freed prisoners, after having recited the Lord's Prayer; after singing "Rule Britannia" three times; after reciting "I Vow to Thee, My Country"; and then marching out from their benches and "desses." The singing of "God Save the King" now ended, the photograph of King George-the-Fiff is saluted, as each boy reaches the door. A smart, swift wave of their black hands before their faces, as their bare feet pound the deal-board floors, marching as to war . . .

And Gertrude comes. Like a ghost, without ceremony; like the Inspector of Elementary Schools, sneaking up on the Headmaster and trying to catch him off-guard; talking to herself . . . "I-myself was just-this-minute going to come in and see if you want me to serve now, Mistress? Wait until Mr. Wilberforce come? Since you having-in guesses, you want me to leave things until you ready to go to the table? Or-if-not, if you want me for something else, like more drinks. Or. . . ? But I really was wondering, Mistress, if I could take-off as soon as I clean up?" . . . There are many things on Gertrude's mind: what is Sargeant doing, talking so damn long; and why the Mistress haven't told her to take-off early tonight, as usual; and as promised; ". . . and I promise myself to pass round by the Pilgrim Holiness tonight, and see if the Sisters getting in the spirit, and hear the word o' God at the same time . . . Lord, what wrong with this woman, tonight . . ?"

"Lock-up before you leave, please, Gertrude."

"Thanks. And good night, Mistress."

"You got somebody to company-you-home? It dark."

"Yes, Mistress. My cousin . . ."

"Be careful . . ."

"Good night, Mr. Stuart."

"Throw-on one o' Wilberforce old black jackets over your two shoulders, Gertrude. To prevent yourself from catching a draught . . . The night cold. And the dew falling, hear?"

"Good night, Miss Gertrude," Sargeant says, very formally.

"Night!" Gertrude says. "Well, I leaving, now, then . . ."

"Night! And Wilberforce isn't even here . . . I had no idea I keep the child so late! . . . to give her a drop to the corner . . ."

"Night!" Sargeant says.

"I going now, then," Gertrude says; and closes the parlour door a little noisily behind her.

"Why you never took-up with a steady woman?" Mary-Mathilda says, now that they are alone.

"After the mother of your two daughters left Bimshire and died, you became a sad, lonely man. We used to wonder, and some people even bet that before-long, you was going to put a end to your life by your own two hands. And when you were telling me about your trip to Trinidad, and knowing you were likely to meet some Trinidadian woman down-in-there, I was waiting to hear if you left some thrildren behind; or if you married to one, hoping some day to bring-she-back to Bimshire; or you return back down in Trinidad. But, nothing, Percy? *Nothing?*

"So, I ask you *why*, as a consequence? Why?"

"Celia DiFranco was a light-skin woman of Porchogeeze-Negro extractions that I meet, when a Trinidadian detective-fellar take we out on the town one night, from up in Toonapoona where we were billeted, all the way down in Port-o'-Spain, by car, near the Savannah. In a place, my-God, Mary-Mathilda, that sold the sweetest ice cream in the whole Wessindies! The Green Corner. Or the Corner of Green.

"This girl—she was a schoolgirl at the time I was in Trinidad, tracking down the whereabouts of Patel. This girl, not more than sixteen when I meet her, 'cause she was still 'tending high school, Bishops High School for Girls.

"This girl, of a light complexion, and with good-hair; long black hair that was straight and silky . . . and when I tell you *shining?* Well, in that heat and sun, and with the humidities they got down there in Trinidad, when this girl walk in the street, and the light hit her hair, oh shite! Well, you know what I talking 'bout . . .

"Her name was DiFranco. My Trinidadian detective-friend tell me that she have Porchogeeze-and-Negro in her blood. I tell you that already.

"She lived in Town. In Port-o'-Spain, right in the middle, near the Royal Gaol.

"Her mother stayed at home, as a housewife. Light-skin like the daughter. The father was a schoolteacher. Headmaster, I think. And black-black-black as a Blackamoor. More blacker than me. I look at that man the first time, that man, tall-tall, black-black as pitch, as a Blackamoor, and just as dignified; his skin smooth as molasses; and the complexion and the texture of his skin, and a *nose!* My God, Miss Mary! When I tell you a nose? Big and long, and hooked; shaped like the nose you see in that movie about Roman senators, at the Olympic Theatre, I think it was *Quo Vadis.* That was all I could think of when I first rested my two eyes on Celia father nose.

"*Quo Vadis.*"

"And I never-before, in my born-days, receive the kind o' hor-spitality and courtesies from anybody that I receive at the hands of Celia mother and Celia father. I had-intend to make my intentions known to Celia father and Celia mother as fast as possible, in regards to marriage and to holy matrimony, due to the way they treated me, a complete stranger. Because I was a man struck by love and sincerity. But before I could do it . . ."

"Perhaps that is why."

"How could they treat me, a complete stranger, more better than I ever get treated here in Bimshire?"

"Some people like strangers and foreigners more better than their own. A prophet is not without honour safe in his own-own country. It is to do with not having to be honest. A father-in-law-to-be, or a mother-in-law-to-be, don't have to be honest with the man who have eyes for their daughter, exactly-because he is a foreigner, a man from a other island, and have no history. Or another Parish. They don't want to know him. The more unknown, the bet-ter. The strangeness, or what Wilberforce calls the 'exotic,' will get in the stranger's blood, and turn his head; and he will start to have ideas . . . Oh, well . . . if you know what I mean."

"I know what you mean . . ."

"One person really don't have to get to know the other person. The distance that separate them, one in Bimshire, the other in Trinidad, and the seawater in-between, which by itself would mash-up things. Doubt and suspiciousness. The one feeling that the other one carrying-on on-the-side. The other one listening for background noises when she is on the telephone to him, long distance. They never really get to know one another. Doubt building on doubt, and suspiciousness, and the suspicion of infidelities-on-the-side, if you see what I mean, will——"

"You are reading my mind, Miss Mary! I was about to tell you that when I came back here from Trinidad, by the *same* schooner with two masts, and suffer the same seasickness on the return-journey back, as had-afflict us on the passage out, I didn't sleep for the first six days of my return to Bimshire. Tossing and turning, as if I was still crossing the Carbean Sea, going down into the Gulf o' Paria. Sleep won't come, no-kind-o'-how! I counted sheep . . ."

"What you mean, you counted sheep?"

"Like, one, two, three . . . Up in the three hundreds, the four hundreds. In the *thousands*! Yes. Counting sheep, as they say in the storybook."

"My God-in-heaven, Percy! You had it bad, in-true."

"Bad-bad-bad! And whilst counting sheep, a funny thing happened to me. The counting of sheep led me to reading fairy tales, every night.

"The first six days, back on *terra-firmer*, as I lay sleepless, turned into the seventh day, and then into the first fortnight, and over above my bed, as I was laying-down flat on my back, over me was a picture of Celia DiFranco, plain-plain-plain as anything, like a painting of angels; suspended over me, above the bed, as if she was a coverlet, or a mosquito net over a four-poster bed, was the woman I left in Trinidad. Celia DiFranco. One fortnight turn into two. Two, into three. When I see the month-end come, Jesus Christ, Miss Mary-Mathilda, I start feeling that I needed serious medical attention. Time to call-in Mr. Wilberforce, for consultations."

"I remember the time. Wilberforce told me. Just the outlines, mind you."

"Can't sleep. The sleeplessness of insomnia turn into palpitations. That is when Mr. Wilberforce first-tell me how serious thoso thingo had become mental anxieties, and were now giving me the nerves. That was the origin of my pressure. Blood pressure and palpitations of the heart.

"During the day, I would be all right. I would do my work and go about my duties. But the moment you see dusk fall, and twilight turn into darkness, *bram!* the sadness of sleeplessness and other psychological insomnias that go with it . . . and then, these heavy palpitations of the heart."

"That was *love*, Percy-boy. That was love. What foolishness you talking? Is love, Percy. You too old to recognize the passion of love?"

"*Love?*"

"Love."

"If that was love. . . ! Anyway, I start writing love letters to Celia. In one week, I write fourteen letters. I remember stanning-up in the Post Office, in the Public Buildings; and the civil servant-fellow selling the stamps, all of a sudden, without word of apology or nothing, just get-up-straight-from-behind the wire-cage and-left. Gone to lunch. Or, went drinking rum. But I had more patience than he have bad manners! I walked out by the Olympic Theatre, behind the very Public Buildings, and went in a rum shop, and buy a rum; and eat a ham-cutter. When I went back, there wasn't a soul in line. And I remember the feeling I had, as I lick-on the stamps on the airmail envelopes, with saliva. I was posting all fourteen letters the same time. I don't know, why I didn't post *one* letter at a time. Or *two*. I posted the fourteen letters the same time. They take me seven days to write.

"I address those fourteen letters to Celia, nice, with my Watermans fountain pen. And written with the best Royal Blue Quink Ink that I could get from Weatherheads the Druggists.

"Man-yes! And I loved to smell that fine English airmail writing paper; stationery, that according to a watermark-seal on the paper itself kings write on. The watermark-seal said, 'By Appointment to His Majesty King George the Fiff!' You know the smell of that quality o' stationery, Miss Mary!"

"English stationery, boy!"

"Man-yes! And soft. The feel of it. Soft-soft-soft, that if I wasn't careful when I was writing those words to Miss DiFranco the nib of my Watermans fountain pen wouldda punch-through the paper, and spoil the flow of the Quink Ink that was, as I said, Royal Blue.

"The paper itself was blue. For airmail. If you hold it up to the light, you could see a drawing of a bird, or something that look like a bird. It could be another animal. Like a lion. The only thing is that it had-on wings, this thing printed almost in a invisible manner, like a mark, was there . . ."

"A griffin."

"What a griffin is?"

"A animal with wings."

"That is right? A griffin?"

"A watermark."

"Watermark? Is that what you call it?"

"It's a watermark. With a griffin on it. One way of telling quality."

"Well, my stationery that I used to write those fourteen epistles to Celia, in Port-o'-Spain-Trinidad on, was royal, and a griffin. And Miss DiFranco was royal, too. She was my princess. My queen, and . . ."

"You didn't married!"

"We didn't get so far."

"She would be a princess, then!"

"I see what you mean! Man-yes! I addressed all fourteen en-velopes in the manner I was taught in by Mr. Edwards' Penmanship in elementary school: the beginning of each line, a half inch to the right of the line above it, and so on . . . like:

"'Miss Celia DiFranco,
      '114 Cambridge Street,
            'Port-of-Spain,
                  'Trinidad,
                        'Trinidad & Tobago,
                              'British West Indies.'

"Man-yes!"

"Yes! I would say, yes."

"Man-yes! And, Miss Mary-Mathilda, I am ashame to tell you, that a woman with a foreign accent, turned my blasted head behind my blasted back, making me look like a blasted poppit. Approaching Mr. Brannford. I am man-enough to admit that.

"This went on for eleven months. What keeping me going was the writing of fourteen love letters at one time, letter after letter, with words more sweeter than a calypso, more sweeter than 'Frenesi' that we just listen to. I don't know where I got those sweet-words from!

"I not telling you the whole truth, though. I got the words in books from the Public Library. And from a few verses in Psalms in the Bible. And from the Book of Proverbs. You would be surprise to see how many words, suitable to love letters, could be found in the Bible. And I mean the Old Testament. Sweet words, Miss Mary-Mathilda. Words like *beauty*. And *fragrance*. Like, *vouchsafing*, *love* and *affection*. *Softness*. *Beatitudes* and *felicitations*. The beating of a man's heart getting louder and louder, as the distance of green seas and mountains of waves get wider, and cut him off, and he vouchsafe that should there be a parting of the waters, he shall drown himself in a sea of loneliness. Love-words . . ."

"Yes, Percy. Yes!"

"Fourteen letters at one time, I send that woman. And in the first eleven months of licking-on stamps with my saliva, and sticking them on 'pon letters and stanning-up in a crowded Post Office, with a blasted unmannerly civil servant behind a wire cage, and my corns burning me from stanning-up half-hour to a hour before I get served . . . *she answer-me-back, three times!*"

"Three times? One, two, three?"

"Three times. Miss Mary-Mathilda, I never knew that a woman could break my heart so hard. She break my heart as if my heart was a piece o' lead pencil, brittle and weak, that when you go so, *snap!* . . . it break.

"When I think back to those days, and always my grief comes at night, the moment the sun sink-down below Flagstaff Hill, and drop in the sea, my heart sinks sudden and deep and low-low, and final like the sun. When dusk fall . . ."

"You was a wreck over love, Percy-boy."

"These woman-problems happened the same year I pass-out as a police Constable, in the Royal Constabulary of the Island of Bimshire Police Force, from Police Training School. With the Baton of Honour."

"That is twenty-something years!"

"Twenty-five. *To the day!* Miss Mary-Mathilda, twenty-five to the very day! Isn't this telling you something?

"What I mean by that is this. Here I am. Here I have been. In all this time. This Sunday evening, and whatever it is that is in my heart, concerning you . . . not concerning *you*, with respect to the matter at hand which I shall not mention, but in the present circumstances for me to unburden myself before you and confess that I fall in love with a Trinidadian woman in Trinidad . . ."

"What happened, after writing the love letters?"

". . . love letters? Unrequited love letters, you mean. I pick-up that word *unrequited* from a poem. I can't remember who write the poem. But it couldda been Keats, a English fellar by the name of John Keats. Maybe Wordsworth, or Tennyson. All those poems I come-across years ago, through private lessons Mr. Edwards give me; and in books from the Public Library.

"It lasted, really, into the second year. I think I came to the conclusion, after my experience, that these kinds of love affairs have a natural lifespan of not more than eighteen months. If that.

"She would write things like *'Dear Percy, This can't work. You there. And I here in Trinidad. I still love you. Celia.'*

"That one came one Friday. The next one came on the Monday.

"*'My dear Percy, This still cannot work, for as I tell you, I here in Trinidad, you there in Bimshire, residing. I still love you. Celia.'*

"And her third letter?"

"*It finish, 'Percy. I still love you. Celia.'*"

"And where is the lady now? This Celia DiFranco?"

"I save-up, and save-up, and eventually I got the passage. On the *same* schooner, with two sails that had take we on the Patel 'Vestigation. I went back to Trinidad. And vomited in the same manner, from seasickness . . .

"Land come up. In the mist. Early morning. Pretty-pretty. The trees, the colour of the skies, the clouds white, and the land. The land. The Land. Mists over mountains. Trinidad! Excitement. Just like how Christopher Columbus must have react when he first see land in these same Carbean waters. *'Land!'* he mustta shout. *'Shipmates, officers, land! We see land!'* I imagined myself saying the same words of destination and destiny.

"My heart in turmoil. Beating like the music I love to hear and always hear when I in Trinidad. Steel-band music. Even though I only see Trinidad two times.

"I must have run all the way from the Port-o'-Spain Deep Water Harbour right up Charlotte Street, trying to reach Cambridge Street. Number 114.

"And then I stopped running. And start walking. And eventually stann-up in the middle o' Charlotte Street.

"Suddenly it hit me. In two-years-and-something-months, after writing fourteen letters at one time, I hadn't seen this woman after our first and only meeting the Friday night, in Green Corner Café, eating vanilla ice cream . . . in all that time, I never rested my two eyes on Celia DiFranco a second time. And now, here I am, in Charlotte Street, less than one thousand, seven hundred and fifty yards away from the object of my affections, and I am behaving like a blasted poppit. And running. Running to what? And to where? Celia bound to be home. *Where* she could go?

"She know I coming.

"I write she to tell she I coming.

"She waiting for me . . .

"So, I buy a roti from a Indian street vendor. And I eat it. I had no appetite on the schooner, on account of seasickness, and my bowels. And then I tried a channah. And I see a fellow selling parch-nuts. And I had a pack o' them, too.

"I take my time. I reach Cambridge Street. I fling a Buckley's inside my mouth. I grind-up the Buckley's and swallow it.

"I press the bell.

"One time. No answer. Two times. No answer. Three times. This time, more longer. Four, five, six times . . .

"I think I hearing movement inside the house. But in things like this, your lack o' happiness and your nervousness, and your fear and your angriness, and in your unhappiness, you don't always hear the truth of what is happening . . .

"And the door open. Celia mother facing me.

"*'Celia gone to play bingo, yes-wee!'* Celia mother say. *'Eh-eh! Celia gone bingo. She did-know you was coming, yes-wee?'*

"My bottom lip drop. My mouth open-wide. I feel I am back on the high seas, tossing-'bout in that inter-island schooner; pewking and bringing up my guts in seasickness. I can't talk . . .

"When I regain my voice, I axe Celia mother, *'She didn't get my letters?'*"

"*'All o' them come,'* Celia mother tell me.

"*'And she didn't open them?'* I axe Celia mother.

"*'I don't know if she open them, Percy,'* she tell me. *'I don't know, Percy.'*"

He stops talking. The old grandfather clock, ticking in self-assured confidence in a far corner, is the only life in the room with them. There is the smell again of burnt sugar canes, as the wind rises and brings the acrid smell into their faces, through the open window.

"Love!"

It is she who has said this.

It is as if she wants to bring him back from those waves, from that sea, from that street in Port-of-Spain where the door was shut against him, where the conclusion of his sea adventure was bound to end in shipwreck, amongst flotsam and in jetsam, concerning his ambition to find a new life that reflected the one he had left in the barracks of the Police Training School.

She wants to talk to him about love. About the love that she has lived without for the same twenty-five years that is the measurement of his loss.

What choice was that, she wonders? Even if the woman did not love the man, what choice is that, to "*go bingo*"; to watch her fortune and her luck fall before her eyes, in numbers matched to letters:

"O—6!" a voice says. And hands move nervously, scrambling over the hopscotch bingo card.

"B—23!"

"N—39!"

"Bing-go! Bingo, bingo, bingo!"

What kind of a life is this, for a woman in love? Matching numbers with letters on a bingo card that does not guarantee fortune and bring luck?

"Love," she says. "I never really understand love. Nor loved anybody. Not if I am talking about a man.

"I loved my mother, Ma. And Gran, my grandmother. And my great-gran, Ma's grandmother. Three people. Three women. But I don't think I ever loved anybody else.

"Particular, a man!

"Wilberforce! I forgot Wilberforce, my God! That goes without saying. My thrildren. William Henry. And Rachelle Sarah Providence. A mother loves her thrildren. It is something that she doesn't have to prove. Something you take for granted. Apart from them, the three women in my life.

"But in all the time you were seeing me, in Church on first Sundays of the month, taking Communion; at certain functions, like the opening day at the Races; on the Garrison Savannah Pasture for parades, like the King's Birthday Parade, Queen Victoria's Birthday Parade, and the annual Gymkhana that the Bimshire Volunteer Regiment and Brigade puts on.

"You seeing me from that distance, at our annual Church outing and picnic; up at the Crane Beach Hotel; once or twice in Town, walking-cross Swan Street, when I had to visit Mr. Bellfeels lawyer, the Solicitor-General before he was a Solicitor-General; you had to have a different opinion of the woman you were seeing.

"What you were seeing wasn't me. You were looking at a person you had invented in your imagination, a person who, as you say, you couldn't approach. And here I was, all the time you were watching me, suffering for the slightest attention I could have got from any man.

"Let me tell you something, Percy.

"This Great House is bigger and definitely nicer and prettier than the shack I was born in. Than any in the Village. But is it a happier place to live in?

"And the things you see inside it. The furnitures. The chairs and tables. The carpets, either brought back for me by my son Wilberforce or else delivered here by mule cart or delivery van from Cave Shepherd & Sons, Haberdasheries.

"The food I eat, that me and Wilberforce eat, doesn't come from Miss Greaves Shop in the Village. When last have I darkened the door of Miss Greaves Shop? I was brought up going to that shop. Ma used that shop all her life, trusting salt fish, mackerel and flour on credit . . . I won't be surprise if she dead, owing Miss Greaves money . . .

"Now, I order things from Goddard & Sons, the Ice House, down in Town. And I have my pick of any boy working in the Plantation Yard, to get him to jump-on 'pon his bicycle and cycle-into-Town, to place my order.

"But is this the happiness that I want? And not to be able to go to a dance if I wanted to? Not only in Queens Park Shed, but even at the Aquatic? Or the Marine Hotel? Even if I was accompanied by Mr. Bellfeels?

"In bygone days. Because dancing gone outta his bones a long time now! But back-then. The dancing!

"Your freedom, your life, is taken from you, as a woman in this Island, for the certainty that you will have food, and a roof over your head, and over your thrildren's head. Yes.

"Loss o' freedom?

"Yes! Perhaps. But if you play your cards right, you will have these things to look at; these things of material value flowing unto you, in abundance, in your direction. Even flowing unto your bed. Under your sheets. Yes!

"But is this happiness?

"Perhaps. Yes-and-no. Perhaps. So, you look at me, and you see a woman you know from small; from when we were growing up together, as thrildren. You stand from across a street, and you fix your two eyes on me, and every time you do that, even from that distance, my body reacted with a tinge, a twinge, and a feeling comes over my body.

"But I couldn't look-back-in your direction. I could not give-you-back the look you were sending.

"There were always eyes following me. Put there by Mr. Bellfeels, to follow. He was never sure of my faithfulness. Yes! But the eyes followed me, even when he no longer had any uses for me.

"You don't know, Percy! It just doesn't fall within your understanding to know. Follow and report. Report sometimes, even without following."

Sargeant is leaning forward from his seat, following her words. She has now stopped talking. From her sleeve, which reaches to her wrist, her left wrist, she pulls a cotton handkerchief. It is white. It has white flowers embroidered into its fabric. Its borders are four strips of lace. The lace itself has no flowers.

She taps this handkerchief to her mouth. Tears appear at the corners of her eyes. The tears remain lodged in her eyes. And it seems to him that when she does eventually feel the tears flow from her eyes and come to her cheeks, only then does she move the handkerchief to her eyes. She closes her eyes as she dries them.

And then she opens them. Her face is smiling again. Her brown eyes are bright. Frisky as a cat's. Her lips are pulled firm and tight over her teeth. And this makes the smile that is on her face even more beautiful. But beneath the beautifulness of the smile, there is a sneer.

Her skin is firm. Pulled back without wrinkle. Her skin is brown. Her hair is long and black, with a few waves of silver in it. Her neck is long, and her swallow pipe bobs up and down when she gets excited, or emotional as she was a moment ago. In the middle of her top lip is a crease that gives distinction and definition to her mouth, and then to her lips. And her hands are strong. Veins criss-cross the smooth dark brown plains of her hands, travelling between her fingers, between the webs of her fingers. Her hands are soft.

They do not reflect the hard work she endured in the North Field for years, years ago. And her fingers are long. Her fingernails are short. They are cut very short.

She does not wear lipstick. And she does not wear nail polish.

She puts the handkerchief back into her left sleeve.

"Would you please make me a drink, Percy?"

It takes him some time to respond. He has been travelling along with her story of personal history, over that landscape, observing the chapters of that journey, as he did then, and even now, from the other vantage point, from the other side of Highgates Commons, on the other side of the counter, on the other side of the aisle, on the other side of the picnic ground, on the other side of the waves at the Crane Beach Hotel, on the other side of the sandcastles the children built, wishing that he had the ability of knowledge, at least that he could have guessed at her unhappiness, and now, tonight, on the other side of this front-house . . . did she say she was unhappy? Or lonely? He wishes he could have guessed at her loneliness. But as he knows, and as she has said, eyes followed, and reported.

Golbourne got a cruel, severe, crippling beating from Mr. Bellfeels. And it was caused by jealousy over Golbourne's girl-friend that Mr. Bellfeels fancied.

Pounce got a severe beating from Mr. Bellfeels for going with a woman Mr. Bellfeels fancied.

Sargeant knows about these incidents.

He knows more. He conducted the two criminal investigations himself; and another: the damage to the Morris Minor of the Vicar, the Reverend Mr. M. R. P. P. Dowd, caused by "deliberate incendary activity," Sargeant wrote in his little black book; "burned"; and the "whole entire car and part of the garage it was park in, butting and bound" on the west side of the Vicarage, "almost engulf totally in conflagration." Mr. Bellfeels had passed one Sunday when it was raining, on his way from the Church to the Great House in which Miss Mary lived with Wilberforce, then a small boy in Third Form at Harrison College, and had seen the Vicar speaking with Mary, and had seen how Mary was holding her body over the Vicar's car door, to thank him for the lift, to say good night to the Vicar . . . It was about eight-forty-five the Sunday night, after Evensong and Service . . .

As Sargeant's investigation found out, Mr. Bellfeels had gone to get Mary, as he always did, after the service; but the rain was falling; and it had been falling all day; and he was delayed by a flat tire, and Mary had waited inside the Church, at the West Nave, sheltering, for half an hour, with no sight of the large black Humber Hawk; so the Vicar, out of the kindness of his heart, was encouraging Mary to wait for Mr. Bellfeels to come. "So, be patient, my child, do not venture forth into this torrential rain, Miss Mary. Wait."

"*Bellfeels coming. Don't despair.*"

"*I want to get back to Wilberforce. Wilberforce has a touch o' the flu. And he got exams in the morning.*"

"*Still, wait. How Wilberforce? Which Form Wilberforce in? Third is it? End o' term. Exams for promotion. Right?*"

"*I should really go. Even walk-through the rain . . .*"

"*Is only thirty minutes since service done. Wait a next ten, at least.*"

"*I should walk home.*"

"*I'll drop-you-off, then . . .*"

That is how it happened. That is the evidence Sargeant accumulated. What Sargeant did not know was the beating Mary-Mathilda got that night . . .

Now, Sargeant is looking at this woman, whose age has stopped still, seeing her in the same years and identical beauty as when he followed her along the beach as she carried the clear liquid in the large glass jug . . .

And Sargeant knows that if he had, over the years, made a move to talk to her, to see her, to send her a message, to make his intentions known, and Mr. Bellfeels had smelled this adventure, had not even discovered it, but had only suspected it, Sargeant knows that the rat of his lust would have tasted disaster . . . demotion, dismissal, death, even.

Sargeant knows of men who have died . . .

But he is too scared to call the names of those who killed them . . .

". . . Not to be able to take the lane from this House, and walk-cross the road there, and visit the Needleworker, Mistress Brannford, Rosa Mary Antoinette Brannford, before Mr. Brannford kill her; and before she poisoned the Governor.

"Those places you would have seen me in, from that distance, were times when I would gladly have-exchange my lot with the poorest woman in this Village.

"Even with Clotelle. With Gertrude, who works for me. Even with *his* wife, Mistress Bellfeels, whom I have hardly spoken to. I have hardly picked my teeth to that woman. Nor her to me. Yes.

"You would have seen me, yes, in various places, and I always came back in here and say to Wilberforce, 'Guess who I saw in Town? The Sargeant. And he never-as-much as acknowledge my presence. Wonder why?'"

"I was scared," he says. "I was ward-off."

"Ward-off? And a little woman like me scaring you? Come-come, Sargeant!"

"You know what they say! A lil woman, but a mob-o'-ton o' woman."

"Me? Poor me?"

"It is your position and status. Your status, Miss Mary. Your image. I was talking about this only this evening, to Manny, before. And your class. And what it is that you stand for, and mean . . ."

"What I mean? What the hell you mean by what I mean? Am I a . . . a-a-a . . . a *thing?*"

"No, no, Miss Mary. Not that."

"Then what, Percy?"

"We were discussing something-altogether-different."

"Do not pity me, Sargeant. Not because I have told you certain things."

"But, good-Christ, Mary . . ."

"In my house, Sargeant, I am Miss Mary Gertrude Mathilda, a lady who . . . if you don't mind, sir."

"I sorry, Mary. I am very sorry, Miss Mary Gertrude Mathilda . . ."

"Thank you, Sargeant."

"I didn't mean . . ."

"I have a Statement you have to take from me."

"Now?"

"*Now!*"

"Now-now? After the conversation we been having?"

"You are still on duty, Sargeant."

"But Mary-G . . . I mean, but Miss Mary-Mathilda, do we really have to . . . Why this change o' heart, all of a sudden?"

"Change o' *heart?*"

"Change o' mood . . ."

"I went too far, perhaps, in our conversation. And allowed you to get a false impression. You took advantage of me, under the circumstances; and I allowed you to see me with my guard down. But I really do not need your pity, Sargeant Stuart. I am still the *mistress* of this Great House."

"I don't feel no pity for you, Miss Mary Gertrude Mathilda."

"You are a Crown-Sargeant of Detectives."

"I still don't feel no pity for you."

"You are in my house. My home. You know what this means? You are sitting in my front-house. And in uniform. You are on duty. All I have to do to remind you of this is get a message to the Commissioner. If Gertrude hasn't left, Gertrude could take a message . . ."

"You would do me so, Tilda? I mean, Miss Mary-Mathilda? You would go to those *lengths*? You would jeopardize my career in the Police? And my life? Expose me naked-naked, to Mr. Bellfeels? You would do this to me?"

She does not answer. She sits with her head leaning slightly in the direction of the open window, as if she is expecting to feel a kiss from the wind, as if she is listening to a noise, a sound announcing arrival that only she can distinguish and hear and know about when it arrives. Her eyes are closed.

He wishes he had the guts, the balls, in this moment of what she called her vulnerability, to stand up, travel the few feet to the chair in which she sits, bend down, take her up, in his arms, and draw her close to him, even pressing her breasts against the rough-edged silver buttons, with the Imperial Crown on each of the five of them, running down the front of his tunic. He wishes he was a man brought up with a stronger sense of confidence, with a background in family and position that was solid enough to make him able to see this woman before him, in the same confidence of presumption as he sees Gertrude; the kind of man whom, ironically, she, Mary-Mathilda, has been dreaming of having, and has been talking about, even if only through implication; but he got the drift of her words; to hold her in his arms, and move her from side to side, take her back to her own infancy and childhood, when it was Ma who did this to her, putting her to bed every night on the mattress stuffed with Khus-Khus grass, her cradle, rockabye, rockabye, rockabye, "Rockabye baby, on a tree top, when the wind blows, the cradle will rock . . ."; hold her and move her, as if he were guiding her in following the melody of "Moonlight Serenade" . . .

She pulls the white cotton handkerchief with the white flowers embroidered into it from the same sleeve as before; and she passes it across her eyes; three times across each eye.

She is crying. She is crying. Her body is shaking, in heaving movements, and she is rocking her body back and forth . . . as she is crying; rockabye, rockabye . . . she is weeping . . . "when the bough breaks, the cradle will fall. Down will come . . ."

"Would you please make me a drink, Percy?"

"Are you sure you want me to make a drink for you?"

"Yes, Percy."

"What kind o' drink?"

"What kind you-yourself want? More rum? Or brandy? Why don't *you* choose?"

"You sure you want me to make myself a drink, Miss Mary-Mathilda?"

"Yes-please, Percy. Don't have to call me Miss Mary Mathilda, any further. Please. Or Miss Mary."

"What to call you?"

"Call me Mary."

"Just Mary?"

PART THREE

THE GRAVEL WAS BEING SCATTERED by the tires speeding over it. And the sound of the flying gravel was similar to that of marbles rackling inside a galvanized bucket; and indeed some of the stones smashed against the oil drums cut in half that served as planters for the croton and hibiscus trees that lined the driveway. If it were still light outside the Great House painted in a creamy pink wash by the man who cleaned the stables and the pigpens, and if Miss Mary Gertrude Mathilda and Sargeant were able to look through the window and pick out anything, they would have seen the gravel rising in swirls of dust, at the speed the car was travelling over the white marl and loose gravel of the driveway shaped like the figure eight. Half of the eight led to the front door of the Main House.

When Wilberforce comes home in this tense, speeding urgency, in broad daylight, the chickens and the fowls, the slow-moving ducks wobbling in the wake of their ducklings, and the gobbling turkeys attracted to noise begin to make louder noise themselves; and all these animals, like members of Miss Mary-Mathilda's family, would cluster and line up, at safe distance, to welcome Wilberforce.

Wilberforce was coming home.

"Drunk!" as his mother would have said, had she been looking out the Dutch window in the kitchen, standing beside Gertrude, sitting on the wooden bench that has no back, peeling eddoes for the mutton soup.

The tires now skid to a stop. The engine dies. The door is slammed. The trunk is banged. Sargeant becomes tense as he hears the door of the car shut. Sargeant can also hear the crickets chirruping. And he takes his hand from her lap. She allows his hands to slip from her grasp.

The kitchen door is opened. And then slammed.

Mary-Mathilda gets up, and runs both her hands along the sides of her dress at the same time, passing them from just under her armpits, down her small waist, down along her full hips, until her hands can reach no farther down. And next she passes her hands over the bun in which her hair is tied. And then she passes her right hand, using the third finger of that hand, over her eyes. Her eyes are closed as she does this. Then she opens her eyes, and with the same fingers rubs them.

The door, down the long hallway from the dining room to the kitchen, is now closed firmly. Wilberforce's footsteps sound on the dark-stained hardwood floor. There is an irregular creak of the floorboards as he comes towards his mother.

"Wilberforce!" she calls out to him. "We have guests."

"Guesses?" he says. His voice rises in laughter; and still laughing, he says, "Guesses? Mother, you celebrating something?"

"Guesses," she says, speaking the dialect, imitating her son.

"What you celebrating?" he says, as his voice grows closer. Wilberforce is at the door of the front-house, where he stops. "*Sarge?* What the arse you doing here, boy? . . . Mother, don't lissen to my French . . . but where the guesses? You don't mean that Sarge is a guess!"

"'Evening, Wilberforce," she says.

"Good evening, Mr. Wilberforce!" Sargeant says.

"The Sargeant is here on business," she says.

"Somebody thief a fowl-cock?" Wilberforce says; and laughs. They laugh with him. "Somebody kill somebody, then? I know one man I would like somebody to kill!" They do not laugh at this.

"The Sargeant is here on business   "

"Well, Jesus Christ, welcome then, boy!"

"On business, Wilberforce," she says.

"Here to lock-up somebody?" Wilberforce says; and laughs. "You here to lock-up Mother?" And he laughs some more.

"No, Mr. Wilberforce," Sargeant says.

"Drop this Mister-thing, boy! My name is Wilberforce. Or, if you insiss on being proper, Doc, then. Call me Doc, man."

"Evening, then, Doc."

"Mother, you looking after Sarge? A good boy."

"Thank you, sir."

"*Doc!* Doc, Sarge!"

"Thank you, Doc."

"How the blood pressure? And what you drinking?"

"A taste of brandy."

"Good! I sticking with rum. Bellfeels Special Stades White Rum. The best cured darrou in the whole Wessindies, boy!"

"What about dinner, Wilberforce?"

"Gertzie cook, or you?"

"Gertie cook."

"You should cook more often, Mother, 'specially on a Sunday, as you uses to. Uh mean no disrespect to Gertzie. The two o' wunnuh going-have to eat without me. Patients. Sarge, it seem that the minute I start enjoying myself with a lil bird, somebody be-Christ, tekking-in, getting sick, with bad-feels! Or they having a pain in their leff side, and calling me in to tek-out their 'pendicitis! A next body getting sick, be-Christ, and deading suddenly, and I got to do the attopsy . . . when um ain' one thing, um is the next, Christ, I don't have time for—"

"You would swear, hearing my son talk like this, that Wilberforce was a lighterman, and not a big doctor, who—"

"Man o' the people, Sarge-boy! *Roots!*"

"So, you're not eating."

"A lil bird waiting for me, at the Club."

He pours himself a large rum in a crystal half-pint tumbler, without chipped ice, without water; and he leans back his head, just a little, and with the mouth of the glass not touching his lips, he lets the rich, white liquid pour into his mouth. He keeps the rum in his mouth, making his mouth look puffed; and with his jaws not moving, he places the glass gingerly back onto the table with the diamond-shaped top, screws up his eyes, swallows the rum inside his mouth, and says, *"Emmm! Uh-hemmm!"*

He moves and stands beside Sarge; and pats Sarge heavily on his back, and says, "Down the hatch, boy! Down the hatch! Watch that blood pressure. As man!"

He leaves as noisily as he has entered.

They can hear his feet climbing the stairs at the back of the dining room; and then they hear his footsteps crossing the ceiling, and they look up, as if expecting to see his footprints reproduced on the ceiling; and then they hear drawers being opened and closed; and water running, travelling noisily through the pipes inside the green-papered wall where they stand, looking at the ceiling.

They just stand, and listen. And they follow the progress he makes above their heads; and can almost feel they are in his room with him.

Wilberforce rumbles into the front-house and faces them.

He has changed from "hot" shirt, cream linen slacks and Clark sandals to a dark grey suit with a fine pinstripe; white shirt, university tie of Jesus College, Oxford; dark brown suede shoes; a freshly pressed and starched handkerchief juts from his left breast pocket, ironed in four points, by Gertrude. These points in his handkerchief are like the sails of a four-mast yacht putting out to sea from the Aquatic Club.

"You really walk-all-the-way up to the Main House last night, as you say you was doing, Mother?" he says to his mother. "What was so serious you had to tell Bellfeels?"

The question takes Mary Mathilda by surprise.

"Sarge, you know anybody who does-address his father by his surname?"

Sargeant looks uncomfortable.

"Calling your father by his surname! Imagine!"

Wilberforce turns his attention to the decanter of Bellfeels Special Stades White Rum and chooses a fresh crystal glass.

He pours the drink, the same size almost as the first one; closes his eyes; holds his breath; holds the rum in his mouth; and finally swallows it; and screws up his face. *"Emmm! Uh-hemmm!"* he says; and then, "Down the hatch!" and then, "As man!"

He stands about two feet from them.

"Well?"

"Well, what?" his mother says.

"You not offering the ipso facto Bimshire Constabulary no dinner? Not even a fresh drink?"

Sargeant is uncomfortable.

"Of course!" she says.

"In this old house, Sarge-boy, if yuh don't brek for yuhself . . ."

"My manners!" his mother says.

"Well, down the hatch, then, Sarge-boy!" Wilberforce says. He has poured another drink—for himself—and turns to leave, and says to Sargeant, "I got some pills for you, for the pressure. Down the hatch, Sarge-boy! Pass-round tomorrow by the surgery . . . Good night." And he leaves, whistling a calypso.

They stand, not too close to each other, and remain like this, looking through a window, as the gravel kicks up, as some animals in the yard, not sleeping at this hour, shift and resettle their bodies on the dried grass in their pens, reacting to the skidding noise of tires over the white marl and the loose gravel.

Sargeant imagines the dust rising like smoke from a field of sugar canes on fire, all along the eight-hundred-and-eighty-yard stretch of the white-marled driveway that joins the entrance to this house and that of the Main House, forming a large figure eight; the same road that leads to the corner of Highgates Commons and Reservoir Lane; and he can see the rear lights of Wilberforce's red Singer sports car getting smaller and smaller, eventually being eaten up in the clouds of marl, in the distance, and in the blackness . . .

Mary-Mathilda raises the mantle of the acetylene lamp, "a gas lamp," and strokes the pump attached to the lamp, two times; and this gives the room a white brilliance, greater than the electric light from the two bulbs that hang on long brown wires, like "pah-wee" mangoes, from a branch. The mantle bears the flame. The mantle is like a child's bootie or the cover Wilberforce puts on his golf clubs.

In the light of the acetylene lamp, the front-house becomes bigger and grander. Sargeant is swallowed-up in its bigness; and at the same time, he becomes part of this bigness and grandness; adjusted and acclimatized: recognizing faces of the men and women in sepia-tinted photographs, all of which are framed in wood and glass; and he is intrigued to see how the glass sends a glare from the frame, and this glare prevents him, temporarily, from seeing the faces clearly behind the glass, unless he changes his position and stands at a different angle to the glass—which he does—to defeat the glare; and study the faces of the men and women—some of whom he sees each day; has seen for years—but who now look dignified and distant as strangers by the formality of the frames; some frames look like silver; some like gold; some like brass; these photographs of the faces of men and women; and the faces of her two dead children, taken in their small, white coffins. In another photograph, little Mary-the-virgin is sitting on the twisted roots of a tree. The tree is the bearded fig tree. It is the tree that is native to Bimshire, picked out by the Portuguese who "discovered" Bimshire, who told the natives of Bimshire to call these trees "barbutos" trees; bearded fig trees; who told the natives they will christen the Island "barbados," then lost interest in "barbadoses" and "babutos"; and allowed the Island to fall into the hands of pirates, into enemy hands, the paws of the English, who renamed it Bimshire.

These bearded fig trees grow in uncountable number round the Race Pasture.

She is about eight when this shot of her is snapped.

Mary at the annual Church picnic, standing like a buoy in a sea of no current, up to her knees in the warm blue waves, which have a crest of whiteness, like cream on coconut pie, on them; or like the froth on the top of a pail of milk, fresh from the cow.

Mary in her school uniform. She is eleven years old in this snapshot.

Mary standing like the proprietoress, in front of a small store in Swan Street, of Cloth Merchants. The background is of people passing and staring.

Mary, standing in the middle of the East Nave, with the iron gates of Sin-Davids Anglican Church open; framing her body, cutting off her forehead and legs at the knees; and still in this picture, on either side of her are the flowers in bloom, in the garden beds amongst the graves; this natural grotto of life and loveliness. She stands straight, but shy. Her left hand is over her face; a cross attached to a chain is revealed round the neck of a white dress; shielding her face from the sun. A book marked *Holy Bible* is in her right hand. It is the day of her Confirmation. Sargeant was present in the Church Yard, that Sunday afternoon, around four—but removed from the field of depth and of focus—when the lens was clicked shut.

Mary holding Wilberforce, in various stages of his growth and development, in many mahogany frames.

"My Wall of History," she says. "Or my Wall of Shame. Wilberforce dig-up these photos from in trunks in the cellar, and had Mr. Waldrond frame them."

And Mr. Bellfeels on a horse. High, above the level of the photographer, and with no smile, with no softness on his visage, his countenance stern and white. The shirt and the jodhpurs and the helmet he is wearing are all white. The sun is shining in his face. It is shining with such force and brightness that even in this black-and-white photo, Sargeant feels he can still see how the sun has burnt the spiteful ruddiness into Mr. Bellfeels' face. His riding boots are shining. Sargeant can see the spurs attached to the boots. In his hand is a riding crop.

Mr. Bellfeels is standing beside a horse. The horse's hindquarters and Mr. Bellfeels' head are at the same level. Mr. Bellfeels looks tall and big in this photograph. Sargeant is surprised to see how the Kodak box camera has conspired in the magnification of Mr. Bellfeels' stature. In real life, contradicting the veracity of this box camera's lens, Mr. Bellfeels is a short, small man; a "five-foot-three kiss-me-arse, fecking midget——if yuh axe me!——who always trying to terrorize the whole fecking Village! That short-nee-crutch son-uv-a-bitch!"——Manny had called him earlier tonight, talking with Sargeant in the Special Clienteles Room; short as a woman; shorter than Napoleon Bonaparte.

Mr. Bellfeels standing in a group of men, in front of a cluster of beach-grape trees. Sargeant assumes it is the beach at the Crane Beach Hotel. The Vicar is there. The Solicitor-General is there. The manager of the Aquatic Club is there. The Headmaster of Harrison College is there. And the owner-manager of a haberdashery store, smaller than Cave Shepherd & Sons, Haberdasheries, is there. The six of them. Like a cabinet. Like a government. Or like a committee. Like a clan. Like merchants involved in the sale of something, of somebody, of lots of bodies, chewing on the prospect of profits. Like a secret society. Like their own Bimshire Masonic Temple Lodge. Young, and healthy, and rich, and cocky; arrogant and carefree. And powerful. And drunk. Privileged. White.

Mr. Bellfeels is sailing a boat in the white sea that looks like glass; off the Aquatic Club.

Mr. Bellfeels standing over a log, a large branch sawed off from a tree, perhaps a breadfruit tree, perhaps a mango tree, perhaps it is the fallen branch of a tamarind tree; the branch is ripped from the rest of its sturdy body by the winds of Hurricane Darnley that scared the Village and the Plantation into believing that they were facing the end of the world. But it was merely the hurricane season.

And Mr. Wilberforce, Doc, "Mary's boy-child," in most of the other photographs.

There are shots of Wilberforce snapped to match and chronicle his development: from cradle, into Church Choir, into the First Bimshire Sea Scouts, into Harrison College, in various ascending forms and achievements; standing in front of the large black Humber Hawk, with a chauffeur dressed in livery, grinning behind the steering wheel, parked in the Yard of the College, under the sandbox tree, near the main entrance to the Hall, where Assembly is held every morning, punctually at nine. Wilberforce and Sargeant would sit in the grass-piece, beside the Great House, in the long vacation, eating mangoes, and Wilberforce would tell him about the "funny ways we do things at Harsun College"; and Sargeant would stop sucking a Julie-mango and listen in awe: the Assembly would sing one hymn, from the book of *Hymns Ancient and Modern*; recite one Psalm; listen to a piece of literature, read by the Headmaster, from the Bible or from *The Pilgrim's Progress,* which little Wilberforce, on his first day, in First Form, a "new boy," did not understand head-nor-tail of this first Assembly, as the Headmaster's thunderous English accent recited, *"As I walked through the wilderness of this world, I lighted on a certain place where there was a den, and laid me down in that place to sleep; and as I slept, I dreamed a dream . . ."*

But he grew to like *The Pilgrim's Progress;* and sobbed every morning the Headmaster read from it; and told his mother when he got home how he cried; on the morning of his last day at Harrison College, the Headmaster, now old and with a voice that was weak and distant, and still English, that faded between words, read the final words of *The Pilgrim's Progress,* his voice matching the trembling of his hands that held the black, leather-bound, gold-engraved tome,

> *As for Christiana's children, the four boys that Christiana brought, with their wives and children, I did not stay where I was till they were gone over. Also, since I came away, I heard one say that they*

*were yet alive, and so would be for the increase of the Church in
that place where they were, for a time.*

*"Should it be my lot to go that way again, I may give those that
desire it an account of what I here am silent about. Meantime I bid
my reader*
  FAREWELL

And Wilberforce cried . . . the poems of the English poets Keats or
Wordsworth or Tennyson or Byron or a devotional section from
"The Rime of the Ancient Mariner" did not have the same impact as
John Bunyan "the prince of dreamers" . . . and photographs of
Wilberforce, going right into and throughout his days at Oxford
University, and then at Cambridge; in gown; and finally in hood,
mortarboard cap and gown; and with the stethoscope round his
neck making him look serious and important, like an African
chief, draped in ceremonial beads: a medical doctor.

"*My God!*"

"What?" she says.

"So many snapshots! Of *every* step the three o' you, Wilberforce,
you and Mr. Bellfeels, take! That is the difference. Me-now, I have
one photo of me in my whole house. *One!* And that photo was
taken when I get *these*!" He taps the three silver stripes below the
Imperial Crown on his left arm with his right hand. The stripes are
edged in red velvet. "That is the only snapshot I have of myself!
There is one of my two daughters, Ruby up in Brooklyn, and
Wanda who pass-away; taken at two different times."

"History, Percy. These people . . . and I wonder if they include-
me-in with them? . . . these people like to know where they begin,
and where they stand, at every minute in their lives."

"That is the difference between me and them."

"They like things to last a long time. Endure. Wilberforce tell
me that the name for this habit is a *continuance*. These people wor-
ships continuances and making things last and endure. The same
thing that you would call history.

"If you look careful, you can map-out Wilberforce life. From cradle, to Christening to Confirmation, to First Communion, to Harrison College, in the Sea Scouts, as you can see from that snap-shot where he look like a little coloured sailor-boy in the Royal Navy, to his promotion through all the Forms at Harrison, right up to Six Form, when he won the Scholarship in Classics. And finally, his life through the countries of his trekking-about in, Away. His travels Overseas.

"Look at him in this one. The clothes he got on. A altered man. A different person, a stranger to me, wearing those damn leather short pants, held-up with those braces, and that shirt, looking more like a woman's blouse than a man's shirt! I swear to God . . .

"In all these variations, in countries, Wilberforce behaving as if he born *there*. As a European! Not like a real man from Bimshire, at all.

"But, Percy-boy, that is the young generation for yuh! Eh? Yes!"

She moves to stand under another row of photographs; looking at them, and having her own thoughts, painting them with her own memories of their history; remembering the pose and the sugges-tion that the head should be raised, just a little; that Wilberforce, or the subject, one of the Six, should move, just a little bit more to the left, yes; to prevent the sun from hitting the lens so hard . . . yes, a lil touch right . . .

"Ma!" she declares.

She takes the photograph of Ma from the wall. A large nail is in the wall. The outline of dust left against the wall marks out the shape of the frame of this photograph.

"I must ask Gertrude to dust more . . ."

Ma is in an oval frame. The frame is made of grainy wood, highly polished. The oval shape on the wall, left by the frame, emphasizes the amount of dust collected round the frame.

". . . must ask Gertrude to dust better."

The face of the woman inside the frame is touched by age: age of the photo itself, and by dark specks and some white ones, too. There is a dead scorpion in the frame with the woman. Its skeleton.

But her face is beautiful and round; and her lips are thick, but not voluptuous or suggestive of wantonness; and her eyes are not staring at you but are held down just a little, in prudence, in shyness, in well-mannered propriety, and as if she could have been distracted by a voice, a movement of the photographer's hand, a butterfly coming too close, or a bee buzzing around, just when the shutter was about to be snapped. Her hair is combed back. Sargeant cannot see the style in which her hair is fixed, for the hair is close to the head and there is not much space in the frame for more hair to be seen. Her dress is white. White because it is probably white; and white because there was no colour formula when this photograph was taken. Everything is either black or white; looks either black or white. There is a chain round her neck, round the neck of her high-necked bodice. A plain, large Crucifix is attached to the chain. The bodice of her dress has workings, gathers, pleats, the design common in those days of prudence and chastity in women's fashions; and it reaches her up to her neck, just below her ears.

Mary-Mathilda holds the photograph to her breasts.

Sargeant cannot make the comparison: of size between the two women, of shape, of gait; for one is a mere photograph, a ghost; while the other is standing beside him, and he can smell her presence, her dress and hair and perfume; and also the scent, the smell, the "stench" of his own sensuality that has been in the room all night; and Ma's breasts are hidden under the heavy, intricate needlework of the bodice of her dress. Mary-Mathilda's breasts, which he has touched in his imagination, are flattened under her brassiere and the formation of her blouse, which fit like a corset, to give the impression of modesty and that there are no breasts at all.

"Ma!" she says; and sighs.

And the love she still has for her mother makes her voice shaky.

"Your mother," he says.

"Come . . ."

She walks up the stairs, slowly, standing for a pause on each step, and studies each of the photographs that become level with her eyes; takes another step, looks, all the time holding her left hand, which is placed into Sargeant's, behind her, towing him as she has seen barges and "lighters" towing motor vessels and inter-island schooners, into the safer waters of the Careenage, to touch the walls of the Wharf, softened by old, black car tires.

With each slow step up, at each pause, he too examines the exhibition of photographs, at his own eye-level.

Wilberforce is standing near a huge waterfall . . .

"Kaieteur. In Demerara . . ."

"And this one?" he asks her.

On the succeeding step, Wilberforce is in a square, in a place that is not Bimshire. "Vincentia! An ancient, small city in the northern part of Italy. He met this girl there. Mirabella. At first, everything was sweet as a brown sugar cake. Mirabella, Mirabella, Mirabella. You couldn't hear your blasted ears for *Mirabella*! Mirabella Vero. Veron . . . Veronesi—I can hardly pronounce the blasted woman surname! Nowadays, I don't hear *one* word 'bout this Mirabella. It seem as if Mirabella *dead*. And a damn good thing, too!

"No daughter-in-law of mine, with a foreign accent, boy! For my only son? Oh, no! I am not so broad-minded!

"Prejudiced, maybe. But I old-enough to bear grudges. Old-enough to be a serrigrationist—if you want to call me one, then! You don't think so? And a lil prejudiced. But a woman with a *foreign* accent! And for my son?

"Yes, man! Vincentia—if that's how you pronounce it. But look what a lovely way they build their houses in Vincentia! Wilberforce tell me that that way of building buildings is a special tradition the Eyetalians have. And the type of buildings they build have a special name. *Palades?* Is it *Palisades?* No, man, that's not the word! I know! *Palladios!* Yes! The buildings in that part of the world, the buildings you see in the background, with Wilberforce standing in front of one them, are called Palladios Architecture. Wilberforce told me that Palladios built his buildings all over certain parts of Italy. Spe-cially, Wilberforce say, in the cities where the Borgias and other families of Popes lived, all the Piuses; and that in Venice, Verona and Vincentia itself, you will find these buildings; and some of the same Borgias, Wilberforce found out in a book, is black people like me and you, and . . . you didn't know that, did you?"

"*No!*" Sargeant says. "Popes? . . . like Pius-the-Third, Fourth and Fiff . . . *black* Popes? What you trying to put on me?"

"Yes!" she says. "Eyetalians are a black tribe, like me and you."

"*Yuh lie!*"

"Read the book!"

"So, the three *V*'s were the birthplace of black Popes, you must be. . . !"

"What you referring to, about three *V*'s, Percy?"

"The Palladios cities! Venice, Veronica and Vincentia! All *V*'s!"

"Never thought of them so! But, yes. The three *V*'s! Must be important. Those Eyetalians are smart bastards, I tell you. They have black in them, that's why. Imagine that these pictures hanging inside this house, on the same wall for years, never touched nor moved safe when Gertrude cleaning and dusting, or when the painter paint the place, once every blue-moon, and I never, never-ever thought of seeing them as the three *V*'s! The three *V*'s . . . But that's why you are a detective . . ."

"A pretty place. I wonder if in my lifetime on this earth I would ever be fortunate-enough to stand up in a square, or a plaza like this, with Palladios Architecture behind me, in the background, and have a snapshot taken of it? I wonder if I would ever see Venice? In the flesh? Or Italy . . ."

"*See Venice and die!*"

"I hear' somebody-else say so. 'See Venice and die.' But what it mean?"

"It means that you could-as-well drop-down dead when you see Venice, because there isn't no-other-place-else-on-earth that can touch Venice! Nothing-more in life, to see. Perhaps it is another meaning to the Palladios Architecture that I was just telling you about . . ."

They are at the top of the flight of stairs. They have climbed thirteen steps. Sargeant did not intend to count them, but he is intrigued by being inside this house; and now that he is inside it, he is not at ease, as he would be at the Harlem Bar & Grill, in the Selected Clienteles Room, and he needs to get his bearings, and perhaps would be comfortable. This is why he has counted the stairs. Thirteen of them. With each step, the stairs creak, groaning under his weight and under her weight. They creak in the same loud way as new shoes cry out in a silent church, where noise is not normal, when the congregation are kneeling and praying.

The flight she has just taken him up is steep. He has run his hand, the one she is not holding, over the mahogany banister; and his hand picks up the sweet smell from the patina on the wood and the polish.

Looking back down the thirteen steps he has just climbed, to the carpets on the hardwood floor stained in brown, he feels he is in the Changing Room of the Choir, up in the Loft. Revern Dowd calls it the Crow's Nest. A slight giddiness suggests itself in his head. He closes his eyes. And in a moment, the giddiness is gone.

She leads him along the hallway. It is about twenty feet long. It has the two large windows that face the fields; and on the side opposite, on his left side, is the whitewashed wall that has two French doors painted white, with frosted panes of glass, covered in lace through which he can see the eight rectangles of glass. She leads him through this door.

He is in a bedroom.

Is this her bedroom?

This room has more space than the house in which he lives. His house is down the hill from this Great House, near the intersection of Highgates Commons and Reservoir Lane, through a set of mahogany trees, one mile from the sub-station, half a mile from the Harlem Bar & Grill, walking distance to the Church and the Elementary School.

He is inside an enormous bedroom. He is standing beside a huge bed. With a canopy. King? Or queen? Four sturdy legs of polished mahogany stand like guardians round the pillows and the sheets and the bedspread. The bed is like a monument in the grave-yard of the Anglican Church: about three to four feet off the floor, and the size of a tomb built for three stout bodies.

Everything in this bedroom is white. The six pillows, three on each side, are white; and brocaded, with white patterns in them, like flowers. The bedspread is white and thicker than the material with which the pillowcases are made. The bedspread hangs on the left side of the bed, on the right side and at the foot. The pillows, high, and fluffed and soft-looking, are as large as four bags of flour, but softer and lighter. The sheets are made of silk. At the bottom of the bed is a folded white clump of cotton. It is her nightgown. There are two large windows in this room. Covered with white curtains, which move from the outside of the frame of the window inwards, as if the wind, like an invisible hand, soft, though, as a kiss on the cheek, is breathing on the lace of the curtains.

She takes him to the side of the bed, which reaches him up to his waist, and from which he can look through the large window down into the valley, where his house sits among thick trees.

What he sees has a dramatic effect upon him. Looking out from this single window, he can see the fuzzy outline of the entire Village and place the location of every house lying within it in his mind.

He wonders if this Great House was built purposely on this promontory of land, in order to observe the Villagers below; if it was placed in this position, to record their daily movements, to be the overseer of their private lives.

She takes him now, out into a short passageway. They walk through this passage, and face another large window, with a seat and a cushion in the seat, and Sargeant sits on the window seat, just to see how it feels; and if it feels similar to the one in the Commis-sioner's home in the Married Women's Quarters, a name for a res-idence which Sargeant finds as puzzling and intriguing as the row of red brick apartments themselves; the Quarters are close to the Savannah Tennis Club; and now sitting on this maroon cushion, as flat as a bake through use, in a window of this Great House, he sees, and he feels no difference between this one and the one in the Com missioner's apartment . . .

The cushions in the window seat at the Commissioner's apart-ment are all navy blue, with buttons stitched in them, the way motor-car seats are made.

"Yes!" he says.

The passageway leads out from her bedroom.

Before she touches his shoulder, pointing him outwards, he has noticed a large black chest, with an oval lid, strengthened with clasps of iron and pointed with large brass studs; and he thinks of children's books of fairy tales and tales of adventure in Indian caves and temples, and the mysteries of the Far East; and treasure chests of pirates; and of Captain Morgan who, like a pirate, seduced tall ships coming from Englund and the Spanish Main and from Africa with slaves and other treasure, to land in shallow waters round the coasts of Bimshire. These ships were captained by pirates; and Cap-tain Morgan caused many of these ships to be beached upon the craggy shore, after sailing with confidence into the bright glare of lanterns placed strategically high up in coconut trees, mistaking them for beacons. Those slave ships and galleons, schooners and tall ships filled with gold were fooled that these coconut trees were the blinking eyes of the Needham's Point Lighthouse; tricked; wrecked; had; *"was took!"*; and run aground; half sinking. Then, in the dimness of dawn, and placid sea, they were plundered by Mis-ter Captain Morgan, wading through the floating bodies of pirates and of slaves, and Western-rolled and crawled with strong swim-mer's strokes, through the quiet waves and oozing blood from the dying bodies; and stole their loot; "stole the shirts from off their black backs," treasures to be pocketed; English sailor-pirates to be buried with hymn and Prayer Book, Churched as if it were a wedding, given benediction and quiet burial in Sin-Davids Anglican Church's Church Yard, following the admonition that "the Office ensuing is not to be used for any that die unbaptized, or excommunicate, or have laid violent hands upon themselves"; hearing the lugubrious words of Job: "*We brought nothing into this world, and it is certain we can carry nothing out. The Lord gave, and the Lord hath taken away; blessed be the name of the Lord*": slaves to be carried back out, into the broiling waves, and fed dead to the sharks. And Captain Morgan became a millionaire. Good ole Cap'n Morg also became powerful and respectable like the clan of men, the Six, in the photograph with Mr. Bellfeels; went into politics; "did good," gave money to the poor and black, and gave his name to a bottle of rum; "Jamaica him come *fram!*"; and ended up as a legislator on the Legislative Council of Bimshire . . . And there is a looking glass, framed in wood, which swings just like the blackboards in his Elementary School. It is large enough for him to see from his black boots right up to the top of his head, in a single glance. The looking glass is poised at an angle of about forty degrees from the floor. And there is a horse; he calls it a horse. She would know it as a valet. On this horse is a dress, spread around the coat hanger that is built into the horse; and what looks like a woman's camisole is thrown over the dress. The dress is of white cotton. The camisole is of silk, and is white.

"Yes!" he says.

She leads him out of the dressing room, and back into the bedroom. She does not know why she is doing this. He walks to another large window with a seat, and sits on it, and wishes it was daytime, and that the sun was shining, and he could see down into the valley, could see his own house from this window, and mark in clearer daylight vision the distance he is from that chattel house in the valley.

"My house gotta be somewhere down there!" he says. "If it wasn't so dark, I could see my house."

"Yes," she says, "and the small piece of land round it. And your pear trees! One day Gertrude brought a pear from one of your trees, and it made a lovely salad. So yellow and thick and fleshy! Chickens your pullet hatched last Saturday . . . all round your yard, Percy . . ."

". . . my-God Mary!"

He shakes his head, in disbelief; but smiling all the time. "You been observing me. *All* these years."

He looks down into the valley, green during the height of day, dark now as the laneways he patrolled earlier tonight, to locate his house; and his eyes in their weak vision travel from memory, in the thick pitch-blackness from the skies, through the half-mile of white marl and loose gravel driveway which Wilberforce had taken earlier, then through the trees in the gully, over the rise of the cane fields and fields of Khus-Khus grass, through the grass piece, and finally down into the valley, and come to a cluster of trees that marks out the boundary of pasture land on which cows and horses of the Plantation graze, on which the Villagers play cricket and football; and run ordinary races, and goat-races every Sunday afternoon; and then, Sargeant can guess, from memory, the location of the Harlem Bar & Grill. In this journey, blindfolded by the pitch-blackness, he expresses some alarm that the Harlem Bar & Grill is hidden almost completely in a grove of fruit trees. But not even this blackness can erase his memory of it. The trees are breadfruit trees, sugar apple, tamarind and a mango tree, a Julie-mango tree; and a puh-paw tree, Manny's favourite that provides him, year-round, with the thick, yellow, nectarine flesh of the puh-paw, abundant with seeds the colour and consistency almost of fish roe, which "move the bowels so nice, more better and easy than castor oil. My puh-paw tree!" And beside the puh-paw tree, a mayflower tree in bloom. From this distance, from this lofty view, in this graveyard darkness—a quite different perspective—he is shocked at the power of his memory, like the game of arranging objects after you have been given two minutes to memorize all of them. He can find his way through any encumbrance, through any maze of evidence, through any entanglement that his presence—the length of time that he is in this House—or any amorous entanglement she, and his physical presence, might conceive.

He is more confident now of his ability to rearrange, from memory, and in total darkness, objects and persons he has been passing in broad daylight.

He walks this Village at the level of the centipede and the worm, on bare ground, on roads in the darkest of nights, patrolling. Now, from this window, he has a new elevated knowledge of his Village. There are more trees clogging-up the land than he had imagined.

"You been looking at me, Miss Mary-Mathilda, all these years! Seeing me *almost naked*!"

"To your right . . ." she tells him now, "I'll be your eyes. To your right, you would see the Pilgrim Holiness Church that Gertrude attends; and to your left, the Church of the Nazarene, where Pounce stands up at the window during revival meetings; and the narrow road, then the alley turning into the lane that leads to the house where Golbourne lives . . . his house need a coat o' paint bad . . . to the one-roof chattel house where Pounce live; the three-roofed-and-kitchen house where once Mistress Rosa Mary Antoinette Brannford carried on her needlework and making pudding-and-souse every Saturday afternoon, and where now, her husband, Mr. Brannford, live alone, on full disability pension from the Aquatic Club, going half-mad; and the tree at the corner of Flagstaff which his wife ordered him to stand and wait under, until the Governor had-finish eating his food . . . stands big and broad, like a fowl-cock fluffing its wings, boasting of its prowess with hens, showing off his colours amongst the encircling hens in the yard; and the intersection of Highgates Commons and Reservoir Lane that divides the inhabitants of the Village of Flagstaff, and their homes, into good and bad, into decent and worthless; into the rich and the poorest, into the Village and the Plantation; and, man-yes, more than anything, you could see, clearer even in your imagination than the blackness of tonight is allowing you, the steeple of Sin-Davids Anglican Church, where you sing in the Choir. In the Church Yard, if it was day, the tall croton trees, with all their multiple colours and prowessness, like the plumes of the fowl-cock, you could visualize. Tall and powerful, even though, with only this light, you can't see it. But it is there. And from this distance, the outline of Sin-Davids, and the way it is built from local coral stone from the Village Quarry, and imported marble from Englund. Isn't it majestic and frightening, at the same time? In this pitch-blackness?"

"The music we have-sing in that Church!" he says. "And almost break-down the walls, and crack the windows, with our voices!"

"'O, all ye Beasts and Cattle, bless ye the Lord; praise him, and magnify him forever.'"

He intones this, imitating Revern Dowd chanting.

"'O, all ye Fowls of the Air, bless ye the Lord,'" she says, in response, 'praise him and magnify him for ever.'"

"The times we have-sing this Psalm!"

"This is Morning Prayers," she says.

"But we are saying Morning Prayers in the evening."

"And a late evening it is."

"When I was a choirboy, and my voice didn't crack yet, I use to spend the whole time, when Revern Dowd standing in the pulpit giving his sermon, counting every one of these verses in this Psalm. They come to thirty-two. All thirty-two begins with the word O.

"'O, all ye Works of the Lord, bless ye the Lord; praise him, and magnify him for ever.'"

"Yes!" she says. "This is the Benedicte. I used to know all thirty-something verses, by heart, too. And once, my Sunday School teacher made me memorize the first three words in each Benedicte."

They stand and look out through the window, humming under their breaths, but not in unison, the verses of the Benedicte, as they come to them. And then Sargeant says, "Lemme see hommany Benedictees you know."

"Man-yes!" she says, smiling. "Man-yes, it's a bet!"

"What are we betting?"

"A kiss."

"'O, all ye Works of the Lord,'" he says.

"'. . . *bless ye the Lord,*'" she answers; and adds, "'*O, ye Angels.*'"

"'*O, ye Heavens,*'" he says.

"'*O, ye Waters.*'" And they continue like this, down, down to "'*Let the Israelites bless the Lord,*'" which is what she says.

"'*O, ye Priests of the Lord.*'"

"'*O, Ananias, Azards, and Misael . . .*'" she says.

And they both cross themselves, making the sign of the Cross, she correctly; he, moving his hand at the first horizontal position to his right, instead of to his left. Their faces take on a satisfied look, like a glow, like an understanding; as if there is affection between them, like the visage of beneficence that he has seen on the faces of the congregation after Communion; and together, concluding the *Benedicte,* they recite, "'*Glory be to the Father, and to the Son, and to the Holy Ghost.*'"

"'*As it was in the beginning,*'" he says.

"'. . . *is now . . .*'"

"'. . . *and ever shall be . . .*'"

"'. . . *world without end.*'"

"'*Ah-men,*'" she says.

"'*A-men,*'" he says.

She forgets to give him the kiss: and he does not ask for it.

"Let me show you this," she says. She takes a red cloth tied with black string, from a chair. Slowly she unties it; slowly, and seductively, and dramatically, looking at him as she does this. He does not know what is contained in the velour folds of the cloth which she peels back like the skin of a banana. Then, he sees it. It is a box. Slowly, for she is performing magic now, she lifts the cover of the box, and shows him a second, smaller velour bag. This contains an instrument. And when she unknots the silk tassel from the bag, she pulls from the cloth a spying glass.

"No, Mary-G! No!" he says.

She places the spying glass into his hands, and goes to a large desk below another window, and from a drawer she takes the tripod for the spying glass. She extends the legs of the tripod, takes the spying glass from his hands, and screws it tightly on to the tripod. She swings the long lens in the direction of the valley below, locks it into that position, and motions him to look.

The spying glass is about one yard long. But when it is extended, to suit focus and distance, it stretches to about four and a half feet. Its body is made of dark brown leather, and marking each joint, or section, there is highly polished brass. The combination of leather and brass reminds him of the smell of the upholstery in the Chief Justice's Jaguar Mark V. That powerful, smoky smell of a man who is sweating. Almost that smell. This spying glass looks as if it is brand-new.

"*Look,*" she says.

He touches the eyepiece warily; and handles the instrument carefully in appreciation of its price and its owner's regard of it. He marvels at its beauty and workmanship. He is nervous holding this magnificent and expensive instrument.

"*Look!*" she says.

He looks through the lens, and immediately takes his head away. The lens is so powerful that even with no moon shining he can make out the outlines of things. His imagination does the rest. At first, it is like seeing objects through steam; or mist. But the lens clears up, and he sees some objects the way he sees congo-eels and lobsters when he wears goggles underwater.

"We used to use ones like this, in the Special Branch, to spot Nazzie submarines!"

Out of the darkness of the valley, where there are no street lights and only a few kerosene and acetylene lamps burning, the occasional headlights on motor-cars indicating turns, like blinking eyes, comes an object. It looms up at him. With the force of a jab. He is rattled by its magnification. The object occupies the entire lens.

"You're seeing your house," she says. "Or should be. Flagstaff Macon Castle, with the Royal Insurance Company shield on it, made outta tinning."

"My God!"

"The sun blinds you when you look at it during the day. But you can still read the *Royal* in the sign."

"My God!" he says.

"If it was light outside, and I keep saying this," she tells him, "you could see the little dent in the Royal shield, beneath the letter *y*."

"I insure the place against all natural disasters," he says, "with a U.S. Money Order, ten dollars it was, that Ruby send for me. And I remember telling Manny, 'Ten hard, cold Amurcan smackeroons!' the afternoon Griffoot the postman deliver the airmail letter. I tell Manny, 'Manny, Ruby getting rich as hell, fast-fast up in Amurca!'

"With part of the Money Order, I take out insurance 'pon the property, with Royal Insurance Company of London-Englund. Flagstaff Macon Castle insure with them. Against fire, storm, hurricane, burglars and the unseen. And the unforeseen. Against every-damn thing imaginable."

"Tomorrow, in daylight," she tells him, "you could see the dent beneath the *y*."

"My God, Mary-G! That dent made by a rock-stone three months ago. I pelt it at a wood-dove. The rock smash-against the house, missing the glass panels I had-install in the front door, by a *khunh*, with the rest of the Money Order."

Flagstaff Macon Castle is painted in reddish brown. He cannot see its colour in this light.

"Spying glasses of a similar mannifacture to this one, is the ones we used to use for spying at night!" he says. "All military people in the Allieds use' them. I even see them use in war movies at the Olympic Theatre."

He uses his imagination more than his actual vision, to see the Royal Insurance shield nailed into the deal board over the front door. He can see the heads of the nails he used, so powerful is his imagination. Why he can see things so clearly as if it was daytime? What kind of science was necessary to manufacture this English-made spying glass that brings objects so close to his face, on so black a night?

He had nailed the shield on to the house, with a claw hammer, using five rusty nails he had got from Manny; and he drove the nails in, proud in the full view of his neighbours; displaying the sign that testified to the fact that he was now a man of means; that Flagstaff Macon Castle is covered by insurance, "'gainst natural and unnatural disaster," Manny told him, with equal pride; for although Flagstaff Macon Castle is a one-roofed chattel house, with a door in the middle of the two windows which open outwards, on a hinge, and propped up with a window stick, the naming of the house, its "christening," had made everyone in the Village see it as a castle. Everyone gives his house a name, written on a piece of cardboard or tinning or three-ply; or, the name is sometimes written straight onto the house itself. The most dilapidated house in the Village has a name. Manny does not know how this habit started. It is probably a custom in imitation of the Plantation. So, the Villagers go on "christening" their houses, just as the Royal Navy christens warships.

Sargeant's mother died twenty-eight years ago; and for the past twenty-five, he has lived without interruption, even before he christened the house, in this house which he "inherited." His mother owned the house when he was a child. She died suddenly one day, overseas. He assumed ownership. There was no Will and Last Testament. There was nobody to whom the dilapidated house could be given. His father had died when he was two years old. From typhoid fever. The house was unpainted; the wood was grey from age; part of the floor had collapsed; and there were holes in the roof, where gaulings and blackbirds squatted. Sargeant painted the house, repaired the roof, replaced the rotten wood with new lumber he bought one length at a time, on paydays; painted the new lumber; and on the Sunday, three days after Griffoot had delivered the U.S. Money Order, gathered all his friends, Manny, his former teacher Mr. Edwards from Elementary School, Golbourne, Pounce, Mr. Brannford and Gertrude, to "christen" the house with a name. Gertrude cooked boiled chicken for the jovial, loud men; and served them dozens of Fray Bentos corn beef sandwiches with a leaf of fresh lettuce protruding from each; and when the work was done, they all drank a shot of Mount Gay Rum, in a toast to the house.

"Let we christen the blasted house!" Mr. Edwards, the school-teacher had said.

"Man-yes!" Manny had said.

"Wha' name we christening this house with?" Mr. Brannford had said. He had drunk three shots of Mount Gay when he asked this question. "Wha' name you giving to this castle, Perce-boy?"

"Macon Flagstaff Castle," Sargeant had said.

"Jesus Christ!" Golbourne had said.

"Wha' shite this is you coming with?" Manny had asked.

"The blasted house belongst to the man," the schoolteacher said. "Let the blasted man christen the blasted house Macon Flagstaff Castle, Flagstaff Macon Castle, or Macon Castle of Flagstaff, or whatever blasted name he choose. And every-blasted-body in Flagstaff Village will walk-pass the house, look up at the blasted name, and laugh-like-shite!"

"Wha' it name?" Mr. Brannford had asked, four times now.

"Flagstaff Macon Castle," Sargeant had said.

"So be it!" the schoolteacher had said. "So be it blasted-well be!"

And they drank the second bottle of Mount Gay empty; and got another twenty-six-ouncer from the Harlem Bar & Grill, which Manny made them pay for; and he drank some of it with them, himself; and they continued into the dusk of that Sunday, drinking rum and repeating the name the house was christened with, and singing Psalms; and then left for Evensong and Service.

There is a "shed-roof" built onto Flagstaff Macon Castle now, two years after Sargeant got the stripes that made him Corporal. This "shed-roof" is his bedroom and his "den." He plays dominoes with his friends every Friday night, in his "den," between "tinklelling" his piano. He can sit in his "den," so named by Ruby, on his "lazy-boy chair" which she sent for him, and watch his puh-paw tree bloom, and pick his puh-paws green, to boil them with no salt, for his high blood pressure. From his "den" he is able to see the pig growing in its pen; and watch his chickens and check under his cellar for the eggs they lay, before his neighbour and his neighbour's dog claim ownership . . .

And occasionally he would glance up the hill, through the valley, to the Great House; and wonder . . .

"Many's the night, sometimes," Mary-Mathilda tells him now, "but more regular in bright daylight, I would come up and sit down here, to study my head, and catch a lil fresh breeze blowing off the sea, and would have a strong urge to see what you are up to. Very-often I would find myself looking down at you, through the trees, wondering where you get the name Macon from? I know the origin of Flagstaff.

"I even asked Wilberforce the derivation of Macon.

"Macon is not a name from round-here. Wilberforce, with his knowledge of dialects, languages and the origin of languages, could not figure-out Macon. Is it French? Or a word from a African language? Nobody in my household, in the Village, even Mr. Bellfeels, could come up with a explanation.

"And now that I have you, where Macon come from?"

"The South."

"South of here?" she says. "South of Flagstaff?"

"More south than that," he says. "The real South. The Amurcan South."

"You named a house in Bimshire after a place in the Amurcan South? After what I told you about my visit to that country?"

"I was listening to the radio. A service from a church somewhere in a Southern town I didn't know the name of, then. It was like a vision, and I was transpose' there in the flesh. A Friday night, just before the boys come over to play dominoes, and I was listening meanwhile to the service. Manny had-tell me things about the South, though he never tell me exactly what he was doing in the Deep South; but Manny had-tell me sufficient, and by only listening to a fellar preach . . . from a Southern Baptist Church . . . I could visualize everything.

"Five or six years afterwards—Manny had return-back by then—Manny inform me that it was a man from Georgia, preaching in that Southern accent; and that he was from a place call' Macon-Georgia. A white man . . ."

"And you sing in a Anglican Church Choir?"

"Was the man's voice, and the music, Mary-G, not his 'nomination!"

"I don't understand you."

"Manny had at-first say that the name of the Southern town sounded African to him, because with the first bunch o' slaves to land in Bimshire, Manny say, Macon was the name of a African slave; and he was speaking a language called Maconese, which the slave masters couldn't speak, and never learn' to speak, hence the broken-English version of the proper African name handed down to we, as Macon, Manny say so. Macon. So, therefore in consequence, Macon isn't merely a word from the Amurcan South, but could-very-well be a African nomenclature. I don't rightly know exactly what Manny was telling me, nor the correct pronunciation of the name of my house. But wha' I going do?

"I christen it Flagstaff Macon Castle, nevertheless. But Macon of Flagstaff is the name I first-had-in-mind to christen it with, having come across that name in a English story I was reading. But what is done is done. I name it Flagstaff Macon Castle, after listening to a man preach about sin and loving thy n'ighbour as thyself, and putting a end to fornication; and stop serrigating people, because everybody born free. Amurca, the preacher say, is in grave danger of becoming two Amurcas. One, a white Amurca. The other, a black Amurca. I still say, be-Christ, pardon my French, that that white man preach a sermon that make sense to me, regardless to whether he is a Anglican, a Southern Baptist, or a white man!

"I was impress' by his voice. When he finish preaching, I remember that I take out my police black notebook, and waited until he axe for donations, and where to send the money and to get the address, when at long last, he said Macon. In Georgia. The Deep South.

"I join-on Macon to Flagstaff, and add-on Castle, to make it more appropriate," he says.

"Thanks for explaining, Percy."

"Nobody never asked me this before."

"Pass me the spying glass," she tells him. "Let me show you."

"If you can see a little dent in a Royal Insurance shield from this distance," he says, passing the spying glass, "you sees *everything* that I do all these years, *inside-out* . . ."

"And outside-in," she says.

But she says it with a smile in her voice.

"But it's such a bad word," she says.

"Knowing a person outside-in?"

"The spying glass. To say that I been looking at you with my spying glass is different from saying, I been seeing you through binoculars . . . all these years, your every move, with it at my left eye, with my right closed, trained upon you . . ."

"Trained on me? But, Mary-G, I don't have nothing to hide."

"One Saturday afternoon, Gertrude went to Manny to get a piece o' pork, and with my spying glass on Manny, I could see the flies buzzing-round the table with the pig on its back, and its head cut off; and Manny now have the pig in the hot-boiling-water, scrubbing-off the hairs. I could see the colour of the bristles, a white spot near the snout of that boar-pig, that had such a big-long . . . *thing*, Percy!

"And the flies. But I was tracking Gertrude. I had just take-her-on as cook, promoted from being kitchen help, and I deliberately ask her to make something for me; as a test. I had to know if she was suitable. Pudding-and-souse, or meal-corn cou-cou; and if she pass either, she suitable. And watch to see if she clean."

"I would have-make her cook split-pea soup with flour dumplings, mixed with cassava flour!"

He knows now that she has been spying on other people: Manny cutting up pigs; Gertrude going to Manny's shop and to Miss Greaves' Shop; and she has picked out Pounce, Golbourne, the

Constable and Naiman. She has spied on all of us, from this window in her bedroom. Just like Mr. Taylor who climbs the fourteen grey cement steps from his green-painted Government house, assigned by the Bimshire Department of Housing, spies on the entire coastline, and deep into the Harbour looking for enemy hostilities; and so long as Mr. Taylor continues to reach the fourteenth step of the Lookout, punctually, four times every day at a fixed hour, in all emergencies and weather, he'll keep his job. He has to climb fourteen steps—plus one step—to enter the octagonal-shaped Lookout; and spy carefully down into the green sea, Bimshire's portion of the Carbean Sea, part of the Atlantic Ocean and the Gulf Stream, this vast body of water that is sometimes clouded by the sprays of waves and clouds that hang low. Mr. Taylor will live comfortably in his Government house, so long as he lifts the telephone and rings the bell, and calls out to his superiors down in Town, Crown-Sargeants in charge of Security, and Crown-Sargeants in the Harbour Police in charge of depth-charges, stationed in the Central Police Station, the Special Branch, and at the Harbour Station . . .

"*A submarine! A enemy submarine! A Nazzie submarine!*"

Yes!

Yes, she has picked out the lives of more people than he had imagined.

"Gertrude left here after twelve that Saturday taking the lane with the dunks trees; and she picked a few, ate some and spit-out some; the dunks are strange, bitter fruits, sometimes; yes; and wipes her mouth with the back of her left hand; holding the basket in her right, the hand she wears two silver bangles on; yes; and I followed her in my spying glass, through the grass-piece to the Pasture, pass cows and a few sheep grazing, where the boys were playing cricket, where she pick a blade o' Guinea grass, and put the blade in her mouth; and chew it. Growing up, you and me couldn't walk ten yards without stopping to lick-down some dunks outta somebody dunks tree; break-off a piece o' grass, and put it between our teeth. Saturday, Gertrude behave no different: break-off a blade o' Guinea grass and use it as a toothpick; near now to Flagstaff Macon Castle; yes; and it came to me before Gertrude even think about it, that she was heading to your Castle; yes; is something that a woman would know about the behaviour of another woman; my mind racing now, back over the years to see if any hint Gertrude had-drop: in the bus going to Town, at Church on first Sundays; being confirmed together, me, Gertrude and you.

"The two o' you always had more freedom than me. But whenever I thought I had a chance to be free, Ma would throw cold-water over it . . .

"I first-began to regret the life that was mark out for me, when I realize they were keeping me far from people like you and Clotelle, Sis, Gertrude, Pounce and them-so, deliberately. Ma, and even Gran, wanted to bring me up different from you, and closer to the Plantation way, different from the Village. So, I was left half-fashioned as a person; in-between.

"Not fish and not fowl. Not white and not black. A half woman. Half a person. Or, as the Villagers say behind my back, 'not knowing my arse from my . . . you know what'!

"So, there Gertrude was that Saturday afternoon at your front door, and I could hear the knock she gave your door, from this distance, so powerful was I imagining what was in Gertrude head; her knock was too confident; too sure, too brazen for me to stomach and bear; because the way she knocked was the way a woman knocks on a door she is accustomed to entering; who has shared *some* thing with the man who lives there; she is a woman with a past with that man. I wasn't angry: just, just . . . just . . .

"After that afternoon, I stopped counting the times I saw her flounce-up to Flagstaff Macon Castle, and open your door and walk in.

"The confidence of that woman, though! Soon after this, she stop knocking altogether, and just walk in. Flagstaff Macon Castle was now her briar-patch. As if she living there."

"Living in *my* house?" Sargeant says.

". . . as if she and you had something," she tells him.

Sargeant is confounded. His speechlessness is more from shame than from shock.

She stops talking. He remains silent. She continues looking down into the valley; and then she looks up into the heavens; and then she says something barely audible, about no stars out tonight.

"I am sometimes at a loss," she goes on to say. "Sometimes I see things but they are not the things that my two eyes are pointing out to me. They are my imagination. But when I saw Gertrude walk-in without knocking, that was not my imagination. Although I did see her walk in, before she actually walked in.

"And, this evening, when she brought the drinks, you didn't notice how she used her body to block-me-out . . .

"But Gertrude don't know I already caught her at your front door. Months, now. Yes.

"And still trying to hide. When she brought in the drinks you didn't notice her nervousness? Because you-yourself were nervous."

"What you saying, Miss Mary-G?"

"Merely that life can play tricks on a person like me in my present position; under the circumstances.

"But hey, listen to me talking about things that have nothing to do with what brought you into this house, in the first place!

"You know, and I know, what we should be talking about . . ."

"And instead we are talking about yesterday."

"Yesterday is the best way to face today. Or tonight. You come across this in your detective work, don't you?

"It doesn't seem like I can come to the point, at all. You shift-away from assisting me to come. When I think it is time to come, take blame, admit, confess, and have you warn me that what I say will be taken down and use against me, you veer-away, and postpone my coming.

"Why I am doing this to myself? Why are you doing this to me? You are here to take a Statement. But a bare Statement can't

convict me. Only God can convict Mary Gertrude Mathilda.
Not another soul. Living or dead.

"They could *punish* me. And I have faced punishments untold.
From the moment the midwife cut my navel string, and I emerge
from inside my mother's womb . . . God bless her soul."

"God bless her soul," Sargeant says; and imitates her as she
makes the sign of the Cross, pleased that he does it correctly this
time.

". . . mercy on the dead," she says.

". . . have mercy on the dead," Sargeant says.

From standing at the window, Mary-Mathilda and Sargeant
retrace their steps back through the dressing room, and into the
ornate bedroom. She stops beside the canopied bed, and passes her
hand over the bedspread, as if she is spreading it evenly; erasing the
creases. The bedspread has been made smooth by Gertrude, who
prepared the bed before she left, a few hours ago.

Gertrude has gone to wait for Sargeant, at their rendezvous.
Tonight is Sunday night. And Sunday night is a night when there is
no revival meeting, when Church ends early, at nine o' clock, early
enough to spend in the cane field, in complete freedom and aban-
don, in complete recklessness and happiness: away from her work,
and from Sargeant's neighbours; and from her two small children.
Her house is too small to have carnal knowledge in it, and contain
Sargeant's voice at orgasm. He woke the children one night.

Something daring and very sexually exciting makes them love
to foop in a cane field. It is the caneblades that make their flesh itch,
and the trash that bites into their arms and legs . . . and Manny
teases him about this predilection: "Sarge, you sure-like to exercise
your fecking carnal knowledge in a grass-piece or a cane field, as if
you not 'fraid of centipees! Remember Golbourne, boy! Remem-
ber Golbourne!" And then he added, "But suppose Bimshire was a
cold country like Amurca?" Gertrude expects that Sargeant will
join her tonight. Gertrude, just to think of her love and her body of
which he is sure, brings a powerful feeling of passion and a need to

foop into his entire body: while Mary-Mathilda, whose love is cautious, and more dangerous, places her body teasingly before him, just out of his reach. She holds her love dangling uncertainly, like a stick on which a cord is tied, with a common pin shaped like a fish hook, at the end. He is not sure he will know her love. And he is not sure he wants to. He is not sure if it is safe and wise to be so close to this woman. He has known her from the age of five. Has loved her secretly from the age of ten. He is not sure he should leave the splendour of this room and go right now, back to Gertrude, who waits for him in a cane field, in darkness.

To locate Gertrude in the North Field is easier than to learn his way walking through all these rooms in this Great House. Through the unbearable heat of carnal knowledge, Sargeant can find Gertrude in the canes with the ease of a dog smelling the path to pussy.

For many years, he has been riding his bicycle on the perimeter of the Plantation's lands; and he would see the fields change from black soil, to green grass-like plants sprouting through the black soil, until they became sugar cane, interspersed with yams and potatoes and eddoes; and sometimes, with luck, he would see Mary-Mathilda from a distance, in her garden, stooping to tend her lettuce and tomatoes, the skirt of her long white dress tucked tightly between her legs, showing from that distance only her white-stockinged legs and her brown laced-up boots; or he would catch her beside the flower beds that run the length of the verandah, along the front of the Great House, and down each side, and almost to the back of the house itself.

She was dressed always in white, and this colour sharpened his lust after her body, endured silently for years, and disclosed only to Manny from since they were young, bathing in the churning sand, at the edge of the sea, in the green clear water. This lust like white heat has remained smouldering in his body.

They are in the bedroom. The smell is of lavender. The sheer waves of white cloth surge over the canopy of the bed; and the stout, brown, sturdy mahogany legs scare him; and the magnificence of the bed draped in its white canopy empties his body of desire; and at the same time, this fear excites his lust.

She takes his hand. She leads him to the bed. The bed is white. The bed is soft. And the mattress is soft and thick, and deep. The canopy comes down into his face, and is like a cloud shutting out the sun. He smells a smell that he cannot define or distinguish from others.

She is flat on her back, looking away from him; lying crossways; at the head of the bed. The space between them is large. He sits at the foot of the bed, in his black tunic buttoned to the neck, wearing his black policeman's boots, thick leather belt with the truncheon attached. He has no cap on. It is downstairs, on a chair.

The urge is there. But he is scared. The fear is like heat, white and searing. And the impetus to rape is there. And this frightens him, to think . . . It is his imagination that saves him: with it, he can do anything. He paints himself into all of the photographs on the wall, that have her in them; dispossessing the man already in the photograph, does so even when there is no man beside her, takes over the space that no man is occupying. In his mad rush to this vengeance no longer lodged only in imagination, he rips the man sitting in her lap in an English deck chair, in the shade, from the frame, and then realizes that the man is Wilberforce, her son, sitting with her on the Pasture, watching cricket. He immediately chastises himself that he can have no moral right to be jealous. And he promptly, but sheepishly, cleanses his mind of this torment, and of this vindictiveness: and goes back to think of rape. He imagines a picture of urgent lust: she is taking off her long, pleated white dress that Gertrude starched and ironed this same morning; beneath the white dress is a white petticoat, the same length as the dress. She is not wearing a brassiere, only a short white cotton garment, like a shirt that has no sleeves; a camisole; a blue flower of cloth is in the middle of the neckline; and he can feel his penis rub against the coarse flannel of his black trousers;

right then, she unties a white string made of the same delicate white cloth that is round her waist; and the long white petticoat falls to the floor, just as he has seen a balloon that has lost its air and its agility collapse and fall, in silent wondrous finality; yes, her petticoat is like a cloud that has fallen from the sky.

And when she steps out of it, and her legs move, and the soft muscles in her thighs shake, he sees how much more beautiful her body is than the speculation of wonder and fantasy; for her legs are shining just like the polished mahogany legs of the four-poster bed that reflects the exquisiteness of taste and gentility; but he does not like this comparison; and he tries to think of what her legs remind him of; when her legs are out of the fallen white cloud, she steps with the lightness of a cloud itself, and stands a short distance from the white collapsed petticoat, as if she had never worn it; as if she is despising it now; and he can see her legs only to her knees. For the undergarment is long, tied with ribbon at the knees, and with another string to protect it from exposing her entire body to him; but he has seen enough; as his penis swells, he puts his right hand into his right side pocket, to hold his penis down, and soften his embarrassment; but he cannot control it, so he takes his hand out, and inhales, holding his breath. Manny had told him, one night drinking rum in the Selected Clienteles Room, to do this: *"Hold your dickey down with your hand inside your pocket, man! You's a man, or a boy?"* Manny said he learned it *"from some Amurcan Nay-groes"* in the South, when he worked there illegally for the three months after he had jumped ship at a port in Louisiana. Manny and Sargeant had been talking about a striptease show that an "Amurcan Nay-gro main" had taken Manny to see, in Macon, Georgia . . .

Now, Mary-G raises her arms, and guides the short vest-like garment over her head; and he sees her arms, and the thick black hair in her armpits, and the form of her neck, and the sculptured prominence of the bone that runs across her shoulders; and more of her neck, long and thin and delicate and strong and with two long strings on either side of her swallow pipe; and then her lips.

. . . and just as the garment is about to be taken completely off, her breasts in their new posture and position become large; become full; become ripe with the throbbing of his penis, which has not fallen, in spite of Manny's prescription; while her bubbies become the colour of olives, dark, dark brown, almost purple, and in the middle of each breast, a nipple erect and hard as a marble; and the passion in his body which he wants to have surge through her thighs with the same force, grows unbearable; and when she drops her arms, and has thrown the garment onto the same pile as the cloud that has collapsed on the carpet, her bubbies are transformed; now her breasts are small; he can hold each in one hand; no, her bubbies are not the size he wants; not the same size as Gertrude's; and they do not have the fullness he had imagined all these years . . . and in the middle of her chest, between her breasts, equidistant from each nipple, is a mark, a spot, a growth of skin, the healed blemish of a wound . . . "Did Bellfeels try to kill her with a kitchen knife?" . . . oblong in shape, raised from the rest of her flesh, and looking like an exquisite brooch, smooth, and well-sculptured, a wound cut out clean in anger; or bestowed at birth. And he wants to feel it, to touch it, to fondle it; but he wishes he could rub his tongue on it; and polish it with his hot wet saliva; and he allows his imagination to do that, and the moment his wet tongue touches the cold, soft skin of her brooch, immediately a rush of joy and trembling and passion and peace greet his tongue, which is more wet and sticky and salty from the resilience of her skin. He sucks her brooch hungrily and wildly, with closed eyes . . .

"*Talking 'bout woman,*" Manny had said one night, when he and Sargeant were talking about women, "*I's a bubbies-man, personally myself! I could fall asleep with a woman's two bubbies inside my mout', all night! You have to take them bubbies in your hand, and full up your mout' with a lil saliva, and then you put them two bubbies inside your mout', and wallow-'bout the nipples inside your mout', and turn your tongue round and round the nipples, oh-Jesus-Christ, Sarge, have you ever do this? And then, with the palm of your right hand . . . always use your right hand . . . you pass the palm of your right hand over the tip o' the woman left nipple, light-light-light like the feather from a guinea hen, and oh-Jesus-Christ, Sarge! I could do this all night, till I fall asleep. Now, being as how I natu-rally different from another man, you for-instance . . . you might be a legs-man, or a neck-man, or a fingers-and-toes man . . . or a plain pussy-man. Some men are like that. 'Gimme the pussy, now,' some men does-snarl! . . . and bram-bram-bram! . . ."* And Sargeant had told Manny, *"Confessing now, and nobody is to know this but you, since it won't look good if this get out. I is a hairs-man."* Manny screeled out, "A *wha'*?" And Sargeant fixed his eyes on Manny, with shame in them. And Manny smiled, and dissolved the embarrassment. And it made Sargeant smile, which made Manny break out into uncontrollable laughter, *"Ho-ho-ho-oh Jesus Christ!"* Manny screamed, *"As man!" "As man,"* Sargeant said. *"The hairs between a woman's two legs? Or, under the armpits? Sarge, you's a fecking freak!"* And Sargeant said, *"But don't tell nobody."* And Manny screeled for blue-murder, again; and said, *"For a police, you weird as shite, Sarge!"* But this is in his imagination. And he does not know what he should do.

Is it her age? Is it her station in life? Is it Mr. Bellfeels? Or is it this house? This Great House, which stands for place, for richness, for wealth, for power, and fear . . .

Real, deep, terrifying, deadly fear. Raw fear. Like the rumours that blow through the Village whispered by the Plantation's servant-women, about the things that went on in this Great House, before he was a policeman; rumours that continue all these years, in whis-pers and in hushed awe. And also things that went on over at the Plantation Main House. They say, even to this day, that Clotelle was hidden in a well, or a cellar, long enough for the Plantation-people to let the anger of the Village cool off, to let the talk die down; and they say she was taken from this hiding place, because the man who was ordered by the Plantation to transport her to the other place and kill her there got frightened by the deed he was about to com-mit; and they say she was brought out from the well, or the cellar, at an ungodly hour in the dead of night; dead; and strung up in the tamarind tree, to make it look as if she had killed herself.

The canopy is white. Thick, white satin. Like the curtain that falls on a scene of fierce Western violence, in cowboy and Indians movies at the Olympic Theatre. Moons and stars and pieces of yellow, gold-like slashes, representing flashes of lightning, are painted onto the canopy, as she lies on her back, and is able to see the heavens, the stars and the moons.

"Here we are," she says.

He cannot concentrate on her words: his mind is watching the hollering, cheering long-haired Indians facing hordes of U.S. Cavalrymen at Little Big Horn; going over and over again, the spectacle of blood and screams, and the craziness of arrows thick as crows in a summer sky, when George Armstrong Custer letting-loose "the full force and pow'r of the Amurcan Arm-Forces" fell, and lay hidden, cowering from the black clouds of arrows coming after him, and hightailed it through the beautiful green fields of Little Big Horn, running from Sioux and Cheyenne warriors with Crazy Horse in front, leading them on a horse that had no saddle and no "*sterps!*"; and this made him sit and watch the movie three times, and marvel at the galloping film as the reinless horses roared and thundered round and round, men shouting at the top of their voices "like Indians," like a merry-go-round . . .

"But did you hear the way that boy addressed his father?" she says. "'*Mr. Bellfeels!*' He couldn't even call him Pop? Or Father? Or even Old Man? But '*Mr. Bellfeels!*' The thrildren of the rich! It must be something about being white. But I will tell you, Percy, if Wilberforce ever come with that slackness to *me! Waps!* One box to his damn head . . . turn his blasted head behind his back! The rudeness! '*Mr. Bellfeels,*' when 'Daddy' sound so much more nicer."

She seems relieved to get this off her chest. Sargeant is not paying attention.

"Did I fall-off so long laying-down on this bed?" she says. "What were you doing, while I was dozing? Just sitting down there?"

"Travelling," he says. "Travelling over life, and over land. A lotta things went through my mind whilst you were laying-down, first on your back, then on your stomach."

"And you didn't take advantage of it?"

And she laughs. But he does not.

"I didn't take advantage of you."

"Good."

"But I wanted to," he says. "Not the way it sound, not like take advantage of you, meaning carnal knowledge, or nothing so. But . . ."

"I am not a child."

He gets up from the foot of the bed, and goes up to her, as she leans against the headboard; and she places her body against his, and draws him close to her; a little rough, through clumsiness; and her body touches the coarse black serge of his tunic and trousers, and she flinches a little from the bristles, and sneezes; then she flinches again, this time with more agitation as he puts his arms round her body. It is not an embrace. As he puts his arms to draw her within the strong, swallowing circle of what he wanted to be an embrace, she draws her white handkerchief from the sleeve of her dress, and sneezes into it, and passes it lightly, in two dabs, under her nostrils as he is circling her body with his strong arms clothed in the black serge; and for the moment his embrace is complete—it lasts for three seconds only—the fear returns to him and he removes his arms from her body, still fully dressed in the long flowing poplin, with her white stockings visible, and the brown-laced leather boots dangling over the side of the bed; contrition overtakes his body, and makes his lust fall, limber. Her feet do not reach the floor . . .

"What are we doing in my bedroom?" she says.

Shame covers his face; and he does not answer. He knows what is in his mind; and he knows why he is in her bedroom . . . he thinks of Gertrude, lying on her back, in the vast cane-brake, on the talkative bed of cane trash; her eyes closed; her arms held out from her body, as if she is on a cross marked into the thick, tickling blades of dried sugar-cane leaves, on a makeshift bed of trash that whispers with each move and thrust he makes into her sweet pum-pum. Gertrude moves away from his coarse, tickling black serge; and she holds out her right hand, and takes him down to her, down to her level, down to the trash; and slowly she unsnaps the shining silver buckle, with the Imperial Crown on it, and releases the thick, brown, highly polished and ugly leather belt, pulling it through the tabs slowly, insinuatingly slow; all the time his pulse is quickening, and his penis is stiffening, and the spasms of anticipation beating almost as fast as his chest; and then she uses both hands, three of four fingers on each hand, to move over the buttons of his fly; over all five black metal buttons . . . And he thinks of his mother as she did this to him, Monday, Tuesday, Wednesday, Thursday, Friday, "fixing" him to face the world, to face his school; and to face Sundays, in his better go-to-meeting clothes, to "march yourself to Church!", to sing in his little angelic soprano voice, in the Choir; conducting this training even earlier in his life, as she taught him how to use the toilet; doing this to him, week after week, into months, until he was thirteen years old, "and old-enough" to have learned all she had taught him about "fixing" himself proper . . . his fly is open; and her hand moves into his sliders, made from the coarse white cloth of a flour bag in which flour comes from Canada, made by the Village needleworker, and before that by his own mother—her hands in his sliders which do not have buttons; do not have a zipper; they do not have elastic in the waist; so, she puts her right hand into the vent, and holds his penis, which is no longer stiff, and is wet and sticky at the head.

And she squeezes it.

"Ohhh, Jesus-Jesus . . . *Jesus!*"

And into her hands splurts the thick liquid white substance of his come, reminding her of Quaker Oats Cream of Wheat.

"Come," she says.

It is Mary-Mathilda talking to him: and not Gertrude.

"Come," she says.

Down the back stairs, down the thirteen steps from her bed-
room, pausing to take a white shawl from a poster at the foot of the
bed, she walks with it trailing, like a bridal train; and the perfume
from her fragrant and scented bedroom rises in his nostrils. This
sensation has a great pull and influence upon his body and his mind.
From here, from this sanctuary, and this prison, she leads him into
the cellar. He is dressed in full uniform, except for his peaked cap.

She is once more lovely, majestic, in her long white dress; and
dignified. He sees her in her true age.

He is safer here, outside her bedroom. Inside the house, with its
splendour, he was collared and encircled, as he had been on the
schooner going to Trinidad surrounded by sea and sharks. Walking
like a blind man now, led by a woman, in this underground tunnel,
he feels braver. Manny, who was working illegally in Amurca,
until the Immigration people found him, and locked him up for
two months, and then deported him back to Bimshire, had told
Sargeant about underground passages and tunnels, sewers that con-
tained water that came at you with the force and speed of a bullet.
Some of this water in the underground channels was plain, simple
water. Water you could drink, if you were that thirsty. The other
kind was water you could not stomach, could not bare to smell,
water that was thick and slimy, and more like a soup with dumplings
and pieces of limbs and rotten vegetables, and pieces of meat in it;
ordinary decayed meat. *"Was a kiss-me-arse saniterry sewer, man!"*
Manny had said. Sargeant put his hand to his nostrils and stifled the
imagined dirty, stinking smell of the underground tunnel. Manny
rested his shot glass of rum on the counter, and blew his nose loud, in
two short explosions. Just like the force of the water in the sanitary
sewer had thundered through the pipes, he blew his nose into a white
handkerchief, balled it up and pushed it into his back pocket. Manny
had tried to hide in the sewer, and the roaring dirty water scared
him, and he crawled out, and the Immigration people grabbed
him; wet, shivering, smelly and smiling . . . "That was one city I
was glad as shite to be deported out of! Philly. Or Philadelphia."

Sargeant feels he is walking in this kind of underground tunnel that Manny had told him about, but without the water. Without the smell of offal. This passage has only the smell of damp coral stone and cement, and the sourness of wet dirt. He feels safe here, although he does not know where he is, or where exactly she is leading him. But he is safer here, outside the encircling house, which has inhibited him from writing down her evidence. The world of the Great House has squeezed the writing down of her Statement out of his mind.

Now he thinks she is leading him to the scene; to the evidence; to reveal to him the motive. He has seen many such scenes, dipped in blood; scenes that are sometimes splattered with pieces of bloodied flesh and bone from the force of the blow or the knife; sometimes just scenes soaked in blood. But always, with these scenes, comes the natural and immediate desire to pewk, as if it is a kind of seasickness developed on land; to bring up whatever is in his bowels, to vomit, recoil from these graphic, dramatic, still-life duplications of emotion, of passion, and of hatred. Reproductions of life.

He walks behind her, in silence.

He wishes that Gertrude had taken him into her arms, that he had got to know her better, and more intimately. After taking her to the fields for the past five months, he still does not know her; foreplay does not alleviate nor soften the brutal fierceness of their screwing and fooping. Gertrude would not know, would not have known the word *foreplay*. She was always, like him, in too much of a hurry; too hot; "I wet-wet, man!"; couldn't wait to get him inside her; too frequently in a hurry against the chance that a man might wander into the canes to fire a pee, and detect them sprawled out, half-naked, her maid's uniform pulled up above her knees, and his policeman's trousers still on his legs, not even pulled down to his knees; two buttons on his fly open; tunic, boots and cap still on. Gertrude was always concerned, when they fooped in the humid afternoon, about being late to prepare dinner for Miss Mary-Mathilda and Mr. Wilberforce. Miss Mary-Mathilda and Mr. Wilberforce both liked to eat at seven-thirty; except on Saturdays when they ate at four; and at two on Sundays.

Cobwebs lick his face, like sprays of rainwater sprinkling him.

The walls of this tunnel are sweating and crumbling; and dust drifts down like flour through a sieve when he touches the wall. She has taken a lantern from a nail on the disintegrating wall, lights it, and he sees that the tunnel is the width of his arms outstretched; and he fumbles in a long pocket at the left side of his trousers for his searchlight; and switches it on; and she rests her left hand on his arm.

"Turn off your searchlight," she tells him. "I have the light."

The tunnel is damp and has loose gravel on its floor. The lantern shows him spiders and webs with spiders in them and cockroaches, brown and long as a thumb, and fat.

He steps on one, and its body cries out in a soft, slightly muffled *crunch*.

She holds his hand.

"I will show you something," she says.

He had never found this kind of solace in Gertrude: not when he took her bubbies into his mouth, as Manny had coached him to do; but at that first application of the lesson, he bit on them, a little too hard, by mistake; and Gertrude screamed, and said, *"Christ, you giving me cancer, with your teeth?"* And then she was sorry. *"Suppose somebody hear?"* And then, she started to cry.

Not when he dug into her, in his strong impatience. Not when she cooked steamed flying fish and cou-cou, for him, one Friday night. Not when they walked the two miles to the Factory, on Wednesday nights in Crop-Season, on moonlight nights, late; like lovers, and not one word passed between them, did he find the peace in their relationship.

Mary-Mathilda, on the other hand, feels as close as an affection that is years old.

She releases his hand. And walks ahead. One step ahead. He feels he is alone in the tunnel; cut off from the world, not the world of the Great House, or that of the tumbling schooner cutting through the waves in the Gulf of Paria, but a world of loneliness and very high-strung resentment. He feels the full meaning of her released hand. And it gets the better of his emotions, and changes the feeling of isolation into a feeling of raw, strong violence.

It is large and dangerous, because in this tunnel, he is also inside the belly of the land, under the North Field, in which he has lain on his back so many times, especially at night when the skies are dark, dark, blue, and the stars come out with a clearer melody as if they were singing to him and to Gertrude; when he would point at the only three stars he could name for her: the Big Dipper, Orion, and the North Star, each time he fooped her in the North Field, and she had said, each time, "Yes, yes. You's a bright man, Sarge. Yes."

"I learn all these things from books written by Amurcans. Astronomers and other men of sciences, send-down for me by Ruby, my daughter up in Brooklyn; and from Mr. Edwards, my teacher at Sin-Davids."

And once, as he lay looking into the black sky at the Big Dipper and at Orion, he emptied his heart to her; and told her his deep secret. He had pulled a piece of sugar-cane trash from the ground, and he tore the dried, brown, tasteless leaf, thick as a toothpick, with his teeth and said, "After me and you done, I like to lay-down 'side o' you here, in this damn cane field, and look up in the skies. And you know what I does-be-seeing?"

"Orion, and the Big Dipper," she says.

"*Amurca!* I does-be-seeing that big powerful land, that land with all that wealth and riches and jobs for people like me, and people like you, Gertrude. Coloured people. Amurca is a country for people like you and me. Black people, or coloured people. A fellar born in Jamaica, by the name of Marcus Moses Messiah Garvey, say so. We should escape to Amurca. And then, Africa. This place Bimshire, where we born-and-raised, as comfortable as it is, is not meant as a habitation for people of our kind. This place, a colony of Englund, is made specially for Plantation-people, and to 'commodate Bellfeels. And your mistress, Miss Mary-Mathilda. Not for real black people, even though Mary-Mathilda isn't a white woman. Whenever people who was slaves are brought to a place like this, rule' by the English, a colony, and then are let-go and freed; after they are freed, you know what they do?"

"I won't know these things, Sarge!"

"They choose to *remain* right there in the slave colony! Those slaves. Those people, now the ex-slaves, could never find peace. It is as if their spirits and their ghosts was telling them that for them to get peace, and real freedom, they have to trace-back their steps, even to re-embarking on ships like the HMS *Bounty*, and journey-back to places like Mali and Elmira Castle that Manny tell me about, where they were first brought from, in chains, in the first place. You understand what I am trying to tell you, don't you, Gertrude?"

"Your words over my head, Sarge."

"I trying to put this simple. I don't believe in this slavery business that everybody say was happening 'bout-here. I don't think it ever exist, in-true. Not on the scale of Jamaica. A couple o' black fellars get their arse lick-in, a couple o' times, yes. But whole-scale slavery like what they have in Amurca, *no*! Not in a English colony, Jesus Christ. I know the English. The English won't do a thing like that. You know what I mean?"

"You using words that you hear from Manny, words 'bout Mali and the Castle. But I don't know, Sarge, I don't know."

"Words have to suit thoughts, Gertrude."

"I don't know, Sarge."

"Words have to suit deeds, Gertrude."

"I never hear you talk this-way before," she said. "And your words frightening me. But I still like to hear them, though. They make me feel . . . well, they make me feel . . . feel like somebody."

"Some people living-'bout-here make the mistake of calling Bimshire a black country."

"I think you should draw the line, there, Sarge. These ideas is Manny ideas," Gertrude said. "These is dangerous ideas. You had-better be careful, 'cause if the Plantation hear you walking this-way, and even you being a police yourself, you don't know what they would do . . . like in the Riots, when they shoot people . . ."

"What you frighten for, Gertrude?"

"I thought you was starting to tell me about the stars. Orion and the Big Dipper. You have to watch your career, 'cause they thinking of putting Crown-Sargeant rank at your disposal. A couple Friday nights ago, while serving dinner . . . I would hate to know that you throw-that-'way . . ."

"But *Amurca*, Gertrude! Amurca. Notwithstanding with all its colour prejudice and serrigation, with all its black fountains for Negroes and white fountains for whites, nevertheless. Water is water. Jesus Christ, Gertrude, water ain't got no colour! At least, not the water we does-drink here in Bimshire. So long as it clean, and cool, 'cause in Amurca, the South does be hot as shite, according to Manny . . .

"But Amurca, Gertrude-girl! I argue it is still a more better place to live, and that it more better for a man to know where you stand with white people than to live in a place like here, where every man must know what his rightful place is; like Golbourne, and Pounce, like Clotelle and even Manny, and like me. Miss Mary-Mathilda over there in the Great House is different. Her complexion with the right amount o' white face powder and cosmetics, could carry-she-cross the Coloured Line. And she could pass. But living in Amurca is different than living in a place like this, where if you was to make a lil mistake in behaviour, and anybody, the Vicar, the Solicitor-General, the managers o' hotels, *anybody* that white, the Plantation, anybody, feel they have a right to tell you that you are stanning-up in the wrong place. I hear a lil white boy, eight years at the most, one day tell Naiman, a big-big kiss-me-arse man, to move off the sidewalk, so he could pass! Naiman is forty-something, going 'pon fifty."

"*If you're white,*" Gertrude said, "*you're right.*

"*If you're brown, you can stick around.*

"*But if you black, you gotta stay a waaaaay back!*"

"*Where* you hear that?"

"Mr. Wilberforce. He says it all the time. He says it like if it's a song he is singing. Says he first heard it up in Amurca. God, I like the way Mr. Wilberforce talk sometimes! If I didn't know that Bellfeels, a white man, was Mr. Wilberforce father, from some o' the things that boy says, I would have argue, before I knew the facts, that Mr. Wilberforce is a black man, even-although he look white. Though, after all, he almost white, and could pass, *anytime*."

"But he is a plain man."

"When Mr. Wilberforce sings it, I like the way it sounds.

"*If you're white, you're right*."

"Bellfeels, that son-of-a-bitch, is almost pure white. He had a mother who was light-skin like Mr. Wilberforce. Then, you have Miss Mary-Mathilda, your mistress. She is the colour of coffee with a lil milk in it. Light brown to brown-skin. Much more lighter than me. Then there is Wilberforce, light-light-light. And you, two or three shades less lighter, maybe four, than your employer. And me, the blackest of them all. What a group we is!"

"We work-out a way to live together, though. We could teach Amurca a thing or two."

"Even that son-of-a-bitch, Bellfeels. I wish somebody would teach *him* something! If I wasn't sure they would want to pop my neck for doing it, I would be the first man, one o' these dark-nights, with a butcher knife placed to that fucker's throat! Yes!"

"You scaring me, Sarge, man."

"Believe me, Gertrude."

"Is more better, Sarge, to talk about Amurca than Bellfeels . . ."

"Those Amurcans!" And so, after they had fooped on the bed of trash, and Sargeant had remained on his back, looking up into the firmaments, as he called it, this is the way it would be between him and Gertrude.

Now, he inhales the stuffiness of this underground tunnel, and can taste the white dust and the dampness in his mouth, and this makes him remember where he is; and he becomes disoriented again, even though Mary-Mathilda is leading him.

"Follow me," she tells him.

"Where to?" he says.

"I am leading you, Percy."

That is all she says. And she takes his hand again.

"Going back to tonight, earlier," she says. "You are to follow me now. So, follow me."

"Where to?"

"Where I am leading you."

She is silent for the next few yards.

"You know, around midday last Sunday I was standing beside Gertrude watching the pot . . . dry-peas and rice, checking to see if the water boil-out, and if it needed more; and I happened to look out the Dutch window, and God bless my eyesight! Such a white cloud! Stretching the whole expanse of the skies, taking up the whole Dutch window!

"You remember Good Fridays, how we would look up at the clouds, and see in those white clouds the interpretations of our future? That was the second thing we used to do as thrildren, on Good Fridays. Midday-noon, sharp. The exact time corresponding to when they nailed Jesus to the Cross?

"And this afternoon, I saw a cloud the shape of a big-big *L*; and I wondered if this *L* was standing for *Luck*, for me? I don't know. Or standing for *Love?* I didn't think so, at the time. Cause, Percy, in all my life, in my present state, and in my past state, the state in which you noticed me, as you been dropping hints, all evening, in that time when it appeared to you, as to others, that I was a woman worthy of envy and lust, the truth is that love, and on my part, lust, was absent from my life. Even then.

"Not even when he bred me. Not even when he lay-down on my belly, every other Saturday night, in his usual drunken stupors. So, the *L* shaped in the clouds that I saw this afternoon did *not* stand for *Love*.

"And you know, whether it went out of my mind, as a cloud would do when it vaporates, or whether it was a temporary distraction from watching Gertrude cooking the dry-peas and rice we intended to eat with the joint o' pork we got from Manny, it never dawn on me to carry that *L* in my mind, as I walked up the road, earlier tonight; travelling as if I was walking through a underground tunnel like this one we're in now.

"And this brings me to wonder, why I am taking you through this tunnel?

"We could have remained in the front-house. Wilberforce won't be back till all hours, but that doesn't matter. And Gertrude gone. Heading to Flagstaff Macon Castle, most likely, or the Pilgrim Holiness.

"Women, Percy! The tragedy with women . . .

"I have not tell you *half* the things that were going through my mind earlier this evening . . . "

She moves beside him, making little noise walking in her boots on the cement steps going down, tightening her grip on his large hand, leading him down, down, down into the darkness of the underground tunnel, in this section with its steps, built like a manhole. Into this dungeon they go.

Not that he is really in a dungeon; not that he is being thrown into the darkness and the cobwebs and the despicable things he himself imagines are crawling over his arms and his face, and up his trousers legs; not that there are snakes and giant scorpions and starving lions awaiting his company in this dungeon, nor tarantulas with bodies the size of his head; things he has read about in adventure stories of the Orient, in *Bible Stories for Children* and Hans Christian Andersen; and library books; it is just that the tunnel and the dim kerosene lamp, blown by a draught that seeps into the tunnel, and clutches him like a close body-lock—he can now smell the smell of dungeons, conjured up in those stories; and smell the taste of old stone, old mortar, old sand and wet dirt; and mould—and choke him to death as if a snake is wrapped round his neck. It becomes difficult for him to breathe.

"The Saturday night that Mr. Brannford, poor fellow, stretched to his limit, had to take his wife's life, that shameless woman, who gave-way all her business, free, to that man, the Governor; and expose, poor Mr. Brannford, her poppit-husband, to all that embarrassment and ridicule and shame; well, the Saturday night when he couldn't take no more, and he finish-she-off, by putting the butcher knife to her throat, *this* was the first place he run for succour, to. Yes. Right here. We didn't know *what* to do, at first.

"We had to call in the Solicitor-General, because it was a case that could have expose the fornications of those two sinners, His Excellency and Mistress Rosa Mary Antoinette Brannford—as she liked to have people address her by—the whore; in her pompaset-ting ways, and damage the reputation of the Governor's wife.

"Mr. Brannford was brought by car here; and we placed him in this underground tunnel, to hide-him-away; and keep him safe outta the clutches of the Law, until the next move was decided.

"Cause *nobody* in this Village never liked Mistress Brannford.

"Mr. Bellfeels came down from the Main House, and he and the Solicitor-General who had been contacted by now, and the Vicar, and the two leading barsters-at-Law—one for the Defence, the next one for the Prosecutors, it appears; and Wilberforce. In his capacity as a doctor. We sat down in the front-house, planning the next move, whilst Mr. Brannford, poor fellow, is down here, in secret, trembling more from fright, certain that his life was now in the Plantation's hand, at their mercy; and at stake and in the bal-ance, than from guilt. Gertrude took a piece of yellow Cheddar to him, that we had-got-in from Australia, a fresh salt-bread baked the very day, and a nip-bottle of Mount Gay Rum, in case he felt a lil peckish. All the time, we upstairs over Mr. Brannford head, spraining our brain in a effort to convince the Solicitor-General not to press charges against Mr. Brannford, nor bring poor Mr. Brannford before the Court of Grand Sessions. Because, in the opinion of the Village, even although murder is murder, and we

couldn't argue gainst that, still, a more greater injustice was perpe-
trated that cause Mr. Brannford to be now having to face the bitter
justice of the Court.

"Plus-again, certain old animosities existing betwixt-and-
between the local whites and the whites from Away, from Englund
and so forth, multiplied by those who claimed they were white.
No love lost 'mongst them tribes, boy!

"So, with this knowledge of this history of vengeance and spite-
fulness amongst Bimshire white people, we poured the Solicitor-
General some of the best prune-cured white rum that Mr. Bellfeels
had been keeping in secrecy, in a half-gallon jimmy-john, under my
bed; and eventually, I think it was after a few shots, well, half-dozen
such shots, that the Solicitor-General took counsel from all o' we,
and agreed to not bring Mr. Brannford before the next Grand Ses-
sions to face justice in the taking of his wife's life, by his hand. May
she rot in hell!"

"Cuddear!"

"But we had what Wilberforce always refer to as a 'contingency.'
I think it is a word use in Amurca, more frequent than here, 'cause I
never heard the Vicar, nor the Solicitor-General, both o' who stud-
ied in Englund, use such a word. *Contingency.* But I love the word.
Contingency. It connotes so much that you could do, on the other
hand, as a alternative; and as a way of wriggling-out of a tight spot.
Like a escape. A secret passage, such as what we are in, this very
minute." . . . Sargeant remembers the Commissioner of Police call-
ing him to his private residence in the Married Women's Quarters,
when the Commissioner placed the bottle of white rum on the
mahogany table, and for a time Sargeant who was then a Lance-
Corporal watched the rings of water form round the bottle con-
taining the rum, and round the bottle of water just taken out of the
icebox, and round the two glasses which found their bottoms
touched by the travelling, slow, comforting water from the two
bottles which themselves seemed to be melting.

"This is shite," the Commissioner had said, finally.

"Sir?"

"*You heard what happen? A man killed his fucking wife. Is pure murder, in the first degree. He got to heng for this,*" the Commissioner had said.

The Commissioner was a white man, born in the Island. And he talked, even at formal events, like parades, speech days at Harrison College, and at Combermere School for Boys, his alma mater— he graduated from Combermere in Fifth Form, with the Senior Cambridge School Certificate, with a Distinction in Religious Knowledge, and three Credits, in Geography, Shorthand and Latin; and was the Island's champion swimmer—and giving evidence in the annual Assizes, the Court of Grand Sessions, and in the Appeal High Court, in the same vernacular that Village men and fishermen used. With a broad, flat, semi-musical brogue that came, so people said, from both Ireland and Scotland.

"*And be-Christ, guess what, Lance-Corporal Stuart?*"

"*Sir?*"

"*Guess what I call you here for?*"

"*Sir?*"

"*You can't find a next word to use? Why you so monnisyllabical in front o' me, all of a sudden? You can't find nothing else to say?*"

"*Sir? But I don't know what to say, then.*"

"*Well, I going tell yuh!*"

It was at this point in the interview that the Commissioner of Police lifted the bottle containing the white rum, Bellfeels Special Stades White Rum; unscrewed the cap; and poured four drops, slowly, one at a time, on the hardwood floor that had no carpet, *tap . . . tap . . . tap . . . tap*. He then filled the first glass up to its sturdy middle, which he handed to Sargeant, did the same thing with the second glass, which he lifted close to his lips, and said, "*Down the hatch!*"

"*Down the hatch, sir.*"

The Commissioner cleared his throat, "*Emmm!*"

Sargeant cleared his throat, "*Uhh-hemmm!*"

The Commissioner emptied his glass.

Sargeant emptied his glass.

"*Water?*" the Commissioner said, hardly able to talk, unscrewing the bottle containing the water.

The Commissioner and Sargeant were sitting in a window seat, on its two blue cushions, facing each other; and through the green-painted jalousied windows, that had a view of the Race Pasture and the Garrison Savannah Lawn Tennis Club; and they could cast their eyes over the shining, black iron bulk of the two cannons left over from the Boer War, and given to Bimshire by a King of England, as a token of loyalty, and see the green-painted clock tower. It was midday.

"*Water?*" the Commissioner said in a clearer voice, now that the sting of the rum had gone.

"*Water, sir,*" Sargeant had said, barely able to speak, "*thanks, sir.*"

"*Good for you. Bowmanston Special good for you.*"

"*Sir?*"

"*Occasional drink. Plain. Not with any o' this blasted soft drink, as if you is an Amurcan. Just plain. And straight. English way!*"

"*Sir!*"

"*So.*"

"*Sir?*"

"*So.*"

"*Yes, sir?*"

"*What we going do? This murder take place inside your jurisdiction. You may even know the man. Good fellow, they say. Wife been horning the blasted man, giving-way the pussy, in front the man nose. Some women, including wives, are like that.*"

"*Sir.*"

"*And in your jurisdiction, I need your . . . you know what I'm saying . . . no charges.*"

"*No charges, sir?*"

"*Blind eye. If you know what I mean.*"

"*Yes, sir.*"

"*But it's inside your jurisdiction . . .*"

"*I am reading you, sir.*"

"*The liss the Assistant Commissioner place' on my dess, Thursday morning, you know anything 'bout this, Lance-Corporal? He recommending you to get the next stripe. Full Corporal.*"

"*Sir?*"

"*Well, drink up. I got to have a shower-a-shit-anna-shave, change-in my cricket-gear, be-Christ, and go and participate as a witness, as them Spartan Club fellows paint our arse in licks, pure licks, in the cricket match, this afternoon! We playing at Spartans, in the Park. You coming, to support the boys?*"

"*I going be there, Skipper. Cheering for Police.*"

"*Charges dropped, hear? Matter o' fact, the Police not laying nuh charges. And congratulations.*"

"*Sir?*"

"*The Assistant Commissioner tell me, early as next Monday, you may be wearing one more stripe over that one pretty stripe you now got 'pon your shoulder, boy! For distinguish service . . . beyond the call o' duty. Congratulations!*"

"*Sir.*"

And Sargeant had stood at attention, and saluted the Commissioner; his right hand hitting the peak of his cork hat, and reverberating like a piece of heavy wire that holds a bell . . .

". . . if we had time," Mary-Mathilda says, "I could tell you the things that take place in this underground dungeon. And this don't have nothing to do with the times of slavery that Ma used to narrate to me, about when even more stranger things took place on this Plantation.

"Always blood being shed. And blood flowing. Ma says one time, when the workers rebel and asked for a couple-more pennies-a-week, in wages, the Plantation pick-out who they thought the ring leaders were, namely Golbourne father, Pounce father, Manny grandfather, brought all three of them down here in this tunnel, strapped them by their hands and legs to the wall, in iron chains, handcuffs and leg-irons, built into the wall, the same time the Great House was built . . . Mr.Bellfeels tell me that this Great House originally was the residence of the Englishman who own the slaves and the Plantation. He went back to Englund. He couldn't stomach the sun and living so close, with his wife, to the slaves. Ma say how she and Gran, my grandmother, the night in question, shelling green pigeon-peas, stood up in the kitchen—the Plantation was having a birthday party that night—and how they could hear the cowskin, the bull-pistle whip—in them days, they called it the balata—tearing-into flesh, *plax! plax! plax!* in a rhythm as if the man wielding the balata was looking at the hand of a metronome, or a clock, measuring-off time in seconds, *tick . . . tock . . . tick*; and in the heaviness of each lash. *Plax! . . . plax! . . . plax!* And the shrieks. The screeling. The cries for mercy. The voices of pain high, high, high, like the fright that comes from a child's voice when a dog snarls; and then the same voice, low, low, low, in pain, like a moaning, exhausted; no voice at all, now; the loss of strength gone out of the cry for mercy, the murmur of the sting and memory of the pain inflicted by the balata. *Plax! . . . plax! . . . plax!* And the echo of the lash, like a giant violin with one of its strings brek. Yes.

"Not knowing, from their distance aboveground, and their place in the kitchen shelling the pigeon-peas, if they could rightly say, or be certain of who the particular recipient of the lashes was, or could they make-out the owner of each pleading cry.

"One man receive forty lashes.

"The second man receive thirty.

"And the third man got only twenty-four.

"Ma and Gran counted all ninety-four!"

"When the last lash, the ninety-four *plax!* landed on that man's back, Ma and Gran say it had the same sound, the same sting, the same echo, the same savageness as the previous *ninety-three*. Delivered by one man. That one man, beating three other big men, could have *such* consistency in his administration o' violence . . .

"And afterwards, Ma say, she had to wipe her hands in her apron, and pour Mr. Lawrence Burkhart, the Driver at the time, in

charge of disciplines and floggings on the Plantation, a glass of cold
Tennent's Beer that she kept in the icebox, which was all the rage
on the Plantation.

"He drank-it-off in three big, long draughts. And then he said,
'Ahhh!' and Ma said a feeling of contentment came-over Mr.
Lawrence Burkhart face, that she herself had a hard time under-
standing: how this Mr. Lawrence Burkhart could remain so cool
and calm, after the screels that turn her blood to ice water.

"Then she had to follow Mr. Lawrence Burkhart down these
same steps. And come to the three bodies of the three men, barely
held up by the manacles and the leg-irons; the whipping had dis-
figured their bodies almost beyond recognition; and if she didn't
witness with her own two eyes, that the whipping had-take-place
in this underground cellar, Ma say, she couldda *swear* that she was
looking at a tableau-type picture of the three men on the Cross
from Biblical times, crucified by that wicked governor, His Excel-
lency, the Roman, Sir Pontius Pilate. The three of those men from
history. With Jesus Our Saviour, in the middle. And two thieves,
robbers, nicodemons, side-b'-side of her precious Saviour . . . one
of them being none other than Barrabas who walked by night,
Ma said.

"Their backs was turned to Ma. And Ma knew then who the
Plantation labelled the ringleader to be. Cross the whole-entire
back of Golbourne father, also named Golbourne, she say she
counted forty slashes going in all directions, formed a kind of star, a
star that she had come-across somewhere, the Star of Bethlehem . . .

"Ma say she had to throw a bucket of saltwater on Golbourne
father, on Manny grandfather and on Pounce father, each; the same
way, Ma say, she used to throw water on the hogs in the pigpen, to
cleanse-them-off. With a few drops of Jays Fluid in it, to bind the
wounds and clot the blood.

"Not a peep came from *one* of those three men, crucified by the
flogging Mr. Lawrence Burkhart gave them."

" '*Get a second bucket,*'" Mr. Lawrence Burkhart tell Ma. '*And when*

*you up there in the kitchen, call the gardener and Watchie. I can't lift
these three heavy sons-o'-bitches, by my-one. These three bastards too
blasted big!'*

"The blood was all over this underground tunnel. Flowing like
rainwater running to reach a gutter, and pour-down. And only
after buckets of fresh water, the yard broom and some crocus bags
that Watchie bring, did Ma and Gran bring back that section of this
underground tunnel to former appearances.

"*'This for you, May,'* Ma say that Mr. Lawrence Burkhart said
to her, using her Christian name, and handing her a bright, half-
Crown, as if he himself had just minted it. *'For your services. And keep
your mouth shut. Nobody will-ever know about this, right?'*

"But he didn't have to seal Ma mouth to that secret confidence.
Ma would be a blasted fool to ever utter a word to anybody. Mr.
Lawrence Burkhart give Gran one shilling.

"I heard this, not from Ma. But from Mr. Bellfeels, after he got
me pregnant the first time, with William Henry. Since then,
pieces of this history, this pageantry of blood, have leaked-out
through various cracks and crevices in conversations at the dinner
table, back-there, back then in the times when times were sweet
between me and him. . . ."

The story that duplicates this strange underground journey
Sargeant is being made to take causes him to feel he is a foreigner, a
stranger in a land in which he thought he had a straight course, but
which he now knows is winding, if not circuitous; something like
the alienation, the hopelessness and the invisibility Manny told him
he felt, when he lived in Georgia and in Florida and in Philadelphia,
working illegally, until that morning when a Trinidadian worker,
himself illegal, bearing a grudge against another Trinidadian, went
to the place of work, late the Friday; payday; and waited until it
was five minutes to five, knocking-off time was five, and then he
screamed, "Immigration!" One time. Just once. "Immigration!" he
screamed. A second time. In one minute flat, the place was empty!
Only the shocked, angry manager-owner of the factory that made

bottle caps remained at the unattended machines, which whirred and ground and rattled to a halt. Manny spent that winter freezing in doorways, after he was chased out of the boiler room of a hospital; and it was after this, that he sought refuge in the sewer until he resigned his fate to the clutches of the U.S. Immigration . . .

But another aspect of her story, the part about men dragged underground, comes in his recollecting it, from *Nelson's West Indian Reader, Book Three*, his textbook in Standard Three. In this book, an animal whose name escapes him now, was burrowing in the mud, making a channel, from which it could not afterwards extricate itself. It was a channel of journey and of death. And he wonders if death underground, below the surface of the earth, hidden from the sun and from the stars which he likes to point out to Gertrude, is to be his fate.

But it cannot be. She is Mary-G. Mary of his dreams, a virgin woman, before tonight. Now, tonight, she is a woman with whom he has made love, in his imagination, making her no longer a virgin.

But it is still imagination, and no matter *what*, she will never be able to know the carnal extremes he has performed over her body, over her.

Sargeant is thinking also of reading exercises in *Nelson's West Indian Reader, Book Three*, about a spider who bores a hole in the ground and covers it with a lid made of pieces of straw and mud, as a protection and as a guillotine. As a weapon. He remembers another exercise in the *Reader*, about an animal, a very small animal, who bores a hole underground and lives in it, with traps laid for intruders; and he remembers another animal, but not by name . . . why can't he call-to-mind these important little animals at a time like this, when he thinks of himself as one of them? Understanding how vulnerable he is crawling through this tunnel, not on his hands and knees, but crawling nevertheless, being led in this slow passage? . . . this animal whose name he can't remember is a worm that bores its home under the surface of soft mud, in tunnels which any intruder would get lost in, tire himself out in,

and give up the ghost of spirit and of strength; drop dead from
frustration, unable to extricate itself; then to be devoured by the
worm. He is this animal. This bug. This fragile spider. "Come into
my parlour, said the Spider to the Fly." He cannot remember
where he first heard this line; but he had to learn the entire tale by
heart, in English Literature classes that were heard orally. Per-
haps, it was Mr. Edwards, his private lessons tutor, who told him
about it at Sin-Davids Elementary School for Boys. Perhaps in
Sunday School. Perhaps on the Pasture playing cricket "firms";
and football with the big boys, who kicked the football made of a
pig's bladder, or a green breadfruit; kicking each other, anything;
all day long, in the hot steaming sun, during the long vacation.

"Come into my parlour,
"Said the Spider to the Fly."

He does not remember who wrote these words. But he feels he
is a fly in her hands.

". . . and, years ago, when Ma worked in the Great House, and
she sent me to the Plantation Main House, in the long vacation, to
buy large tomatoes and cucumbers and carrots; and walking by
myself, it would take me twenty-five minutes to get there, from
the Great House.

"Earlier this evening, it took me *ten*. To travel the same distance.
Perhaps because I am a big woman. And can walk faster. Perhaps I
had a reason for getting there quick. But I was telling you about the
three men . . .

". . . after Ma brought the salt water to pour on the three men,
branded as 'bastards,' for raising their voice to ask for a raise,
the Plantation-people start whispering outta the hearing of the
field labourers that Pounce father, and Manny grandfather, and
Golbourne father were trying to overturn the Plantation, in spite
of all the good things that the Plantation do for the Village and
the labourers and the poor and the cripple; and here now, comes

these 'bastards'—the Plantation label them-so—plunging this decent, harmonious, law-abiding Christian community into chaos, into rebellion, in their imitation of an Amurcan Nigg-rah, one Nat Turner; ". . . shouldda shot the ma'-fecker, when we had-eem cornered," the Commissioner of Police said, in a conversation on the cranked-up telephone, to as many Plantation managers as he could reach in the heat of that night. "Make a fecking example of, I say. What? Well, that's all for now . . . keep your powder dry, if you know what I mean. The barracks have ammonitions, as much as you need . . . an example of, I say. Bellfeels have a cousin up in Southampton keeping us abreast of . . . meanwhile keep your powder dry . . ."

"Even his Christian name, Nat, was a strange name to hear in these parts. We christen our thrildren—and even our houses— in particular, our male thrildren, with proper English names. Like Wilberforce. And Waddington. And Chesterfield. Nobody, in all the days that this Village of Flagstaff exist, nobody ever had the historical effronteries to christen a boy-child with a name that reflects slavery. Like Nat. *Nat?* Nathaniel, Washington and Jefferson are not names that are native to this Island of Bimshire.

"Ma never told me much about the reasons the Plantation had for sociating the three 'bastards' to the name of this Nat Turner fellow. She only told me about the blood. Blood on the walls. Blood on their bodies. Blood on their clothes—what little they had-on, what little was left-on after the balata peal-off their flesh, and rip-up their flour-bag shirt and short pants. Blood on the ground.

"Ma standing in this blood covering her two feet, and having to mop it up, because people had to walk along the same underground passage later in the week, bearing barrels of rum, and barrels of pig snout, and cuts of beef that were slaughtered and had to be cured in brine and pimento, and put there for curing; and all the other provisions that had to be stocked-up-on, and stored, in case of hurricanes, like Hurricane Darnley; against a rainy day.

"Ma's two feet walk through all this blood, to get to the three 'bastards' still lassoed by chains against the wall. The six pieces of iron chains, the handcuffs and leg-irons is still in the wall . . . I will show you them.

"So, the Plantation accused Pounce father, Manny grandfather and Golbourne father of *forming insurrections.* Nobody hadn't use the word *insurrections* before. It was only an Amurcan thing, an Amurcan word before this. A word that somebody who had-went to Amurca, working on a ship that dock in the South to take-on fruits and cotton, had-heard and brought back.

"But it wasn't that we knew much concerning the Negroes and coloured people in Amurca, those who were slaves and those who were free; or freed.

"Ma, in her small way, used to tell me a narrative about a slave name Frederick Douglass who ended his slavery through what they called *manomittance*, and became a newspaper reporter and editor, and a speaker, and who ended up in Buffalo, the place I visited with Mr. Bellfeels, years ago . . .

"Booker-Tea Washington is another such narrative. And there you have it, those Amurcan names that Negro and coloured mothers love to name their boy-thrildren with. Named after some great white Amurcan, such as a President, a doctor, a Senator, a abolutionist, or a Confederate general. Somebody big and important; so long as Amurcan Negroes can trace their history from the name to a person who exists, everything is proper.

"So, through Ma, and then Mr. Bellfeels, and through Wilberforce travels, I got to know all these things. The Plantation label them insurrectionaries. And the Solicitor-General at the time would have henged them all, all at the same time through spite, as a example to others, to show that English law reigned in Bimshire, had it not been for the Vicar, Revern Dowd, not this present one, but the father who interceded on the 'bastards' behalfs, and said it was not Christian, or charitable, and certainly not English, to heng three felons, called 'bastards,' at the same time, back-to-back. His exact words. 'It isn't English to put the three insurrectionaries to their death, in this uncivilize and savage manner.'

"But the boat to take them out in the sea, and push them overboard, was waiting. There is a section to this tunnel . . . I never ventured so far inside it, by myself before; but Ma told me, and later Mr. Bellfeels concur himself, that fifty to a hundred yards down from where we now are, there is another passageway, more secret than this, leading to a junction which they were going to use to take the three insurrectionaries through, after binding them with rope, hands-and-knees; and the skipper of the boat was waiting, and they had the cement already mix and the bags waiting, and they were going to stuff crocus bags in their mouth, to prevent alarms and pleas, and then tie-up their mouths with pieces of their very-own clothes, those that was not shredded from the lashes, and stuff the 'bastards' in the crocus bags, pour the ready-mix cement, the mortar into each bag, tie the end in a reef knot, and without waiting for the cement to dry, push each body overboard. The plan was to go out in the sea, off the Aquatic Club, in the dead of night, when the tide was out, and *out-goes-you*! Jesus-Christ, and in the silence of secrecy, no sign of the Cross, or without saying 'ashes to ashes,' the Vicar say he didn't intend to give them Last Rites, nor read a word from the Bible to bury them in a Christian manner. 'Just bury the bastards!'

"It was the Solicitor-General who had-wanted Captain Frazer-Small, the owner of the motor-vessel, to take the three 'bastards' far-far out, out beyond the horizon, and throw them overboard, and leave them to the mercy of the lion sharks. But the Vicar prevailed. Warning them of their own salvation in the face of the brutality of such a deed, in case the sharks was full, and didn't have appetite to eat the three 'bastards,' right-off; but just *toy* with them, biting off a foot this morning, nibbling-way at a toe in the afternoon, and leaving-back the bulk of their dinner, the torso, for the dead of night, when lion sharks really get hungry and mean. How would that look, the Vicar ask them? How would they feel, if they were one of the three 'bastards'?

"That did it. That turned the tide. They settled for a more painless and merciful death. Suffocated in cement, in the crocus bag, and thrown overboard . . .

"So, this Amurcan Negro, Nat Turner, after who the Plantation-people swear the three 'bastards' had-pattern their rebellion after, intending to burn down the entire blasted Plantation, molest and rape the women, not sparing even thrildren, male, female, and old women, allegedly; cutting-off the heads of horses and mules and donkeys to prevent pursuit into the hills and gulleys of Sin-Thomas and Sin-Joseph; and Chimboraza; keeping the rest of the stocks in the Yard, after getting blind drunk offa their violence, and offa Bellfeels Stades White Rum, and vengeance, according to the Plantation, for meat, and roast-goat; the Plantation said they had to punish the three 'bastards,' it was their bounden Christian duty, 'bliged-and-bound,' to make a example of these insurrectionaries.

"That is one story. There's more."

"And I, a policeman, never heard nothing about none o' these, before! At least, that they ever happened."

"You are a stranger to the truth, to the history, and to the actions of the powerful in this Island, Percy.

"You will certainly remember a certain Commissioner of Police, not the one you presently serve, but another one. You must-know who I mean!"

"I don't know if I know."

"No need to call his name. But he walked with a limp."

"I don't know, if I really know the person!"

"Skip. I may as well tell you. He dead, anyway. Well, Skip come home one day, for his lunch, and found his wife in bed. With the gardener. And Skip took his gun from outta his holster. Hold it to the gardener head. And *blam!* All this time, the wife naked as she born. In the bed. Can't move. Don't know if to move. Stricken

with fear and fright. With the blood splatter-over her body. Scream-
ing her head off. And Skip take off his Sam Brown, take off his
police uniform, the short-sleeve khaki tunic he take off; the short
khaki shorts he take off. Roll down the three-quarter khaki stock-
ings. Off went the brown leather shoes; and of course, as he was
inside the bedroom, he wasn't wearing the peak cap that police
commission-officers wear.

"And without saying a word, he climb on top of his wife. And he
gave it to her. Going and coming. From the back, from the front, and
donkey-style. Ride her till-thy-kingdom-come. And when he had
his full, he say to her, *'You satisfied, now?'* And she say, *'Yes, darling. You
always satisfies me, more better than anybody-else.'* And he tell her, *'Good.'*

"He went out the bedroom, and come back with his Sam Brown.
Draw his police revolver. Cock the trigger. Put the barrel to the
wife head. And pulled the trigger. *Click!* the revolver said. He put
back the barrel of the revolver to her head. To her left temple, this
time. She screaming like bloody-hell, now. And pulled the trigger
a next time. *Click!* Then he put the barrel of the revolver to her pri-
vate parts, her pum-pum, her pussy, then. And pulled the trigger,
and *blammm!*"

"Jesus Christ!"

"But before he put the revolver the last time, to her, he axe her,
"You think I is a fecking cunu-munu?"

"*'No-no-no!'* she say. And that is when he put the revolver to her
pum- . . .

"Wilberforce was acting as Coroner. And suppose you had heard
Wilberforce describe the scene of the blood and the body he seen!
Wilberforce say such demolition of a human body was unknown
before. Her entire body disfigured. Wilberforce said it was as
much as to make a horse pewk!

"The Plantation gathered up the wife's body after the attopsy,
in the same two white sheets she had lay-down on, to foop the gar-
dener, and they wrap-she-up in them, and took her through the
secret tunnel, and out to sea.

"Disappeared. Off the face of the earth.

"You ever hear anybody in this Village, or in this Island, mention a Mistress Burke, Skip wife? Outta sight: outta mind. Wipe-out. Forgotten.

"This time, they followed the advice of the Solicitor-General. Far-far-far out to sea, they took her, and left her there. The sharks had a field day."

"And the gardener?" Sargeant says.

"The gardener? Well, they didn't invest summuch time in his disposal. The nearest dry-well to Skip's house. Wrap-up in a crocus bag. And carried in a donkey cart, like a bag o' brown sugar. And down the first dry-well they came to.

"Likewise, do you hear anybody asking for the gardener, even though everybody know that he disappear? And how. And then, one morning, nobody didn't see him. Gone! The whole Village and the Island, police and Sin-John Ambulance Brigade set up search parties, even some of the same white people who drop-heem-in-the-well, join in on the search. Nobody couldn't find the gardener, poor fellow."

"I don't see the Commissioner so often, these days."

"In the mental hospital. In Jenkins. Telling the other madmen there with him, that the end of the World is nigh, and at hand . . ."

"I heard so, too."

"Percy, but didn't people say the gardener was a distant cousin to you? I am sure I heard word that he was to call you a third cousin."

"A second cousin o' mine did disappear. They say he store-'way 'pon a ship going to Curaçao; left Curaçao for Cuba where they needed gardeners; jump ship in Havana, and then get-deport back to Curaçao. Nobody don't know what happen to him, since."

"The exact man! A gardener. One of the best this Island ever produce. Used to be head gardener at Guvvament House, when the Governor was the same governor who had a feast off Mistress Rosa Mary Antoinette Brannford's pudding-and-souse. Later, worked at the Crane Beach Hotel. Thence, gardener to the Commissioner of Police."

"Maybe," he says.

"Maybe. Maybe not. But it's a long time."

"Long time. Maybe."

"We're coming to the end. Not much more farther," she says.

The underground passage is not pitch-dark, as he had thought it would be. There is a strange kind of light in this passage below the ground. And a strange angle in the way the light strikes the wall, then bounces off the white cement and touches her face.

As she talks, and their two bodies move in the light thrown by the lantern, her face takes on an animated look. It is all excitement in her voice, and in the story she is telling him. She tells the story with such gruesome detail, as if she is reading and getting its horribleness from a book of narratives about slaves.

But there was never any slaves in Bimshire, Sargeant argued only a few days ago. "I wasn't taught nothing-so at Sin-Davids Elementary School. Nor in Sunday School at the Church, when we listened to stories of the Israelites in the Bible. Mr. Edwards never tell me 'bout slaves, to my knowledge."

Manny who lived and travelled throughout Amurca for a couple of years, and returned with an Amurcan accent, calling a man "a main"; and using *boy* instead of *fellar* and *chum*; and who had visited many cities in the South, including Nashville, Macon and Louisville, and Lynchburg, without picking up the connection, Manny never told Sargeant very much about slaves or slavery in Bimshire; and all he said about that was that some of the "Nigg-rahs" he met in towns in South Carolina, talk with something like a Bimshire accent; but he didn't know why. "For-sure," Manny told Sargeant, "the nigg-rahs I butt-up-with, down in the Amurcan South, were former slaves." And yet, once in jest, he called Golbourne *"you blasted nigg-rah, you just-pass to sixes! How-come you got another six in your hand?"* And Golbourne said he never thief at dominoes; and laughed at the word, and its strange sound. And Sargeant laughed at the funny

name. And Pounce laughed at the word and said, "Why you bring-
ing that Amurcan foolishness 'bout-here? People who was slaves
are called nigg-rahs. Slavery never touch Bimshire. We don't have
insurrectionaries nor nothing-so, 'bout-here. Anybody ever was-
lynch' in Bimshire . . ."

And Manny, who had used the word, and who was the only one
who lived in Amurca, said, speaking in a Southern Black Amurcan
accent:

"When you're white,
"You're right.
"When you're brown,
"You can stick-around;
"But when you're bleck,
"You gotta stay a waaaay beck!"

And they all laughed, and went back playing cutthroat domi-
noes; and drinking rum chased with ice water.

"Those Amurcans could talk real sweet!" Sargeant said. "My
daughter up-in-there, now six months, and you shouldda hear the
way she talk! *Pure* Yankee twang."

"I prefer to hear Amurcans, more than the English, talk. Those
Limey bastards're always talking-*down* to a man. The Amurcans,
now, with the real low-down twang they speaks, puts you in the
same category as them!"

"Except for their love of lynching Nigg-rahs and coloured
men!" . . . Mary-Mathilda stops suddenly. She releases Sargeant's
hand. A hardness comes over her face. And in this subterranean
light, with its dramatic picking out of detail in the most cruel man-
ner, Sargeant sees now, for the first moment in the long day, with a
force that frightens him, that Mary-Mathilda is really not a very
attractive woman. He sees her hardness in this light below the
ground, in light that is really no light at all, and he thinks that Mary
Gertrude Mathilda is a very ugly woman. "You are wrong . . ."; but

it takes Sargeant a moment to realize that she is talking, and that the
silence, the hum, the strange reverberation of sound in the under-
ground tunnel is not the wind, nor the echo that tombs and caves
and sepulchres give off: it is her voice. "Let me and you sit down
here and rest for a while, whilst I tell you a story that Ma told me,
to let you know that the names that the Plantation-people in this Is-
land used to call us by were the same names the Southerners used
in Amurca, showing, as Ma always said, that there is no difference
between those brutes who enslave us here in the Wessindies, and
the ones that enslave other coloureds in Amurca. They could be
our brothers and our sisters. "

"You feel related to them?"

"Most do not feel we are related. And in a way, we are not. We eat
English food, and they eat Amurcan food. Is a case of pudding-and-
souse versus hot dogs. But the name they use to address us by, is the
same. Negro is just a soften-up term for nigger, spoken with a English
accent! So, nigger for them in Amurca. And nigger for us in the British
Wessindies. Though here, the word is spoken under the breath.

"We don't remember being called that, because our memory
is short. And the lash was not delivered as frequent or hard and
didn't bite-in in our backsides, with the same sting. But a lash is a
lash. Whether it be delivered by a cowskin, a balata, a bull-pistle,
here in Bimshire; or by a cat-o'-nine tail, as they did to Nat Turner
in Southampton. Or with a lash from their tongue. Or their lips.
Remember Mark Anthony and Judas . . .

"And how many different Southamptons do you think they are?
There is only one. Up in Englund where they used to stop-off with
the slaves in mid-shipment to the Wessindies. From that one branch,
that one root, from that Southampton in Englund, sprung-up all
the other Southamptons in the world; Southamptons in Amurca
and Southamptons in the Wessindies, and oh-loss, Southamptons
in Brazil. There must be Southamptons all over the world!

"Ma told me a story, as I said, before I got distracted by the name
of Southampton, to prove to you that a white man in Bimshire and

a white man in Georgia is one and the same white man, from the
same branch and the same root.

"For instance. Mr. Bellfeels has a brother, by father—not
by mother—in Englund. In Buffalo, where I travelled with Mr.
Bellfeels to, some years ago, there is a Mr. Bellfeels, right there
in Buffalo-New-York, who is Mr. Bellfeels great-uncle. And it
was this Bellfeels who told Mr. Bellfeels during that visit—I didn't
hear it for myself from his lips, because Mr. Belfeels stayed in a
hotel, whilst I stayed in a house called a "bread-and-breakfast,"
owned by a coloured lady; so, I didn't hear the words straight from
Mr. Bellfeels great-uncle lips; but I was told that the main branch
o' Bellfeelses come from Southampton in Englund; finally settling
in South Carolina where they had five cotton and sugar plantations,
populated with thousands and thousands of slaves.

"That is how Mr. Bellfeels was able to link the little disturbance
here in Bimshire to the bigger Amurcan insurrection that Nat
Turner started in Southampton.

"Just as these people keep photographs and snapshots of their
life, and write-down every damn thing that happen to them in a
book, good and bad, keeping records, and writing journals day-by-
day, it is for the same reason they write letters and send signals to
one another, all over the world where they keep slaves.

"I won't be surprised if this little underground passage that we
are walking through now doesn't have some link and terminal, some
connection, to the United States of Amurca, travelling unknown to
every person in this Island, under the Carbean Sea, and the Atlantic
Ocean, 'cross all those miles and miles of sea, to some secret port,
some cove, all the way up in South Carolina. Charleston.

"Stranger things have happened in this Island.

"Ma told me that her mother, my great-gran, was a slave on this
very Plantation. Ma didn't know where she come from, neither.
Africa-somewhere. Or Charleston-South-Carolina. They sent all
the rebelling slaves, following the Southampton Resurrection, I
mean Insurrection, here to Bimshire, which has the reputation, Ma

say Great-gran told her, of having the most cruel slave overseers and slave-drivers, famous throughout the world of slaves, for successfully breaking slaves that the Amurcan plantations didn't have the skills to break.

"So, I don't understand how anybody, particular a coloured person, could have the gall to say there wasn't slaves in Bimshire!

"Perhaps, not in the droves they had in Amurca. But to put a thing like this in two scales and weigh one against the next don't make sense to me. They must think I is a cunu-munu, or something.

"Slaves is slaves. Bimshire slaves are Bimshire slaves. And Amurcan slaves are Amurcan slaves. But slaves are slaves.

"I was telling you of a narrative told to me by Ma, which she heard from her mother, Gran, who I am sure, heard it told by my great-great-gran, and finally handed down to me. These narratives are the only inheritances that poor people can hand down to their offsprings. The rich people and the Plantation-people have land and trees, pigs and cows, money in Barclays Bank, Dominion, Colonial Overseas, and money hidden in wells all over this Island, on this very Plantation and throughout the Village, to lavish-way on their inheritancies. But all that we possess to hand-down is love. And bitterness. And blood. And anger. And all four, wrap-up in one narrative. Stories I would hear at night, in kerosene oil light, with mosquitoes coming and going, like commas and punctuation marks, and I under my crocus-bag blanket, shivering from the cold and from the blackness in the stories, and . . .

"We are halfway in our journey. We don't have much more to go . . ."

The underground tunnel turns left, not a sharp left, but left-incline, going away now from the cellars of the Great House. They are walking slowly. The closeness of the air, the strange light that seems to come in through the pores in the coral stone and the grates give a magical, timeless feel to the surroundings.

It is this left-incline turn that she points him in; and the moment his body is dealing with this change of direction, he smells the smell of the sea, fresh and raw and with the taste of saltiness. It is a surprising sensation: to smell seawater when he is underground. And the breeze that lives over the sea, comes into the cavern, and he feels less anxious about where he is. And about her. The previous, burning sensuality she drove into his body has dissipated. He walks now, as if he is entering the short lane that comes off the main road leading to the clump of hard, short, deciduous trees at the edge of the sandy beach, at the edge of the sea. And he knows he shall enter the sea, and let the rich, warm water crawl over his body and overwhelm him, like a womb. And he feels as if he will not return from facing the horizon in his long bath, swimming in the welcoming water.

"But even if we in this Island do not see ourselves as slaves, the treatment that Ma tell me about that she suffered through, and what my great-great-gran went through, you would have to invent a new name for it, if not slavery.

"Thomas Jefferson, named after his master, and bearing his master surname," she says, "is only one story of a case from Georgia; but if you substitute Flagstaff for Georgia, um is the same narrative. So, listen to this, and tell me if you don't see a connection? As I said, Thomas was born into slavery, and at the age of fourteen, escape and walked all the way from Waycross-Georgia, way-way up North, until he found Canada, with the help of some people on the Underground Railroad. His master was about to whip him the second day running, because a pepper-coated Smithfield ham went-missing from the curing house; and the day before, the master had-give him forty-two lashes, four-two, with the cat-o'-nine tail, when, *wuh-loss!*, the slave master wife came running, out-o'-breath, from the Main House, and tell the master that is she who had-take the Smithfield ham, and had-give the ham to her brother who live on the neighbouring plantation. The next day was the Fourth of July."

She is leading him to a door. The door is made of wood. It is roughly hewn, with large nails securing the horizontal strips of

unpainted wood to give the door more strength, to make it im-
pregnable. It is like a door Wilberforce told her about, in an Ital-
ian palazzo in Vincentia which he visited. Through the spaces in
the wood come shafts of light. It is like the light of moonlight. Or
of the high beams of a car. The light similar to the blueness of dawn.
Or like smoke clearing from a cane fire.

"This is the secret passageway leading to the sea. Years ago,
when Ma was still in the fields, this gate was used to smuggle men
wanted by the police, and hide them in neighbouring islands. And
to bring in contraband goods, particularly during the First World
War. And I understand from Mr. Bellfeels that some Germans who
used to live in the Island, who, when War broke out, this is the Sec-
ond World War now, these Germans were renamed as enemy spies;
these Germans, the four of them, were smuggled through this pas-
sage to a German boat waiting outside the Careenage, in deeper
waters, out in the Harbour.

"There was a English boat full of foodstuffs that was in the Har-
bour once; and all of a sudden, the whole island was black with
smoke and burning oil, and shaking to its foundations, after a shot
from the same German boat used to smuggle spies hit the blasted
merchant ship, as a signal that the four Germans was now safe on
board, and to show all o' we living in the Wessindies, and in the
Island of Bimshire in particular, that Churchill and the Allieds, *our*
allies, were nothing but hypocrites. They left we Wessindians
starving and at death's door: whilst ship after ship in a long convoy
of food was bypassing the Wessindies and heading straight for the
various theatres of war to feed Europeans.

"This simple little underground tunnel played a very important
role in the outcome of the War. Simple as it is . . .

"But it was put to more bigger uses in the history of this Island.
Thieves who dressed in white shirt and collar-and-tie, clerks and
managers, specially Englishmen, stole millions of pounds whilst
working for Barclays Bank, Dominion, Colonial & Overseas, for
Plantations Limited, for the Lumber Yard, for the various sugar

plantations all over this Island, even for Cave Shepherd, and were smuggled into the Plantation Main House, hidden in secret rooms, and then taken through this passage to a waiting yacht, which would take them later to a schooner laying at anchor, which would in turn take them to Trinidad, and from Trinidad to Venezuela, to their final destination, Brazil.

"Brazil is full of Englishmen who have stolen from Barclays Bank-DCO, Cave Shepherd and the hotels, whilst they lived in luxury here in Bimshire. Mr. Bellfeels know all of them."

She opens the gate. The hinge creaks. She lowers the wick of the kerosene lamp. And places it on the ground. A burst of air, like cooling wind, comes in from the darkness outside.

Sargeant looks up, although he is not yet outside, in the wide, dark night, to see if he can see the stars. There are no stars. They are still in the underground tunnel, although they are climbing the ten cement steps to reach the exit.

She smells the night. It is like it was hours ago, when she took the ten-minute-long walk from her own house to the Plantation Main House, to confront Mr. Bellfeels as he lay slouched in rum, and heavy from food, on the verandah. From that same verandah, Mr. Bellfeels could see the hills to the north that cut off the parishes which touch the sea in that part of the Island; and to the south, he could see right down onto the beach, over the plains and lands and fields of Indian corn, and Guinea grass and sugar canes grown privately by small landholders and farmers; and beyond, to the sea; if it was a clear day, he could see a merchant ship, or a ship filled with "tourisses" coming over the placid Carbean Sea. Farther to his right, south-southeast, he could see the Union Jack flying on top of the Aquatic Club. From his verandah, Mr. Bellfeels could see three-quarters of the Island.

"There was a time when this Plantation owned three-quarters of all the land and property in the whole of Bimshire."

Now she is before the second wooden gate. It is stiff. Its hinges swing inwards, towards her. There is a roughly made handle. The nails that hold it are now loose, from age and rust. She pulls, and pulls, and it seems as if the gate will hold its secrets and remain shut, and block her entry into the wider world that lies before her, buried in the darkness and the vast fields of sugar cane, wide as the Carbean Sea, vast as the Atlantic Ocean itself . . .

And, all of a sudden, the gate swings open. A new world outside this wooden gate opens and faces them.

There is the smell of the earth, after rain. The soil. Thick, wet, black soil. The fields planted in yams are like waves.

The smell that greets her is a smell she thinks is of flowers.

If it were not so dark, she would be able to see these flowers. That Sunday afternoon she had lingered over her lunch, and could find no appetite for the dry-peas and rice, boiled chicken, local sweet potatoes, pulped eddoes, cucumber sliced as thin as the pages from a book and pickled in lemon juice, fresh red hot peppers and generous amounts of fresh parsley; she had sat watching the steam from the other serving dishes rise like fingers of smoke she would sometimes see moving over the North Field, when the canes were on fire; sitting and "studying"; and she had found, sitting there, some solace from the thoughts that were interrupting her appetite for her Sunday lunch; thoughts that provided a temporary postponement of the suggestion that entered her head: that after all these years, she should choose this Sunday to correct the injuries she had suffered, swollen through the passage of the years themselves; find the motive, and prove to herself that he had, through the narrative of her mother's life, and the tales handed down from her great-great-gran's life from a time even before that; that in spite of the Great House in which she lives, the reward for his use of her body; giving him three children, two dead before they hardly saw the light of day; and all the gifts for which a woman would normally kiss the dirt on which the giving-man walks; or kiss his arse; but no; not she, after all these years of success, in the eyes of the entire Village of Flagstaff, in the eyes of Sargeant who always loved her, and who wants her now, but could not have had her then; not because of her circumstances, but because of her own decision—she could have sneaked him a foop even in spite of Mr. Bellfeels' "following and reporting" eyes; no, nothing had erased from her mind, the way the riding-crop moved from her neck, from the neck of the cotton frock which belonged to his own daughter, Miss Euralie . . . She has been in this underground passage before. Mr. Bellfeels brought her here, once a week on Fridays, when he was repairing the green-painted gate she has just closed, when he had first promoted her to work in the kitchen of the Main House.

Here, in this underground tunnel, Mr. Bellfeels did not make love to her, if he could ever call his rapid "firing of blanks" making love; when he brought her here it was to foop her; but not foop her in the normal sense, the sense she knew by instinct, and by listening behind the cloth curtain in her house to the stories Ma and Gran told about women on the Plantation.

Mr. Bellfeels brought Mary-Mathilda here into this underground tunnel, and pulled up her dress, and pulled down her cotton panties, and pushed his index finger on the left hand as high into her pussy as it would go; sometimes beyond the second joint. And then he put the same finger into his mouth; licked it dry, noisily, regardless of her time of month; and then he took the flask of rum from his khaki jodhpurs, which he always carried, and held his head back, and let the strong, burning white liquid fall into his mouth. When he put the flask back into his side pocket, the silver in the flask gleamed; and she could see the initials, DARB, marked deep into the beautiful sterling of the flask. He drank only white rum. The rum he himself would learn to cure.

"*Young pussy and mature white rum, the best anecdote for a man! Eh, Mary-girl? What you say?*

"*I grooming you for later. I waiting till you get more riper, girl,*" he told her always, on these Fridays.

He would put the flask back into his jodhpurs, push the whip into his waist, and with his hand round her shoulder—she reached

him to his chest—they would walk back through the one-mile un-
derground tunnel, with him pressing her head against his strong
virile body, not saying a word, just breathing; he with a more pul-
sating rhythm, as she could feel from her closeness to his body; she,
in the rushed, uneven pulsation of fear.

"*Good night, Mary,*" he would always say as he locked the entrance,
the trap door which led into what is now her kitchen, in the Great
House.

"*Next Friday again, hear?*"

"*Friday,*" she would tell him.

"*Don't tell your mother.*"

And he would smile. And she knew. She knew enough of life
that she knew she could not tell her mother. And if she did, she
knew what would happen.

"*I forget,*" he said one time. "*Sorry, Mary-girl. Not next Friday. I
seeing May.*"

"*Yes, sir.*"

May was her mother's name. Everyone who worked or who
lived on the Plantation called her Miss May.

"*Friday's May's time. When you get home, tell May I want to see her.
Hear?*"

"*Yes, sir.*"

"*Good night, Mary.*"

"*Good night, Mr. Bellfeels, sir.*"

"I am taking you this way, leading you through this gate, to show
you something you wouldn't probably've seen before," she tells
Sargeant now, closing the gate behind them, but not latching it.

They are now walking in a passageway cut out like a deep trench
at the side of a road, but much deeper; and covered. Their heads do
not reach halfway up the sides. The sides are of concrete. It is plain,
rough concrete. It has the toughness of a fortress. It is like the
trenches described by the BBC as the place where English soldiers
and soldiers from the British Commonwealth fought in the War.

It is dark in this trench. The path on which they are walking is hard, packed mud; hard almost as concrete.

"Field hands were lashed and tied to a stake out in the hot sun; and one afternoon I saw, with my two eyes, how Mr. Lawrence Burkhart the Driver brought a bucket of water and placed it *three* inches out of that poor man's reach; and the Driver stood there, laughing and smoking a cigarette, with his whip under his right arm-pit; and every time that that man made a attempt to reach the gal-vanized bucket of water, Mr. Lawrence Burkhart snap his balata, *plax!*

"Ma say that when bad field hands were beaten, just for fun, and when they were no longer any use to the Plantation, this is the road the Plantation had them take, while waiting to be carried out in the sea, to feed to the sharks. Ma say this was the way things were, in my gran's time, because for one thing, as damaged goods and spoil-property, it was more cheaper to throw them to the sharks than to pay a doctor, if there was one on the Plantation, or pay the gravedig-ger to dig-down six feet; or the carpenter to nail-together planks of deal board for a coffin, to bury them in. To-besides, the graveyard, christened Coloured Valley, was getting full-up too quick, during slavery, with dead black people.

"We had five great tragedies in this Island of Bimshire. The Typhoid Fever Outbreak. Was like a epidemic. Killed great and small. The firm and the infirm.

"Then the Hurricane. The weatherman out on the Hill didn't have time, the hurricane lick-down summuch property so quick, to think of a name to christen it by. We did that ourselves. Darnley! What a brute-beast! It devastate practically half the Island. Flagstaff Village almost didn't exist the third day. All the houses where the poor people live, were toss-'bout, and went flying all over the place, like dry leaves. Houses near the sea went in the sea like kites that pop their cord. And the waves from the sea left the sea, and came over the land and destroyed all that the hurricane winds had spared. Ma say it was as if God had-christen Bimshire by a new name, a Biblical name, and called it Sodom and Gormorrah.

"After the Typhoid Fever Outbreak, and Darnley the Hurricane, there was the Hunger. Caused by foodstuffs becoming, all of a sudden, scarce; scarce-scarce-scarce. Churchill wanting all the food for the Allieds to fight the Nazzies on the beaches, in the lanes, on the high seas, in the air, and on the ground with; all over. Ma say all that effort took food to be successful with, so Churchill send the food up in Englund for the Allieds.

"We had to cut and contribe.

"Even the inferior salt fish that Canada, a member of the Commawealth of Nations, and as a consequence *our* Commawealth sister, sent down here was scarce. Lining up for three hours in Miss Greaves' Shop to buy rotting, stinking salt fish, with such a awful smell to it that when you put it in a skillet to boil it, it was like cooking offal. But it showed, Ma say, what artists black people are. I don't only mean in singing and acting, like Miss Ella Fitzgerald, and Billy Eckstine, Nat King Cole and Fat Swallow, Cab Calloway, Jesse Owens, Count Basie, Joe Louis and Duke Ellington . . . incidentally, I wonder if Duke Ellington is a real Duke like the ones up in Englund, or if he is using the Duke as a alias or a nomenclature, one of those names common in Amurca, amongst Negroes? Or, Trinidadian Calypsonians. But we were artists in a lot of other ways, too.

"Sweet potatoes which we only boiled or roasted before was now grated and made into flour. Flour remained on the merchant ships that stopped here, but was not off-loaded. Churchill ordered the ships to stop here, *only* to take-on fresh, clean water; and rum; and then run straight for Englund.

"Cassava, which we used only to make starch to starch clothes with; or cassava-pone, or cassava-hats, a local delicacy; or sweet-cassava boil and serve with dry food, we now realized we had the genius and had-possess the *same* stamina, ability, and determination as the English of Englund, and we could turn this cassava into flour, cassava flour.

"We turned poison-cassava into starch.

"And we turned ordinary sweet potato and the other variety of cassava, sweet-cassava, into flour.

"And had a hell-of-a-time eating 'hats' cooked in a iron buck-pot, yes! We ate to our hearts' content! Forget Winston Churchill, man!

"The tamarind, gooseberry, puh-paw, all the fruits that we used to take a bite outta, and then throw-way, well, we now turned those fruits into preserves and preservatives, rivalling the best from Englund, Seville Orange Marmalade made by James Keiller & Son, Dundee, and them-so. Yes!

"How did I get on to this? The mind, Sargeant-boy, the mind going . . . Sometimes I sit down, and call-to-mind travelling on journeys; and then, the more I am studying, I afterwards realize that I could not have been on those journeys at all, because I don't even know where the particular country is. But it is the mind. It is in the mind. My mind, when not occupied with Gertrude, would take me on these journeys, and then I would have to tell myself that it is purely imagination.

"I have never really left the shores of Bimshire.

"Uh lie! *Once.* Once, though, I travelled to Buffalo with Mr. Bellfeels. I remember landing in Miami-Florida, and travelling by train all the way up to the North. I remember the coloured women in the same comport—partment . . . compartment as me. Mr. Bellfeels, being a businessman, had to sit with other businessmen, to talk business. Sugar-cane yields, machineries for the Factory to get larger yields with. He taught me to look at life as a matter of yields. Everything have its yield. Or its possibility of yields.

"So, the businessmen sat in a different comportment, compartment, talking about yields; and smoking cigars. Apparently, cigars were not permitted in the compartment where I was, with the other coloured women. God, I loved the way those coloured women talked, though; so slow. We coloured people in this part of the world talk fast-fast.

"And when we reached Buffalo, we were serrigated in two different places again, because as I said, businessmen have a way of talking about yields long into the night, and I was a woman in-the-family-way, pregnant then, with my first child, and I needed my rest. And I surely didn't want, through pregnant complications or something happening, to have to remain in Buffalo, and have a child of mine born under the Stars-and-Stripes! Oh-no!

"My child had to be English.

"So, Mr. Bellfeels went his way with his businessmen-people, and I spend my time in the place called a 'bed-and-breakfast'; and at night I sat me down in a little restaurant to eat, and hear a coloured lady with a voice like Marian Anderson, singing 'It's Nobody Business,' and other blues. From then on, I fell in love with the blues. Give me the blues any morning; for breakfast, for lunch and dinner; and before I go to bed at night, give me the blues as a nightcap . . . with a lil brandy. Give me the blues anytime, before I would listen to this hilly-billy music from the South, or to cowboys from out in Western Canada.

"I related this journey many times to Wilberforce. And Wilberforce tell me that I am imagining things, that I am conducting a psychological recall, spurn-on by certain things. I am conducting a journey of imaginary reality. I ask Wilberforce, *'What the hell are you telling me? What language you speaking?'* That's the trouble with having thrildren who are more brighter than their parents! They embarrass you all the time.

"Wilberforce tell me that there is a section of the mind, or the brain, that holds things that the person in question cannot control. He actually didn't use the word *person*. He said *patient*, insinniating that something was wrong with my head, although he didn't come right out with a diagnosis, and say that something *was* wrong with his mother's head! That would be convicting him too, won't it?

"A person can be anywhere she wants to, Wilberforce tell me, even if the person has never actually been there. And this is the kind of journey I am taking you on.

"We are at the end of the passage, and what you see in front of you is the field in which I started my life.

"Ma started her life here, too. My grandmother, Gran, started her life here, and before Gran, my great-gran, who was taken from a different place. And Ma never really found out if Gran came straight from Elmina-Africa, or was transship from Waycross-Georgia, and then here. I used to hear Gran sing 'Steal Away to Jesus,' and 'Swing Low, Sweet Chariots.' And many a night, as I had occasion to tell the Constable, I sang 'Ole Liza Jane.' I told the Constable this.

"Ma always told me narratives about life in the barracks of the men and women who didn't work in the fields, or in the sugar-cane fields, the house servants, some of who were coopers and car-penters and blacksmiths; and Ma say that in the barracks of this very Plantation, Saturday night was the night that the master visited his slave woman down in the barracks, to get his weekly dose of his *thing*. Pum-pum time! Driver-time. Overseer-time. Bookkeeper time. Assistant Manager time. Manager time. White-man time . . .

"Ma's time came. And she had to deliver. Either stanning-up behind the shack where she lived with Gran; or inside the house, with Gran inside the house, too, hearing every move, every push, every juck, every cry which was muffled, because the massa, the driver, the overseer, the bookkeeper, assistant manager, manager had-place his two hands to cover Ma's mouth, as he did it from behind . . . and Gran pretending she wasn't hearing nothing, nor her own history repeated; spend the hush, wet, soiled time pre-tending she wasn't hearing nothing.

"Performing just like two animals.

"Every Saturday night, when things were sweet, and Wilberforce was at Harrison College, Mr. Bellfeels, as his habit was, as the custom was, would visit the Great House. And on these Saturday nights, there would be so much food. Good food. Rich food. Chicken fricassee. Long-grain rice that was clean, you hardly had to pick or wash it; not like what Demerara exported here. Ham. From that place I told you about, in the South. Smithfield. Bully-beef. If a ship hadn't come in with beefsteak from the Argentyne, 'cause the Argentyne being Latin-Amurcan, was always a favourite of Germans. And fried pork chops. You wouldda thought we were having a feast. And that it was Easter or Christmas. Or Wilberforce birthday. Yes!

"Only the three o' we. Little Wilberforce, Mr. Bellfeels and me. And Gertrude serving.

"I must confess that Mr. Bellfeels wasn't a bad-looking man, being not pure-blood. He had the same body, that nice, strong, sexy—is that the word young people use nowadays?—mannish body that you and Golbourne and that I remember Pounce having.

"So it wasn't all that bad, absolutely. It wasn't a choice that I made. It was more like one of those Indian arrangements of marriage where the woman have no voice in the man she will get in bed with.

"Ma chose Mr. Bellfeels for me: and vice versa.

"On Saturday nights, you shouldda seen me and my son, with me holding my son's two hands and we turning round and round, spinning; with our mouths wide open, laughing; at the top of our voice, doing these dances. Jigs, Wilberforce call them, after travelling in the South himself, to a conference in Tuskeegee. Tuskeegee was named after an Amurcan slave who told other coloured people to follow agriculture and learn how to grow crops, and that when slavery abolish, the very white people would come buying the crops that these same ex-slaves produce. But you know all this. Yes. Tuskeegee!

"I wasn't even thinking of the man from Tuskeegee when I mention the habit of contriving, during the War years. It must be something in us, in we people, coloured people, Negroes, *whatever* you want to call us, that connects us together, no matter which Plantation we are to call home-prison, as Ma always referred to her life, on *this* Plantation, as.

"Dancing those Saturday night jigs caused Wilberforce to see the likeness of me and him in *Little Black Sambo*, a book he happen to buy in Tennessee.

"Wilberforce could not wait till he returned from Tennessee. He send *Little Black Sambo* by airmail, special delivery, with this note attach: *'I have marked page 150 of this book to show you how we used to behave. Isn't it ironical?'*"

They are standing now at the edge of a large field. There are no lights from the labourers' shacks surrounding them. The houses are too far away, behind the phalanx of mahogany trees, down the slope, down the long drift of land that leads gently and gradually in the distance, into the sea. And on the other side, the side that could have afforded them a vision of the Main House, the distance is too far.

The noise now, of her feet and Sargeant's, on the dried trash, even at this time of night, when dew is already forming, is still sharp and loud.

But when she thinks of the way her feet strike the trash, and the way the trash responds to her weight, it carries her back, farther back in her childhood, to the time when Ma would shake her mattress every evening before spreading it back onto the six pieces of board that were placed crosswise, in place of bedsprings, after the mattress had been hanging on the clothesline in the sun all day; to get rid of bugs, chinks and other little things that bite during the long, sweating, tossing-and-turning humid night. Walking on the trash in the field now, takes her back to those evenings when it was her duty to spread the mattress, stuffed with dried Guinea grass, evenly over the six boards.

The night has begun to get chilly. It is a skin-piercing chilliness that is noticeable because the day was so hot, and now the sudden change in temperature is like a change in disposition, from passionate confidence, to sly gossip and deceit.

It has changed from a night of passionate confidence, to a night of deceitful negotiating.

She pulls the neck of her dress and the shawl tighter round her neck, but there is no relief from the chilliness of the night.

Sargeant tramps on the trash in the same way he would track a suspect. With silent, deadly determination. But Sargeant never calls them suspects: they are all criminals to him, even before proven guilty. It is with this steadfast determination that he is walking now. He no longer feels the power she had over his body. His flesh is no longer weak. He is going along with her, out of courtesy. And because he is a policeman.

"We're going to stop here," she says.

"I think I know where we are," he says.

He looks around into the thick, heavy darkness.

"I think I know where we are."

"The North Field."

"That field?" he says, still looking around.

"You should be well acquainted with this field, Percy."

"Why?"

He does not see the sarcasm.

"Why?" he says again.

Perhaps, he does not want to see it.

"Are you a bat?"

"Bat?"

"A night-bat?"

"As against a day-bat, like in cricket?"

"Seeing in the dark, Percy. Seeing in the dark."

"You had me there, for a moment."

"This is the spot," she says. "The best spot."

They are standing now. The trash comes up to their ankles. Each time they move, change a posture, the trash grumbles.

"Wilberforce will be thirty-two, tomorrow," she says. "What a funny thing to come into my head, at a time like this."

"Thirty-two?"

"Monday. That makes me fifty-something. And pushing sixty," she says, looking up at the skies. "At fifty-something years of age, I feel like a woman for the first time. And it scares me."

"Fifty-something," he says, still trying to see through the blackness of the night that surrounds them. "You don't look so old, Mary-G," he adds, and immediately realizes how stupid is his comment.

"If that's a compliment, thank you, Percy."

"I didn't mean it so," he says, not knowing really what to say. This kind of delicacy, this kind of sophistication, the confidence to sweet-talk a woman, as Manny had tried to coach him, just stanning-up and throwing sweet-words at her, even to do this with Gertrude, is not his *fortay.*

He is a man of action. A man of deeds. A man of force. And drive. A man of hardness. Even in his fooping. In. *And* two flings. With his eyes shut. And *bam!* Climax. Done with that! And out.

He is a man on everlasting missions, usually in the dead of night, when all Christian-minded people are sleeping, leaving him to roam the Village, in the company of bugs and worms and centipedes, with the "unrighteous," as Manny calls them; in this kind of blackness, having to track down criminals; catch criminals; paint criminals' arse with blows from his bull-pistle, to assist them in confessing "and don't waste my blasted time"; lock up criminals; beat them some more; and "throw-'way the blasted key, if it was up to me. But it ain't up to me. I is only a lil Crown-Sargeant. Not even a Inspector. But if-only. Only-if I were a acting Inspector, if um was up to me, all like you-so would be dead. Beaten to death. And then thrown in the sea, for the sharks to feast on, be-Jesus Christ, mark my word!"; and Boysie-Boys, to whom these words had been addressed, harkened; and Sargeant would forget them, until the next criminal is being tracked down, and beaten into pulp, and into confession.

But is he really such a man? A man who, as he says, likes to do a little "tinklelling" of the ivories on Friday nights, who likes to cook for Naiman and the Constable, and Gertrude, when she is off duty; a man who reads, not only crime magazines, and travel brochures about Amurca, but library books. Is this man the kind of policeman you would call by the nickname "Hitler" or "Goebbels" or "The Gestapo"?

He is a man "who love woman," as he confesses to Manny. "'Nough woman. The more the merrier." But, as he also confesses, "a man who don't know very much 'bout woman . . ."

"Sit down, Percy. You're so stiff!"

And he laughs, and she laughs, too.

"This is awkward for me. I haven't done this, since . . ."

"You don't have to tell me, Mary-G."

"A lot I have to tell you, Percy. Both to you, as Percy my friend; and to you, as Percy the police Sargeant."

"This passageway that you bring me in," he says, looking back in the direction they have come, "this passageway. I was listening all the time you was talking, and I say to myself, whilst you are telling me the uses this tunnel was put to, nowadays and in days of yore, I been thinking, Mary-Mathilda . . .

"And this is hard for me, a lawman, to say. But this is life. And I know you. And you know me. And this is hard . . ."

"What, Percy? What?"

". . . hard to say. But there isn't *one* man, *not one* . . ."

"Who, Percy?"

". . . not one man in this whole-entire Village and n'ighbourhood who won't want to . . ."

"What, Percy?"

"There isn't one blasted soul in this whole Village or n'ighbourhood, who won't want to pelt a few stones, or one big rock-stone, at Mr. Bellfeels, a man you got yourself involve with, not that it was any fault of yours. It wasn't your fault. And it wasn't your choice.

"And according to Manny, who, as you know, spend time in Amurca, working in the South, Manny always say that your life was ordered through the destinies of paternity. I don't know exactly what Manny mean by that. Do you? But, as he try to explain it to me, and as my brain retain what little it could, Manny mean that your life, and not only your life, but the life of anybody who dwells within the precincts of the Plantation, any Sam-cow-or-the-duppy, man, woman, child, girl or boy, would regard it as a honour to drive a deadly lash in Mr. Bellfeels arse.

"I know your connection to Mr. Bellfeels, and I hope you will pardon my language. And I can understand your loyalties to a man like Mr. Bellfeels. And I can't say nothing against that. But, as Manny say, it is a matter of the destinies of paternity.

"I know you. And you know me. We grew up together. And played together, before your mother thought you were, well, you know what I mean. And that is when Mr. Bellfeels came on the scene.

"But I trying hard-hard, all this time, to see if I can't forget what occurred, that cause me now to be here with you. To see if I can't on purpose forget to take a Statement from you. If I can't pretend that neither me, nor you, nor the blasted Statement exists . . .

"I feel like, like doing something to Mr. Bellfeels, and this whole case, to exterminate him from existence. You know what I mean? If it was possible, for me, or for you, or for any Tom-Dick-and-Harry, to do something to Mr. Bellfeels, to make him disappear. Just disappear off the fecking face of the earth—pardon my French, Mary-Mathilda. And nobody won't miss him. Like invisible. Like a kind of extermination. You know what I mean?

"And I wonder if it is possible, and as soon as we visit the scene, which I should have visited hours ago . . . there is a scene to visit? . . . visit the scene with you long-side me, I been here wondering if when I visit the scene of the crime . . . if, as I said, there is one? . . . if I see him in the scene, whether dead, be-Christ, or alive, if I couldn't snap my fingers and make him *disappear*. Like in music and in witchcraft. Or like the movie I saw once at the Olympic Theatre in Town, where a woman who didn't want the man who was following her, begging her for a piece, to continue humbugging her, all she did was fling some drops from a special vial she had in her purse, right in his face, and all over his body, and *snap!* he disappeared; from sight. Disappeared from off the face o' the earth! *Invisible*. The movie in question was *Gaslight*.

"That is what I would like somebody to do to Mr. Bellfeels, and make my life easier, from having to write down a lotta evidence in a Statement I have to take from you; and hand-in to the Commissioner, first thing tomorrow, Monday morning . . ."

"And you haven't taken down one word, Percy. Not a word."

"I am derelick in my duties."

"And I always wondered how you and other policemen go about questioning a suspect . . ."

"There ain't no suspects, Mary-G. Excepting you, of course! But they ain't no fecking suspects, to talk plain to you. They's *all* crooks, and criminals. And guilty as shite! There aren't no suspects. At least, not in my books. In all my years policing, I haven't come-cross none. Not one man who, as a suspect, was not also consequently guilty."

"But I always wondered how you could question a suspect, for hours and hours, in a room, with the door lock; and listen to the suspect's evidence, and retain all this evidence in your little policeman notebook that have a elastic band round it, word-for-word, and without a knowledge of Pitman's shorthand."

"What I don't remember I invents. Between me and you."

"With a man's life at stake?"

"We are train to have good memories."

"Without Pitman's Shorthand?"

"My brain is like a machine. Like a big piece o' blotting paper, sucking up every word and phrase and sentence that a criminal utter when I 'vestigating him, with the door lock, and I stanning in front the door. And I don't even worry no more, not at my age, to warn him 'bout his rights and all that shite 'bout what he say will be taken down, and used in evidence against him, and further bullshit like that, when the time comes. I don't make no difference between a suspect, *if they exist at all*, and a criminal. One and one is two!"

"You did-ever learn Pitman's Shorthand, at school? Or in Police Training School?" she says, sitting on the trash. "Sit-down here, with me. And talk."

"Have I ever been in this field before, you asked me earlier?"

"I wanted to learn Pitman's Shorthand, so bad, when I was a girl. But Ma, poor soul, couldn't afford the sixpence-a-month for tuition. In those days, I wanted so bad to be a secretary. A private secretary. I read about a private secretary in a *London Illustrated.* To be a private secretary, dress in a grey woollen suit, with grey stockings, with a seam in the middle of the back of my two legs, and high-heel shoes, that black. And spectacles. A private secretary have to have-on spectacles; tortoiseshell spectacles. And to a person like the Solicitor-General. To keep his business private; and confidential. Not that I know what a private secretary have to do; further-less, what a Solicitor-General does-do. Even to be a secretary to a Plantation manager, then. It is just that the name sounds so good. Private Secretary!

"To sit at the desk in front my boss, and take down the most serious and confidential things; personal things, too, in letters he dictates. In my Pitman's Shorthand. Circle-s, and hooks, and dots! I saw this in a book, *Learning Pitman's Shorthand, the Fast Way.* Matters of serious business. Plantation business; mortgages; deeds; and rental of tenantries on the Plantation. Matters of importance. Matters of Law. I always had a weakness for the Law, for Wilberforce; and for my son that dead. Wilberforce couldn't make up his mind between Law and Tropical Medicines. Law is the greatest thing, particular if you have a deep strong voice, like some of the English barsters-at-Law I see in the movies at the Empire Theatre, like in *Witness for the Prosecution,* starring James Mason. Something like a strict discipline, to remind you of your rightful place in this Island. The Law. But, nevertheless . . .

"I could see myself taking a letter, like this:

"Dear Mr. Bellfeels, The letter herewith addressed to you, Sir, in confidence, and without prejudice, is to inform you that we have

been investigating certain instances relative to you, and sundry
behaviours of yours, over the years . . .

"'*Over the years*'? Or should we put a figure to the number of
years and state how many years, in question?"

"State the number of years in question, and aforementioned . . ."

". . . *for the past several years, namely and to-wit, twenty-five*
years, and in your capacity as Manager of the Plantation that have
the nomenclature of Flagstaff, to-wit, Flagstaff Plantation, it is
my honour, Sir, and my duty in representing my clients, Sir, to
inform you that Miss Mary Gertrude Mathilda Paul, also known
under the alias of Miss Mary Gertrude Mathilda Bellfeels, and
hereinafter referred to as Miss Paul, herewith and by these tidings
wishes to inform you that the said Miss Paul, of the Parish of
Sin-Michael, in the Tenantry of Flagstaff, an area of habitation
butting and bounding . . . butting and bounding . . .

"Should we tell him what we are suing him for? Or let him find
out when he is hauled into the Court of Grand Sessions?"

"Disclosures, Mary-Mathilda. The fundamental thing about Eng-
lish Law, which is not found to the same extent in Amurcan Law, is
disclosures. Disclosures, Mary-G. It mean that yuh can't blindfold
a defendant's defence, meaning, in other words, that the man him-
self that is charged, even though you catch him red-handed in the
act, or with his pants down, in regards to being caught in the act of
committing the act, to-wit, the crime . . . Even if um is murder,
and in the first degree, and he tell you that he going kill she, there-
fore admitting premeditation, disclosures still have to be disclose
to the defence."

"Thanks.

'*We regret to inform you, Sir, that Miss Paul has taken actions*
against you, your person and persona, and your properties and your
chattels, servants, maids, cooks and sundries, to-wit, she has evidence

through disclosures, that you have committed the following unlaw-
ful acts and deeds . . .

"What acts and deeds we should charge him with?"

"Murder."

"Murder?"

"*Murder!*"

"But he has to murder somebody first . . ."

". . . figure out that later. And in the first degree! And ravishing, in the second degrees. Carnal Knowledge, in the third degrees. His misdeeds remind me of a story in the Latin textbook, *The Rape of the Sabine Women*."

"But he didn't commit . . ."

"Murder? And rape? We still going-charge him with murder, in the first degree; and ravishing, in the second degrees. Carnal Knowledge, in the third. If one fail, we got him on the next. We have to tighten the noose tight. He is a' important man, a man with powerful contacts in this Island and overseas; a man of influence; and he could easily, through his friends like the Solicitor-General, like the Vicar, like the two leading barristers-at-Law in the Island, like the Dean, and like the Headmaster of Harrison College, he might— as easy as my snapping my fingers—wriggle-out from justice, by means of the privilege of those friends, and plea' not guilty to murder in the first degree, and rape in the second degrees; and, consequently, cop a plea of guilty to a more lesser degree. Like insanity. Or unfit to stand trial, by virtue of. So, if we hit him in the first degree, with murder, and with rapinage, in the second degrees, and with Carnal Knowledge, with these three degrees, seeing that all we have in mind, regarding motive, and want, is to lock up the son-of-a-bitch—pardon my French, Miss Mary-Mathilda! If we can't heng him!—well, you understand? Or I have to state the obvious?"

"But it isn't Mr. Bellfeels who has committed the murder!" she says.

"Who, then? You? You telling me that a season detective like me, a Crown-Sargeant in the Royal Constabulary of Bimshire, who passed out with the Baton of Honour, and who take special 'vestigative techniques and police strategy in questioning witnesses, plus a' intensive course in the Island of Trinidad and Tobago, in the district of Toonapoona, you telling a big man like me that a lil woman like you—not referring to your natural self, real size or avoirdupois—but lil in the ways of influence, compared to Mr. Bellfeels, you telling me that a lil woman like you could commit this big crime, namely murder? And in the first degree? Jesus Christ, Mary-Mathilda, be serious with me now! I beseeching you. Who in this Village going-believe that a woman like you, could ever commit murder? And all jokes aside. Concerning you wanting to be a private secretary . . .

"There ain't nothing you could say about your act, alleged; nor nothing that I could write-down in my report as your Statement, that will make anybody in this n'ighbourhood blame you, Miss Mary Gertrude Mathilda, for carrying out such a' act, allegedly . . . You's a saint in the eyes of the people, even if your act, allegedly, is a' act that break a Commandment. You know what a Commandment is, in terms of this matter? Lemme tell you, then. A Commandment is more important than the Law; a law in Comma-Law, or a statue passed in the Legislative Council of Bimshire that is then turn-into a Law? 'Thou shalt not kill . . .'"

She piles some trash high, to make a pillow for her back.

"Let's lay-down here."

"You could tell me your side o' things," he says, "and I could write it up in a certain way, advantageous to you, that will . . ."

"Sit down, Percy, and face me. Face me, and talk to me."

She rearranges some more trash to make a thick, fluffy mattress; and then she lies on it, on her side; and then she moves her body in it, like a cat or a dog searching for the most comfortable, enticing trough in which to lie, in the spread of cloth on a floor in a corner of a room.

She has found her trough of comfort. He just lies on the trash.

Above them, the stars are blinking. Some are out; and are bright, like statements, like accusations.

"Do you know anything about the stars?"

"A little," he says, making a trough for himself on the trash, which, on his side, is spread thinner. He is so much closer to the bare earth. He can smell the rich, pungent smell of mould. Of soil. The fragrance of dirt soaked by rainwater, and drying out slowly. And he can smell the smell of the things that are growing in this field.

He makes up his bed, and he thinks he feels an object, a stick or something, a discarded handle from a tool, a wooden handle, beneath him. But it could be a piece of sugar cane. He does not get his side of the bed of trash fluffed as thickly as she has done her side; but he is content.

He unbuckles the heavy, thick, brown leather belt from round his waist, and he places it on his chest, after unbuttoning the five silver buttons of his tunic. She cannot see the grey undershirt that he wears.

If there was a moon, she thinks, lying beside him—the first time in a long while that she has lain beside a man—if there was a moon, this closeness could have been so soft and tender, touching and bathed in the goldenness of the moonlight; and she would be impelled, seduced—not seduced . . . *inspired*—to tell him stories, like the story of the Greeks who were in battle with the Romans . . . Was it the Romans? . . . in battle with the Romans; and the Romans retired behind their city walls; and their walls were about twenty feet high, and as thick as a man's arms outstretched; and the Greeks could not break down the gates to the city, further-less scale the wall; they were never good at high jumping or pole-vaulting; and the Romans would spend the nights, which were all moonlight nights, looking through holes they had bored into the wall to see these Greeks working hard, building a toy horse for Roman children to play with; but the toy was too big even for the biggest child of noble Roman birth; and the Romans laughed, and were convinced now, for the second time, with proof, that they were superior to the Greeks, not only in their knowledge of Latin, and building ruins and monuments and statues of naked men and naked women, and fountains and aquariums, but that they were also superior to the Greeks in their knowledge of philosophy, the philosophy of War and Warfare; and the manufacture of wooden horses, and equestrian toys; and they laughed and laughed and had parties and orgies and drank wine and chewed grapes and olives and spat the seeds into fountains and pools of water, while the Greeks continued, outside the city walls, moonlight night after moonlight night, to build the toy to be given to the children of Rome, but which they must have known was much too gigantic for any child to play with; and one moonlight night led to another, and the Romans forgot that they were at war with the Greeks. And then, certain that the Greeks were stupid, the Romans opened the gates to the city, just to see what the Greeks were doing; and with the help of real, live horses, the Romans hauled the stupid, oversized child's toy, the Greeks' gift of a wooden horse, into the city gates. And the Romans drove the iron bars back into their sockets, and closed the gates. With the toy horse inside the gates. And the Romans drank some more wine; and made love to the women at the orgies. It was a night of the full moon.

"The rest is history," she says.

"I remember reading this story at Sin-Davids Elementary School, in private tuition from Mr. Edwards who was preparing me for the Secondary-to-Second-Grade. He said that he read the same story in the original Latin, in a book written by Julius Caesar, called *Caesar's Gallic Wars*. I remember the story, but I can't remember the moral Mr. Edwards tell me was in the story, nor whether it was the Greeks versus the Romans. Or the Greeks versus the Trojans. Is a Trojan a Roman?"

"Or I could tell you the story of Bathsheba."

"Bathsheba? The resort area on the East Coast of this Island?" he asks her. "The place where Miss Enid Maxwell does-cook for a fellar by the name of George Lamming, only 'pon a Sunday, after twelve? *That* Bathsheba? I didn't know there was a history to Bathsheba, and Miss Maxwell, and Mr. Lamming."

"Bathsheba the woman! And David, man!"

"Oh! The Bible."

"The Holy Bible says that it was David who was peeping at Bathsheba bathing, spying on the poor woman's nakedness, without her knowledge. But I have a different version, giving the interpretation that says that it was *Bathsheba*, knowing her husband was away at the front in the Wars of Ammon and Rabbah, fighting battles and killing other women's husbands, she, Bathsheba start feeling a lil peckish for the absence of her husband's warm body side-o'-her, in her bed, got her maid to move the basin with the water she was washing her face-and-hands with, more closer to the window where King David could see her more clearer. Naked as she born.

"She was invited the night before, as a dignitary, along with other political and military dignitaries and wives of soldiers and of politicians, and the King, David-the-First, gave her a tour of the castle, including his bedroom; and you could imagine that when nobody was looking, the King, being King, pinched Bathsheba on her behind, and she bit her lip in ecstasy and in surprise that powerful King David was feeling-her-up; and that is how she knew which position to put her basin and ewer of water in . . ."

"It is not only kings who behave like David. The Commissioner is *so,* too. Manny tell me the Vicar is so; but I don't believe so. We had, as you well-know, a Governor of the Island, who was *so,* in the worst way. He caused the woman in question to lose her life, he was so much *so.*

"I know a lot of men in high society who are *so,*" she says.

Her hand is on his baton. She removes it from the holster, and places it on her stomach, between her breasts, and absentmindedly runs her left hand down the smooth object; and when that hand has reached the smaller end, she makes her right hand travel from the smaller end to reach the larger end. And she removes her hands, leaving the baton resting in the middle of her body   and she knows that there has been, has always been, a lot of gossip about her, and about some of the powerful men, friends of Mr. Bellfeels', who played poker for large stakes—some men lost land, some men lost houses, some men lost racehorses, some cars and businesses, and one man lost a woman, on the fall of a card at the Friday night games of Five Card Stud, no limit, that Mr. Bellfeels hosted at her Great House (as his wife detested card games; even bridge); yes, a lot of stories are told about her: how during games, a man, wanting a break, a change of luck, would go into a bedroom, or an adjacent room, and Miss Mary Gertrude Mathilda would be sent by Mr. Bellfeels to follow the man; and in fifteen minutes, the man would re-emerge, with a smile on his face.

Gertrude told this story to Sargeant, who told it to Manny, and from there, it spread throughout the neighbourhood, and then beyond; but there was no truth to the rumour . . . No, she must certainly not appear as if she knows what to do with the baton lying on her belly; and how. When this thought came into her head, like the recollection of an item on a long list of things to do, momentarily her body went limp. Her thighs became dry. Her nipples returned to their unexcited calmness, like a flat land over which many have travelled. For that moment, desire went out of her body. And the smell of the earth came through the thick mattress she had made out of the trash. She could smell the freshness of the canes, and the distant sickening fragrance of crack-liquor, the hot, sweet juice squeezed from the ground canes. She could smell the soil, the land, the ground in which she had worked so hard at the beginning, so hard and with such brutality at the hands of the overseer, the driver, and the male leader of the field gang; and then, at the hand of Mr. Bellfeels; and she remembered the leather riding-crop as it lifted her dress one afternoon, when she was made to follow him to a deserted section of the North Field, while the other hands were eating their flour bakes and drinking molasses water that had pieces of chipped ice in it; her dress was lifted by the riding-crop, and his jodhpurs crushed the trash and the land itself, that vast field that was so large that a woman could not walk it in two hours, the North Field; the land seemed to shake as he unbuttoned two buttons on the fly of his khaki jodhpurs, pulled his "tool" out—he himself called it that—and it assumed a size and brutishness and an ugliness, such an ugly colour, that she thought her bowels, her stomach, her guts, whatever you call that part of her insides, was going to erupt.

It took him three minutes. He came inside her.

"*Jesus Christ!*" he said.

And he left his semen and the stain of his semen on his jodhpurs. It lasted three minutes.

"*Jesus Christ!*"

And the rest of that afternoon, weeding the six-weeks sweet-potatoes and the young yams, she ached; and had to bend over many times, practising regular breathing, in order to stifle the excruciating pain that crawled through her body.

"*Jesus Christ!*"

She was sixteen years old then. She became pregnant. It was the first of three abortions that Ma and Gran induced with herbs and other bushes recommended and selected by the older women in the neighbourhood, and that grew wild behind the palings of their houses.

Ma said nothing. No word of pity or of reproof, or of consolation, passed her lips, as she administered the potion. And Mary Gertrude Mathilda cried secretly, and made a promise to herself.

When she had walked the mile home that evening, at six o'clock, Ma prepared a hot steaming bath for her that had herbs she had picked from the gutter and from the overrun growth behind her house . . . and she soaked Mary-girl in the wooden tub of scalding water; and the water was enervating as seawater first thing in the morning, at the Crane Beach; and Ma gave her the bottle that contained seawater, to drink. No dinner that night; nothing solid; just piping hot Miraculous Bush tea. . . .

It seems a long time, long enough to tell a story in, that she is lying flat on her back; fumbling in the darkness to touch his hand, and his fingers, to hold his hand, holding it in such a tight but loving manner that it is an exclamation of discovery and of beneficence, also.

She can feel his body shudder at her touch . . .

He shudders because his mind is running ahead of him. He cannot extend his hand and touch hers, touch her body: he imagines and paints in dreams the things he wants to do with her . . . He must learn to control his orgasm, and not have his semen spew out too soon, as it happens when he is in this same field, but at another corner, with Gertrude. And he must put aside all his reservations, and his feeling of inferiority, and foop her good, as he would foop or would want to foop any other woman whose presence has caused him to melt, in spirit, in toughness, in masculinity, in man-talk in Manny's rum shop, amongst his friends, in the Selected Clienteles Room . . . "Help me, God," he says to himself. He closes his eyes as he says this, and he means it, sincerely as an exhortation for help; for he knows, with the instinct of a detective, that he really is incapable of giving Mary-Mathilda love; the kind of love she deserves; no matter how she should define love.

On the other hand, she wants to give him her body; but she feels that he feels she has been touched too often, by other men; that she is *different*; that there is something wrong with her. She wishes that he would be a man, behave brave; mannish; fondle her, take her, go deep inside her and flood her with his sperm; "explode inside me, oh-God!"; wish he would behave like the man she imagines. All the men she has known, and she has loved not one of them, are men who knew what they wanted; powerful men; and men who took it.

She can feel his body beside her shudder; and she lies and hopes he will behave mannish; natural . . . but since she cannot take his hand and guide it over her body, she gives over that desire to her imagination. She is safe and untouched imagining this: she remains whole. She lets her imagination portray her desire, and in this way she can now guide him, at her will, over her body: *it seems a long time, long enough to tell a story in, that she is undoing his fly. And it is done now. And she fumbles inside his sliders, and holds his tom-pigeon tight in her hand, holding it in such a tight but loving manner that it is an exclamation of discovery, and of beneficence also.*

She can feel him shudder.

"No," he says in a voice soft as a wisp of smoke over a field; soft as the voice of the first wood-dove's cooing in the morning, "I will get on top." . . . Mary-Mathilda fumbles in the darkness and finds the baton which has fallen off her belly; and she takes it up and rubs it along her body, beginning at her breasts, down in the middle of her chest; past the raised dead skin of her brooch-wound; down down, slow-slow now, until it reaches the tuft of hair covering her pussy; and she makes the return journey, too full now of passion for words that will let him know how hot she is; and this upward journey, this journey North, is like an expedition, an exploration towards freedom; for the baton is moving slowly round her breasts, massaging the brooch of flesh on her body, that old wound overgrown with flesh that is dead, then over her nipples, which are getting hard as two small peanuts sewn into her breasts; and when this is beyond control, and is controlling her, expressing how uncontrollable it is, she moves the baton in its journey back South, and it stops in the tuft of hair; black, shiny hair that has remained black, and not like the hair on her head; and she is careful now; moving the baton with some determination, but in that determination, with gentleness round and round, as if she is measuring the labia; and she knows she is getting wet; the baton glistening with the fluid from her body, she takes the baton out from her lips, and she places it into his mouth.

He closes his mouth over the baton. He says nothing. He does not like the taste. Or the stickiness of the baton. But it is a sweet smell. A thick, sweet, mouth-licking smell that has a breath of boiled salt fish on its fragrance, and of a perfume that he does not know the name of, immediately.

She lifts her dress with her hands. The coolness of the night bathes her buttocks in a tantalizing, relaxing feeling.

And she gives him the gift she wants to know he has never received before. She passes her left hand over the wetness of her pussy, and then

passes the same hand, in a gesture very much like a gesture to be silent, to
keep a secret, an indication agreeing to be confidential, over his mouth.

"My body." She says it barely audibly. "This is me, for you."

"Thanks, Mary-G. Thanks very much, Mary-G."

"This. Yessss."

"Yes, Mary-Mathilda. Yesssss!"

She is on top of him. And he is hard, and stiff, and long, and deep inside
her, and she feels like a gymnast would, balancing her entire body on a bar
that is pointing vertical. And she does behave, in way, precisely as if she is a
gymnast, moving in circles, wide and small; small and wide; and feeling his
tom-pigeon bend, pliable, in her gyrations, in her circular movements.

She does not talk.

No word, no sound escapes his lips . . .

The smell of the earth is strong. The dampness of the trash
makes her feel as if she has awakened from sleep; disoriented; and
confused, realizing, perhaps, that she has wet her bed during the
night; for she has reverted to childhood . . . or as if she is sick with a
fever and the bed is wet from her body heat, and is not her urine . . .

The smell of the earth is of rotten sugar cane. And she is walking
through the trash, in a hurry; and it is night; and it is dark; and she
must get to the place she is heading to, in a hurry; but she cannot
hurry, because in this rush that is anxious, something always happens
to delay the time of arrival and destiny. But the reaching of destina-
tion is precisely the cause of her anxiety . . . *Even though he does not*
move, to help her keep the rhythm, she can feel the liveliness in his body . . .

The sky is dark. He is looking at the stars. They are far away.
Music comes into his mind. He cannot say the name of the tune he
hears. The music has no name that he can put to it. It is heavy
music; martial music; powerful music, the kind of music, he sur-
mises, that would be played at a funeral, at a public hanging, at a
ceremony to accompany an execution; or just pure, simple, raw
violence, like killing.

He remembers the name of the music. He heard it earlier
tonight. "The Ride of the Valkyries." He does not understand why

this is the music that comes into his head, at this moment. And under these circumstances . . . *And a sound comes independently into her head; and it is the sound of water running, water pouring in volumes of magnificence over a precipice that is higher than the rest of the land, and there is a noise from the water which boils in its churning, from the fall of the water, like thick clouds, like mist, which pours everlasting over the Falls; and the name of the place comes to her, far, far from here in this cane field, far in the North of New York State, in Buffalo, across a lake from Canada, the closeness making Amurca and Canada one country.*

The roar is the quickening of her heart; the injection of violent thought, violent action. Her body is out of control. Her eyes are open, wide, wild, staring; and her hair is standing on end, and as she moves, it flares outward; and fearing she will lose her balance, and her perfection of style on the gymnastic bar, the bar that is vertical, she must hold on to something; and she grabs him, in the darkness . . . But the darkness is not so dark that he does not know she is grabbing him, with both her hands, by his neck.

Tight. Choking. Violent. Wild.

"Jesus Christ!"

It is her voice.

"I'm going to kill you!"

It is her voice.

And as the words fall out, like the water tumbling over the tall, high, misty precipice, all the passion, controlled successfully for so many years; all the feeling that place and position, and the neglect had caused her to stifle, came pumping out.

"Jesus Christ!"

This is his voice.

Her grip on his neck is still tight. And she has bent over, collapsed at the second after her scream of climax; and her mouth is at his throat.

She can taste a saltiness in her mouth. And a thickness. And a revulsive sensation.

It is his blood in her mouth.

"Jesus Christ!"

It is his voice.

Her hand, with her own linen handkerchief in it, is passing over his neck. It is not a wound. It is the hotness of blood that has caused the puncture . . .

"Mongoose," she says, at the sound of feet darting about in the cane field in which they are. She is lying on her back.

"Mangooses, you mean."

"Or men who are sly like a mongoose?"

"That would be man-gooses? Or men-goose."

He is lying on his stomach. His arms are propping up the rest of his body. She is flat on her back, as if she is floating, as if she is in the sea at the Crane Beach, floating like a dry beach-grape leaf. He cannot see the expression of relaxed happiness, approaching joy, that is on her face, for it is still too dark. It is not entirely dark though, not like the time of night he roams throughout the Village, on his bicycle, looking for criminals. The light is the light of foreday morning, the light that begins soon after midnight, but hours before dawn, that dreary, dramatic, graveyard type of light. It comes in on their left. And soon, he will be able to see the expression on her face, and gauge her various moods, and see her face, and see if the softness he saw in her face years ago, and knew, when she was young, the softness that came and disappeared in impulses tonight, is still there.

"Do you know anything about astronomy? The stars?" she says.

"No," he tells her, lying deliberately.

"Not since I was a little girl, have I lay-down on my back, looking up into the skies. Certainly not with a man side-o'-me!

"And it is a long time since I even worried to look up, to see if there are still stars in the skies over Bimshire.

"Orion. The Big Dipper. Jupiter. The Three Sisters. The star that tells you when you are getting rain. And the North Star.

"Do you know anything about the North Star, Percy?"

"I didn't know you know so much about stars yourself! Did you study astrology? I don't know much about the North Star. Nothing unusual, except that it shines in the North."

"Me? A simple, uneducated woman like me, an expert in the stars? No. Everything I been telling you, about paintings and travel, about life, even about how I feel, I picked up from library books. And Wilberforce, to a extent.

"Years and years, when things between me and Mr. Bellfeels was still sweet, and he could get away from his work, and from his wife—he had just got married to her—he would steal away, and me and him would go for moonlight walks sometimes; for at that time I wasn't in the Great House yet; but we were still thick; so, late at night when nobody was around and walking the road, and we couldn't be seen, or identified, or picked-out in a motor-car headlights; and bring shame to Mistress Bellfeels, his wife, we had the whole place to ourselves! But on moonlight nights, even though they didn't last so long, those nights were still . . . Still.

"On those nights, few and far between, always having to dodge people even when it was dark, we never could risk to hold hands while we walked; or nothing so that lovers do; so the walks would take him and me through the fields, where we could hold hands; through the canes, where he would pinch my bottom, and run after me, climbing trash heaps that were like castles and hills, jumping in the trash-heaps as if they were waves in the sea, 'cause I always liked climbing; with not a word passing between us, walking in trash, up to our ankles.

"Now and then, once in a blue moon, along that portion of the front road where few cars pass, he would tell me things about the stars, and what they mean in regards to travel, to science, to witch-craft, and in the foretelling of weather; and fortunes. And naturally, the season for planting; and for reaping. A long time ago.

"The Star of Bethlehem is the most important star. Because it is about Jesus Christ, our Saviour. But the North Star is my favourite star. Do you know why?"

"Isn't the North Star only another name for the Star of Bethlehem?" he says.

"The thing about it," she tells him, "is its direction. The North. A compass point, as Wilberforce pointed it out to me. Columbus went East. Or is it West? He certainly end-up West, down here with us in the Wessindies, completely lost in the Carbean Sea, without knowing his arse from his you-know-what. And yet, Columbus get all this credit for discovering all o' we, including Amurca; but according to Wilberforce, Amurca was already discovered for *donkey years*, by people who Columbus called Red Indians; but peopled by those people, nevertheless. What discovering did Columbus discover, when he didn't even know his armpit from his arse!— pardon my French, Sarge! What discovery would you call *these* discoveries?

"But Columbus was concern with the East. And ended-up West. In other words, from where he came from, Columbus travelled South. And discovered people that were already discovered, and that had discovered themselves, in one way or the other.

"The South has come to mean freedom, and escape, even today, with all the blasted North-Amurcan tourisses that crowd-up the place, certain months of the year. Coming South means escape and freedom; and other things too, from the coldness of the North.

"But the North. The real North, Percy! And the star that stands for the North, the North Star! To me, and I am not a historian, or a well-enough-read person to be pointing you to this point, but from listening to Wilberforce, the North Star is the star that led my ancestors, and Gran, from outta the clutches of men like Mr. Bellfeels, and point them straight-straight as a arrow, out of Canaan Land, cross the Nile River and the Sahara Desert, and up inside the Promised Land, after forty long years perishing in the desert, safe. And free.

"Ma say that her grans on the mother and father side come from a place in Africa call Elmina; was haul-off ship in Amurca; and then was transship here to Bimshire, in transit from crossing the deserts in the forty years that it took to escape bondage.

"And talking about Ma's grans strikes me as strange. Because we don't go back too far in lineages; not in this Hemisphere. I never come-across *one* soul in this Village who could say she have a grandmother who born here in Bimshire, to match Mr. Bellfeels bragging that he 'have family here in Bimshire from the year 1493, A.D.'! That bastard!

"I don't know one coloured family, or coloured person in the whole of Bimshire, perhaps in the whole Wessindies, who could match that claim, who could lay-claim to that claim, and trace-back his ancestries to 1493! You?

"And it seem to me, when I think of these things, that we go back, if we go back at all, only just round the blasted corner, to the first chattel house standing on the Plantation land. Rented; and beyond that, to the last slave ship to cross the Atlantic Ocean, which my son calls the Middle Passage, and which lay-anchor in the Careenage of Carlisle Bay, down in Town. Or we could go back to the forty years it take us, like the Israelites, to cross the desert, outta bondage.

"Wilberforce argue strong that this time span of forty years isn't accurate; not when you take into consideration the measurements of the desert; allow for sickness, and death, marriage and even childbirth; for wagons brekking-down, and the horses and mules dropping like flies in the heat of the Sahara Desert, their flight from Pharaoh's Land should be a journey of one week. Nine days. At the most!

"I wonder where that boy gets his ideas? Learning is a funny thing, Sarge, isn't it? But Wilberforce allow me to understand that his calculation is based on science; something that proves this argument.

"Yes! The North. Guided by a star pointing to the North. To the land of real, true-true freedom. Namely, Canada!

"And when I went up to Buffalo that time, with Mr. Bellfeels, looking for second-hand machineries for the Factory, as the machineries here was always brekking-down, I happened to look across the lake, the Superior Lake, I think they call it, and I saw the

beauty of Canada, the white fields of snow, the white trees covered
in white snow, and the houses, and the heads of the people, those
who didn't have-on fur hats, *white*. All that snow symbolize to me
the freedom that my ancestors, Ma's gran-parents, were seeking
when they followed that North Star in their journey from out the
clutches of Amurcan slaveholders and owners and drivers like Mr.
Lawrence Burkhart, into Canaan Land.

"Do you remember that there used to be a passenger bus line in
this Island, by the name of the North Star?"

"The *Lone* Star Bus Line, you mean," he corrects her.

"Yes! My mistake. But much of a muchness. The name is close-
enough for you to grasp my meaning. In the eighteen-hundreds, if
not centuries before that, the people who were disembarked and
put-off on the shores of Amurca, those who had endurance, all of
them who could, embarked and got-on on a underground railroad,
travelling by foot in whatever weather they slipped out of captiv-
ity in, in winter, storm, deluge and summer; and from Pharaoh's
clutches; dodging and escaping and outwitting wolves and hound
dogs and guns, state troopers, bounty-hunters and Kloo-Klux-
Klans, bloodhounds like the Alsatians the Nazzies employed in the
War, that we see in BBC newsreels, at the movies; and walking
practically barefoot, in the deepness of winter and snow; and not
taking the kind of transportation, like a Greyhound Bus Line, that I
see in Buffalo! Nor a motor-car! Not even a Model T. To say noth-
ing of a plane! They had planes then?"

"Planes existed in the First Whirl War."

"Imagine, just imagine a man with a bag, with fried chicken in
it, a slice of watermelon, no change of clothes, hardly a penny to
raise ransom, or pay a tribute, with a hand-roll cigarette in his
mout', and *walking* from the town of Waycross-Georgia, or Miami-
Florida, straight up to Canada, following the North Star, putting
all his trust in astronomy, since he couldn't put his hand on a road
map . . . They had road maps in those days?"

"Not to my knowledge," he tells her.

"Is there any wonder that the black race produce such great runners, and athletes? It must reside in what Wilberforce calls the *genes*. Isn't that something?"

"Maps didn't exist, to my knowledge."

"Isn't that something, then?"

"They had maps that a person could draw from memory of having travelled that route before. But not maps in the sense that you could go in Cave Shepherd & Sons, and ask for a map o' Englund, and the clerkess hand you one. Maps didn't exist in that sense."

"Isn't that something?"

"Maps didn't exist, to my knowledge."

"But you have given me something very precious, Percy. Precious as having a map to show the escape routes and passages and byways for flight out from under Pharaoh's hand. You have on this night given-me-back confidence in myself. And some of my dignity. I used to be a woman who could move mountains, not blowing my own horn.

"Mr. Bellfeels knew that. He let me try my hands at certain things in the running of this Plantation. Little things. Things like telling him which labourers was reliable, which was troublemakers. I will never take that from him, bastard that he is still.

"You also gave-me-back my disposition, my disposition to even out things.

"But I want you, Sargeant, to show me no favours. After we get up from laying-down in this trash heap, I want you to tell me *straight*, what I have to do; and what I have to say to the authorities, in the best way, to get this thing over-with."

"I already gave you a hint."

"A hint is not advice, or a solution. I am waiting on you to take down my Statement, word for word, in full, showing the motive, the motivation and the intention.

"I wish you had-learn Pitman's Shorthand, though. That way, what I tell you, and what they report Monday morning in the *Bimshire Daily Herald*, will be my words and nothing but my words.

And not like the words the authorities in Northampton put in Nat Turner mouth to say, and then say that his own words condemn him."

"Who is Nat Turner? He used to live 'bout-here? Was he one of the 'bastards'?"

"A man from a place in Amurca, called Southampton. You don't remember hearing or reading about Nat Turner?

"When we were talking about the family ties between Plantation and Plantation, and between owners living in this Island and those living in Amurca, in places like Waycross, Charleston-South-Carolina; and the City of Lynchburg, we end up always talking about Southampton. Not Southampton-England, although they are related, like Trafalgar Square in Bimshire is named after the Trafalgar Square up in Englund, the Mother Country.

"We talk about Southampton and we always end up talking about Mr. Nat Turner, who led the insurrection that burn down Southampton Plantation, where he worked; and a few other Plantations as well, surrounding; and lick-off the heads of his owners; and likewise a few other Plantation owners heads he chop-off. In particular, the drivers. And a handful of the wives, and the girl-thrildren. Yes. Mr. Nat Turner, whose Statement is the name of a book, Wilberforce say.

"The authorities sent a Mr. Thomas R. Gray, a authority, to take Mr. Nat Turner Statement, but Mr. Gray had no understanding of the way Nat Turner speak; and Mr. Gray didn't care, since he was a authority, cause it didn't take no skin offa his teet, so he take-down Nat Turner words without understanding the language Nat was talking to him in; but being a authority, he put his own words in Nat Turner mouth; and in so doing, produced a authentic confession, not paying no mind that he altered Nat's sweet, nice Southern Negro twang, that I heard those coloured ladies speaking on the train going North, into a Statement he call *The Confessions of Nat Turner, the leader of the late Insurrection in Southampton, Virginia, as fully and voluntarily made to.* And had it printed, and published in 1831."

"I following you."

"The year my great-gran born!"

"I following you."

"Yes. The authority from the authorities say that Nat acknowledge the Statement 'authentic.' But he altered that sweet Negro language."

"He could do that and get away with it?"

"Because he is a authority."

"I following yuh."

"The full date of the publication is the Fiff o' November, 1831 . . .'"

"The Fiff o' November? *Guy Fawkes Day?* That is a day of real fireworks. How Nat Turner know about Guy Fawkes Day?"

"No master, nor overseer, no driver nor ordinary inhabitant of Waycross, of Jerusalem-Southampton, Charleston or Lynchburg and no Mr. Thomas R. Gray, authority or no authority, ever entered into a ordinary conversation with a man like Mr. Nat Turner, or Golbourne father . . . or even with you . . . to exchange common pleasantries or courtesies.

"There wasn't no 'Good morning, Mr. Nat. How you and the wife and the thrildren? Things all right with you, and them? Your roof leaking? I not working you too hard, is I? Okay, well look wha' I gonna do for you. Ahm gonna slice-off a few working hours, without penalty, tha's what Ahm gonna do. Now, boy, the hours you accustom working, five in the morning till six in the evening, all that gonna change from today. You gonna begin at ten o'clock sharp instead, hear? Just like me and the overseer. And you gonna knock-off at three in the afternoon, so's you can go fishing . . .'

"You think there was any such dialogue with a authority? No, man!

"You see now, why I worship Wilberforce for his brain."

"I didn't know you know so much about history, *and* astrology," he says. "Morning is coming, though."

"Yes. Let it come. Morning soon here, as they say."

"I have to get back to the station. And report in. Constable must be snoring by now. And go home and have my morning tea. And I have to write a report, before the Commissioner come round on his rounds. He doesn't know nothing, at least not from me, 'bout this accident, which is what I calling it.

"The Commissioner don't have no evidence of this accident, this incident. And I intend to keep it that way. I keeping it from him, until we, me and you, figure out something . . ."

"Morning breaking, soon. A new day coming. But I don't want favours, Sargeant, because of what we almost went through . . ."

"What we almost went through?" he asks.

"That is separate from anything . . ."

"Was above and beyond."

"That could have been a big mistake. Not that I am blaming you for anything. I will forget it, anyhow."

"Forget everything?"

"It is like a person who needs to satisfy herself, and after having herself satisfied, right at the moment of satisfaction, at the point of, well . . . what I want to say is that, well . . . after a man bring a woman, the man might not know that the woman doesn't have any more use for him. It is so. Not that this is my philosophy. But the woman out-outs the man. *Extinguish.*"

"There is a family of stinging bees that Manny tell me about that does do that to the man-bees. Sting-them-to-death."

"The queen bee," she says.

"There is women and there is women. Some women, if you don't mind me talking straight to you, but there is women who, according to Manny, regardless to-what they do, and how they do it, could always come out of it, whatever it is, clean, and untouch. I not saying, Mary-Mathilda, that you is this type o' woman, 'cause I don't know you that-good, I only making a point. For argument sake. And then, alternatively on the other hand, there is the other kind of woman, who . . ."

"Which kind is me?" she says. "Which category you put me in?"

He is uncertain about the way she wants him to take this.

"You is the kind o' woman that . . ." he begins. But he cannot continue to tell her the truth that lies in his mind; but he completes his comparison, nevertheless, using her as his model, but only in his thoughts . . . *You is the kind o' woman who have already travel beyond this trash heap, a journey that didn't last too long; and though you is the one who bring me here, who choose this spot to come to, in the cane field . . . I don't know if you want to be the same as me, simple and low-down and nasty, to make me believe that you are on the same level, in making me take you in a cane field; I know, though, that you's still the kind o' woman who could, and will, wipe-off the trash from offa your dress, could get up from this trash heap anytime, and with a flick o' your wrist, brush-off the last speck o' cane trash, wet from the dew falling on it, clean-clean-clean from off your white cotton dress. The minute you leave this cane field, you become Miss Mary Gertrude Mathilda again. Miss Bellfeels. Wilberforce mother. The lady who lives in the Great House . . . I not so foolish not to know this . . .* "But supposing, Mary-Mathilda, supposing. Supposing, for argument sake. That I have feelings for you. What I mean is, supposing, supposing that I could be having certain feelings for you?"

"The feelings that King David had for Bathsheba? Or Romeo for Juliet? Or Caesar for Cleopatra? Which of these three couples you are imagining the two of us, me and you, to be?"

"I only know David and Bathsheba. You-yourself introduce them to me, in a story."

"They are all the same. They're European stories, about European love. They are different from stories of love that originate here in Bimshire and the Wessindies, or stories that come from the Amurcan South. Only the names are changed, depending on language. Romeo and Juliet in Eyetalian is the same as David and Bathsheba in the language of the Hebrews. I just don't want you to have the idea that . . ."

"But supposing," he says. "Supposing right now, you tell me how you feel, and I was to tell you how I feel. In the morning, a bright new day, we can start fresh. A new day, a new dawn."

"Like playing house? Like when we were thrildren? Yes, why not play house? I will be the father. You mind playing the mother?"

"House? Why house?"

"Because."

"What?"

"Or we could play Court. A game is a game, isn't it? Or is this game of house, really a game of Court? Well-yes! Let us play Court. I am in the box. I am the Defendant. And I demand disclosures, as you call it. I demand disclosures from you.

"You be the Chief Justice."

"Sir Gerald Chester Jones-Kirton, KC?" he says.

"Yes, Sir Gerald, Lord Chief Justice."

"My God!"

"But who will be defending me? Who my Learned Counsel, or my barster-at-Law will be, to defend me?"

"Why don't you play the Defendant *and* the Defending barster-at-Law, at the same time, to save time and legal resources?"

"Can I be both? And who you will be, then?"

"Lord Chief Justice, Sir Gerald Chester Jones-Kirton, King's Counsel. And while I at it, I may as well play the Solicitor-General, too. And the Juries. I may as well be all three. For the same reason. To save costs, and time.

"If this Court of Grand Sessions, a play-play Court, is to be well constituted, in accordance with the Jurisprudence of Law, I have to be them-three. 'Cause time is money. To save time is to make money. And vice versa. And since good justice is swift justice, it is better to save time. *Quod a-rat demonstrandum!*"

"Can one man, a policeman, be Chief Justice, Solicitor-General and the Jury, all-three, together?"

"In some courts," he says, "in certain other jurisdictions, and in some real cases, it does be that, when all is said and done. But I don't need all three roles, because I will try honestly to act honestly in upholding the Law; and in view of the shortage of manpower in this Island, I am acting as Chief Justice, and the prosecuting police officer, namely with powers of the Solicitor-General, and the twelve men honest and fair, who are your peers."

"Twelve men? Where the women on this Jury?"

". . . it makes for cleaner, cheaper Jurisprudence; and the Jurisdiction of the Law."

"It doesn't sound too-fair to me!"

"It is a *play-play Court*, Mary-Mathilda!"

"Call to order, then," she says, changing her voice to suit the stern, legal manner of the Court of Grand Sessions. "Call the Court to order, Officer."

"You mean, 'Court is in sessions.'"

"Is this why they call it *Grand Sessions?*"

"This is the Law, Mary-Mathilda. There is nothing play-play 'bout the Law, even although we are conducting a play-play Court. Remember that. And this is a serious case on the Docket. And that's why it have to be tried in the Court of Grand Sessions, in the Annual Assizes."

"This is a murder case, then . . ."

"We don't have a body, or what is known in Jurisprudence as a *habeas corpus*. And with no *habeas corpus*, I not sure of the degree to give to this case."

"Give it the third degree."

"Murder in the first degree!" he says.

"Okay," she says. "Who begins first?"

"I have the floor," he says. "I's the Solicitor-General. I going first."

"God go with you."

"*Muh-Lud*," he says; and bows extravagantly, "*in the midst of the presumption that a man's home is a man's castle, in the declared accepted and universally Christian presumption that no harm comes in a man's way, when that said man is sitting in his den, his front-house or his verandah on a Sunday evening after eating his supper, when the candles are glowing, and the lights are low, when the breezes waltzes over the fields of sugar canes, present in its description, an English landscape that is ideal, and for*

its tranquil-ness and serenity, in this hushed moment, on a night when
the vision is reduce' by the thick, velvet blackness of having no moon shin-
ing, into the sacred atmosphere, into the pure environment of deserved peace,
up crept, Muh-Lud, like a thief, like a robber of civilization, like a sinner,
like a veritable Iago . . ."

"'*Verago*'? Or did I hear, '*Iago*'? As in The Tragedy of Othello, the
Moor of Venice?"

Sargeant says, in his role as Crown. "*The very same, Muh-Lud . . .*"
he answers himself.

"*Iago, Iago . . . Iago!*" the Chief Justice says; and recites:

"'*O, Sir content you;*
I follow him, to serve my turn upon him:
We cannot all be Masters, nor all Masters
Cannot be truly follow'd.'"

"*And with an instrument, Muh-Lud, which as you might have gathered*
in my prelimary remarks, represented, if only in a symbolic way, the very
uninterrupted horspitality, generosity and English dependency that the
Crown is arguing for motive and motivation in this dasterly act prepe-
trated, Muh-Lud, with the very instrument which, when the Accused was
given employment on and by the said Plantation, as shown in documents,
was used by the Accused, namely a hoe . . .

"*A who?*"

"*Hoe, Muh-Lud. The* h *is silent.*"

"*Oh-ho! Ah-ho!*"

"*A hoe, Muh-Lud. An agricultural instrument, implement with the sacred*
and indigenous oral and cultural history, like a scythe, in local parlance, a
sickle, the instrument that is used in all the religious and historical por-
traits and portraitures, by who I am made to understand is the Renaissance
artists of the European school of painters, symbolically to suggest industry,
to suggest bounty and to suggest honest labour. By the sweat of thy brow,
Muh-Lud, shalt thou . . ."

"Whose *brow?*"

"*Not thy brow, Muh-Lud, surely. Your labour is of a more intellectual and jurisprudential nature . . . metaphorically, Muh-Lud, metaphorically speaking . . .*"

"*Proceed.*"

"*A hoe, Muh-Lud, a common hoe . . .*"

"*Did you say* whore, *again? A common prostitute? Surely, the Crown are not addressing this honourable Court as a whore!*"

"*Most humbly, Muh-Lud, in sorest estate, do the Crown tender apologies for the misapprehension of the term used to describe the instrument used in this, in this, this brutal, dasterdly crime. Referring to the hoe.*"

"*And who now is the whore?*"

"*The* r *is still silent, Muh-Lud.*"

"*Who else is silent, may I ask Crown?*"

"*Referring to the weapon used, Muh-Lud.*"

"*Proceed.*"

"*Muh-Lud would have read in Kinnergarden class at the Ursuline Convent, and later at the Lodge School where Muh-Lud was educated, of the speculative sayings, of the local rumour surrounding the shape of the seeds of the fruits from a certain tamarind tree, located on the property of the Plantation owned by Mr. Darnley Alexander Randall Bellfeels, namely that these tamarind seeds are all, each and every one, in the shape of the head of a man allegedly whipped to death by an ancestor of the Bellfeels family. But this is pure folklore, speculation, Muh-Lud . . .*"

"*Indeed! Indeed! As a boy growing up in Bimshire, during the long vacation of 1902, which I spent on the Plantation in question, referred to by Crown, we lads, the two Bellfeels, the father and uncle deceased, of the Bellfeels referred to earlier, to-wit, Bellfeels still in the quick, and I climbed the said tamarind tree, and devoured, with brown sugar from the Factory added, the fruits of this tree just introduced into evidence. Tambrin-balls we called them in the local jargon, as natives of Bimshire use the term. Despising the English pronunciation* tam-mar-rin *balls . . .*"

"*Indeed! Tambrin-balls, indeed! Clerk, show the Crown the object at the end of my watch chain . . .*"

(Clerk of the Court takes a watch from the hands of the Lord Chief Jus-tice, and crosses the Court, to the right of the Chief Justice, and hands the watch to the Crown, who admires it. The members of the Jury, all men, all white, all from the administrative levels of other sugar-cane plantations in the Island, lean forward to catch a glimpse of the beautiful gold watch with a matching chain . . .)

"Do the Crown see the ornament on the chain?"

"Muh-Lud."

"And are the Crown aware of the origin of the said ornament?"

"Muh-Lud."

"And what, may I ask, is the origin?"

"The seed of a tambrin-fruit, Muh-Lud, the ornament is a tambrin-seed."

"Proceed."

(Crown hands the heavy gold watch back to the Clerk, who gives it to the Lord Chief Justice, who replaces it back into the buttonhole on his black waistcoat, the tamarind seed hanging outside, over the waistcoat, glitter-ing in the light coming through the tall glass windows. The watch is inside the pocket.)

"May I proceed, Muh-Lud?"

"Proceed."

"Muh-Lud, it is the Crown's position that this crime outstrips any case in history, in any jurisdiction where Law rules, where civilization based upon the democratic principles of the British Empire reigns; where fair play exists, in Comma-Law and in Statue Law; Muh-Lud, it is hard for the Crown to cite a single case, not one precedence where there is the expression of such vile brutality and violence, coming against the tide of long his-torical, practised generosity.

"Muh-Lud, this crime makes the beast of the Defendent. This crime has incensed the Defendant's kinsmen and kinswomen. And this crime has plagued the Defendant with flies . . . fleas . . . flies. Muh-Lud, from this Sun-day forth, beginning with that Sunday night when the deed was done, the Crown cries out, 'Thieves, thieves, look to your house . . .'"

"'*What is the reason of this terrible Summons?*'" the Lord Chief Justice continues. "'*What is the matter there?*'

"Ah, Shakespeare! I remember it well. I had to learn it by heart, '*by rote*,' to use the proper term. Othello, *Act One, Scene One*, lines eighty-nine and ninety. In the Variorum Edition, of course. . . ."

"*Muh-Lud?*"

"The Moore of Venice. *Act One.*"

"*May I proceed, Muh-Lud?*"

"The Tragedy of Othello, the Moor of Venice."

"*Thanks, Muh-Lud. The Crown will show, from witnesses . . .*"

"*There isn't any witnesses, Muh-Lord,*" Mary-Mathilda screams, in one of her roles, the role of Counsel for the Defence. "*Nobody didn't there! Nobody wasn't there, I mean. Nobody but me couldn't see nothing that happened that night, and therefore bear witness.*"

"This is a play-play Court," Sargeant reminds her.

"Not from the things you were saying about me! And the way you were talking-so in favour of Mr. Bellfeels, I had to wonder about the justice of this Court. Jesus-God, Sarge! Suppose it wasn't a mock-sport Court! Jesus Christ, man! I would have gone! Send-way to His Majesty's Glandairy Prison, for life. Loss-away behind bars, facing the gallows. If not *henged* immediately . . ."

"This is what real Crowns and Solicitor-Generals and Officers of the Crown does-do; have to do, in cases heard in what we call a Mute Court. We are only practising. We are in Mute Court."

"Proceed then, under those conditions," she says.

"*Muh-Lud, the Crown intend to call Ma, the Defendent's mother, Gran, the Defendent's grandmother, and Gran-Gran, the Defendent's great-grandmother; and boys who grew up with the Defendent, to show the irascible temperriment and character the Defendent have, and moreover, had from youth; namely, and to wit, Pounce, who was a' apprentice gardener; Golbourne, who went into the joiner and cabinet-maker trade, also as a' apprentice; and Manny of unknown employment, seeing that his father, Manny the First, had money and was his own man; and consequently as a result, Manny the Second didn't have to lift a straw, nor find work; also, the Crown intend to call the Vicar of Sin David' Anglican Church, Revern Dowd, and the Headmaster of Harsun College, and the Comma-dant of the Bimshire Aquatic Club . . . the Comma-dore I think the proper term is, I've just been inform . . . Revern Dowd who was afore-mention' above . . . and the Manager-owner of the Crane Beach Hotel. These latter shall show, Muh-Lud, and it ain't really necessary for them to show, with all the evidence we got against the Defendent; and their evidence bearing the heaviness along with the burden of this tragedy, the exemplary character, the affectionate dispositions, the generosity of spirit and of pocket, of the, of the . . . man, the late gentleman . . ."*

"Muh-Lord, I asking for a step-out, not a step-out. I asking for a recess, man," she says. *"I axe-ing that we adjourn. I mean, recess."*

"Please rise."

"Court adjourn," Sargeant says. *"Recess, I mean."*

"Couldn't be soon-enough!" she says. "You do-me-in, good! You show your true colours to me. Is something I do? Or say? Or didn't do? You do-me-in real good!"

"Is a play-play Court, Mary-Mathilda."

"Play-play, my arse!" she says. "I was Mary-G to you a minute ago!"

"To me, you's always Mary-G, Mary-Mathilda!"

"You change fast."

"Is a play-play Court, Mary-Mathilda."

"You did-me-in! But I suppose His Lordship have to go to the lavatory. To relieve himself. And the Juries, too. To fire a pee, and refresh themselves. A glass of ice water, in the canteen. And a shot o' rum, in Chambers," she says. "And I have to pass water myself."

"Lunch," Sargeant says.

"Already? So-soon? In real time, it is not even breakfast-yet. But morning coming."

"Breakfast, then," he concedes.

"My God! How can a person, if he want to, get comfortable in the strangest of places! I don't want to leave this cane field," she says. "But, before I do get up from this makeshift bed, almost as comfortable as the Simmons in my bedroom, I want to show you the stars.

"Over there, where you can barely see the light getting ready to break, to your left, is Orion.

"Orion. In astrology books, they say that Orion came from the urine of three people, two men and one woman. But I don't know if I believe in all that urine-business.

"If you look good and hard, you will see the Big Dipper. Some people refer to it as the Great Bear. And once again, something I could never explain is why all these stars in the zodiacs were originally people, like me and you. When they got tired living on the earth, of being killed, or poisoned, they all went up in the heavens, and became stars. And change their names from earthly names into heavenly names.

"I can't remember what-else Wilberforce say is the relationship between the Big Dipper and the Lil Dipper, his relative; and who was father, and who son . . ."

"The Big Dipper had a son?" he asks her.

He has already decided that he will give this information, in turn, to Gertrude, next time they lie in this same cane field, on another bed of trash.

"Big Dipper and Little Dipper," she tells him. She places her right hand on his stomach, and leaves it there. "I wish I could remember what Wilberforce say is the Latin names for the two Dippers."

The stars seem to remain bright, as she points with her left hand, and shows him the beautiful constellations, the figurations of those heavenly bodies, which appear in the distance, simply as sparks from starlights that she and he used to buy from Manny's father's shop, before it was the Harlem Bar & Grill, and was just a shop that sold salt fish and flour and box matches and cigarettes and "bombs" which she and Sargeant, Pounce and Golbourne threw against a wall, or against the stone foundation of somebody's house, on the night of the Fifth of November, Guy Fawkes Day, and then covered their ears with their hands, waiting for the explosion. *Boooomm!* Yes. And burning starlights.

She can see plainly, the sparkles coming from the starlights, like a fountain of water illuminated, burning too fast, and then its stars disintegrating into the hot, black stems of wire; and she can smell the smouldering pieces of wire; and feel the heat; and feel the sadness for the disappearing "stars"; and she throws her wire now black into the gutter; or if they are home, dips the wire into a tot of water, and hear it fizz. *Ffffzzzzzz!* And watch the starlight die.

"Nor can I remember, so I could tell you, the distance one constellation is from the other. But they are not as close as they look with the naked eye, to us.

"But if you look over there. There! There, by the top of the breadfruit tree, with its leaves just touching the tip of the first star in the group. If you look good, without blinking your eyes too much, you will see stars that form the shape of a saucepan. I call it the Saucepan. I don't call-to-mind the real name. Nor the name in Latin. Ask Wilberforce.

"And all I try, as I lie here studying, I can't remember what he told me is the proper name for the Saucepan.

"You want to hear something, though? You sure you won't be shocked? Mr. Bellfeels, still only the Bookkeeper at the time, used to swear by the stars. I think I told you this before.

"Am I making you uncomfortable talking about Mr. Bellfeels? Under the present circumstances, I should be concealing any reference to him. Imagine! Here I am, in a field of canes, lying down on the trash, beside a policeman sent to take my Statement. This is more *ironical* than my constant mention of that son-of-a-bitch.

"Strange, eh? Strange. Strange. Strange. Nobody would believe it.

"And that is why I can be here. Nobody would ever believe it. That I was here. Not only because there's no witnesses, as they are not, but because nobody could imagine I would spend a night in a cane field. With you. So, it hasn't happened. And in a way, before I brought you through the underground tunnel, I must have known this . . .

"I even dare you, Sargeant, that when you leave the House, after we get back, and I make you a little green tea, I dare you to go and wake up Manny, and tell Manny that you just come from spenning the night with me, in a cane field. I dare you to even tell Manny that me and you was . . . were what you call it . . . having *carnal knowledge*, then! As you-yourself been hoping to . . .

"Or your Constable. Or even Wilberforce. Or if you were not still so scared of Mr. Bellfeels, Mr. Bellfeels. No. *Nobody will believe the truth.*"

"You think I so stupid as to try!" he says. "To-besides, this is between the two o' we. Our business. What I would wash my dirty linens out-in-public, for . . . I didn't mean to put it the way it sound, but . . ."

"There is *nothing* between us, Sargeant! Perhaps it is your business. But not *our* business."

"I get what you saying," he says, "though I can't agree."

"False oaths and evidence."

"False oats and evidence?"

"That is a threat?" she says. "People will only believe what they want to believe.

"And the play-play Court that we conducted for my benefit, in imagination and in play-play conjecture, but with the harshest words a Solicitor-General could dream of using, there still was a, a . . . a doubt."

"I didn't know you knew the stars."

"You changing the subject?"

"Am I?"

"You are changing the subject."

"But I still-didn't-know you know the stars."

"Just something I picked up. Nobody would believe that I was with you, in a cane field, the same cane field, incidentally, I know is where you take Gertrude, to show her the stars."

"Which Gertrude?"

"My Gertrude."

"Gertrude isn't interested in astronomy. She don't know nothing about the stars."

"She doesn't. That's true. You didn't teach her good. She asked me about The Three Sisters. I thought she was talking about the Solicitor-General's three girl-thrildren."

"Gertrude told you so?"

"You know where we are now?"

"Where?"

"Where we are?"

"In the canes."

"But *where* in the canes? What is important and ironical about where we are?"

"We are together?"

"What else?"

"I give up."

"Guess again."

"In a trash heap?"

"*In the North Field.*"

"The North Field?"

"I took you in the North Field."

"What so serious about being in the North Field? I pass this field, this North Field, sometimes nighttime, either going to work, or going home; and sometimes, on my days-off. Or to visit friends in the next village, in the daytime. I grow up knowing the North Field. My mother, as you know, worked with your mother, in the North Field, before she went away. I know something about this North Field, too."

"But not enough."

"What more to know there is about a ordinary field o' canes? There is a more deeper meaning that is personal?"

"Good!"

"Tell me?"

"The North Field is where my life began, and caused it to end. And is the motive."

"You want me to include this in your Statement, as part of your disclosures?"

"I mentioned it only because it is ironical and strange. One beginning is much of a muchness to another beginning. I just wanted you to know.

"You understand that we could have-remained in my bedroom. We went first into my bedroom, didn't we? But with my mind working in such a strange way, I had to go back in the canes, to be in a cane field; get close again to the trash, and smell trash, sweat; the smell of mould and the soil. Honest and like life. I wanted to go back, as a condemn man, going-through with his last wish.

"For when you spend as many years as me, living so close to cane fields, surrounded by canes, you have a strong pull to go back into cane fields.

"Cane fields can take on a life of their own; and they become a extension of your own existence. That smell. Mould and soil. Of centipees. That smell of death, too.

"When I returned-back from the Main House, earlier tonight, I took the back-way, leading-down directly from the verandah; crossed the circular driveway with the white marl and the loose gravel; down the little incline, and into the gully where the dunks trees and the hog-plum trees grow; through the lane that cuts across in one direction to the girls Elementary School, and in the other direction, to the Church; and it is getting dark now; and the light isn't too good, because there is no moon; but I know this area like the back of my two hands; and when I realize where I was, for I wasn't thinking clearly anymore, with all the things on my mind and in my conscience, it was right here, not exactly here, but right here in this same vicinity, where destiny it appears and the fates brought us back to. And I say fates and destiny, because we started-out, you taking my Statement, me giving it to you, in the front-house; and ended-up taking the journey of the Statement, beginning in my bedroom, then in a underground tunnel, in darkness, and ending-up in the open air, but in similar darkness. Yes.

"But I haven't fail to remember that you arrived as a policeman. And me, I greeted you as the lady of the Great House," she says; and laughs. "And end up in a cane field. Now, I am more a woman; and less a lady."

And without saying any more, she removes her hand from resting upon his stomach, as she would take a bookmark from a page, or as she would withdraw a small bone needle from an intricate pattern of flowers she was knitting; and she sits upright, and then gets to her feet, shaking pieces of trash off her white dress, holding the dress at its hem and fluffing it; adjusting her shawl round her shoulders; and then she walks off.

He follows her. As he follows her, he is "fixing himself": putting his testicles into the same side of his trousers, inside his sliders; putting his penis flat inside his sliders; putting the thick, dark-stained ugly baton back into its leather sheath.

The light is far away. It marks the edges of the North Field. It shows them, barely, the colour of grass, and of canes, and of pigeon-peas on trees, in pods that are turning from dark green to spotted brown; and there are beads, jewels, specks of water on the leaves of the puh-paw trees that line part of the North Field.

Against the sky, the large breadfruit trees are like towers, like fortresses, protecting the fields beneath them; and she and Sargeant can see the large green fruits hanging from the breadfruit trees, like huge Christmas balls, only green.

A wind comes up. A dove, far away in another tree, coos, *"Moses speak God's words, Moses speak God's words . . ."* This is the translation boys and girls in this Village of Flagstaff have given to the eye-cleansing, mouth-washing early morning "face-and-hands" voice of the brown wood-dove's cooing.

"Moses speaks God's words," she says.

She holds out a hand, and takes his; and softly the trash, being trampled and walked on, hardly reacts, as if it denies it is chastised by their feet; but the trash itself is made less prickly, and cannot tickle the neck anymore, because of the dew formed on it. The trash speaks softly to them, in answer perhaps, to the declarations of the wood-dove.

And she stops. And stoops to the ground. And removes some large stones from a spot in the ground over which she is standing. When the wet trash is cleared away, stones in the shape roughly of a cross are disclosed.

She kicks the stones away with her boots, as if the stones are small footballs. Beneath a thin layer of trash is a hoe. Her hoe.

The handle is shining, but with the dew that has formed on it.

"Here it is!" she says.

"I don't want it," Sargeant says, "even as a disclosure. And I not leaving my fingerprints on it, neither. I not touching it."

"Then, I will put it back under my bed, where it belongs. After I give it a cleansing." She picks up the hoe, and the two of them walk on in the breaking morning, back to the entrance to the secret underground passage.

Sunlight now pours in from a grate in the ground, which is above their heads, under which they are walking. They come to the portion of the underground tunnel where it gets to a higher level, the height of two steps, and which he remembers having descended hours earlier. Now, as he is about to lift his feet, he can feel the fatigue and the tightness in his legs; and he realizes the number of hours that have passed, and the weariness that has crept into his body, like the formation of dew on the trash and plants and grass and bushes in the field.

They walk on, with no word from her. He watches her body as it moves before him, like someone who is blind and still walking with certainty. He cannot claim that he has contributed to her certainty of gait that is so self-assured; it has nothing to do with him; it was not his body that induced this glow in her posture. It is all hers. The gait of a woman who knows what she wants. And how to get it. He cannot be arrogant and boast, as a man might boast, that he has anything to do with her independence. Her independence seems bigger than when he arrived; and stronger, too.

All this time, from the moment he propped his black Raleigh three-speed bicycle against the side door of the Great House, he knew he could play no significant role even in the taking down of her Statement in longhand, in his careful, tidy, well-rounded handwriting. His knowledge of her is second-hand through rumour and gossip, and glimpses of her over the years; and from Gertrude who speaks mainly of her with love, bordering on adoration. All the things Gertrude says are said with deep affection, but are nevertheless things that singled out Miss Mary-Mathilda as a woman of determination, toughness, iron discipline, wilfulness, even bitchiness—"and don't cross her, if you value your life!"—and yet a loyal, religious woman who kept her word. "But for all that," Gertrude told Sargeant, "she always strike me as looking a bit crazy-crazy. Tetched a lil, in the head; and frighten like a little girl, yuh-know-what-Uh-mean . . ." And listening to Gertrude sing Mary-Mathilda's praises, as he looked at the stars, wondering what fate, what future, what luck they held in their distant sway and sparkle for him; it made him uneasy to hear such personal things about a woman he had lusted after since that Easter Monday bank holiday.

He knows he has to make his move soon: take her Statement, get it over with; and then arrange for the Black Maria to take her down the hill, to the police sub-station, and book her, and then, because she is Miss Mary Gertrude Mathilda of the Great House, immediately release her upon her own recognizance; "release and without bond on her own recognizances," words he has been going over and over, aloud to himself, all night; words that take some of the sting out of the duty that insists on being done. And yet, he

knows she is a woman loved by all in the Village, this Mary-
Mathilda, daughter of a field hand, mother of the most brilliant
and well-loved doctor in the Island. Who would want to be the
man to place the iron handcuffs on her delicate, beautiful wrists,
and snap the bolt; and turn the key?

Who in the Village did not know, and wish for, and hope that
"the son-of-a-bitch who inhabits the Main House, don't deserve his
throat slit; and the sooner, be-Christ, the better"? And who would
raise a hand of censure, or answer a call from the Plantation, or the
Solicitor-General, to take an oath and give evidence against Miss
Mary-Mathilda, alias Miss Mary Paul, a. k. a. Miss Paul; also known
as Miss Bellfeels, and still continue to live in Flagstaff Village?
Or remain in the Island of Bimshire? Best to leave; disappear;
"drop out o' sight, for-your-own-good, for-good!"; take a slow
boat to China; or to Panama, or Venezuela, or Brazil. Or Brooklyn-
New-York.

Sargeant knows there is no one.

Not even the juiciest bribe or inducement could produce one
man to arrest Miss Mary Gertrude Mathilda; and condemn her.

In many serious and puzzling criminal cases, the authorities
easily found a first-hand witness, who at the time of the crime was
in another parish of the Island, to come forward, and with a little
coaching, and the promise of gain, or the threat of loss, be induced
to spill his guts in the rehearsal of precise facts and interpretation
that the authorities had taken him through, swear "on false oats":
and always the Defendant was found guilty on this evidence manu-
factured in a rum shop; and then, presented in Court.

Such a "false-oats taker" would then leave, and never return to
the Island, even if he thought, as reason ought to dictate, that the
time gone-by, in silence, away from these shores, would have con-
tributed to loss of memory, or the dissipation of the scandal that
had followed the sentencing, based upon his "duty as a citizen, to
tell the truth, the whole truth, and nothing save the truth," that his
manufactured evidence had caused.

No.

Sargeant had at first thought, when the telephone call came and interrupted the afternoon game of cut-throat dominoes that he and Constable and Naiman were playing in the sub-station, that this kind of a case would guarantee a promotion . . . but a promotion to what? He was already at the highest rank a man of his class, education, social status born in Bimshire, and colour could ever dream of achieving: he had no further round to climb. He was soon to "conclude, as a result, therefore" of these circumstances that the detective who took part in the 'vestigation of this case, to say nothing of solving it, could not be rewarded by a promotion. Perhaps, by a new Watermans fountain pen . . .

Walking through this tunnel now, with its tricky light, Sargeant imagines he is behind the wheel of the Chief Justice's large, black Jaguar Mark V. He has been sent by the Chief Justice to fetch his dress suit at his home on Belleville Avenue. The Chief Justice liked Sargeant because he was a young and bright policeman, prosecuting simple cases successfully; and Sargeant liked the Chief Justice for his sternness and his classical education, and his sense of humour; and Sargeant tried, whenever possible, to make the Chief Justice his model, imitating his mannerisms, and his love of Shakespeare, and more than once cursed his fate and his family, that he was not born with the necessary background to be rich and able to attend an Inn of Court in London, and become a barrister-at-Law . . . Now, ahead of him, with the light on her body brighter, showing him her thighs as she takes one determined step after another, is this mysterious Mary-Mathilda in better focus, in this strong light . . . and Sargeant remembers fumbling, for no reason, just maliciousness, in the glove compartment of the Chief Justice's Jaguar Mark V, where he finds an envelope marked IN STRICTEST CONFIDENCE; EYES ONLY. The size of the capital letters, and the colour of the ink, something resembling the squeezed juice from the berries off a spinach vine, mauve or deep red, makes him curious; and makes him want to open the envelope. The envelope is not sealed. So, technically, "and consequently, as a result there-fore," he is not breaking and entering. Breaking and Entering was the topic of the lecture the Commissioner of Police had given that morning to the non-commissioned police officers. The Chief Justice gave a few words, then whispered something to the Com-missioner; and left. Immediately after, the Commissioner said a word to Sargeant, in private; and dropped the car keys into his hand.

"Don't drive-'bout the CJ car showing-off," the Commissioner warned Sargeant. "Return-back prompt. You hear?"

The envelope is the colour of khaki, and has a window through which Sargeant can see part of a pair of legs; and when he shakes the envelope, the legs drop in full view in the window; and the legs are the legs of a woman; and his eyes and his hand now ease the photograph out of its envelope; and more photographs are dis-closed; and the woman's legs become her waist and then her thighs, and finally, her entire body, naked as she was born. He looks up and sees a cyclist in his path; and swerves, too late; and in his rearview mirror, he sees the cyclist on the ground, and his legs caught in the bicycle wheels; and the fallen man is pointing at the Jaguar, with his right index finger.

"Haul your arse!" Sargeant tells the image of the man in the rearview mirror.

He looks at each of the snapshots of the woman and a man, in various sexual positions; and suddenly facing shame for looking at the snapshots, and for "breaking and entering," he replaces them, using one hand; and worries: "I hope that blasted bicycle didn't scrape the CJ Jag!" and speeds on.

A swelling, a lightness, came to Sargeant's head, making it swim with this new sensation of seeing a man and a woman in the act of lovemaking, with the man doing it in many positions; performing cunnilingus; spanking her buttocks; squeezing her breasts; and from behind—a position Sargeant had *never* contemplated, a posi-tion Manny had never suggested; captured on film; and he wondered how the photographer made the arrangements to take these acts. All the twelve snapshots leave out the head of the man and the head of the woman.

Sargeant drove like a speed-demon through the streets of Town, from the Law Courts on Coleridge Street, where the High Court is situated; past Cave Shepherd & Sons, Haberdasheries; past the statue of Lord Horatio Nelson, standing in stiff naval erectness, in bronze, at attention, looking out to sea, his line of vision passing over the shallow Careenage, over the Rum Bonds and the Warehouse Bonds, and focusing instead on the wide Carbean Sea and on the vastness of the Atlantic Ocean, over which he has himself sailed, years ago; past the Esplanade where the Police Band plays the martial music of Sousa every Wednesday night; past the Aquatic Club, past the Garrison Savannah Lawn Tennis Club; past the Hastings Rocks, his heart beating fast, an unsettling feeling in his groin, wondering what Manny would say about these dozen positions, ignoring the accelerated RPMs registered on the polished mahogany dashboard, until he comes to a screeching stop in the uneven driveway, in front of the Harlem Bar & Grill. The Chief Justice's mansion Sargeant deliberately passed on his way to Manny.

"Look at these. Fast, Manny," he says. "I have to take-them-back. I find them in Sir G's Jag, out there!"

"The Chief Justice?"

"Look at the things, quick, man!"

"Jesus Christ! Jesus Christ!" Manny says, as he looks at the first two snapshots, as Sargeant back-backs the large motor-car into the small, rocky, muddy space in front of the rum shop. "Jesus Christ!" Manny says, rolling his eyes, and looking at the third snapshot. "This position is call the Baked Fowl, for your information."

"What bake-fowl?"

"This next position, I think, the Amurcans call the, the . . . the Missionary Position."

"How the arse you know these things, Manny?"

"They is both white people. Perhaps from Bimshire. Or they could be English . . . the English like these kinky things," Manny says. "I know. You is a police; you should know, too. Sometimes I axe myself, 'Sarge is a police? Sarge is a real police?'"

Sergeant thinks of the Lord Chief Justice who is waiting to be driven to luncheon at the Bimshire Club, whose members are the powerful men in the Island; and he has twenty minutes to pick up the CJ's suit and get back; and as he speeds through the crowded daytime streets, all he hears in his head are Manny's exclamations, "Jesus Christ!" as he flipped to another snapshot; and the spewing of mud and the noise of stones run over by the wheels of the powerful Jaguar, as he points it back in the direction of Town, and the CJ's mansion on Belleville . . . Sergeant passes passenger buses, belonging to Eckstein Bus Company, to the General Bus Lines, Reid's Buses, and Miss Madame Ifill Bus Company, painted in various colours, like the flags of nations and independent islands, on their way into Town, like a caravan, in droves, early in the morning, as if it is an Easter Monday bank holiday; and men are dressed in white as if they are heading for the cricket fields of villages, of Harrison College, and Spartans and Combermere School, or to Kensington Oval, and now going to the white-marled Yard of the High Court, where they will stand for hours, under the berry trees that give the only shade from the sun which comes down at you, with a vengeance, even as early as ten o'clock in the morning. Everyone lucky-enough to be an early bird already has a seat inside the Court, in the Gallery.

The Court is large and sedate and with large windows covered in jalousies, to keep out the heat and the sun. The jalousies are painted green. Everything that belongs to the Government of the Island of Bimshire is painted green. Thick, deep, shiny green. Everything that is important in this Island is also painted green: the shutters of all the buildings on all the plantations; the eaves and the shutters on the windows of the Garrison Savannah Lawn Tennis Club, windows which hang out from the wall like sleepy eyelids;

the windows of the pavilions of the First Eleven cricket clubs, and of the Aquatic Club; the windows of the Bimshire Club, whose verandah overlooks Broad Street, the main street in Town; on everything that is English and important is this green, shiny paint.

On the walls of the High Court are portraits of all the preceding Chief Justices.

A portrait of the King is on the wall behind the seat of the Chief Justice. This seat looks like a throne. It is high. It is made of stained wood. It has markings and images, like small sculptures of heads of beasts, ugly, prehistoric monsters that do not live in the Island of Bimshire; and a replica of the Goddess of Justice; and there is the head of a lion that is about to eat some small animal, or the nearest, careless human. The heads of gargoyles.

Below this throne, upholstered in crimson velvet, are seats, on the left and on the right, for the two sides of the Court. Rex versus Accused. Crown versus Defendant. And long tables at which the solicitors and clerks and barristers and juniors of both sides to the argument are seated.

All are dressed in the black of undertakers, white dress shirt stiff at the winged collar, white tie that is two two-inch wide strips of cotton, black silk jacket, black silk waistcoat and dark grey striped trousers, black shoes; wearing wigs which stand out against their natural hair, and their dark skins and white skins, or the reddened complexions, from sun and rum.

They all look very intelligent and very sleepy; and very stern. Some look cruel.

There is a railed, squared-off section, lower than the throne, in which sits the man, or the woman, before the Bar, "the Accused"— the condemned man or the condemned woman—"the Prisoner"; no one escapes lightly from the clutches of Sir Gerald's encompassing, thorough knowledge of the Laws of Englund applied in classical pronouncement of the English language, straight from his head, to the lawlessness of Bimshire; and without looking into the pages of the huge leather-bound books, whose backs are carved with letters of gold print, and which sit on his desk, piled like cement blocks, to provide protection from the rabblement in his Court, or like huge domino seeds, as if these books of heavy jurisprudence and precedents are placed there to protect Sir G from contamination from the prisoner in the dock; no; no one escapes Sir G's clutches.

And in the balcony, or the Gallery, the few fortunate local, native historians of murder cases who will tell you, from memory, years afterwards, precisely which argument it was that swayed Sir G to don his black cap, the second the Foreman cries, "Guilty, sir!"; when Sir G will pronounce Judgement: "*You shall be taken from this place, and conveyed to another place, where you shall be held until the day of reckoning come, thence, you shall be taken to the proper place, and hanged by your neck, until you are dead, dead, dead, and may the Lord have mercy on your soul*"; these historians, fortunate to be seated within hearing distance of argument and judgement, will stand afterwards in the Yard, under the berry trees and talk, and ignore the yellow sticky berries falling on their heads, will go on talking, reciting the heavy arguments made in Court; and will move from the Yard only when night falls, to the public Standpipe, under a street lamp, in a rum shop, and disclaim, almost word for word, the complicated citing of Law and legal precedents argued by the Solicitor-General, and Torts cited by the Defence, the Island's leading Barristers-at-Law.

The names, Christian and surname, including initials, of every barrister, law clerk, solicitor who represents Rex or Defendant— there are no women barristers—involved in any aspect of a murder case is known, by the second day, by the onlooking historians in the Gallery. His mother's name, and his father's name are already known. It is known on what day he was born; which elementary school he attended in which corner of the Island; and it is known "how he came" in the Secondary-to-Second-Grade examinations; in which year; what marks he got; and in which subjects in those examinations; and similarly, about the Senior-to-First-Grade exami-

nations; and when he finishes either at Harrison College or the
Lodge School, it will be known by these "members of the Gallery,"
mostly men—and some women, too—that in Latin Distinction he
reached Scholarship level; that in Greek he got a Distinction; that
in Ancient History, likewise; and that "he went up," afterwards,
to Oxford—or Cambridge—and "lick' all-them English-boys,
and *teached* them Law!"; and "came back with a *One-One!*" First
amongst all those in the University, and first of all those who got
First Class Honours in Jurisprudence.

To the last man, his credentials are known by the entire Gallery.
They are known with the same ferocity of retention as cricket
scores of batsmen from Englund, Australia, Ncw Zealand and the
Wessindies, are held in the memory, and spewed forth at the small-
est challenge.

It is a contest. There is no interest in the rightness or wrong-
ness of a murder case. Nobody really cares whether "a woman
kill a man; he was a worthless son-of-a-bitch, anyhow"; whether
he deserved to have his head chopped off; and his "dickey" jammed
into his mouth. No one standing in the Yard under the berries is
concerned about the horribleness of a crime. Not really. They are
here to hear legal argument. They are here to hear "*talk*." They are
here to hear Sir Gerald interject his wisdom, with humour and
quotations from Shakespeare and from the Classics, Livy, *Book
XXI,* and Virgil's *Aeneid,* and Tacitus' *Histories*; and listen to Sir G's
wit, "dry as a cassava-hat." They are here as they would be in a
cinema, watching a cowboy film that has the longest fight in it in
the history of cowboy films.

The words they will hear, words from the Latin, and with a gen-
erous sprinkling of words from Greek classical literature, and from
Shakespeare, are words they would not hear every day in their
neighbourhoods, on the beach, in the fish market, or at a cricket
game on the Pasture, on a Saturday afternoon; but they will like
these words, although they do not know Latin, or Greek; or would
not have read too much Shakespeare, they will fall in love with

these words; and make them their own, by repeating them, even when their usage is not exactly relevant, or exact. It does not matter. It is the word. And these men have always loved the word. And the sound of the word being spoken. For the word is God. And is like the Law. And like the Law, which is English, the *word,* too, is English. Yes. "Talk-yuh-talk! Yes!"

"Muh-Lud, humbly I beg leave to proceed in my examination of the person before the Bar . . . Thank you, Muh-Lud."

It is more than play-play Court. More than Mute Court.

"Now, I put it to you, did you, or did you not, depart your domicile on the night in question, and with malice aforethought, did you not in fact proceed at about thirty-five minutes after six o'clock in the evening in question, on the thirteenth instant, going into a direction which alone of itself could only have brought you within the boundaries of the private property of the Plantation referred to in the Docket of Evidence before this Honourable Court; and did you not, by that trespass, intend to, and have motive, to carry out the dasterly act of which you are hereby charged? I put it to you, did you, or did you not?"

One man leans closer to the man sitting beside him, and with a hand covering his mouth, whispers, "Words, man! Words."

"Too-sweet!" the man replies.

. . . and she carries the hoe in her right hand, imitating the Lord Bishop with his Staff of Office, holding the end with the blade, pushing little pieces of paper out of her way, wondering how they got here in this subterranean passage; poking the holes in the masonry of the wall, with the handle of the hoe, and bringing down a small gust of white dust. She is holding the hoe with the care that its meaning would insist upon. She carries her hoe with the aplomb and arrogance and dignity of the Bishop's Staff. A staff of rank. Or like the polished African stick she saw an African walking with, in the *London Illustrated News;* and this is what it means to her now.

Perhaps she is carrying it with this exaggerated importance and imagined symbolism because it has been with her for the same comparative length of time as the wishbone she had carried pinned

into the hem of the tunic of her school uniform, when she was in
Primer Standard—and later on, in her navy blue bloomers, when
she went into a higher standard in Elementary School—for years,
touching it during difficult moments in Geography, when it took
her some time to remember the capital of Australia; and once,
when the name of the highest mountain in India slipped her mem-
ory; once again, when she did not spell in time to suit her teacher,
the name of the biggest river in Amurca . . . "M-eye-double-s, eye-
double-s, eye-double-pee, eye! *Mississippi*, ma'am"; and that sad,
rainy Friday afternoon in Scripture, when she could not remember
what the First Commandment warned against doing. But she knew
her wishbone was there, to help, in case of some serious problem.

And it did come to her aid, on another afternoon, when her
teacher Miss Blackett was hearing Standard Two in oral Mental
Arithmetic: *"Class, listen good! A breadfruit and a half cost a penny and
a half, hommany breadfruits I will get for three cents?"* She put up her
hand high up in the air, indicating she knew the answer.

"Well, Mary, then?" Miss Blackett said. *"Yes?"*

"T'ree!"

"Tree?" Miss Blackett said.

"T'ree, ma'am! They cost t'ree cents!"

"You bright as a new shilling, Mary-child!" Miss Blackett told her.

And afterwards, the girls in her class branded her *"the most
brightest girl in the whole class, among all of we."*

And Miss Blackett singled-her-out, for the balance of that week,
telling the class, *"Mary-girl is going far; far in life."*

No, she did not forget much; not Mary; and she did not forgive
much, either.

Here she is, in her white dress that was so well pressed by
Gertrude, which she wore at lunch one day ago now, the Sunday
afternoon, sitting at the table covered by a lace cotton tablecloth
that she herself had crocheted; the sterling service set precisely
and in proper arrangement by Gertrude, whom she had trained in
manners and in the art and etiquette of table setting. And at that

time of Gertrude's first engagement as a servant, Mr. Bellfeels
would bring his friends to the Great House on Friday nights; and
they would eat and laugh and sing bawdy songs and the Blues; and
then play poker until all hours of the night, until the sun started to
peep over the green cane fields the next morning; and she wanted
so much at that time to please Mr. Bellfeels, and make Mr. Bellfeels
look good in front of his friends; to be proud of her; and how she
looked and contributed to his status, in the presence of his power-
ful friends: the Solicitor-General, the Vicar, the manager-owner of
the Crane Beach Hotel, the Commissioner of Police and managers
of the Aquatic Club and of Cave Shepherd & Sons, Haberdasheries,
down in Town; and the Chief Justice, to make them like her; and
on those merry nights, not always happy nights for her, a guest
would wander into the kitchen where she was standing beside
Gertrude, showing Gertrude how she wanted the edges cut off the
enriched white bread, to make Fray Bentos corn beef sandwiches
with, and cucumber sandwiches; and this guest would come up to
them, ignoring Gertrude's presence, and place his hand on Mary-
Mathilda's bottom, and squeeze her well-spread bottom, until it
seemed his thumb met and touched his index finger, beneath her
soft perfumed flesh; "*Mary-girl, lemme feel-you-up a lil, girl, nuh? Yuh
feel good, girl! Sweets! Thanks*"; and in her pain and agony, caused as
much by the suddenness of the assault as by the pain from it, Mary-
Mathilda would not utter a sound, but would smile pleasantly, and
remove the man's hand. And Gertrude, who saw trouble setting
up like rain, by the man's approach, would of her own will, for the
sake of self-preservation, leave the room. But Mary-Mathilda, in
her silent disgust, masked her anger and her promise of vengeance
in a blank visage as if she were sitting with them, at the table,
poker-faced; clutching her wishbone, she wanted Gertrude to
remain, and bear witness; to cause the guest to shorten his assault.
"*Looking good, and feeling more better, girl!*"; and the guest would him-
self take the platter of corn beef and cucumber sandwiches, and

another of fish cakes, covered with a damp linen cloth, with him back into the front-house, for the other men to devour.

In all these times, she hosted these parties, which could not be held in the Main House, because Mistress Bellfeels, his wife, disapproved of his gambling, and of his friends. She herself told Mary-Mathilda on the one occasion that they spoke, "Mary, for too long I have endured his crude manners, and the uncivilized behaviour of *those* men. It's despicable, the way those men treat women, including me, *and in front* of my girls!" And Mistress Bellfeels added, "I hope that for your sake, Mary, you will never be exposed to their *lawlessness.*" This was soon after Wilberforce won the Bimshire Scholarship in Classics; when the Plantation and the Village were rejoicing; and everybody was friendly. But Mary-Mathilda did not have the same legitimate excuse as Mistress Bellfeels. She was not the Mistress. She was plain Mary. Mary Gertrude Mathilda. *Not* Mistress Mary-Mathilda Bellfeels.

One night Mr. Bellfeels himself came into the kitchen.

"Give we a minute," he said to Gertrude.

Gertrude took off her apron; wiped the sweat on her face with it; the oven was filled with joints of pork, to be served in a few minutes, so she checked the pork in the oven first; and then left. The back door slammed two times, and then it became very quiet, and Mary-Mathilda thought she could hear Gertrude's bare feet striking the cement steps that led into the yard, and then moving over the wet grass; and she could picture Gertrude standing beside the garden bed that held the Rachelle Rose; and it was at that moment, hearing Gertrude's retreating footsteps, that Mr. Bellfeels came right up to her, beside the large iron oven, giving off the smell of delicious pork and heat; and raised her dress, lifting the delicate white sea-island cotton material from her ankles up her shins, past her thighs, over her waist, exposing her well-shaped legs and round belly with the sunken navel, tearing apart the cord of her short delicate camisole . . . and when the minute was up, he told her, "Tell Gertrude she could come-back-in." And he returned to the poker game; and she heard him laugh, with a deep-throated joviality; and then she heard his voice say, "I raise two hundred!" She did not know the poker game of Five Card Stud.

Standing beside the hot iron stove, she heard the other men laugh; and Sir G's voice speaking in a foreign language; in Latin: "*Missus Hannibal in Hispaniam adventus primo statim adventus omnem exercitum in se convertit; Hamilcarem iuvenem vigorem in vultu vimque in occulis, habitum oris lineamentoque intueri.*"

"*. . . and I see that you still remember yuh Six-Form Latin, eh, Judge Jeffreys!*" she heard the Vicar say to Sir G.

The laughter in the front-house rose like fresh waves hitting against the rocks at the Crane Beach Hotel.

"*Bellfeelus nec temere credendum nec asperandum ratus,*" Sir G. then said.

"*Oh God, oh-God!*" the men screamed.

"*Sweet-sweet!*" the Vicar said. "*Too-sweet!*"

And the men roared. She could hear the ring of glasses tipped against one another, and the rattling of ice in the glasses, as the men toasted Sir G's versatility and application of Livy, *Book XXI* to Mr. Bellfeels' situation. They had all—except Mr. Bellfeels—studied this book in various Forms at Harrison College, or the Lodge School; most of them, however, had forgotten the passage . . .

It was a warm feeling. And some of this warmth, whether of anger or of passion, she could feel in her face, in the area round her neck, as she touched herself there, the way she does when she touches her neck with the back of her hand, checking her temperature for fever.

She did not, at this time, put her life under strict scrutiny, nor did she bend her behaviour under the critical eye of self-reproach and doubt. Years after this, after the riotous nights, when Mr. Bellfeels visited, as a parent and as paramour; on Saturday nights when he played the piano, and the three of them, father, son and son's mother, sang and danced to the beautiful songs from the Amurcan South, songs she later came to know were Negro spirituals and Negro blues and Negro minstrels and Negro gospel music, she would throw her head back and laugh, and spin little Wilberforce, no more than five or six years old then, round and round, and watch his body flailing round, out from her own body, as if he was a merry-go-round; and his head would be thrown back in abandon, in security, in confidence that the woman holding his two hands, his mother, was not so reckless as to release her grip on his hands, in that merry turning world, in the security of the Plantation, in the front-house; and she would laugh as she swung him, and laugh as she heard the tantalizing yet mellow songs which Mr. Bellfeels told her were sung by "Nig-groes," and by slaves; and she had no thought nor feeling for those Negroes and those slaves; for she was in Bimshire, in this solidly built Great House, square and tough, two storeys high, whose walls were built thick and redoubtable, "like a brick shithouse," Mr. Lawrence Burkhart the Driver said; just like the walls of His Majesty's Prison at Glandairy, or Dodds Reformatory for Boys; like the Sin-Anne's Fort, near the Garrison Savannah, something like the toughness of the walls of Troy which the Greeks could not penetrate by force of arms, or catapults; this Great House, as it is called by everyone, standing, it seems, since time began; for it has been here, like a curse, like a smile, like an insult in the face, from the time people came to live and work on the Plantation; so, in this circle of love, and wealth, and sensuality, and violence and raw unadorned sex, Mary Gertrude Mathilda Paul (taking her mother's maiden name) made her life with her only surviving child, Wilberforce, whom she worshipped from the time the midwife told her, "This one going-live, this time, darling!"; while the child's father, Mr. Bellfeels, provided the means of her elevated status, *condoned,* though circumscribed, in his social circle; and he maintained her livelihood, servants to cook her food, servants to wash up afterwards; servants to wash her clothes; maids to iron her clothes and keep the house clean, and sew the blinds when they got ripped by hurricane winds, and darn the shirts Wilberforce wore to Harrison College, and iron the doilies and clean the cushions; and a boy to sweep the yard, and "mind the stocks," and a girl to run easy errands. But when she got accustomed to this help, and realized that her servants ate more than they worked for in wages, she asked Mr. Bellfeels if she could dismiss all but Gertrude; and he surprised her, and said, "Man-yes! They does-only-thief the fecking food! I did-waiting to see how long before you catch on!"; and so she kept Gertrude. She loved Gertrude, and did not treat her as a servant: she assisted Gertrude in the kitchen, and round the house.

She did not know that Mr. Bellfeels was fooping Gertrude, too.

This is Mary-Mathilda's life. Paid for by Mr. Bellfeels. But in a more serious manner, in a more deep and romantic way, her life is paid for by her body. Has always been. It is therefore *her* life; and her life only. She owns it.

Mr. Bellfeels took her, as his right, in his natural arrogance of own-ership, as a part of the intricate ritual and arrangement of life on the Plantation—"if it wasn't you, Mary-girl," Ma told her, "it wouldda be somebody-else daughter. And even though it is what it is, I still feel more better to see that is you getting some o' the sweets that goes along with it, if you know what I mean!" Ma had told Mary-Mathilda this two years after she had introduced Mary-girl to Mr. Bellfeels that Sunday morning in the Church Yard, when he towered over her from the saddle of his horse.

Mr. Bellfeels had had Ma, too, for years; "taking what he want"; and their affair; no, not affair, for it could not be called that, since there was no bargaining power on her part; and even if she had thought of exchanging her body for power, or for privilege, or a simple thing, like having to work less hard, in exchange for "a piece o' pussy"; or receiving an extra shilling in her brown wage enve-lope, when she stood with the other field hands in the large Plantation Yard, covered in white marl and loose gravel, under the tamarind tree, and heard how she was addressed by Mr. Lawrence Burkhart the Driver, "*Eunomia Irene Paul, here?*" and then have to hear the number of times she was marked late; and the number of times she "didn't show-up," including when her monthly sickness was too painful for her to walk the mile to work; and listen to the number of pence she was docked for this "*blasted unpunctualness, too often, hear?*" Ma knew, and would get to know even better, since she was a member of the field gang and the Plantation system, that this coming Friday afternoon late, Mr. Bellfeels would come and have it; rough and ready; and there was nothing she could do to make it not happen.

"Fair exchange," Ma began to tell herself, as she limped home a little later than the other field hands, sore from the throwing up and down of her hands, like a machine, with the hoe in her hands; and driving it, with venom and hate, "I going-kill yuh, I going-kill-yuh . . . one o' these good days . . ." into the ground which was hard as rock, sometimes; hard as a piece of coral from the sea; sometimes hard as soft mud; and her thighs sore from Mr. Bellfeels' brutal prick which dug into her without mercy, without the lubrication of love.

It was a glance of his eye, a command of silent determination, threatening a flogging, if Ma had not seen the wink, or if she seemed not to have observed the signal. The large, chestnut-coloured horse, smelling like urine and straw mixed and left out in the sun, would tread on the thick black soil, with the pieces of corn stalk and ruts from the cut sugar canes, roots from the plants of sweet potatoes and eddoes, spread like a Persian carpet from the way the colours were arrayed on the ground, and the horse would shit on the stalks and on the ruts, and add to the smell of terror and of despair—with the smell of horse seeming to guide her behind him. Barely out of sight and hearing distance of the eleven other women in the field gang, Ma would see him standing just two rows from the edge of the growing canes. The canes were still young. They reached him to his waist. They reached Ma to her chest. The fly of his khaki jodhpurs was already unbuttoned. Ma saw the ugly brownish red head of his circumcised prick. She had seen it many times, and as many times had thrown it from her mind; or had imagined she would bite it off, hold it in her teeth, close her eyes even tighter than they were shut, at the touch of his hand on her breasts; and bite, and bite, and hope there was no blood; she couldn't stand blood; and spit it out the moment it was severed from his high-smelling thighs . . . retaining only, more in her body than in her thoughts, the burning sensation of unfulfilled tension, and another burning feeling in her vagina, as if his semen was seasoned with hot nigger-peppers.

"Fair exchange," Ma grew to tell Mary-girl, her daughter, "is no robbery. Get something for it. You are a pretty girl. With a lovely complexion. Nice hair. If I was the woman o' means that I wish I was, you would have your own hairdressing place. Or a dressmaking place. Or even be a teacher. But this is our lot. I can't even buy a second-hand, or a t'ird-hand Singer sewing machine for you!"

Ma had told him what she had wanted to tell him for years, from that time she stopped having her menses. The second time. The first time she found out she was pregnant, her own ma, Gran to Mary-girl, was too scared to try her hand at abortion, for Gran's mother was poorly; lying on a canvas cot all day, waiting for God to call her home; but in her weak voice, she whispered the "ingreasements" of the portion; for only she, with this knowledge which she said she brought from Africa, knew what to do. Great-Gran had an apothecary's brilliance with herbs. Great-Gran told them the right herbs and bushes to use. And she knew, from trial and error, the correct portion of engine oil—". . . jest a drop to a drop and a half, two at the most"—to mix with the thick, bitter, black liquid that the bushes were boiled down to in a tea.

"Eunomia-girl, this going taste like hell, like p'ison," Great-Gran told her, "but that is exactly what it suppose to be. P'ison-out the

infirmities inside your system, girl. So, hold your nose, shut yuh
two eyes and swallow *hard*. Good! Now, sit in this bush-bath . . .";
yes, she had gone through that.

But this Friday afternoon, about two, a few hours before she
would assemble with the other hands, in the Plantation Yard, to
answer to her name—*Eunomia Irene Paul, here?"*—and walk for-
ward, take her brown envelope from the hand of the bookkeeper,
and mark a mark that represented her name, her special Mark,
her mark of identity and identification, in the large ledger, PLAN-
TATION LABOURERS, that has a black cover, red vertical lines
and black horizontal lines, and the names of everyone, man,
woman, child, animal, who worked on the Plantation, written in
it; with her mind full of the thought that she could reason with
him, risky in itself; for her to seem to have a mind, this dangerous
disposition, similar to the uppitiness her cousins in Southampton
had seen in Nat Turner, this, this "blasted facetiness," "this circum-
stance," this rebelliousness, this talking-back . . . well, Ma had
hardly got the words with which she wanted to negotiate out of
her mouth when she felt the searing, tearing, biting tongue of the
riding-crop across her back, *whap!-whap!* It was as if the two lashes
were sewn into her flesh, like the two strings of cloth which served
as braces that kept her skirt in place.

"You ever whisper *that* one-more-time, and I fecking kill you,
like shite!"

"Sir," Ma said.

"Don't-fecking-sir-me! Or play with me! You hear me, woman?"

"Sir."

"You really understand what I fecking-well telling you, Eunomia
Irene Paul?"

This was the first time he had called her by her full name. And
hearing her name called by him shocked her into temporary
dumbness; and he had to repeat his warning.

"You really understand what I fecking-well telling you, Eunomia
Irene Paul?"

"Yes, sir."

"Feck-yuh-up! Shoot yuh, like-feck! Point-blank, too!"

"Yes, sir."

And he flung the riding-crop at her, in a vicious lash. Part of the riding-crop caught her right breast; but the longer part, like a striking snake, ripped into her back.

"You heard me?"

Whapppp! it cried out again.

"Yes, sir."

"You understand, now?"

"Yessir . . ."

"Be-Christ, how it would look, for people to hear that I fooping my own daughter! You want to send-me-up to Glandairy? Or cause a fecking scandal pon this Plantation? You hate me summuch?"

"No, sir."

"Good. Well, lemme tell you wha' I going-do. I putting-in a' extra piece o' change in your envelope today."

"Thank you, sir. Thank you, very much, sir."

And Ma, from that moment, knew that Mary-girl was fixed. Was saved. *Taken-care-of.* Just as—and Ma could not have known this—Mary-Mathilda had taken care of her wishbone; and of her hoe. And Ma knew that she herself would carry this damning, indigestible information within her heart, for who would believe such blasphemy, such, such *wirthless* behaviour; so she would carry it to her grave.

It is this thought, this nagging, raw supposition that comes up now, like the first swelling on the arm that you watch after rubbing it with your hand, hoping it will disappear, or else stop hurting, but which becomes in three days, always in three days, an open festering sore, which brings pain; and you cannot any longer rub it with your hand, but have to lance it, or cover it with Elastoplast, or use the Village remedy, ordinary dirt that is dry, mixed with ashes from the coal pot or from the fireplace; but whether it is healed in three days after its bursting out, it leaves a scar. A little smooth roundish skin, darker and smoother than your normal skin, and for life, perhaps, or for a long time, but long enough to be a life, you walk about with this mark. This mark.

This is the mark that Mary-Mathilda would see when she walked up the stairs from the front-house, when she had sat in her favourite chair, reading the Bible, or letting her hands guide the bone needles, absent-mindedly, or "just studying"—for she had now mastered most patterns she had taken from *Ladies' Home Journal*, the English edition—and would, when the light changed, or when Gertrude brought in the acetylene lamps and lit them, before the house was run with electricity, Mary-Mathilda would see, as if for the first time, the smiling countenance of Wilberforce, as a small boy, and then look at the face of Mr. Bellfeels, erect, formal, handsome, in a suit of black, with a high, stiff, white collar that looked as if he has been made breathless by its tightness, and see clearly the obvious fact of patrimony: who had fathered her son, her only living child. And then she would look at the photographs of herself, at age five, and seven, and nine, exactly the three ages of Wilberforce in the triptych in the oval-shaped silver frame, and see the resemblance which struck her always as the resemblance of the son "taking after his mother." But when she looked at all three together, this is when the thought of a mark, of a silent sin, first entered her mind.

But who in this world, in this Christian world of such small space, but with so many souls living in it, would do a thing like that, and still remain living amongst the other Christians?

She had heard about it, from books and from stories told round the dining table, when Mr. Bellfeels brought his friends on Saturday nights, for relaxation. But these were stories that took place in the back-lands of the Amurcan South; and in the Amurcan Wild West; and in Canada on the Prairies, in the wilds, in the North, in the bitter cold of long winters, on winter farms, where farmers, as Sir G explained it, "needed the superabundance of hands to work the land, before the mechanization of tractors and ploughs, in that unredeeming cold which lasts nine months out of the year, what do you expect, to be reasonable, I put it to you, what do you expect nature to do, to accommodate this phenome-non? Of natural passion?"

Sir G answered his own question.

"The farmer fooped his own daughter, after having exhausted the limited usefulness of his poor loving wife, poor dear," Sir G said. "I won't vouch for the farmer's moral obligation, however, in solving this predicament, but I put it to you."

All the men roared with laughter, including Mr. Bellfeels.

"And the poor dear, the wife, overworked with the milk pail, the chicken coops, and baling, and at last relieved of her bounden duty, was placed in the position to supervise, to supervise at least, since she could no longer be a participant, the wife had knowledge of (the dark, cold bedroom where the wind howled through the comforters made of cotton) this act of deliberate economic contribution to the theory of employment, within the cemetery of her conscience."

The men did not laugh at this . . .

Now, in this underground tunnel, where Sargeant and Mary-Mathilda are still walking, these thoughts which are now pressing upon her consciousness and her conscience, slides of her life, make her sad and very angry. But in her mind, now having to think about the act that she "had perpetrated," as Sir G would say, she knows the reason why . . .

She can feel the difference in the sound of her footsteps, in this section of the underground tunnel; and there is more hollowness in the sound of her footsteps, and this makes her feel that the tunnel is approaching the cellar of her house.

She walks with the hoe, putting it down a few inches ahead of each stride, step after step, just as she had seen the Vicar walk with his umbrella.

Sargeant walks slowly behind her.

At the sound of his snoozing, she emerges from her reverie.

"I have told you things you didn't know existed before. And these things are things that will remain right here," she says.

"You told me things, yes," he says.

"The things I have told you, am about to tell you, I want you to forget, and have them remain here, in this underground passage."

"You could trust me, Mary-Mathilda."

"Okay, then. But did I tell you that Ma's name was Eunomia Irene?"

"Close to one o' the Bellfeels girls," he says.

"I asked Ma the origin of Eunomia.

"'How come you have this name?'

"And she told me that her Mother, my gran, saw it written-down somewhere, and liked it, and gave it to her, when she was christened. In Sin-Davids Anglican Church. And her second name, Irene, I don't know what that means, either. A hundred women in this Village name Irene. My guess is that the English must-have-bring it here. But don't you think Eunomia is a very nice name; and then, Irene?"

"Pretty like the Bellfeels daughters."

"Ma never knew who her father is. In those days, on the Plantation, women didn't pay much attention to thrildren bearing the names of the father—if the fathers were known, at all—excepting if the father was living under the same roof with the mother, and the child, which was rare.

"No. Ma didn't know who her father was. Could be anybody. He could be dead, anyhow, before she born. That was Plantation life.

"She knew mine. But she never told me. She never told me who. She just drop hints. Always hints.

"'Well, girl, it could be that he is your father!'

"Or 'What I would be doing with a ugly man like that for?'

"Or yet-again, 'I haven't told you a thing, hear? Not one thing. You hear those lawless bitches in Miss Greaves Shop, talking; with nothing more

*better to do than telling you that the overseer at the Plantation is your
father? What right would I be doing with a Plantation overseer, fathering
the only child I give-birth to? And if that was the case, why you and me still
living in this blasted hovel, whilst your father living in luxuries, in the
third-biggest house 'pon the blasted Plantation estate? That mek sense to
you, Mary-girl? Not to me!'*

"So, Ma never gave a straight answer. I know who he is. And it
came to me from the most unusual of sources. After Wilberforce
was born, after I had-had the two very painful and tragic child-
births, as a woman herself, Ma must have had pity on me, and made
a attempt to tell me. But I wasn't in the mood to hear that kind of
story. It wasn't what I wanted to hear at that time.

"Sometimes, in my bedroom, looking through the spying glass
out to sea, tracking the sailing boats from the Aquatic Club, or inter-
island schooners, or straining my eyes to see the exact minute a
merchant ship, or a boat-full o' tourisses come over the horizon, I
would take a peep at Flagstaff Macon Castle, your house, to see if
I could see you; or I would search the horizon and search the hori-
zon, looking.

"But what am I looking to see?

"Sometimes I see a flying fish jumping in the sea. Sometimes
my two eyes would rest on a fish, larger than a flying fish, and from
that distance, I would say it is a dolphin. Or a kingfish. And my
mind is not on the flying fish or the dolphin, but on the meaning of
my life, from Ma refusing to tell me who my father is.

"It was a Saturday afternoon. The men were playing cricket
on the Pasture. It was, if I remember rightly, a big game, our fel-
lows against the best team from down in Town. I think it was the
Spartans team. Spartans versus Flagstaff. And it was Tea, teatime.
The Plantation always provided Tea, and Lunch. Wilberforce
was a toddler then. I had Wilberforce holding in my arms, as he
was running all over the Pasture going on the field, and humbug-
ging the cricketers. And *she* was in the pavilion, with the other

ladies. Mistress Dora Blanche Spence Hyphen Bellfeels, I mean.

"Mr. Bellfeels was Captain of our team, Flagstaff. I hadn't told Wilberforce who his father was. He wasn't talking yet. Just muttering a few words, including 'Da-Da' and 'Ma.' But there is something about thrildren and their parents, when they are small. In time, after he became a doctor of Tropical Medicines, talking about things, Wilberforce explain this same behaviour about thrildren and parents to me, as genealogy. Or progeny. Or could it be that *genes* is the word he used? Anyhow.

"He always argued that from neither progeny nor genes can any father hide from owning-up to fatherhood. No matter how hard he try to hide, he can't cover-down or deny fatherhood, according to the meaning Wilberforce give to progeny and genes. No man can hide . . .

"And Wilberforce was embarrassing me so much that Saturday afternoon, with his running up to the pavilion behind Mr. Bellfeels, even when Mr. Bellfeels wasn't batting or fielding. And the minute Mr. Bellfeels start to bowl, and whilst he was bowling, that boy would be pelting from outta my two arms, right on to the playing field, then on the cricket pitch itself, and right up into Mr. Bellfeels face. Only up in Mr. Bellfeels face. Mr. Bellfeels pick him up once, in his arms, and run his face against Wilberforce face, making funny noises, and giggling. This was early-on, and many of the people living on the Plantation estate didn't know exactly who fathered Wilberforce. It was too early to tell. I didn't let-on, neither. My philosophy was 'who know, know; who don't know, is none o' their damn business, anyhow.' Yes . . .

"Well, this didn't happen only during the special match be-tween Spartans and Flagstaff. Whenever our fellows were playing at home, and the Plantation made this big lavish Lunch, serving cucumber sangwiches and corn beef sangwiches; and at Tea, cheese sangwiches and plain old butter sangwiches, made with sweet butter from Englund, that boy would choose this time to run up to

Mr. Bellfeels, to Mr. Bellfeels only, and pull at the man white flannel trousers.

"Those Saturdays of cricket playing on the Pasture! Beginning from the Friday night, Gertrude, already tired as a ox, poor soul, and me, just as tired, ironing the linens for napkins, and cutting the bread in slices, leaving-back the crust and the edges to mix with pollard, for the ducks and the turkeys; and putting the sangwiches under a cloth that we had dampened first, to keep them soft and fresh till in the morning, because there was no refrigerator, only a icebox; and that was already full; and picking long-grain, dirty rice from Demerara, cause the Plantation has the habit of feeding people with so much food, at the slightest drop of a bat, as if they thought food was going get scarce again like in the War-years; and cricket in Bimshire was not just cricket, but our lifeblood; cricket was cricket; and me and Gertrude picking mounds and mounds of Demerara rice, to get out the weebulls, weevils, as rice shipped here came by schooner from Demerara—and you never know what could get in the cargo that them Demerara people put in the blasted hold!—and picking-out the dead worrums, and the living little green ones from the pigeon-peas that Gertrude had-pick fresh from the trees round the edge of the North Field the same afternoon; and all this food, because there is eleven men on each team, plus one Extra each per team, plus two empires. Umpires. Plus the Water Boy, and the groundsman who took six days preparing the pitch; watering it, rolling it with the heavy-roller, watering it again, putting the light-roller on it, flinging dry-grass on it, and after a final watering, hit she with the heavy-roller again, the Saturday morning, just before eleven o' clock; and the special guests, or as Wilberforce calls them the 'guesses,' the Vicar, who loves to eat; and the Solicitor-General, who once played first-class cricket for Bimshire, I am told; and the various managers of the surrounding sugar plantations, men with big appetites; and then, for the last, the servants, or 'Staffs,' as Mr. Bellfeels used to call us, by

a English word he pick-up from up in England, after a three week
visit to Wilberforce at Oxford, coming back here talking as if he
had a hot hard-boil egg inside his blasted mouth. After the crick-
eters and the invited guesses came the Staffs. But everybody eating,
and drinking, as if it was Doomsday. Staffs and guesses. Yes!
Those Saturday afternoons with cricket was like Easter Monday
bank holiday with a sea bath!

"And you should have seen Golbourne! Golbourne who licked-
down so many wickets of the Spartans team in one afternoon!
Licking-down all them wickets in less than forty-five minutes!
Clean-bowl! Every time you raise your two eyes and look up from
your knitting, or a magazine you happen to be reading, or from peel-
ing a Julie-mango, intending to eat it, *plah-daxxx!* Golbourne have
another one. Another Spartans-man wicket lick-outta-the-ground!
It was too-sweet! Spartans was a all-white team. And Golbourne,
who as you know was apprenticing to the joiner trade, under the
watchful eye of Mr. Waldrond, was the only man of colour playing
for us, on the Flagstaff team, picked by the Plantation.

"Golbourne was our star-boy. And when Golbourne was still
suffering the aftermaths from rum he drink the night-before, on the
Friday night, meanwhile me and Gertrude are here preparing the
peas-and-rice and the pork chops; and on the day of the match, the
Saturday morning, oh-loss!; and Golbourne still stale-drunk; and
My God, Golbourne get mad and mean and nasty, from having-in
his liquors, he start bowling bumpers, wuh-loss! look-out, boy!
Bram! A Spartans-man get hit by a bumper, right in his chest! And he
bend-over. In pain. And all of we, the Staffs and me, hoping that
Golbourne didn't really kill-he! Only touch-he-up, to soften-he.
And members of his own team, the Plantation-people, like Bellfeels
and the Vicar, saying how 'Golbourne wrong-wrong, wrong and
vicious,' to lick-down a Spartans-man, and that *'this isn't cricket'*
to lick-down a visitor of the visiting team; but we the Staffs, all the
time having sentiments in the opposite: *'Lick-he-down, Golbourne!*

Lick-he-to-hell-down!', in whispers, under our breaths; because, after all, bowling body-lines and touching-up the oppositioners with bumpers wasn't cricket, meaning it wasn't English . . .

"But the minute the two Umpires say, 'Light! Stumps draw!', and the game done, and the various Plantation managers already gone in the verandah of the Plantation Main House for drinks—Mistress Dora Blanche Spence Hyphen Bellfeels prohibited them from crossing her front-house—and we the Staffs begin cleaning up things, and are in the Great House kitchen preparing the food, and they can't overhear what we saying amongst ourselves, boy, you should hear the way we begin to carry-on; and laughing-out loud-loud-loud at the top of our voices, and getting-on-bad, and imitating the way the Spartans-men bend-over, and grit their teeth, and wriggle up their body, struggling to rub their two balls, or take-out the protective box from their jockstrap, riding in bare agonies. *'Lick-he-down, Golbourne! Man, lick-he-to-hell down!'*

"And Golbourne would tack-back to the Great House, to enter through the back door, out of sight of the verandah-full of men up at the Main House, cause he couldn't let Mr. Bellfeels spot him; and he would eat with me and Gertrude.

"Golbourne was our star-boy. And he would sometimes bring-back Pounce and Naiman, and whoever-else he could find, with him. I always wondered why you never took that opportunity, on those Saturday afternoons of cricket. Perhaps you were otherwise engaged . . .

"But those Saturday afternoons! Imagine that. Golbourne, single-handed, and by himself alone, defeated all the Spartans-men, now up at the Main House, enjoying themselves on the verandah: whereas Golbourne was *never* extended a invitation. Not a blasted invitement! Never extended the courtesy, after a cricket game, to sit down in the verandah with the rest of the team, to drink a Bellfeels Special Stades White Rum. The man, who alone by himself, and single-handedly, brought victory to the Flagstaff team, over Spartans! And now, look at them up there! Mr. Bellfeels hosting the host of Spartans-men. Talk about blood more thicker than cricket!

"And I wonder what those men found to talk about, in celebrating their victory, when the general of the battle was not present. When the star-boy was *serrigated* from them! And for what reason. . . !"

"I heard these stories about Golbourne," Sargeant says.

"This took place before he had his little accident, naturally. His tragedy. Before his two testicles start to spread and grow. And the swelling, good-Christ, that no amount of WinterGreen, Sersey-bush tea, the rubbing with fresh coconut oil, heated tepid to a certain temperature, alcohol, and fresh limes could bring-down the swelling. *Nothing* was effective. Consequently, and sadly, concluding in goadies!

"Those Saturdays were like little weddings, little ceremonies, little Services-of-Song, little receptions on account of the hospitalities. And when the cricket game is over, the food! The different courses of food would come out. The Staffs carrying the trays. And there would be music. There always was music. Live music. From the few instruments the cricketers and other guesses could manage to play. Fife and drum. And a flute. If the reception was outside in the open air.

"If the rain had-fall, then the reception would be-move-inside, on the verandah; and I could stand from where my House is, all hours of the night, and hear the piano, and somebody playing a trumpet and another visitor on the saxophone. Tenor saxophone. Till all hours, going into Sunday. And then, one by one, you would hear those guesses trooping-out, talking at the top of their voices. The swear words! The vulgarities! And profanities! And getting in their motor-cars . . .

"Well, all the time before I had the privilege to witness this behaviour amongst Plantation-people, I thought that we, the locals and the Staffs, and the field hands in general, could swear real stink, and use dirty language! We are infants compared to them!

The vile language. And the noise they make when they are happy.

"And then, all of a sudden, it is quiet. Peaceful. Golbourne in a corner, on the floor, sleeping. Sleeping-off the rum, cause first thing in the morning, as a apprentice, he got to fork himself in Mr. Waldrond Joiner Shop, six o'clock! Even on a Sunday, to start sawing-up logs o' mahogany tree trunks and cure chair legs in water.

"But the silence that fall over the Plantation on Sunday mornings!

"You could almost smell the silence. And then, the wood-doves starting to coo, *'Moses speak God's words; Moses speak God's words,'* and then the fowl-cocks begin their crowing, and the peace of Sunday overtake the whole land. And it is time for Church. Yes!

"Yes, those Saturday afternoons when they played cricket on the Pasture! All that is gone . . ."

"Yes! Manny's father pass-down the stories about those Saturdays."

"But getting back to what I was about to tell you . . . On those Saturday afternoons, when Golbourne, like a freight train, would run through those Spartans-men like a dose of Glauber Salts; and Mr. Bellfeels would see little Wilberforce coming towards him, and he couldn't lift a hand to ward-off Wilberforce, or give him a slap; and I not knowing which it was, whether he saw his son with the eyes of guilt on his conscience, or whether it was the embarrassment of having me living in a Plantation house, so close to his other household, butting-and-bounding, as they say; so close to his wife, Mistress Dora Blanche Spence Hyphen Bellfeels, and his two daughters, Miss Euralie and Miss Emonie respectively; of whom both of the two daughters remained spinsters, *untouch* to this day . . . sins of the father! . . . with those two young ladies still living at home, and me and Wilberforce so close, must have been a lil difficult, if not pure hell, for that man, Mr. Bellfeels. Poor fellow.

"I don't have no pity inside my heart for Mr. Bellfeels, but I can understand.

"Say anything about him. Say he is the biggest crook in the world. Say he has no respect for women. Say that he could be more better, particularly in certain things and ways. You know what I mean. Say all those things. You have to still admit that never once, not once, in the thirty-two years that Wilberforce born, has Wilberforce lacked for anything. Not one damn thing. Food. Clothes. Pocket-money, even when he was a child, he had his florin every Friday. As if he was getting wages for working, like the rest of us; only difference, his money, which Mr. Bellfeels called "an allowance," was brought to him here, by the chauffeur, and he didn't have to walk from the fields and line-up under a tamarind tree, in the Plantation Yard, like the rest o' we, to wait till when a blasted bookkeeper ready, before you hear your name called out, and then answer to your name.

"'*Mary Gertrude Matilda, here?*' No title, no entitlements, no surname, *nothing*, and you having to answer-up, plain and loud, and all the other hands, giggling and holding-down their heads, some in shame, some in glee and jealousy, although the whole blasted bunch o' we was in the same so-and-so bucket. *Crabs!* In the same skillet! Yes!

"You had to answer '*sir*' and hear your work history for that week advertise: the times absent; the times late; the times the overseer caught you sitting down under a pigeon-pea tree, in the shade. The times you sick. The times you had to take-off that particular week, because of the time o' month.

"'*Eunomia Irene X?*'"

"'*Present, sir!*'"

"'*Two pence off, for lateness!*'"

"'*Yes, sir.*'"

"'*Mary Gertrude Mathilda?*'"

"'*Here, sir . . .*'"

Sargeant remains silent, stunned by her narrative. When he was fielding tennis balls; and learning to enjoy women running after the yellowish tennis balls; she was in the hot broiling sun, weeding fields of potatoes and sugar canes, with her hoe. He can feel and taste the shame of her labour.

"Wilberforce hasn't lacked for nothing. Education. Nothing. Private school when he was a infant. Private tuitions, like you, from Mr. Edwards. Harrison College, on full scholarship, from First Form.

"And then, when it was time to go abroad, Oxford. Wilberforce win the Bimshire Scholarship, granting him free tuition fees and living-'lowances; everything free except travel-money, which Mr. Bellfeels provided, gladly. Pocket-money, clothes-allowance, travel-money and liquors, in case he start drinking now he ain't home, Mr. Bellfeels was willing, and able, to foot the entire bill. And after Oxford, Cambridge, as if he was greedy for more higher learning, or if Mr. Bellfeels was out to show the world, or the whole o' Bimshire that his *son* . . . remember he had only girls from the wife . . . Wilberforce could-go-on to the other-best university on the face of the earth.

"And as for me. What about me? The woman who gave him this only son?

"Whether it was because of Wilberforce, or whether it was mainly on my own account, but nevertheless, I too stood in need of nothing. Because having to feed one mouth, namely Wilberforce, he might-as-well feed the other mouth, at the same time meaning me. How yuh like that? *That* is what Ma did-mean by telling me I was fixed-for-life. I stand in need of nothing. To this day. To this night.

"I stand in need of no material needs. In need of nothing.

"But I believe in One, Holy, Catholic and Apostolic Church, and I acknowledge one Baptism for the remission of my sins. So, even if two wrongs don't add-up to make one right, and even though I carry such deep hatred and animosities inside my heart for that man, that I could kill him . . .

"I could kill him dead," she says. After a pause, she says, "Dead-dead-dead. And not shed a tear for him. Not one drop. Not one drop of cry-water will leave my two eyes.

"Not one drop o' cry-water will leave my two eyes

"What has he done to me? From the beginning, from that Sunday after Church, when I saw him step out of his seat in the Plantation Pew, two rows from the front, under the pulpit and to the left of the Font; and he bend-down on his left knee; and made the Sign of the Cross; and then walked slow-slow-slow, up to face Vicar Dowd; and kneel a second time on the long white stool that stretched from the front row of the Choirs on the right; to the window on the left that has the garden scene of Jesus and a little child and a little white lamb; on the stool that the Mothers Union— including Ma—embroidered; Mr. Bellfeels kneeled down and took his Communion wafer from Revern Dowd hand; and when Revern Dowd pass-back the second time, with the silver chalice, I was just being ushered along with the other thrildren from the Plantation and elsewhere from the other estates, field hands included, out of my seat, by the Sunday School mistress to proceed through to the Lady Altar, so that I had the second chance to see Mr. Bellfeels, first from the back, and then from the side—his right side turned to me—and finally, from the front; and Revern Dowd passing back the third time with the chalice-full of wine, for other kneelers, Mr. Bellfeels took the cup from the hands of the Vicar, and held his head back, just like how he drinks Bellfeels Special Stades White Rum, he took the cup and nearly drink-off all the Communion wine; and then, he made the Sign of the Cross a second time. And I ask myself, as I ask God nightly, what has he done to me—meaning Mr. Bellfeels—what has he done to me? That was the first Sunday, at eleven o' clock Matins.

"And you would think that as a Christian, or a man just taking Holy Communion, and then coming back down from the chancel, with his two hands folded in front of him, resting on his chest, and looking as if he really had-just-had the Holy Ghost inside him . . . 'Take, eat, this is my Body which is given to you: Do this in remembrance of me . . .' you wouldda thought being so close to God, would have-touch his heart!"

And she stops there.

"'*Likewise after supper,*'" Sargeant says, "'*he took the cup; and, when he had given thanks, he gave it to them saying, "Drink ye all of this; for this is my Blood of the new Covenant, which is . . ."*'"

"Thank you, Percival," she says, cutting him off deliberately. "Thank you very much, Percy. And coming back down the marble of the aisle, his riding boots creaking like hell, every inch of the way, until he reach-back to the Plantation Pew, serious and innocent now, as a mouse. And not ten minutes later, that man is standing over me, tall as the water tower over there on the Plantation stands over the fields, passing his riding-crop over my body. And then for me to find out why Ma, 'Miss Eunomia Irene X,' could not raise a hand in defence of me, her own daughter, when that ridingcrop, and then his two eyes strip me naked-naked, *naked*; and pass his leather riding-crop, like a cold hand, like cold water, back up, all over my body. And then for me, for I, I, me, to find out, to find out that he is . . .

"Forgive my tears, Percival. But I can't control them, no more . . .

"But those Saturday afternoons! When Wilberforce would roam the Pasture and the cricket grounds and invade the playing field, heading straight for Mr. Bellfeels, the same minute that Mr. Bellfeels took the ball to bowl; and to the amusement of all those gentlemen on the two teams who must have smelled a rat, some who thought they knew and some who had a hint, since it was common practice on most plantations for the overseer, the driver, the bookkeeper, and don't mention the manager, to breed the slaves, any slave-woman, from age ten to forty, fifty, sixty . . . we were common preys; you snap your finger and a slave-woman come running, and end-up laying down under you . . . '*Hey-you!* . . . *Cumm-ere!*' Yes!

"It was common practice on plantations in Bimshire for a Plantation Manager to breed *any* woman he rested his two eyes on. As many as he could climb.

"And so it was with me. And with Ma. And with Ma's mother,

until we get far-far-far back, get-back on the ships leaving Africa, sailing on the high seas, crossing the Atlantic Ocean, trying to reach Amurca, before more rape and suicide and deceit and betrayal, and desperation overtake them. And they decide to jump overboard, and face the broiling green waves of the Deep; and God; taking suicides, which was better.

"Wishing that the Atlantic storms and hurricanes would have no mercy on us! That they would *wash-we-way overboard* . . .

"And here I am. In this underground tunnel, just like on one of those ships, reeling in the middle of two waves, in a trough of the ocean, with the wave over my head, waiting to swallow-me-up and drown me; and I am wasting my breath, asking a stupid question, *'What has he done to me?'* I must be out of my blasted mind, Percival. Mad. Percy, I must be stark-goddamn-crazy. Mad! A *cunu-munu*.

"You can understand what I am talking about, can't you, Percival? That I am talking about blood. Bad blood. And blood that have a taint to it. A awful smell that not even Jays Fluid could erase.

"When Wilberforce reached ten, and from ten-onwards, he never once-again in public went up to Mr. Bellfeels, or sought him out. Never in company. Nor in public. And he didn't have to do it, in private. It was like Wilberforce had-develop a strong-enough smell of the man, and that the memory of that first smell remained in his memory. Poor boy! And that he couldn't any more stomach any further reminder of that scent. That smell. That taint. Perhaps, that is why he is so formal, even in addressing him—Bellfeels.

"And then, one afternoon. I caught him. A Wednesday afternoon. Just home from Harrison College, waiting for his piano teacher. Standing up by himself in the front-house, looking at a photograph he held in his hand, and holding it up to his face; looking at it, holding it to his face, looking at it, when quick-so, I spotted the empty space on top the piano, where I kept photographs of the family . . . Or was it top of the mantelpiece?

"Wilberforce had Mr. Bellfeels in his hand, examining! Mr. Bellfeels in a khaki suit, standing-up beside his horse.

"And Wilberforce is holding this photo to his face, and he turns his face to one side, and then to the next; and then is looking into the looking glass, over the mantelpiece, studying what the looking glass is reflecting back to him; and then, as if not satisfied with what he is seeing, again he starts examining and scrutinizing the photograph in his hand.

"You could see the concern on that poor boy's face.

"I remain outside the front-house at the door, and I am shaking with, with nervousness, not knowing what to do; cause I don't want Wilberforce to see me watching him, nor hear a peep outta me, saying a word to let him know that I am looking at him, taken up with his inspection, and in his examination. And through my mind, sudden-sudden-so, pass the words he might-have-heard passed at Harrison College, by other boys, or even by his Form Master . . .

"But what he did next frightened me. *It stopped my breathing.* I am holding my breath against detection. Wilberforce takes up *my* picture, and place it on the mantelpiece beside the picture of Mr. Bellfeels with the horse, and Wilberforce turns his head to one side, then to the other side, trying to make his sight and vision come into perfect focus, and tell his mind what his little heart was show-ing him.

"I saw my son that afternoon, worrying-over this question, probably said in a cruel remark at the College; and there he was, in front of me, searching in his own way for the answer to the ques-tion that every child should know. Now-remembering the remark that Ma had drop to me, years before, *'who my father was'*; and me not being sure myself if I wanted Wilberforce to ever ask me that same question; and that afternoon, in order to make sure that Wilberforce didn't put that question to me, I pretended that I was angry with him over something. And I rushed into the front-house. Screaming something. Or the other. At him.

"Hearing my voice, and seeing me in that state, was a shock to him, poor fellow; it was the first time in his life, I raise my voice to him; and the shock caused him to drop the picture, oh-my-God; the picture with me in it, oh-my-God, *and break it!* Wilberforce looks up at me. In this scared innocent way. Not even understanding why my voice was-raise against him. In anger.

"I got Gertrude to sweep-up the glass. Mr. Waldrond reframed the picture the next day.

"He left the room. Wilberforce. I stayed back, sitting down for the longest time, in my chair, studying; my knitting in my lap untouched, until the shadows of evening came down upon the front-house, and Gertrude brought in the acetylene lamps, and lighted them; and raised the mantles. Night catched me there, still sitting, and studying; surrounded by light, but with my heart still darkened and saddened by watching Wilberforce search for the answer; studying.

"My two eyes filled-up with cry-water. My belly burned me. I knew, even without knowing it, that I knew the answer.

"Looking back now, I was very glad that I had the presence of mind to pretend that I was angry at Wilberforce, the minute I suspected what he was searching for; and in my anticipation that I did not want him to ask me *that* question . . . and I would have lied to him, rather than tell him the truth . . . I therefore made-sure he would not have to ask the question I could see his little brain was revving-up to ask of me: *'Mother, could Mr. Bellfeels, my father, be related to you?'*

"What could I do? At that moment? Tell Wilberforce? What could I tell my child? How could I break the truth of the news to Wilberforce? So, I kept it to myself. And in my heart. In the same way that Ma kept it within hers. Until it almost burst her heart.

"And me-now. Nobody will ever know, but you. Never.

"Ma tried her best to tell me the truth, no matter how hard it was; but as a member of the Mothers Union, and knowing what the Mothers Union stand for, Ma must have went-through pure hell, day in and day out, for all those years, keeping her secret.

"Back there in the cane field, laying down beside you, on the trash, which was a stupid thing on my part, and something I already regret . . . and I wish you could understand . . . back there in the North Field, when we were playing Court, and I was in the role of the barster-at-Law for the Accused, defending myself, I was going to try, if I had the chance, to show why I did it. Why I had to do it.

"Here was a man who you could say was such a loving father, never allowed any differences to be made between his two inside spinster-thrildren, Miss Euralie and Miss Emonie, and between Wilberforce. Not counting my two who died soon after child-birth. The same standard of education he gave the three of them. The same clothes. The same allowance-money. The same bank accounts held in trust. The identical money in each.

"It is true that neither of the two, Miss Euralie Bellfeels or Miss Emonie Bellfeels, ever had to use their university education, nor lift a straw, apart from substituting for one week at two different times, at Queen's College teaching Latin, when the full-time Latin Mistress was on maternity leave to have a baby.

"What a waste of good education!

"But the Plantation is very rich, and powerful. And it have more money and has made more profits off the backs of slaves and the sweat of coloured people than what you could read about in any of the Gospels. Both of them are highly educated women, for women in this day-and-age, in this Island. Both studied the Classics, Latin and Greek, Cambridge University, at a high level. And Music. The piano you can hear all hours of the night, sometimes, is the two of them. Nothing but waltzes. And 'I Vow to Thee, My Country.'

"I am sure that if I was able to get my two hands on the documents that the Solicitor-General wrote-up for Bellfeels, and if I could understand the legal terms and their terminologies, and if I could break-open the safe that he keeps in his bedroom in the Main House, I would see that this Great House I am put to live in, to bring-up his son in, is already left-back, in those legal papers and in Mr. Bellfeels handwriting, witnessed-to and stamped for Wilberforce. Seal-and-sign!

"Of course, expecting that I will be six-feet-under before Wilberforce deading-off, soon. And I sure-sure that the two fair-sized wall-houses, on the edge of the Plantation Estate, the two with the upstairs verandahs and the fruit trees surrounding them, that look down into the sea, the two on the cliff, those two also already have Miss Euralie and Miss Emonie names witnessed-to and stamped, on them. So, why?

"Why?

"Why I had to do it?

"I will tell you why. This is the truth. The God's truth. The whole truth. And nothing but the truth."

"So help you, God?"

"So-help-me-God!"

"Let me hear the truth, then, Miss Mary Gertrude Mathilda Bell—" Sargeant says.

She cuts him off before he can complete the name.

"*Don't!*" she says.

Her tone is high, raised beyond her normal speaking voice; and her manner is without softness and emotion; and is threatening.

"Don't you *ever* address me to my face by that name! Not even behind my back. It is not a name I want to have!"

"Well, you could tell the truth by using *any* surname, Miss Mary Gertrude Mathilda," Sargeant says.

And he smiles: he knows this is the surname she is called by openly, in the Selected Clienteles Room, in the sub-station and throughout the Village, by Manny and his friends; and just as openly by the Constable and Naiman.

When the telephone call came that afternoon, disturbing them from their game of dominoes, Naiman had announced, "The Great House, Sargeant. Miss Bellfeels want to speak to you."

"Bellfeels deputy-wife? I wonder what Miss Bellfeels want?"

And she knows that his wife is called Mistress Badfeels.

"Don't ever use that name for me!" Mary-Mathilda says again.

And this makes Sargeant stiffen, and become formal like a policeman on duty.

He opens his small black book with the elastic band round its back, to keep its contents safe and secret; and he begins at last to take down his notes, already headed *Evidence pertaining to the Case of Miss Mary Gertrude Mathilda BELLFEELS, at the Great House, Sunday the 13th Instance.* He puts the pencil into his mouth, and wets the lead in the pencil, and he screws up his face, making his large eyes into slits, concentrating; and looking like a man with bad eyesight.

He is poised now. To take down her Statement.

"I ready now, Miss Mary," he says.

"A word or two, before you go from here," she tells Sargeant. "I did some good things about here, in all this time you know me. And I talking to you in this Statement, as if I am addressing the Court of Grand Sessions. All I ask you, Sargeant, when people, including the Commissioner of Police, ask you to repeat what my evidence is, tell him what you know about me. Just as I am. Without one plea. You would know what to leave-in, and what to leave-out. Let your conscience be your guide. Tell him about me, not out of malice, but as a woman who did what she do, did, to save her soul."

The formality of her words, and the ponderousness of the thoughts inside her head, seduce her; and she assumes the posture and rhetoric and "silks" of a King's Counsel, whom fantasy has chosen as the barrister for her defence; and easily, she slips back into this role, giving evidence, in defending herself . . .

"It is not as a murderer that she stands before you. Even if on the night in question, murder was the only occupant of her mind.

"If it was in her mind when she set out, it had vanished from her mind when she entered the Plantation grounds, and approached the Main House.

"Not in stealth, even although it was a dark night. The Plantation's three German Alasatian dogs and the two Doberman-Pincers ran up to her, to greet her, licking her feet and fingers, and jumping up to kiss her.

"*Standing in the midst of the five dogs kissing her, she had a strange sensation dealing with sacrifice. I can only identify that sensation as a kind of sacrifice.*

"*She was sacrificing him. She has lived under circumstances for the past thirty-eight years that was unworthwhile.*

"*She is a woman with a past of strangulation. Her future ended with each setting of the sun every evening.*

"*She could not continue to live in that situation, as she could not breathe in it; so, she had to change it. And she changed it in the only way that she knew how.*

"*Her act is the act of self-defence.*

"*Mixed-in with the act of sacrifice.*

"*She wanted to sacrifice herself along with the other-mentioned sacrifice she has made.*

"*She is a very ordinary woman, possessing education not beyond Standard Seven, at Sin-Davids Elementary School for Girls. But that education served her well, and proved to be good-enough.*

"*Good-enough to lead a Christian life.*

"*Good-enough to understand what's going on round her.*

"*Good-enough to read the* Bimshire Daily Herald, *every morning.*

"*Good-enough to follow what people of a better station in life than she are saying to her.*

"*Good-enough to understand the meaning of Church.*

"*Good-enough to raise a son.*

"*Good-enough not to bear malice, nor vengeance for the stillbirths of another son and a daughter.*

"*Good-enough not to cross the paths of, nor show disrespect to, the other lady.*

"*Good-enough to respect those lower than her in state, estate, and station.*

"*And good-enough to know her place on this powerful estate.*

"*So, she stands before you, naked; as a woman; not jealous in spite of cause; but when pushed, she becomes real mad. A straightforward woman. Plain. Simple. Not highly educated, as she has stated. But deeply religious. And consequently, not a fool, as a result.*"

She changes her stride, and walks with the hoe in her right hand. The alteration in her stride matches the rising of her voice. Her words flow behind her, and hit him like the pelting of dust in the wind, armed with fine specks of gravel.

He wonders if this is the working of his imagination, or if the dust, the white specks, the accidental rubbing of his shoulders on the coral stone wall, as he follows her in this subterranean tunnel, is the reason his mind might be inventing all this. Whatever it is, his attention is cemented to her words. He has put the notebook away.

He will omit as much as possible of the evidence from the Statement he has to write. He intends to begin writing it from memory and from his notes, on official foolscap-sized paper provided by the Police Department, at the sub-station; and the moment he leans up his bicycle, and has his cup of strong loose-leafed green tea, with a thick, three-inch slice of coconut bread (which Naiman prepares for him, every morning, at six o'clock), he will begin. He can taste the tea, whitened by fresh cow's milk. Perhaps, if she is in a better mood, when she reaches the door that leads up into her kitchen, and if she has the time, and if there is time before Gertrude arrives, and if Wilberforce is not awake and ready for his own breakfast, she might prepare him a cup of strong green tea. And a slice of Gertrude's coconut bread.

In the bedroom, the light of morning comes in like spray through the white voile curtains. The smell of fresh cow dung comes in with the light. And the wind sweeps in from over the hills, passing the Plantation Main House, through the fruit trees of mango, pear, ackee, breadfruit, puh-paw and tamarind, down the incline that leads into the fields, the North Field and the South Field, through the gully, and finally again up the slight incline to her house, and her bedroom in the Great House.

The voile curtains fly like kites, crash against the glass in the half-opened windows, collapse like burst balloons, and they billow out from the glass, like the sails on yachts leaving the Aquatic Club.

The morning light makes the fields give off a haze that looks like smoke rising from a starting fire. And the morning has in it, at this hour, the signalling small fires from the labourers' chattel houses that mark and dot the green land.

In her bedroom, once again, and with the full light of the morning sun sprinkled over the bed, Sargeant paints a picture in his mind of a man's body on the white bedspread; and the form left by the body identifies itself in his mind as Mr. Bellfeels' body. All desire that had ridden his comfort during the long night has left his body. All he can see in her bed, with its seductive smell, the dainty pillowcases, the feminine touch of colour and the softness of cloth, sheets, nightgown and pillowcase, soften his heart, but point out the discomfiture that the richness of this room brings with it. But the image of another man's body in the bed he himself had wished he could occupy with her beneath him is too strong. Sargeant cannot think of love, or lust, in this bedroom any longer.

Sargeant's mouth is like sandpaper; and he does not wish to think of the fragrance of his breath. Nor the smell of his armpits. Small grits of dust seem to move round his eyeballs. The weight of the night descends upon him, as he watches her take a towel from the stand that contains a wash basin and a ewer, and pass it up and down the handle of the hoe, and make the shine return to the wood. He watches as she passes the same towel across the blade.

The sun streams through the window upon her, and rests on the blade, and makes it easy for Sargeant to read the name of the English manufacturer.

"This was made in Englund," he says.

"What isn't," she says. "What isn't?"

"The blade," he tells her. "The blade of this hoe!"

He writes a note in his small black notebook, after flipping back the rubber band that keeps the pages in place. *Make in Englund*, he writes. And then, he adds, after wetting the lead pencil in his mouth, *Note bene. Reference: the hoe blade! Important.*

"Made in Englund," she says, noticing the concentration in his face as he writes. She cannot see what he has written.

"Mannifactured up in Englund!" he says. He says it as if it is an earth-shattering conclusion he has come to, the solution of a long, nagging problem to do with this case.

Mary-Mathilda puts the thoughts about the manufacture of the hoe out of her mind. And looks instead at the clouds falling thick and dark over the blueness of the morning skies, like a slow curtain at the end of a play.

The storm is coming, she knows. Living so close to the land, she can feel it in her bones. Ma said that, too. *"I can feel a storm coming, in my bones."*

She hears a roll of thunder in the distance, which she gets a scent of, a warning of, like the sound of a whistle from a train still coming round a bend; and then, in full sight, at full speed, bursts through thick, short bush, and a field of almost ripe Indian corn. It is the first report of thunder; and the windows in the bedroom shudder.

The thunder gives no warning of its third explosion. It bursts in a glorious reverberation, like shattering glass, retaining its sharpest sound for the last moment, and this suddenness increases its sound and puts a trembling fear into Mary-Mathilda's body.

The fourth crack of thunder is not so sudden as the third, as the lightning flashes one or two seconds before, as if it is warning her and Sargeant to prepare for the coming explosion.

She is waiting for the next explosion; and she waits for it standing before the window that looks directly through the grove of fruit trees to the Main House. In the gathering storm, she cannot see the trees, nor the Main House. Sargeant is sitting on the bed, near the foot, looking into his notebook, waiting in case she continues with her Statement.

He hopes her memory will bring the words in easy flow, so that he does not have to urge them on by asking any questions.

She seems to be reading his mind, and she begins to talk. She moves a little away from the expanse of glass in the window just as a flash of lightning illuminates the fields and the trees, in a dramatic green setting; and a portion of the Main House.

"Before the storm comes-on more," she says, "I should go on with my Statement. Before the morning gets too old."

"Before."

"And as I was saying, with the lovely smell of the lady-of-the-night, there was me, turning off the Front Road, going along a track between the North Field and the South Field, flat for the most part now, now that most of the cane's cut. All that those fields have in them now is young plants, yams and eddoes, and a few holes of eight-weeks sweet potatoes . . . and the Plantation Main House, with its lights on, facing me. The bright lights reflected-back on to me, was like a big wave coming towards me, rolling over my head; and the feeling that came over me tonight, was the same feeling I had that first Sunday in the Church Yard, when the sun and the height of the man looking down at me from the saddle of a horse knocked me to one side, as if indeed it was a wave. The bright lights in the Plantation Main House earlier this evening was like lights on a steamer sailing over the waves on a dark night. Like the brightness of the sun that Sunday morning in the Church Yard.

"This big powerful House, which have such an effect on me, and which to enter the driveway, and walk up the white marl and loose gravel path, and approach the verandah, I trembled to do.

"The dogs were barking, at first; and the horses shaking their heads; the donkeys making noise, and the chickens and the fowls scattering like leaves in a high wind; and the land covered in the darkness of night.

"And then, everything changed. Time itself changed.

"And I found myself in new and different circumstances, with a change of heart, kind of; as if I was becoming . . . well, as if I was falling in love with the Plantation Main House and the Plantation itself all over again; and wanting to visit it, and walk up the same circular path of the entrance of white marl and loose gravel, admire the chickens and the fowls, and the donkeys and mules and horses which are still swaying their heads with a mouthful of grass in their teeth; and behind the Plantation Main House, and behind the garage and the sheds and pens and Servants Quarters, on the left side and the right side, fields and fields and fields in a expanse of wideness which at this time of year would be cane arrows like plumes, like silver garlands and diadems that I had read about in books Wilberforce subscribe to, swaying in the breeze. And the smell of freshness. Fresh cane blades cut as fodder for the animals. Eddoes dug fresh from the ground, and smelling strong and musty, like with the smell of the earth, ready to be cooked in mutton soup. Fresh Guinea-grass and Khus-Khus grass cut and dried in the sun, then to be stuff into mattresses and pillowcases, for the bedrooms. Fresh, big-big tomatoes for slicing and putting in sang-wiches. And the smell of fresh bread coming from the oven. The penny loaf. White bread with a crispy outside, and a strip of leaf from the palm tree on the outside. Or from a cane blade, four by a half inch; and baked into the dough. And the white insides of the loaf warm; so warm that with a daub of yellow butter that loaf of bread becomes a meal fit for a king! Yes!

"The smells of early morning in Crop-Season!

"I grew up to like the Plantation Main House. And though time have passed, with no change of heart on my part, it is still some-thing I feel so shamed about.

"I can hardly raise my head in certain circumstances, as I con-template my transformation . . .

"The lights were on in every room.

"I knew from experience, they had come to the end of their Sunday supper. I-myself, over the years, cooked and served those Sunday-night meals. And before my time, Ma. Yes.

"I knew what they would be eating.

"Mash potatoes imported from Englund. And when, because of the War, English potatoes was scarce, we got our English potatoes from Prince Edward Island up in Canada, on the East Coast. I used to take so much pleasure watching Mr. Bellfeels eat mash potatoes. Table manners is the only thing he retain from the training he must have had at his father table. Mr. Bellfeels-Senior was a white man from Englund. A Englishman. But to see Mr. Bellfeels-this-one, with fork pointing down to the plate; and not moving a inch from where it is placed. Knife in right hand. Knife moving into the rich, white landscape of the mash potatoes shining from the Australian butter that I basted them with; and then to be pasted on to his fork; now knife rested on the side of the plate. Back straight. White damask napkin placed on the table. And the food lifted to his mouth. And the mouth covering the fork, and the jaws moving slow-slow, as if Mr. Bellfeels had-memorize the number of chews Mr. Bellfeels-Senior had instructed him to chew his food. It was a sight! Yes.

"English mash potatoes, green pigeon-peas and a piece o' roast pork. The two girl-thrildren, Miss Euralie and Miss Emonie, would be served carrots instead of sweet potatoes. After the main course, which Mr. Bellfeels would have three servings of, his appetite was always without limits, and big in all manner of ways, he would walk out to the verandah, and stretch out in the Berbice chairs. It would take two to commodate his bulk, magnified now by the amount of bittle that he had-eaten. Two Berbice chairs. One chair to commodate his two feet in; and the other for his bloated body to squeeze-in. And beside him, on the concrete of the verandah floor covered in straw mats, or spread-over with a tarpaulin, if it was the rainy season, his bottle of overproof white rum which he bottles himself on the Plantation. Bellfeels Special Stades White Rum.

"And with the radio on. To the BBC. The radio would be playing Church services from Sin-Martins-in-the-Fields, up in Englund. Or the Choirs of Westminister Abbey. Or some other place in the

Commawealth. But preferably, a Church service. From Englund. Eveningsong-and-Service.

"And he would doze-off a minute after dropping his weight in the two Berbice chairs, plunked in a heap of flesh, from the food and from his gluttony.

"And in no time, the rest of the Main House, including the verandah, would be in darkness.

"Mistress Bellfeels, the wife, have to have her sponge bath and wash her face-and-hands before the BBC programme *Calling the Wessindies* start, at nine o' clock; and she have to make herself look nice and smell sweet for that bastard—pardon my French— dozing in the two Berbice chairs; and yes, he would remain in the Berbice chairs, dozing-off with the glass in his hand, and start one snoring like a water buffalo till the wife ring the bell to summonse-him-in. It is the same bell that the servants ring to call the family to meals. Sunday after Sunday, and for years, I ring that same bell. This time, though, it was like a gong to raise him from the dead. Yes.

"But, this evening earlier, I pause for a moment, remembering; picturing things that I am seeing in front of me that come to me all of a sudden, without rhyme or reason. With ironies, ironical things. And I found myself surveying the whole place, the circular drive- way of white marl and loose gravel; and the path-walk to the front door; and the verandah on three sides of the Main House. And in the darkness, I am just barely able to make out images . . .

"Mainly the greenness on a dark night like tonight turning into a deeper green like the sea round this Island; and the sheds and pens for the animals, the stables—no horses in sight—donkeys and mules sleeping; and even the bloodhounds, those Alsatian brutes and Doberman-Pincers, beasts that Mr. Bellfeels keeps, were covered in this blackness of night. Everything is quiet. And in my hand is my hoe. My polished hoe. The blade shining even in the dark. Yes.

"My only fear was not the fear of what my intention was. Twas not the fear of being alone in this big place, with the circular drive-way and the front yard as big as the Pasture where the Flagstaff First Eleven plays cricket. Nor because of those three vicious Alsatian dogs and the two Doberman-Pincers, now come awake. The brute-beasts. Those dogs didn't make a whisper. After all, those dogs was part of *my* family, too. Those dogs know me. But they are still vicious bastards. Guard dogs.

"And I stand up there, between two croton trees, in the dark-ness, not ten yards from him. Watching him. Looking at Mr. Bellfeels as he light the first cigar. The strength and the smell came at me. Powerful. And nearly knocked me out. I sneeze; and barely cov-ered my nose in time. Mr. Bellfeels cigar smoke burn my nose, as it used to burn my nose during his conjugal visits, when he still pined after me." . . . That Sunday afternoon, after Church, in the Church Yard, comes into her mind . . . and the leather riding-crop is travel-ling down her body, as it has just lifted, barely touched, the cotton dress at its hem; and raised it . . . Never, in all the time that has passed since she left her house and walked up the road has she dismissed reason.

"His head was turned from me, when I walked slowly up to the two chairs, his favourite Berbice chairs; and he was looking out towards the sea, in the direction of the Crane Beach Hotel, from the lofty rise of the land, where I-myself had sat when I was nurse-maid to his two daughters, when I played with those two girls, Miss Euralie and Miss Emonie, when I was regarded as part of the family, as workers on the Plantation sometimes are . . . yes! . . . he was looking out to sea.

"He could see the tops of trees, and the very top of a sail of a yacht from the Aquatic Club, gliding back to port; and the sea, the sea, a wide unmoving—from his distance—sheet of peacefulness. That is the moment I struck him in the head with the handle of my hoe. And he lay harmless at my feet. He was wearing his khaki jodhpurs, starch-and-ironed; and instead of his Wellington riding boots, he was wearing English felt slippers, lined in a white fluffy fur; and Scottish plaid socks.

"I held the hoe by the blade, and passed the handle over his khaki jodhpurs, intending to unbutton each of the five buttons of his fly; but I soon realized this was madness to try to open the five metal buttons, so . . . I would have to touch his fly, and touch him with my hands . . .

"He stirred once. And I panicked.

"But it was just a spasm, a stirring in the sleep that sometimes comes over a person's body. Holding the handle, I moved the fly back. And exposed his white homemade sliders, his underwears. They were of cotton. Sea-island Cotton. And starch-and-ironed.

"Ma used to wash them, years ago . . .

"The dogs of the Plantation had come up to me, and kissed me; and one jumped on my body, and seemed to want to embrace me. They walked around, keeping me company, and greeting me; and it was at this point that he strained his eyes, in the blackness of the night, at the disturbance caused by the dogs in greeting me, to see if he could make out the intruder. And he must have guessed who it was, for the night where he was on the verandah was not too black that he could not see.

"'*May? That you, May-girl?*' he asked in a weak voice that no one inside the house could hear. This was before I struck him the first blow. '*What you doing here, at this hour? You want some——?*'

"It was too late for him to complete his question."

Sargeant is not writing down any of this. It is too much for him. He sits on the bed, still at the foot, with his notebook in his hand, with his index finger of his left hand between the pages of the book.

"It was easier than I thought, getting his instrument out of his fly," she says. "It barely heng enough, in its limber state, outside his fly, it was so small . . .

" . . . But I knew it for many years. It was now the colour of liver left too long off the icebox, looking as if it was 'tetched,' as Ma

called spoiled meat; and it was the same ugliness, with the circum
cised head in the shape of half of a beach almond; yes, and having
that colour too of the beach almond when it is dried." . . . She
closed her eyes, measuring the distance of his fly and the size of the
opening and the length of the handle of the hoe; she closed her
eyes, and delivered the first swing. A noise came from him. And
two seconds passed—her eyes were now open—before the blood
came spurting from his instrument. Time was against her now.
The head was still left. And again, with her eyes closed, but know-
ing where the head was, she swung the hoe a second time, and a
third, and a fourth . . . countless in her madness. This was the
easier act . . . and it was very bloody, like a spoiled slaughtering . . .
"One last blow. And more blood came. I panicked now. The dogs
came closer to their master, lying on the floor of the verandah; and
they began to smell his body, and lick his face, until they reached
the blood pumping out from his severed instrument; and when
they reached this part, they moaned; and I panicked again.

"And immediately, I regretted I had done it. And wished it was
a dream. And I had dreamed about this so many nights in such
graphic detail that I might very well have imagined I killed him; or
that the dream had been so graphic, and so much like wishful think-
ing, that on waking from the dream, I did not have to carry out my
intention that the dream had, by itself, already satisfied.

"I panicked. And fled. Dragging the hoe behind me. And think-
ing that I had gone mad.

"It was not murder. It was a sacrifice. And did not demand
motive. Motive was born on that bright Sunday morning, in a
Church Yard. Motive was the continuation of events through years
of carrying the wishbone tucked into my cotton petticoat, in my
cotton bloomers, in my blue school uniform, taken from the body
of a pullet killed by a lorry carrying sugar cane to the Factory; car-
rying the wishbone through all these Easter Monday bank holi-
days, through all these interludes in the canes of the North Field,
beginning with the Sunday after Matins, in the Church Yard, when

for years I knew by heart the Collect that was read; and now, I can no longer remember a word of it to save my soul; or where in the Bible it comes from.

"But wait! It is coming back, in a whiff of its first reading by Revern Dowd: '. . . *and that through the grave, and gate of death, we may pass to our everlasting resurrection . . .*'"

Sargeant closes his notebook.

"Please stay, Percy," Mary-Mathilda says. "Stay with me till you get the end of my Statement. Please."

"I will stay to the end."

"The Collect for that Sunday . . . I will remember it better now, like The Lord's Prayer. It will be my prayer for forgiveness, and I hope you will understand."

The Plantation bell has just banged two times, to herald the start of a new, long day of toil, and labour in the broiling fields, just as the short-lived storm has come to its end. They can hear the bell over the fading roar of the thunder which roams throughout the tenantries of the Plantation.

"Clean and pure," she says.

"What?" he says.

"The morning . . . I am ready, now, Percy. Take me, please."

They hear Gertrude moving about in the large house; and they pick up the sound of her bare feet going down the steps; and Mary-Mathilda Paul opens the bedroom door and leads Percy down the stairs to the kitchen.

Going down, he counts thirteen soft, carpeted safe steps, watches the way her body descends, and he smells the fragrance of her perfume that lingers.